Knowledge Waits

James Goddard

Knowledge Waits

James Goddard

Pick a town. Any town. Your own town, if you will, and imagine the school in this tale is on your doorstep. If you look out of your window any morning of any term, you may see some of the staff and boys from these pages on their way to another day of leaving the frontiers of mediocrity exactly where they found them.

ZITEBOOKS
LONDON

This edition published 2017 by ZiteBooks
www.zitebooks.com

ISBN 978-1-910697-03-0

Cover Design by flamin ape © 2017
Cover Photograph by Norbert J. Hetherington

Some of the names and places in this book have been changed to protect people. All events described are the truthful recollections of the writer. In all instances of quotation, every opportunity has been made to contact the author.

A CPC catalogue record for this book is available from the British Library.

Typeset by flamin ape
Printed and bound in Great Britain by CPC Group (UK) Ltd, Wiltshire, SN16 0NX

Acknowledgements

I am grateful to the following people who read and commented on various versions and parts of this book: Pas DiLella: Sian Francis-Cox; Martin Godleman; Bob Gallagher; Nathan James; Andy Larter; Greg Morse; Ron Morton; Cilla Paget; Donna Reader; Nick Smith: Steve Tuffin and Bob Young.

I am also grateful to Sue for not reading it. For wholly different reasons she could not bring herself to read Ian McEwan's The Child in Time, and no matter what her reasons might be, I am pleased to be in such exalted company.

For Sue.

For Ever.

Contents

Chapter One
Gerry McMullen : 1

Fuck knows how I ended up here.

What a shit-hole.

When I think of how I used to hate life in County Cork, I am sickened to my core. How could any man ever want to live anywhere other than Clonakilty? And yet, as a younger man, I could not wait to make my escape.

At night I dream of the coastal walks, the purity of the air, the people and the Guinness. Ah, the Guinness! And don't believe that shite they tell you at the Guinness factory in Dublin; it is most definitely NOT the same all over the world. How can it be? It's not even the same in bloody England. And when I don't dream of County Cork I lie awake thinking about County Cork.

Oh, don't get me wrong, I HAD to leave all those years ago, and for a long time I didn't miss the old country. Not a bit. But how did I ever get stuck here, mid-forties, divorced and in this fuckin' job?

For years now this country's education system has been flushing itself down the toilet with all the haste it can muster. Once there was an aim, an ideal, a dream to instil in young minds the fervour for science that once possessed me. But almost twenty years have ground that out of me and the worst thing is that I didn't see it happening. The journey from idealist to cynic may be a slow one over the early years of your life in this miserable world but even travelling the route, I didn't see where I was heading.

Does everyone feel that way? The rest of those bastards in

the staff room? Barely a friend amongst them now. Those in management are so far from teaching and so far up their own arses they couldn't see a two-headed jackal if it was biting their bollocks off.

The younger ones remind me of myself twenty years ago but, Christ knows, the fuckers at the top will soon kill any joy in their young hearts and they'll be out of here just like the good guys I started with, all of whom had their eyes opened and saw a way out when I wasn't even looking.

All except Ian, of course. How I miss Ian. Such a funny man. Even before he opened his mouth, people were laughing. They laughed at his extreme gangliness, his ill-fitting suits with trousers that were way too short. Nobody makes trousers that length, and on a young teacher's pay he sure couldn't afford the made-to-measure suits worn by those bastards who finally drove him to an early grave. At his funeral I wept without shame. Since then I've not shed a tear for anyone but myself. Thinking about it though, those tears that day were tears of self-pity too. Shit, Ian never heard them. Don't give me that bullshit line.

God, I still hate those bastards and their perfect-fitting suits. And with an appointment with the Head Bastard in ten minutes, my hate isn't abating. And what is it all about? Some snotty little shit whose parents put in a complaint to the Head Bastard about my disciplining their Perfect Little Peter yesterday. Let me tell you, if you're on playground duty in the freezing fucking cold of a freezing fucking Friday and twenty bloody kids are pissing themselves with laughter because their football has just caught you smack on the side of your already-stinging face, you too would do as I did and put a quick end to their game. Now, however, it seems the poncey and over-protective middle class parents of Perfect Little Peter are of the opinion that a Chemistry teacher at an all boys' school should not be carrying a knife. Silly sods, you need a knife here more than I ever needed one after hours in Dublin. Not that it's a real knife, mind you. You'd struggle to inflict much real damage on some nutter, hell-bent on giving you a good seeing to, but it made short work of Perfect Little Peter's plastic football. That deflated ball took the smiles off their smug little faces. Mind you, I probably shouldn't have smiled back with quite so much glee.

But kids like PLP really do get on my tits. I swear it was him who reported to management that incident with the glass beaker.

'Come in!' commands the Head Bastard.

I wait an extra second or two before entering. Never seem too anxious.

'Hello Gerry. Good of you to come along.'

As if I had any choice in the matter.

'Like you, I'm sure, keen to get to the bottom of this matter as soon as possible for the benefit of all concerned.'

Is he fuck! Well we're certainly not here for my benefit; it's for the benefit of Mr and Mrs Parent of Perfect Little Peter that I'm here. They're here to see me suffer; the complete opposite of any fucking benefit to me whatsoever. They do not rise from their chairs.

'I understand you have met Mr and Mrs. -,' HB whines in his best impersonation of some cocktail party fucker.

'Yes, I have had that pleasure.'

They remain seated. Have probably been to a fucking seminar on body language I shouldn't wonder. Handshakes are clearly not on the agenda here. Suits me.

Drone, drone, drone… Drone, drone, drone… Drone, drone, drone…

My explanation of a knee-jerk reaction to being hit by the ball and various concocted memories of life on the more dangerous streets of Ireland cuts no ice with PLP's perfect little parents. However HB plays Henry Kissinger - anything to avoid a scandal – and they have little choice but to accept the formal apologies from HB and Yours Truly – equally insincere I'd say – as well as HB's offer of a new ball. The very least we can do… Drone drone drone… 'He can pay for that,' I think.

When they're gone, HB says he'll take the money from my salary at source and that he feels duty-bound to buy a top-of–the-range ball, and he'll throw in a replica shirt as a gesture of goodwill. Do I know which team PLP supports? Fucking private schools.

Still, the cost of a new ball to see the look on PLP's face? I call it a bargain. The upshot with the knife, however, is less rewarding. Apparently it IS against school rules, and I should purchase, for myself, a conventional pencil sharpener.

Chris Adams who teaches Biology and is, therefore, one of the current staff I am more or less obliged to talk to on occasion, seems, strangely for him, sympathetic when we meet in the prep room the following morning. Normally he's such a sycophantic little tosser with his woolly religious beliefs and his inability to formulate an original opinion on anything. I mean he's such a fucking Yes Man that it's a wonder he hasn't left his bifocals firmly jammed up HB's arse. But today he does seem concerned on my behalf and contributes, almost enthusiastically, to my vicious diatribe about HB.

I should have known better of course, for five minutes

into my rant he's off about his dominating fucking wife again. As if I could give a shit about that poisonous bitch. I've only met her once and even then I felt contaminated. For such a short woman she sure can look down on you. When I mentioned my divorce, you'd have thought I said I fucked the queen's corgis. All of them. All she said was, 'I see.' But with that pause between the two words.

It seems Chris thinks she's seeing someone else. My mind thinks, 'Good fucking riddance.' My body language says, 'I don't give a shit,' and my mouth says, 'Surely not, I wouldn't have thought so, Chris.' Talk about mixed messages. But bored with Chris and his domestic humdrum drama I make up some bullshit about checking the lab and leave him to his misery.

You'd imagine I'd feel sorry for anyone whose wife was playing around, but a big part of me finds huge consolation in such sob stories. Someone else's fucking turn for a change.

Back in the safety of the lab, I feel calm and secure again. No Chris Adams, no HB and, for the moment, no blue-eyed little shites. Is it me or have they really become so much worse over the past twenty years?

Used to be you'd have your trouble makers: always the cocky ones taking the piss out of your accent and the nutty ones igniting the gas taps or sticking their thumbs under the taps and soaking the little shites in front of them. Nowadays most of them just can't be bothered. It's the fuckin' apathy that gets to me. They just sit there bored as fuck no matter what I throw at them. I guess it can't match the splendour they can watch on their HD flatscreens, or their state-of-the-art laptops. How the fuck am I supposed to compete with that, armed only with a strip of magnesium and a match? 'Passive receivers' is what Don from Maths calls them. As long as they don't have to think, they can soak it all up and spew it all out again and, all in all, that's pretty much good enough nowadays to get them through this gobshite education system.

Gradgrind doesn't seem like a caricature these days. The kids aren't expected to think and neither are the teachers. Initiative? Individuality? Personality? Forget it pal. If you think these are important qualities in the job, fuck off and become a stand-up comedian 'cos they're no fuckin' use here.

And what do you have to do nowadays to acquire a teaching certificate? Looking at the trainee they sent me a couple of years back, it's all form-filling and arse-licking. Doesn't matter if your lesson renders them comatose just so long as you've met the waffly-worded aims and objectives of your lesson plan. And not just that. Take a look at this list of bullshit you're supposed to blend into your lessons:

1. Equal Opportunities
2. Learning Styles
3. Awareness of Other Cultures
4. Awareness of Gender
(thank fuck we 're not bothered with that one here, though looking at some of the boys I do wonder on occasion)
5. Political Correctness

...and probably about a dozen others I'm not even aware of.

It used to be that you taught them the contents of the syllabus. They learned it and passed the exam, and everybody had a laugh along the way. No more my friend, no fucking more. One of HB's hench-men/arse-lickers came to watch one of my classes last term. Came along with more blank forms than you'd need for a North Korean visa.

Could he see my lesson plan? Could he see my scheme of work? Could I tell him how I'd integrated the school's Equal Opportunities Policy into both of these? And did I have a list of the questions I would be asking throughout the lesson?

No, no, no and no – in that order. One of the best lessons I have taught all year and still the cheeky bastard judged it 'inadequate' because of 'No, no, no and no'.

It was during his *feedback* – surely feedback belongs to Jimi Hendrix, not Malcolm Malaprop – that the limp-wristed tosser brought up the glass beaker incident. Was it true that I had viciously smashed a beaker on David Gale's head? I, of course, immediately and honestly denied the charge. No. I wouldn't have said it was done 'viciously'. And it wouldn't have smashed at all had the silly sod not stood up so rapidly, practically head-butting the beaker in the process.

Once the rest of the class and, I must admit, Yours Truly, had stopped pissing ourselves, I removed the shards from his greasy hair, generously applied lashings of Savlon and the class had carried on with their experiments. All forgotten I'd thought. But here was Malcolm Malaprop quizzing me like some SS officer, but of course with all the wrong words. Was I aware of Health and Safety Regulations? Did I believe I had *assorted* the boy? Had I had the boy's written permission to touch his head? Touch his head? Trust me, you'd not willingly touch that head. For a kick-off it's the strangest head I've ever seen. It's not for nothing that the other kids call him 'Box-Head'. It's almost a perfect cube and it's a pity that John Hurt copped the role of John Merrick because Gale was made for that role. Maybe a remake one day?

'Well Gerry, tell me what you think.'

Rapid return to the moment. 'Think? Sorry Malcolm...

About what, exactly?'

'About the incident with young David Gale. Now that you've had time to simulate the details.'

'Simulate?' *'Simulate?'* What was the tosser on about? *'Stimulate?'* Surely not.

'Now that you've had the chance to look back and review the whole business, Gerry.'

I'm with him again now: *'assimilate'* of course. How did this weaselly ignorant shite ever make it to the senior mis-management team? Rhetorical question of course. You only have to watch him and HB together to work that one out. Thick as thieves. Only Malcolm is even thicker, with his wrong words and his Bisto tongue.

Malcolm's smooth-talking tongue, so unlike my accent which I've never really lost. I know the kids take the piss mercilessly behind my back, and see me as some kind of senseless bog-trotter. Not that it was always such a bad thing. I remember when folk in this country had never heard of Al-Qaeda and when the IRA was the enemy. Those days when the nutters had got bored blowing to buggery their fellow countrymen and had decided to export their fun. In those days an Irish accent, north or south, it didn't matter, was something to instil fear into the kids. And I played on it at times.

The night some piss-artist Tottenham thug decided to pick on me helped too. There I was at the bar getting them in while Ian had gone for a slash, when out of the blue this pillock started. No idea who he was, but for some reason he had taken a dislike to me. Maybe the accent, maybe I reminded him of someone, maybe he was just too pissed to know. Before I had really got a grip on things we were outside in the car park and he'd caught me with a lucky right hook to my left eye. But that was the end of his luck. I soon got the boot in a few times and down he went. I was about to pull my knife on him when Ian came and bundled me into his car. We just left the tosser there. I've hated Tottenham Hotspur ever since.

Mind you, the eye did swell up and turn a lovely shade of brown and yellow. Monday at school, rumours soon spread amongst the kids that my swollen eye was the result of some IRA activity. I didn't have to say a word. All that shit about the power of language?Never underestimate the power of silence.

Not that silence is always a sign of strength. You only have to look at Dozy Derek Humbrell's Geography classes to see that. What they learn in there is quite beyond me. Every time I go past all they seem to be doing is colouring in another bloody map. Those that are doing anything at all, that is. Most of the time it's like a fucking zoo in there with kids screeching and jumping around. Not that Dozy Derek notices. Just sits there at his desk seemingly oblivious to it all. Now and again one of the more conscientious kids will approach him with a minor query or to seek approval for having used the correct colours but mostly it's chaos and cacophony. All of his classes are the same regardless of the kids' age or syllabus requirements. Just colouring, colouring, colouring. Jesus Christ.

Sometimes I wonder why Dozy Derek ever went into teaching. What possible job satisfaction can there be in doing that, day after fuckin' day? Someone told me that he worked as a postman before he entered teaching. Beats me why he quit. Surely better to walk the streets than watch kids colouring in maps of streets. Apparently he's married, though nobody has ever seen Mrs G. Much staffroom speculation concerns what sort of woman might have wed Derek. The most common view is that she must be a mouse of a lady who probably spends every evening, weekend and holiday colouring in Derek's maps when there are no kids to do so…

I disagree. I'm convinced she must be a monster of a woman who's scared him to the point where he's too feeble to think or talk for himself. It seems they own a touring caravan. I'd hate to be sharing that for two weeks with Derek. Whoever she is I actually feel sorry for the poor cow.

Does he satisfy her sexual needs or does he just ask that she colours in the pictures of the bearded man and his lover in 'The Joy of Sex'?

We used to have a copy of that book. Read it together like it was a work of holy scripture. Tried everything in it except growing the beard.

It's hard to reckon how much we got from that book. I wonder what the kids I teach now would make of it. I can just see them pissing themselves at what today would seem like some old-world quaintness. They don't even bother with tit 'n' bum mags any more. No, it's all back home, lock the bedroom door and straight onto the net. Even the obvious virgins talk in ways I wouldn't have known at their age. What would my old man have made of internet porn back in old Clonakilty?

But what views of women and sex must these kids be developing? Especially in this place where the only female they ever see is the school cat. Christ knows I was never too sensitive, but the internet as a role model? I'm no fucking feminist but it seems to me their golden days have been well screwed by online porn.

I'm beginning to hear Annie's voice now. I've no idea where she is today but I can hear her disgust. Not that she was some retiring wallflower back in the day, as our worn and battered copy of Dr Comfort's paperback would testify.

I soon learned that what she wanted was not that you'd kept your promise to love her the morning after, but that you still respected her.

And I did.

Chapter Two
Chris Adams : 1

Why am I still here?

This is something I find myself saying with increasing frequency both at work and at home.

Nobody seems to want me.

My colleagues seem to just suffer my presence and if I ever try to talk to any of them about my life they make some excuse to walk away or change the subject. And Rachel does the same. I even think she has lost her faith. She seldom comes to church now and has become quite dismissive of any opinion on any subject that I might dare to offer.

She was always what my mother would call 'pushy for a woman'. She would shout at any MP on the television; she would rant at articles in The Daily Mail that Mum used to leave lying around whenever she visited; she would complain for weeks after Mum's departure, and she keeps cold callers on the phone for ages just to pick a fight.

'Just leave it, let it go,' I used to urge her, but she simply could not. I remember one double glazing company who kept calling with their offer to replace all of our windows. Instead of just politely telling them that we already had UPVC windows throughout the house, Rachel went to war with them. Eventually, sickened with their calls, she arranged for their engineer to call round, one day when we were out. The following day the company rang to enquire why nobody was in when they'd knocked. Rachel responded with anger and indignation. Where had they been? Why had she waited in all day? What did they think they were playing at? Were they going to recompense her for her wasted time?

Of course compensation was out of the question but they made another appointment for the following day and offered us even more of a discount on their already low prices.

The next day we went out again.

This must have gone on for at least one more arranged visit until they finally got the message. Rachel often says she wishes I would get the message but until she tells me clearly what that message is, how can I?

It's not unlike that hairdresser who, I must admit, made a right mess of her hair not long after we were married. She came home one Friday looking like Medusa's half-sister; it was frightful and frightening. She fumed around the house all afternoon before ringing to demand that he return her hair to its former glory and refund her money. The hairdresser was apologetic but seemingly insistent that he had done exactly what Rachel had asked, and it was not his fault if she didn't look like Jennifer Aniston.

Saturday morning Rachel was out of bed long before her usual 10.00. She didn't wash, she didn't comb her hair, she dressed in her scruffy gardening clothes and slammed out of the house.

Later I learned that she had quietly entered the hairdresser's and stood in the middle of the salon telling all of the ladies there that if they knew what was good for them they would be up and out of that salon before the thieving charlatans could ruin their hair and their weekends as they had hers. She made a great play of showing her hair to all the customers and playing the hurt card. If the ladies were shocked to be addressed in such a way at 9.05 on a Saturday morning, it was nothing compared with the effect her performance had on Mario (real name Trevor). He promptly refunded all of Rachel's money and actually doubled the amount so she might get her hair fixed at another salon.

Mario (Trevor) had Rachel to contend with for fifteen minutes. I have had rather longer.

She can be a bitch, but I love her. We used to laugh over the time she emptied a pan of cheese sauce over my head while I was watching football on the television. I had forgotten to buy a cauliflower and the only possible reaction was to tip the cheese sauce over my head. She screamed. I ate the sauce and continued watching the television. She screamed some more. I laughed and so did she, we made love and went out for dinner. I worry that one of these days she might heat the cheese sauce first before pouring it over me.

I am sure she is seeing someone else but I am not sure whether to warn him, kill him, or thank him.

Of course I do not mean two of those. If I did not love her none of this would bother me in the slightest. But I do love her and sincerely believe in the sanctity of our marriage vows. Till death us do part. It is God's will that we are together. I just wish God would convince Rachel too.

She is threatening not to come to the end of year school celebration and though I naturally understand her reluctance, I feel a wife should support her husband on such occasions, even when it entails listening to Gerry McMullen pouring his heart out. She was burdened with him last year and although I know she would have listened with great sympathy, I also know she is not at all fond of the man and does not relish the role of his agony aunt. But then I genuinely feel sorry for Gerry. It cannot be easy living in a foreign country and to then have your wife run off. There are of course always two sides to any argument so I cannot blame her without reservation, as he could not have been an easy man to live with. It is well known that he drinks too much and that his appearance and personal hygiene leaves something to be desired. And if his behaviour at school is any indication, he has violent tendencies that may well transfer to a domestic situation. Once I had to return to the staff room to collect some boys' homework and from outside the door I am sure I heard him on the phone to someone, probably his doctor, talking about impotence. I did not listen too long before loudly entering. His wife always struck me as a demanding woman and heaven help him if he was letting her down in the bedroom department.

Not that I have ever had any problems downstairs. From time to time there have been occasions when school workload or church commitments have been very demanding but I do manage to find time for Rachel most weeks.

In passing, is it not strange to note that we talk of the 'bedroom department' whilst simultaneously referring to 'problems downstairs' when most bedrooms are upstairs? Perhaps Rachel had the answer that one time when she bizarrely suggested lovemaking on the stairs?

If it sounds as if carnal relations are not overly important to me, I suppose that may be the case. Naturally the act of bodily union is the physical manifestation of true love, but I can never fully forget St. Paul's words here. And there is far too much emphasis on the pleasure of the body in my opinion.

I might think differently if we had children. It is ironic in many ways our not having children. I went into teaching initially because of my love for children. Not that I would ever profess so much in the staff room nowadays. Talking of one's love for children is only likely to raise eyebrows and provoke distasteful comments but I try to overlook such vulgar cynicism. For me it was the pure love of children, and the desire to help innocent minds that brought me into teaching.

It is with a heavy heart that I see so little of this in my colleagues today. So many of them seem to harbour an actual dislike, often bordering on a hatred of young people, and Gerry McMullen comes to mind here. Others choose to call themselves 'career teachers', which generally means that their aim is to move with as much haste as possible into a management position where contact with children is minimal.

One only has to look at poor Malcolm Davies to see this. Why on earth does a man like that ever come to work in a school? I am not even convinced he has any qualifications to work in a school. His arrival was quite sudden whilst most staff were away on our summer break. I never saw the post advertised. Marketing might be more suitable for Malcolm. The new school prospectus looked quite impressive, once the proof-readers had worked on it. Malcolm exceeded himself with the way in which he presented the school. So well, in fact, that initially I did not recognise it as the place I work. Even the boy he chose for the front cover picture is no longer a pupil here.

When that year's prospectus came out, David Gale quizzed me on this when I was on playground duty. The poor lad wanted to know why Simon Gore was on the cover when he was now a pupil at the local comprehensive. Poor David also wanted me to explain to him why he had not been asked to be on the cover. Poor lad. He's definitely suffering with a whole plethora of problems and is, I fear, quite delusional. He is always telling me stories about other boys and other members of staff. He told me once that McMullen had smashed a glass beaker over his head and, whilst it is common knowledge that McMullen is a violent man with a quick temper, he is surely not capable of such an act. Not to a boy and certainly not to one so in need of help as young David.

Were this a comprehensive school there would be systems in place for him to be referred to some outside agencies, some counsellor or therapist, but the Head here does not encourage the use of outside agencies and I fear it is already breaking David's parents to send him here so any further expenses are likely to be beyond them. But I know he needs help.

I did try to help throughout last year. Gale's odd behaviour first came to my attention on an occasion when I was on playground duty, one lunchtime as it happens. Some boys choose to bring their own lunch or go into town to buy lunch and Gale is usually one of them. On this particular day he sidled up to me.

'Want one, sir?'

'Sorry, David?'

'Jaffa Cake, sir. For lunch.'

In one hand was half a packet of Jaffa Cakes, in the other he had a half-eaten jar of cockles in vinegar.

'No thank you David. I had lunch before coming on duty.'

'Suit y'self sir. More for me,' he cackled.

As his upturned face grinned, his left hand proceeded to dunk a fresh Jaffa Cake into the open cockle jar. He swirled it around for a few seconds before retracting it dripping with vinegar. A couple of splashes landed on his tie as the soggy Jaffa Cake made its way into the gaping mouth, bisecting the poor boy's large head.

One grin, one wink, one gulp, and the vinegar-soaked

Jaffa Cake had gone, leaving one stray cockle that temporarily attached itself to the Gale chin before tumbling to the playground floor. Stunned, I could only watch in horror as young Gale scooped up the lost cockle and crammed it into his still grinning mouth. I had witnessed nothing like this outside of a David Attenborough documentary and with a mixture of pity and nausea, I could feel my school lunch unsettling itself.

'David, are you alright?' I offered. 'I mean did you just do that for a bet or something?

'Bet? Whadd'ya mean, sir?

'That Jaffa Cake. Did you eat it like that for a bet?'

'Don't be silly sir, that's my lunch, my favourite lunch.'

'Your favourite lunch?'

'Yes sir, I have it every day, except Fridays.'

'Except Fridays?' I was struggling.

'Yes sir, never Fridays.'

'Too much of a good thing?' I suggested.

'No sir, I've spent most of my week's lunch money by Friday so all I get Fridays is a Mars and a Twix.'

Is it any wonder the boy has problems?

For the rest of the year I kept an eye on David whenever I could. Some days I would select an extra piece of fruit from the bowl as I left the house. At first he used to take it, but I stopped when I caught him throwing one of the apples across the playground at one of the younger boys. That and when Rachel complained about the amount of fruit we were suddenly buying every week.

One day recently, however, I realised that it was too late for me to be able to help David at all, and that an occasional apple or satsuma would serve no real purpose.

His form-room was one of the mobile classrooms that had been set up near the staff car park as a temporary measure some years beforehand. My way from car park to staff room that morning was impeded by what appeared to be most of the boys gathered around the mobile. Most were laughing. Inside the room was David who had doubtless arrived at school early as he always did; I knew his father dropped him off every day before the school even opened. I could see David gazing out from one of the classroom's upper windows so he was clearly standing on a desk. As I edged my way through the crowd of boys, so that I might remonstrate with him for what was surely a reckless act likely to endanger his personal safety as well as school furniture, the real reason he had attracted such a large audience dawned on me. Nearly all of the windows were festooned with glossy pictures of naked young women. The older boys were making lewd comments and the younger boys were awe-struck. I had never seen so many naked breasts. And above the top row of gaudy women was David Gale's massive head adorned with the smuggest smile. It was a smile that seemed to suggest Claude Monet's observation, 'I believed I could educate public taste.'

Over thirty pairs of breasts and that face, this was probably the closest that face would ever be to the naked female form. He was savouring the moment pretty much as he had been savouring those Jaffa Cake and cockle combinations all term.

What had possessed him? Some form of vicarious exhibitionism? Some need to assert his 'manhood' to the other boys? And where he had obtained all of those pictures?

Later that day he admitted finding them in Charlie Dyer's boiler house. The caretaker had taken to reading glossy girlie magazines in his solitude and had left a pile just inside the door which a curious and wandering Gale had chanced upon. What a foolish and lewd man. I call it highly irresponsible to leave pornography lying around where young boys might come upon it. Gerry McMullen did offer to dispose of them but the Head declined his offer and delegated the task to Malcolm Davies who did not seem at all interested in such a chore.

David went home that day and the incident was largely forgotten by the time the summer term began, but some nights I am still haunted by that face and those breasts.

Chapter Three
Malcolm Davies : 1

I don't imagine I will be here too much longer.

This was only ever a halfway house, a stopping-off point before a suitable opening at the BBC, or even ITV. Father keeps telling me that with my qualifications I am lucky to be here and that it cost him quite a few favours with Gordon Albert, the headmaster, to take me on. Fortunately, Gordon was able to turn a blind eye to my academic record and was able to slot me in as part of his management restructuring programme a few years ago. With early retirement on 'ill-heath' grounds, his two deputies were on their way and I was on hand to step in.

Sometimes I feel he was happy to take me on as he knows that, unlike the two who retired, I am no threat to his power. He largely keeps himself away from the school most of the time. Most of the problems seem to land at my door and Gordon is not too bothered how I go about solving them. This is why I need the move into the media – somewhere I won't be a fall guy for some big-wig. Father says I am green and wet behind the ears but I can't imagine the BBC is run in the way Gordon runs this school. After all, my very appointment could be seen as inappropriate and smacking of nepalism – is that the word? I sometimes get my words wrong, but who doesn't these days?

I am aware that some of the staff ridicule me behind my back, especially that vicious paddy, McMullen. It appears he has taken to referring to me as Mrs Malheurprop, or something. I have no idea what he is on about. As far as I can recall 'malheur' is French for bad luck. It certainly is bad luck having to deal with a man like him on a daily basis. He is a violent man and it would not surprise me at all to learn that he has IRA connections.

Teaching Chemistry gives him access to all he would need to blow up innocent folk. I know some of the boys can be unpleasant at times but nothing justifies the way McMullen treats them. Since I have been here I have known him to stab one boy's football, break a glass beaker on top of another boy's head and there was even a rumour last term that he confiscated one boy's lunch on health grounds only to eat it himself in his prep room. I wouldn't put that past him at all. He's a rat of a man both in his behaviour and his appearance.

Most days he comes to school in his scuffed, dirty brown desert boots, and shapeless grey trousers that appear to be held together with a mixture of food and urine stains. He is always in one of the two shirts he possesses, both of which are faded with worn collars, and a jacket that may have been new once, but not since the Second World War ended. To top it all, his ferret face, nicotine-coated teeth and sad last grey strands of hair do not make for an attractive figure. At least I have a smart suit, a well-pressed clean shirt every day and impeccably polished shoes. Always look the part, Father says. He tells me that if you look the part, others will treat you as if you are the part. I know that if I came in to school looking like McMullen I would not last ten minutes. People expect deputies to look smart.

If I were not smartly dressed how could I expect staff to treat my initiatives as smart? As an example there is my new ABC programme. Gordon wanted me to come up with a catchy slogan to impress upon boys and parents the way he wishes the school to be moving upwards in the league tables. I love tasks like this, tasks that involve me in the promotion of good education throughout the school without having to get my hands dirty with actual teaching. I fear for myself whenever I am obliged to enter a classroom. The boys are so noisy and so unpredictable. I am not even sure they see me as a member of staff. One stopped me once in the corridor in my first term here and asked if I was lost.

Gordon is very impressed with my ABC scheme and tells me that it will present exactly the image of the school that he aims for. He is thinking of replacing the outdated Latin school motto with my ABC. To tell the truth, it's not entirely my ABC as Gordon changed it a little. Originally I had planned that ABC would stand for:

ARRIVE
BEHAVE
COMPLETE SCHOOL

But Gordon changed that.

'It's got legs Malcolm, it really has. But I just feel it needs snap.'

'Snap?'

'Yes, something to give it a little lift. Something to convey the idea that we're a cut above the rest.'

'And my idea doesn't do that?'

'Well, I'm taken by the snappiness of your ABC tagline. It has a resonance of the 3 Rs and we shouldn't forget that the alphabet is important in education.'

'So, why not go with it?'

'Oh I am, my dear boy, I am. I just feel we need to come

up with some words that better reflect the dynamism of the school. After all, the pupils all arrive as a matter of course, don't they?'

'Well actually, Gordon, it was our high absenteeism rates that I had in mind here.'

'Yes, yes, yes, but really the pupils' arrival at school ought to be taken as happening a matter of course.'

'But it's not...'

'Yes, yes, yes, but we don't want to be broadcasting absenteeism rates and drawing attention to them in any way, do we? No, no, no, let's go for something that smacks you in the solar plexus and gives you a lift.'

'Surely a smack there is likely to have the opposite effect?'

'Oh come on, Malcolm, stop being so literal all the time.'

'I wasn't trying to be a great novelist Gordon, I was just trying to help the school.'

'What?'

'Like Dickens, you know, or any of our great literal figures.'

The phone rang. For five minutes, Gordon talked in hushed tones making me feel as though I should have left.

'No, no, no, Malcolm. 'Arrive' just will not do. Let's think now. How about 'Achieve'? Or 'Ascend'?'

' 'Ascend'? Sounds like we're running a mountaineering school. And 'Achieve'? Bit hopeful in the light of recent exam results, don't you think?'

'For heaven's sake, Malcolm, you're right!'

'So we'll stick with...'

It was the point of triumph. Gordon was going with 'Arrive'.

'We'll go with 'Aspire', bellowed Gordon, clearly struck

with Damascene inspiration.

'But the school doesn't have a spire.'

I felt pleased with myself again.

'What?'

'It would be misleading. Parents might sue us under the Trade Descriptions Act.'

' 'Aspire!' It's one word. And it's a verb. It means to stretch oneself, to aim high.'

I hate it when this happens.

'But of course, of course. I know that, Gordon. But to what are you suggesting they might aspire. You've got to aspire to something. Like 'Aspire to Arrive'. That would be good. That would combine my idea and yours, Gordon.'

Gordon looked down at the proposal I had given him, put two thick lines through 'Arrive' and in its place wrote 'ASPIRE' in bold capitals, smiling as he sat back in his chair.

'And the other two you came up with are pretty woolly as well, if you ask me. Let me think, let me think, let me think…'

'How about...'

'LET ME THINK, MALCOLM!'

For an eternity I watched Gordon think. As he did, he picked his fingernails and excavated some wax from his right ear.

' 'ASPIRE, BELIEVE and CHALLENGE'. That's it, that's it. That's what we're going with. Snappy, powerful and strong.'

Silently, I thought, Believe what? Challenge what? But I kept this thought to myself. No point riling Gordon. If he wants a nonsensical slogan, as Derek Bentley might have said, let him have it.

I looked up. Gordon seemed engrossed in demolishing my proposal. I left his office. I needed a coffee anyway.

He is considering a new design for the school badge to include these words. Last week there was talk of bringing in a marketing agency. I admit this upset me a little, as I had done so much of the preparatory work.

I still prefer my version.

I should like to break off for a moment here to stress that there was nothing hands-on last term between me and Simon Gore. Rumours were quietly circling the school, all of them, I am sure, enervating from that vile bog-trotter McMullen. It would be typical of him to slander my good name. It is true I am a homosexual and it is also true that Simon Gore is an attractive boy. That is precisely why I chose him to be on the cover of our prospectus. I am sure prospective parents do not wish to send their boys to a school for spotty idiots, which is what so many of our pupils seem to be. But I never laid a hand on him. I am appalled that anyone could think I would.

Not that at a different time, in a different place with a different culture… Simon is handsome and clever. And the way he looked at me with those brown eyes. No normal homosexual man would feel differently. Difficult to resist, especially when it was just he and I after school when I took the photos. I admit that I took more pictures than were absolutely necessary, but I always feel self-conscious looking at him face to face. From behind the lens of a camera my eyes could linger. I could even ask him to alter his pose, to turn his face this way and that, and to ask him to hold a pose while I shot a few just to be sure of getting the best picture. But that was it. Always behind the camera, never in front.

I know for a fact that whilst Gordon is quite content to indulge me, there is no way I could keep this job if there were ever the slightest scandal involving a boy. At present I still need the job. And I certainly do not wish Father's first knowledge of my homosexuality to be from a tabloid headline.

It may be unethnical but I still have those pictures.

For the present, however, and notwithstanding McMullen's guesses, my sexuality is a secret at school. Once he did make a pointed remark about who I might bring to the end of year celebratory meal but I managed to silence him by asking if he would be accompanied by his wife. Sometimes it is good to have access to staff files. If McMullen were ever to find out about my weekend trips to distant towns and the strangers I meet there! That is too much to dwell on and another reason a media position would be so much more suitable.

But most of my time these days is to be spent promoting ABC within the school. I am chairing a staff meeting soon at which my aim will be to get all staff on board with the programme. They will need to incorporate it into their lessons and to make it a watchword – or three watchwords to be exact – for all of the boys.

Chapter Four
Mike Redfern : 1

Now I really should not be here.

Not at all.

Not *in any sense* should I be here.

First, I should, by rights, be in some top-rate university department. Not here in this third- rate private school. And secondly, by all that is normal and natural, Ian should be here, not I.

The agency promised to place me in a red-brick university where I would teach my specialisms: namely the rise of the novel and American poetry since World War Two. Just a few hours of teaching each week, they said, and plenty of time to read for my doctorate. I still have the working title: The persona of the ageing male in the work of the homosexual poet Craig Burgess – how grayness and gayness inspired creativity in Middle America's Bible Belt in the mid twentieth century.

Choose a career, they advised me in the sixth form. I chose a career but fate has ordained that another has chosen me. Instead of trips around the world researching and lecturing, I have been teaching poetry to the insane for six years. How did it occur that in lieu of working with some of the nation's brightest I am now correcting semi-legible and semi-literate essays on the role of Friar Laurence in *Romeo and Juliet*? Who cares about this character? It's one of the least interesting parts in one of Shakespeare's least interesting plays. But *Romeo and Juliet* is deemed fit for young minds and what might be the alternative?

Imagine explicating *King Lear* to some of these poor

intellectually stunted pupils. They cannot master the apostrophe. One can explain it until one is blue in the face. Perhaps GBS was right and we should consign the apostrophe to the bin, rather that than breed an entire nation of greengrocers. (Or should that be greengrocer's, perhaps?) It is not just the apostrophe: what of effect/affect? Who's/whose? were/where? the different usages of the colon and the semi-colon and the universal inability to grasp the concept that the word separate comes from the same source as apart and apartheid? And that, as a consequence, it should never, *never* be spelled with three of the letter e? It's a losing battle – only they would call it a loosing battle.

And it's not only the pupils. Some of the staff have a literacy level just one or two steps in front of that of the children. I am appalled every term when I come to write my form teacher comments at the bottom of reports. Staff cannot distinguish between its and it's. Sentences are finished with prepositions and infinitives are split. In some cases it is only the abysmal quality of their handwriting that disguises their woeful spelling. Perhaps the scrawl is deliberate to mask their uncertainty over whether to write *independent* or *independant*. Hence the proliferation of the multi-purpose vowel amongst the staff. We would have more complaints were it not for the fact that Malcolm Davies, whose responsibility it is to run random checks, is himself lexically challenged. The low reading age of many of the parents also ensures complaints remain artificially low. One would write to the BBC or The Times but these organisations too appear to be staffed by folk whose grasp of basic grammar and spelling rules is that of a nine-year old.

I believed in coming to a private school, albeit as I had

thought on a temporary basis, that at least some of the staff would be well-read and with an interest in literature and the arts. Alas, no. Chris Adams' only reading would appear to be The Bible. Nothing wrong with The Bible of course. It is after all the basis of so much Western culture, but one only has to engage in conversation with Adams to realise rapidly that his reading begins and ends with the Good Book. This is, however, at least one more book than has ever passed through the hands of that philistine McMullen. I can imagine no more unlikely scenario than McMullen curled up with a copy of The Romantic Poets. But I do have a soft spot for Gerry. He has been here quite a while and his life has been hard, and he is at least honest. He will call a spade a spade, especially if he were taking it to your head at the time. Some of the staff fear him, possibly because of his maverick qualities. He seems to pay no heed to school rules whatsoever. However, his classes achieve above average results and, not wishing to rock the boat, school management tends to leave him to his own devices. They also seem anxious about singling him out, lest he play the race card. He has never given any indication that he would do so but I sense that in this time of political correctness Gordon Albert and Malcolm Davies make every endeavour to avoid offering him the chance for a confrontation opening with, *Is it 'cos I'm Irish?*

Political correctness! What is happening here? Quite naturally one cannot go around calling pupils N- or Pakki, any more than one might address them as *Spotty* or *Short Arse*, but when one is advised that one cannot introduce certain literary works into the curriculum for fear of causing offence… Can these myopic dunderheads not see that there is a world of difference between offending a Black pupil by calling him N- and a rational study of the way Twain, writing in 1880s America, uses the word in Huckleberry Finn to reflect a society emerging from the ravages of The Civil War, a conflict fought largely to emancipate the slaves? Context, I keep attempting to explain to Malcolm Davies, but the notion of reasoned debate is clearly anathema to the man. He sent me this email when he realised my intention to press on with a study of Huck Finn was serious:

Dear Mike, Without wishing to intravene in your proffesional desision, might it be better not to caught controversy in teaching this book? I read in the press that it has been banned in America and they are usually ahead of us. Lets talk.

Malcolm Davies
Director of Quality and Cultural and Equality Officer for School

Atrocious spelling, incorrect usage of words and, precisely like the pupils, a complete ignorance of the apostrophe. How is one expected to treat his ideas – even were they serious ideas - with anything other than complete disdain, especially when they are expressed as if in a poor translation?

Lets talk, indeed! That is Malcolm-Speak for, Let me convince you over a cup of my freshly-percolated coffee to agree with me, because I am right.

We talked.

'This 'N' word Mike, it appears quite a lot in this book?'

'Yes Malcolm. It does.' Mike played a straight bat.

'And yet you still feel it is suitable to teach in this school? Might it not offend some boys?'

'How so Malcolm?' Let him think for once.

'Well, it's an offensive word, Mike.'

'Do you think they will not have encountered it before?' Clearly a new thought for Malcolm.

'Well... no... but it doesn't do to give approval to such language.'

'And how does Clemens do that?' Mike playing the smart-arse card now.

'Clemens?'

'Yes, Clemens. The author of *Huckleberry Finn*.'

'Forgive me Mike, we seem to be at cross-purposes here. Or I've got the wrong end of the stick, Mike.' Malcolm has been on a management course which teaches managers to demonstrate their awareness of staff names at all times. 'I was talking about *Huckleberry Finn* by Mark Twain, I didn't know there were two novels with the same title.' Mike gloats to see such stupidity and discomfort.

'No Malcolm, the correct end of your metaphorical stick is firmly in your hand.'

'Pardon me Mike?'

'Clemens and Twain are the same man. Twain was his pseudonym, his nom de plume. I thought everyone knew that.'

Pause.

'Well, you know I'm no great expert in this field. That's you, Mike.'

'I agree.'

'I'm right?'

'Yes Malcolm; with all due respect,' - (none) – 'you are not the literary expert here. I believe you will concur that literary expertise is my particular forté and the raison d'être for my appointment. With this in mind, ought not I to be the one best placed to assess the literary, cultural, linguistic and artistic merits of the works taught in my classes?'

'Of course Mike, of course, but we do wish to avoid any scandal. Anything that might hint at racism in the classroom. We can't be too careful these days. Only last month...'

'I read about that. Like so many of those cases one has to read rather more than the salacious gossip peddled by *The Daily Mail*. Have you read the novel in question – McEwan's *Enduring Love*? No? Anyone who has read it all is fully cognisant that it is not a novel endorsing homosexuality. Would you like to borrow my copy?'

Malcolm, flustered and transparently embarrassed, rapidly changed the subject.

'Very kind, Mike. Very kind indeed, but I'm afraid my position here gives me little time for light reading.'

Good heavens! Quite a decent riposte. I was not anticipating this. You have ever so slightly and ever so briefly gone up in my estimation Malcolm.

'I would not call it 'light reading' but should you change your mind, just drop round to my flat. You are always welcome.'

More camp than necessary; advantage back with Mike as Malcolm fears flirtation.

'No, trust me and let me assure you that the boys here, and all over the country I would suggest, are not in the slightest uncomfortable with the word 'nigger'. Indeed, I would theorise that most of their generation are blessed with clearer thoughts on the word's connotations than we are.

'We must not lose sight of the fact that they have reached adolescence after a period of puberty spent listening to rap music and its like. This has educated them, if in nothing else, to the point where they are fully conversant with the ways black artists have re-appropriated the word and through constant usage have robbed it of the derogatory white supremacist overtones of former times.'

Safe in the knowledge that he would decline this offer too I also offered to lend him a few albums by *Niggaz with Attitude*, spelling it out for him rather that calling them NWA. Of course I do not possess any such music but far better to let him credit me for my supposed 'street-cred'.

I left Malcolm's office with his conditional approval to teach *Huck Finn*, his conditions being that he reserved the right to drop in unannounced to any of my classes, and that I would not force any pupils to read aloud the 'N' word should it offend their sensibilities. I decided it was best not to seek his views on the episode in the novel where Huck and the runaway slave Jim spend days naked in Eden-like bliss on a river island, as they both seek to escape the constraints of 'civilised' American society.

Chapter Five
Derek Humbrell : 1

I never imagined my life would be like this. At Oxford the possibilities seemed endless. My parents had wished me to read PPE and follow Father into the Civil Service, but I had observed first hand what that had done to him. By his mid-forties he was completely integrated into the institution and was, in many ways, the archetypal Telegraph reader so lampooned by the left wing. The job became a career and the career became his life; the two became inextricably linked and I even believe the Civil Service paid, in part at least, for his funeral costs. By the end he had become entrenched in his ways and his views and was increasingly intolerant of so many things.

But it had not always been that way.

When I was a boy he had time for me. We had long walks in the country together, and went to test matches at Lords and The Oval, after which he would return my efforts at spin-bowling, before launching his fast over-arms at me in order to improve my batting strokes. We would play in the garden until poor light forced us in for a late tea.

By the time Father reached the higher echelons of the Civil Service, I was immersed in my grammar school studies and he was less frequently at home. He still went to cricket but without me, and invariably as part of some office outing. I even stopped playing at the grammar school, though I rarely miss a test series on the television. I could go to the grounds, but with whom?

I am not at all sure how my life has ended up as such a solitary existence.

As an only child I soon became accustomed to my own company and, with hindsight, found I had relied too much on Father for too long. Before I realised it, he had become too occupied, and I had no close friends of my own age.

It is the same at work nowadays. Whilst I was never particularly intimate with my colleagues, there were at least chaps with whom one might have a decent discussion over lunch or tea. Politics, gardening, the financial markets and, invariably, cricket. Men who were always informed and with a world view that was not obsessed with football and drinking like so many of my younger colleagues.

When I started at the school the boys were different, too. I do not believe it is a case of my memory adopting a rose-tinted view. I am genuinely of the opinion that the boys were once interested in Geography. But in those days so few had travelled, and what I offered them was no doubt more exotic than is the case today. My slide-shows of France must now seem so very dull to boys who have already circumvented the globe.

So, my colleagues are of a different colour altogether. The boys may be more worldly than I am, but the headmaster and his assistants are doubtlessly the most significant difference. I felt privileged to be appointed by George Baxter, or George Baxter OBE to give him his full title. He was the old school. By that, I mean he was old school but he was also the old school. Its very essence seemed to spring from his core and his influence pervaded the building. I sometimes, even today, see him marching business-like towards me down the corridor, before common sense demands that dead men, no matter how permanent their lifetime influence, do not wander school corridors in their quiet moments. George Baxter did this regularly to remind staff and boys alike that the school had a headmaster.

The current chap cocoons himself in his office most of the week. It is more a suite of offices, with his acolytes in smaller offices through which one might walk to reach that of the headmaster if one were permitted. 'Labyrinthine' comes close to describing it. He resembles some queen bee surrounded by workers or perhaps some deadly spider enmeshed in a web of smaller spiders. Whichever image one might choose to adopt he is quite impossible to reach. Orders and rulings are issued through his chain of command. One can even imagine the paper trail making its way from hand to hand from him to those of us on the outside. Except, with progress, it's an e-mail chain nowadays. Just so many fingers pressing buttons for a trivial end, reminiscent of the butler and the juice machine in *The Great Gatsby*, an image that lingers from one's own A Level studies.

I suppose he might regard it as his way of establishing and maintaining power. One renders oneself reclusive and elusive and one's rulings cannot be challenged if one makes direct communication from below an impossibility. Staff meetings are the only occasions most of us ever see him. He never ventures into the staffroom and his contact with the boys is minimal. Beyond his twice-termly appearances at assemblies – beginnings and ends – he is a remote figure and one cannot conceive of his ever engaging in a casual conversation with one of the students. The very fact that on the school's letter-head he refers to himself as 'Chief Executive' and his acolytes 'Senior Managers' reveals all. They are not masters or teachers, they are managers. As if this were some company selling parts for used cars.

I'm so dreadfully sorry sir, madam, we aren't here to teach your son, we are here to manage and direct his studies.

George Baxter must be weeping in his grave.

His office door was always open. If the green light was on, one simply knocked, entered and received a warm welcome. If the red light was on one knew he was giving his time to someone else and not to disturb. A sign of good breeding he would say. If he was speaking with you he would finish before allowing himself to be distracted by another. This was whether he was talking with a member of staff or a pupil. He was not to be interrupted except in cases of absolute emergency. Certainly not for telephone calls. He would always return the call at some point later. So unlike today when conversations are left mid-sentence whilst one party jumps at a ring.

Manners Maketh Man was one of George's favourite maxims. I mourn the passing of such good manners. Only last week I was tackling the school's financial director (once the bursar) about my tax code, when mid-sentence some atrocious pop tune on his mobile phone took him away. After five minutes I could wait no longer as I had to be in class. I am still waiting for him to get back to me.

So, George Baxter talked to people. If nothing else, it was this quality that made him human and brought to the school its great sense of humanity. A quality that is long gone.

I am glad to say that the present headmaster – I cannot bring myself to use any of the titles he bestows upon himself – did, despite all of his failings, become involved in that sorry situation with young Peter Greenaway, and that vicious man McMullen from the Science department. He has been here quite a while, McMullen, but I have never taken to the man. He is violent and impulsive, and I sense that he does not care for the boys' welfare and academic progress in any way whatsoever. If he were to ever discover that it was I who suggested to young Greenaway that the only way to resolve the situation would be his parents' involvement at the top level, I should fear for myself. Not physically, for such men as McMullen do not approach their victims directly, but he would feel no qualms about shredding my car tyres or pouring brake fluid over my bonnet and allowing some anonymous pupil to take the blame. He is a sly and devious character. Using threatening behaviour towards colleagues is in quite a different league from doing so to the boys, and McMullen's type are inveterate cowards.

I have also become aware of McMullen wandering around the school during his free periods. More than once I have glanced up from my desk whilst helping some lad understand the principles of relief rainfall, to see his shadow going past. I am convinced that he and Mike Redfern from the English department were slandering me recently when I walked into the staffroom. From outside I could hear loud voices but upon entry the pair of them went silent. Nobody else was there. The sudden silence was dreadful.

Mike Redfern is another of those colleagues to whom I cannot warm. He came here with an MA and a very large chip on each shoulder about having to take the post until a suitable higher position in the HE sector became available for him.

That was six years ago and it would appear that the universities are not head-hunting him in quite the droves he imagined. Not even the newer universities. And so he holds forth in the staffroom pronouncing on anything and everything with all of the authority of a third world dictator, and the oratorical skills of a mute. He talks and talks but if one sits back and listens one soon realises he is saying nothing of real substance. He sounds convincing and I suppose if you have no well-formed views of your own – as is the case with so many of the younger staff – he may seem a chap worth heeding, but lamentably his views would even embarrass a clear-thinking sixth form pupil. The other day I chanced upon something like this:

Phil Stonehouse: Have you heard they're gonna ask us to come in next Thursday for an extra parents' evening? They can't do that, can they?

Gerry McMullen: Not on a fuckin' Thursday they can't! That's my rifle club night. I've paid my fuckin' subs until the end of term and I'm not missin' that. I missed one night for that other fuckin' evenin' they dragged us in for. I'm not losin' another fuckin' night, so bollocks to that for a kick-off!

Phil Stonehouse: But they're saying it's contractual and they'll dock our salaries!

Mike Redfern: Listen, listen. They can't just arrange an extra evening and expect us all to attend. And they can't stop our salaries, either. One word to that effect and we'll have the regional rep in. Gordon Albert is a charlatan and if we give in to him on this we'll be in every time he says the word. We know it is just part of his obsequious image-making with the parents. And the governors too, of course. He likes them to regard him as the iron hand of educational management. As soon as he attempts to make it an official duty I shall…

Redfern rambled on with his empty rhetoric. I did not contribute or involve myself in any capacity, just pretended to be engrossed in some marking. My view is though that we should attend parents' evenings. It is an integral part of our work, and clearly a major responsibility one assumes upon entering this vocational career. If I had children, I should be wishing for weekly feedback from teachers. As it transpired Stonehouse had got it wrong, again. There was no proposed parents' evening.

In my own silent way I was saddened as I always find these occasions fruitful and a valuable way of maintaining contact with the parents.

Chapter Six
Gerry McMullen : 2

Maybe the trouble with Annie was I respected her too much in the end. Christ knows I'd met no-one like her back in the old country and maybe I was just overwhelmed by her difference, her classiness, her Englishness. She had graduated from the LSE with a first and was one clever woman.

When I met her she was working as a commodities broker in the City, making a fuckin' shedload of cash and I don't deny that it was part of the attraction but there was so much more to her too. I know I'd have fallen for her if she had been fuckin' penniless. But, as luck would have it, she had her own flat, a new Japanese convertible and a ravenous sexual appetite. What the fuck she ever saw in me I have no idea.

I used to tease her that one day she'd be off with some rich chinless City type but she said they were all wankers with flash cars to compensate for their tiny dicks. In her case, she said, there was no way her car was a dick substitute so she felt entitled to drive it and at whatever speed she wanted.

She often said that I didn't value myself enough, that I hung on to the myth of the ignorant Irish paddy almost as a badge of honour but that teaching Chemistry was a laudable and vital career. I was, she said, at least contributing something to society, not just making money from buying and selling stuff I never actually saw. Good teachers, she said, were essential for a nation's well-being. I should be proud of the effect I was having.

Maybe I did feel inferior in some ways and I know that I should have had pride in what I was doing. In those days, though, I didn't see that I was making a difference. I should have been proud. Nowadays, however, the kids are mostly little shites and the staff,... Well, don't get me started on that fuckin' bunch of spineless tossers.

In the old days kids still took Science 'cos they were fuckin' curious and they wanted to know stuff and at times it was difficult keeping up with them. *Yes sir, I see that but what if you change the amount of oxygen?* and, *What happens if you exceed boiling point?* These days it's *Bollocks to that - who gives a toss - if I ever need to know I can Google it.*

Google? *Fuckin' Google!*

I can't tell you how much I hate the fuckin' internet. Turned us all into lazy fuckers who just press buttons and hey fuckin' presto! You'd think access to that much information would create a generation of knowledge-hungry fuckers but, oh no, it's just bred a take-it-for-granted brigade who can't be arsed. And what do they do with this wealth of fuckin' knowledge at their fingertips? I'll tell you what they do – fuck all is what they do. No, they choose instead to spend their days looking at porn, playing dozy fuckin' games and watching clips of dogs getting run over by dim-witted American retards who can operate a digital recorder but can't find the right gear on their fuckin' cars.

Jesus Christ! What'll happen in a couple of generations' time when everyone is sitting alone clocking a screen all day? There'll be nothing to look at except the ancient clips they are watching now, 'cos no-one will be arsed enough to drag themselves away from their passive and fuckin' idle lives to get out on the streets and film more stupid fuckers doing stupid fucking things. They will all be stuck inside in their so-called virtual realities as real reality just ceases to exist. Thank fuck

I'll be dead by then.

Annie used computers all of the time at work. She could follow the markets without ever moving from her chair, her screen and her phone. Looking back, I'm convinced that's what made her so lively and demanding in bed. Spend all day at a desk and a screen and you'll be desperate for action. Annie never played any sport or ran so I guess sex was her release. Sex and poetry, of course. She used to recite poetry afterwards. Sometimes it was stuff she made up on the spot. Nothing special I guess, just impromptu doggerel about what we'd just done and which I don't care to repeat here. But often it was famous stuff. No idea what most of it was or who wrote it but I liked the sound and for me it used to give our dirty sex some sort of literary validation. Some sonnet about love meant that great writers had done it too. We were in good company. Most of it I can't really remember but I do recall *Ozymandias* by Shelley which was Annie's favourite. She'd recite it all, building up to a climax where she'd boom out the words written on Ozymandias' pedestal. Then she'd pause. And the final part she'd read in a slow, hushed, almost silent tone and as she reached the concluding line, her voice would fade to barely audible, and I would usually weep.

Not that I'd confess any of this to anyone else! Wouldn't fuckin' do to have those bastards at school think of Gerry McMullen as having a soft side. And, anyway, my love life has got fuck all to do with them.

After morning love and poetry Annie would shower and while I showered and cleaned the bathroom she'd make coffee and pancakes. I lost count of the times we'd need a second shower to wash off the maple syrup. God, she was some fuckin' woman.

On Sundays Ian would often come across and we'd walk by the river, take in a pub lunch and drink away the afternoon in a vain attempt to put off the end of the weekend. As I say, it's not that I hated the job back then, just that sex and beer has got to be the better fuckin' option.

If Annie and I were so happy together why did we spend so much time with Ian? Weren't we enough for each other? Let me tell you, Annie loved Ian as much as she loved me. I'd met her through Ian one night when she was staying with him and he brought her to the pub. We just clicked, she laughed at my gags and, having once been travelling around Ireland with her university mate, we talked about all of the places we both knew. She too loved Dublin and we'd both spent hours reading at The Winding Stair. To think of us both in the same seat, possibly drinking coffee from the same cup, not only seemed to unite us but gave me a thrill as if we'd shared something intimate, something physical before that first meeting. That real sexual intimacy was bound to follow this weird kind of foreplay seemed just natural.

Ian laughed at our shared memories, coincidence he called it, one of those things that happen all the time but don't usually get noticed. He just couldn't see what we were so excited about and, for all that, I loved him too. He never really had an ounce of fuckin' romance in him, the lanky tosser.

Ian's funeral was the last time I ever saw Annie. I've never seen such a huge fuckin' coffin. He wasn't fat, there was nothing of him in that way, but he was one helluva lanky bugger. That bloody coffin must have weighed too much for the pall-bearers as they nearly dropped it coming up to the altar. For a second I could see it sliding back along the aisle, out of the church doors, which opened straight on to the street, and down the hill to town. A few people audibly gasped amidst their tears but I know for a fact that had it happened Ian would have pissed himself laughing. Had he not been the poor bastard in the box. Anything absurd, anything that smacked of black comedy and he was off. His sense of humour was satanic.

Once at a parents' evening a particularly old mother, it may well have been one of the boys' grandmothers now I think of it, paraded across the hall dressed up as if for the opera rather than a school parents' evening. As she walked past us, Ian passed me a note that simply asked: Talcum powder or dust? I had to feign a coughing fit and excuse myself from the room. God knows what the parents I had been talking to made of it.

Another time some of the kids put together a school magazine and for one piece they interviewed Ian with a number of facile questions of the sort you find in teen weeklies: favourite band, favourite film, you know the pattern. One of the questions was, Why did you become a teacher? and Ian's response was simply, *Because they would not let me be king*. That sort of stuff doesn't happen today at school. But I can imagine Malcolm Malaprop's answer: *Because they would not let me be queen*.

I retold those stories to various people after the funeral. Keep laughing Gerry. Keep the tears away. Annie barely said a word to me. She kept her distance. She'd read a poem during the service – something by Shelley apparently but not, thank fuck, *Ozymandias* – but other than stuff about the day's business, not a word to me. When it was time for her to leave she gave me a clinical half-kiss on the cheek, no eye contact whatsoever and the single word, Bye. The emptiness tore at me and I stepped outside to call after her.

She'd gone.

The following day we were all back at fuckin' work. The whole school had been closed for the funeral and all of the staff and several of the boys had attended. There'll be no such fuckin' turnout for my funeral. I know that for a fuckin' fact. But as I say, the day passed. I kept thinking Annie would ring. I kept intending to ring her. But nothing.

Ian's classes were taken by Mike Redfern who'd come from an agency to cover until the end of term. He's still here. He's a fat sod but not such a bad bloke and he does try to stand up to Head Bastard. But he's not Ian and that's his fault.

Chapter Seven
Chris Adams : 2

Rachel was away all weekend. I really could have done with her help on Sunday as it was my turn to serve the tea and cakes after the service, but she insisted the tennis tournament had been pencilled in on the kitchen calendar for weeks and was it her fault if I did not occasionally take note of it? Nottingham seems quite a way to go to play tennis for the weekend, but she was adamant that it was too late to withdraw, that she was part of a team and that there would be no chance of finding a replacement. And she wanted to go.

So on Saturday I cleaned the house thoroughly and in the evening I wrote some school reports. After church on Sunday I was shattered so a simple dinner of eggs on toast sufficed. I had just settled down to eat when Rachel arrived home. She threw her kit bag into the corner of the room and wondered aloud in a vexed tone where her dinner was. My attempts to point out that knowledge of her likely hour of return would have made it easier to prepare something for her had little impact, and she curtly informed me she was off to bed.

She did not really seem too bothered with dinner and ate nothing before breakfast on Monday morning. Before getting into bed I had offered to bring her a tray but she was asleep, or pretending to be so. I used to think being given the cold shoulder was a metaphorical phrase but sharing a bed with Rachel had often proved otherwise.

On Monday at school my first job was playground duty. Barely five minutes before assembly David Gale came to me in tears. Would I please help him retrieve the contents of his pencil case from the toilet where some of the older boys had thrown it? I welcomed the opportunity to escape the biting wind that was cutting across the playground and told Phil Stonehouse, my duty colleague, that I would be gone two minutes.

How is it boys can be so vile and spiteful at times? I know David Gale is not the most charming of boys but what on earth would possess anyone to jam all of his pens and pencils down a dirty toilet and attempt to flush them away? Clearly some had been flushed at least part of the way round the bend and one red pen had emptied its contents so that the bowl looked blood-filled. No-one was ever going to want to use those pens again, and the way David constantly chewed on his pen in class reinforced my decision not to attempt their retrieval. I took David to my lab and issued him with enough pens and pencils to last him the week and sent him to assembly before phoning Charlie Dyer. Unblocking toilets is his responsibility, and it would take him away from his dirty books in the boiler house for a good half hour.

Kevin Fitch always used to bully me. It was never anything quite so comprehensive as flushing away my pen set, more just a loutish attempt to shove around a smaller and weaker boy. Whenever it was my class's turn to be on second sittings for school lunch, I would be in a state of nervous anxiety from morning break onwards. Even today I am convinced that for almost two years I learned nothing between 10.30 and midday, so tense was I awaiting my daily humiliation by Fitch. He was a year older than me but much taller and stronger. No matter what Jesus said about turning the other cheek and loving one's neighbour, my thirteen year old self hated Fitch.

One of his favourite tricks was picking me up by my

school jacket lapels and in one movement removing me from my place near the front of the queue. 'Now piss off to the back where you belong,' he would order, and I would go. My good friend Simon Walker would step out of the queue to accompany me only for Fitch to shout, 'Where are you going Specky? No-one told you to move!' and Simon would meekly return to his place where he would be the butt of Fitch's insults until the queue started to move again.

Why did Fitch force me to the back? Why not simply push in front of me? Did it make any difference to him so long as he had his unwarranted spot near the head of the queue? After all, Simon kept me a seat next to him so I still managed to sit where I always intended.

Outside of my daily dining queue humiliation Fitch completely ignored me; it was as if I did not exist outside of that queue.

There is something vindictive in boys like Fitch and the person who threw Gale's equipment down the toilet. It saddens me that these bully-boys get away with it.

I pressed Gale on the identity of his assailants, but he feigned ignorance and said he would rather not make a fuss. No doubt my wanting him to point the finger was to atone in some measure for the fact that I never reported Fitch to any of the masters at my grammar school. If only poor David could see that such horrible children probably grow up to be adults like McMullen.

I arrived slightly late at assembly to find McMullen taking the reading and prayers. Having this blasphemer in charge of a religious assembly does not seem right. Hearing him read of Jesus's miracle at the wedding in Cana turns my stomach. What ought to be conveyed as an act of loving kindness becomes, in his debauched mouth, the slaverings of an alcoholic.

The King James text of John reads, 'but thou hast kept the good wine until now' with the emphasis clearly on the italicised 'but'; in McMullen's sick rendition he emphasizes the words 'good wine'. The accompanying leer leaves me in no doubt which aspect of the Messiah's miracle McMullen most values. I wonder the Head stands for such behaviour but then I am not sure he even notices. I am all for democracy in school and a sharing out of duties but to let this man read from The Bible! He may not believe but he should show respect. I certainly did when I read from The Koran as part of Malcolm Davies's Cultural Diversity Week. Beforehand I was anxious lest some of the boys reacted inappropriately but I need not have worried, as most seemed not even to notice it was a different creed. Afterwards Mike Redfern said that had I been reading from Snow White and the Seven Dwarfs it would have elicited much the same response.

'Not that it's a story which seems to uphold strong Christian values,' continued Redfern.

'Bloody right there,' interrupted McMullen, 'all those little fellas living with one young girl in the middle of nowhere. One every day of the week for her I guess. To me the miracle here is that she wasn't totally knackered all of the time. The poor girl probably looked forward to when it was Sleepy's day so she could get some rest.' Redfern guffawed.

'I was thinking rather more of the necrophilia it seems to endorse,' he went on. 'My main concern has always been what on earth possesses a handsome young prince, coming upon a seemingly dead girl in a glass coffin, to dismount his horse, prise open the coffin and commence necking with her. A most unlikely and unconventional way of obtaining a wife I'd say.'

It is little wonder the boys see women as they do when one considers the values held by such people entrusted with their education.

'I'm surprised he'd be bothered with her at all.' McMullen again. 'First off, to all intents and purposes she's croaked and secondly she's been shackin' up with these midgets for god knows how long. No wonder she looked dead. Probably shagged senseless. So much for virginity being so fuckin' prized.'

Everything with him is sex. And such coarseness. One would think that a professional body of educated men would not need to adopt such language and that they might rise above the common urges and the common vulgarity of the common man. Alas, no.

I sometimes fear the contamination from being so close to a man like McMullen.

Is this something Rachel can sense?

Chapter Eight
Rachel Adams

Looking back, some of my friends' comments about Chris over the years have started to take on a darker tone and now suggest a warning left unheeded.

At the time I was too caught up in the silly-girl giddiness of the marriage. The event I mean, not the lifetime commitment. The white dress, the diamond engagement ring to flaunt before the eyes of anyone and everyone, The planning, the reception, the presents and, most of all, silly cow that I was, the notion of being the gorgeous bride and the centre of attention for the whole day.

A fairy-tale dream peddled by television. The cheap press and the whole parade of people likely to make money out of the day: florists, car-hire companies, couturiers, hotels, musicians, the list goes on and on. And the fact that this has been sold to so many of the girls and women you class as friends ensures that you too will be ensnared by the trappings for which the bill will run into thousands.

It's odd really that once all of the flowers have died, the cars have been garaged, the dress has been stashed back in its box in the loft and all that booze and food have long since been consumed that you are left with nothing other than the man, the husband. And, mind you, not your husband in a morning suit making romantic speeches about his beautiful bride and his great fortune to have her. This is a man much more likely to write glib comments on schoolboys' Biology exercise books than he is to praise your beauty, your cooking or even the way you treat him in bed.

Before the wedding day everyone talks of nothing but the wedding and rarely is any advice offered on the marriage. Wedding planners, yes, but marriage planners? I suppose the closest thing is *Relate* but no-one talks to them before a wedding, and my husband refused to talk to them afterwards when I suggested we might benefit from their help. At one point I even suggested we seek the advice of a sex therapist.

Such matters, for him, are not the concerns of a third party other than God and so he trusts in the Lord and the power of prayer rather than refers to anyone who can most definitely be with you in the same room at the time and who may even have some first-hand experience of the love and sex between a woman and a man.

My friends observed that he was 'quiet'. I took this to signify the absence of the brashness and coarseness I had noticed in so many other men. My friends said he was 'hard-working'. I saw this as an indication of security and steadiness rather than a lack of ambition and imagination. My friends said he was 'respectful' of women. Never did I see this as timidity or an unwillingness to acknowledge that women have desires for their own lives and interests, for a wide set of friends and, yes, for a fulfilling sex life- though you will have to believe me when I say this was never at the top of my list.

Like so many professional couples we met at university, or, to be exact, at the uni's Christian Society. We were both eighteen year old virgins straight from good schools, both from stout Church of England families who had encouraged us to join the Christian Society for the support and friendship it offered teenagers away from home for the first time.

'You'll be bound to have more in common with them from the start,' my parents had advised, and child that I was,

I dutifully obeyed. Why should I not have? I still believed then and regularly read at the services at home. I still believe, in a way, but university and life have a tendency to make you challenge what had previously been meekly accepted, even embraced as a child. Not that this usually happens overnight. Few of us have a blinding flash like Saul of Tarsus, but one day you realise that you have changed. It's not usually easy to say when, but over time external factors work on you and one day you react differently and, just maybe, you stop and ask yourself why this has happened and when did things change.

One Sunday soon after the wedding day, I woke with a searing period pain like I had never felt before and stayed in bed and missed church, leaving Chris to go on his own. It was the realisation that he had left me alone to go that made me start to question why a husband would leave his wife in that way to go and pray for her. In my view cups of tea, fresh hot water bottles and a sense of care would have suggested greater concern for the one you were supposed to love 'forsaking all others'. Maybe he was praying for the relief of my pain, but would not a loving God have answered his prayers with the message to go home and look after his ailing wife? Wasn't Jesus always the one to help out practically in times of need? Sorry Lazarus, can't do much for you today but I'll keep you in my prayers. Not that I ever expected Chris to be Jesus but on that day at least some concrete love and warmth would have been appreciated more than abstract prayer.

Gradually, perhaps not that gradually, I realised the ever-caring husband is another myth like the unicorns and fairies I once believed in, and that I would have to look after myself if I wanted to be looked after at all. At home and at university there had always been someone, some person or some institution to refer to in times of need or want. But how could Chris ever take the place of two wise and loving parents, a caring school or a whole university? I do not blame him for this at all. I used to, of course: why was he not the heroic knight in gleaming armour astride a magnificent horse who, with one word or action, could solve all of my problems? His background was little different from mine and he was as unsure of himself as I was so I no longer set the blame at his door. But excusing his weaknesses does not mean I can love him. That myth too, that myth of the happy-ever-after has vanished, and nowadays even the thought of a torrid, passionate night with no holds barred sex is no longer important. It's a cliché but these days I would rather suck on a bar of Cadbury's. And that is not something I would ever have felt able to say in my university days.

I am sure Chris suspects me of seeing somebody else. There is no one else but I fail to see any point in trying to tell him so. He would take any such statement of denial as an affirmation of guilt. I see lots of people socially nowadays. I play tennis, I go to parties with people from the tennis club and I once spent a weekend in a cottage in Hampshire with several members of the club when I had told Chris I was staying with my sister. Pointless deception I know, but at the time the little lie felt right. But I am not seeing anyone in the sense he suspects. I am just not interested in that sort of relationship. Or I have not yet met anyone. But if I do Chris will be the first to know.

In the meantime I see little choice but for our lives to go on as they have for some while. I have my tennis and he has his work. It certainly is not what I had in mind on that glorious, sunny, happy wedding day when the world seemed about to begin. But these days it will suffice. There are many women far worse off. And blissfully I am not married to someone like that awful man McMullen who works with Chris. Last year he cornered me at the school's summer party and without even meeting her I soon realised why his wife had left him. His language is from the gutter and from the smell of him, so are his clothes. This year I shall definitely not be attending. If Chris wishes to make an excuse for me he can tell them I am suffering with acute period pain.

Chapter Nine
Mike Redfern : 2

Gerry McMullen took assembly today. It might seem beyond the bounds of credibility, but as he read about Christ's first miracle at the Cana nuptials another miracle seemed to be occurring. Contrary to all expectations he delivered his reading with life and colour and, for once, the boys listened with rapt attention. The pauses at key moments of the narrative created an air of genuine anticipation, and even that idiot boy Gale who, yet again, arrived late, was entranced by the miracle. Afterwards I jocularly mentioned to McMullen that Gale might request such a transformation in his next Chemistry class. Typically, Gerry's reply might have been anticipated. 'Do you think for one minute if I could do that I'd be wasting my time with that fuckin' square-head?'

I must check what the antonym is for 'miracle' because the creation of Gale's head patently falls into that category. The boy is cursed with a cranium of nigh-perfect cubic capacity and whilst I cannot be seen to condone the callous way the other boys refer to him as 'Box-Head', I am desperate at times to incorporate such linguistic originality into my classes on the use of metaphor. The coining of such an aptronym gives me hope that our language is not, after all, in terminal decline.

Not only is his head very much proportioned like a box, but it is, lamentably, a most hideous box. His blond hair seems to have little life and style of its own and it sits astride the top of the box like sparse grass forcing its way through some rocky outcrop, defiant to reach the sun but leaving one with the strong sense that the effort might have better not have been made. Its texture is redolent of the plastic grass so beloved of greengrocers rather than anything that passes for natural human hair.

Beneath the hairline violent acne rampages across an already sanguine complexion. Were the other boys not already attached to the soubriquet 'Box-Head', they may well have adopted 'Stop-Light' instead. And this acne seems a mutant skin cover specific to Gale. His visage is one huge screen of red protrusions, some larger than others, but the whole giving an overall effect of a moonscape photographed through a red filter. Across the middle of this is his mouth. It took me months to ascertain what is so curious about his mouth and it is this. It is approximately fifty per cent too wide for the head, even a head of such unlikely and gargantuan dimensions. Its breadth serves to underline the most anatomically impossible manner in which the chin beneath tapers to a virtual point. My first reaction to Gale was one of both disbelief and pity and, in the days that followed, extreme wonder at what kind of suffering the passing of that head must have inflicted on his mother at the birth. Surely no gynaecological training in the world can prepare a midwife for that? One understands the usual practice is to comment on the appearance of the head as the child prepares to make its arrival, but hospital staff must have speculated what was being delivered by Mrs Gale. 'I can see a box coming towards me,' seems a more likely reaction at the Heathrow baggage carousel than in a maternity ward.

There's no sign of Malcolm Davies at my lesson yet but I have every confidence he will soon appear. He has yet to forgive me for the incident that occurred soon after he took up his appointment. It had not taken us long to realise what a dithering charlatan he was. Being short of exercise books for the boys, I approached him with a request only to be informed that Gerry McMullen held the keys to the school's stationery cupboard.

'McMullen? McMullen? What on earth possessed anyone to put that man in charge of stationery? He can barely read and write, and would probably not have a clue as to the likely purposes for which one might use an exercise book. Or a pen for that matter. To put McMullen in charge of anything to do with the written word is not dissimilar to giving responsibility for twins in the school to Dr Mengele. No good will come of it.'

'Mike. Please, Mike, I don't think that's a very professional manner to adopt. I would thank you to keep your views of colleagues to yourself. Mr McMullen is very officious in his handling of the stationery cupboard.'

'Officious' was actually closer to the truth than Davies' intended 'efficient' and, to a large extent, explained why the school stationery cupboard never ran short.

'I have no doubt of that Malcolm, but I would still question the wisdom of giving any cross-school responsibility to that man.'

I was warming up for a protracted session of Davies-bating.

'I am going to pretend this conversation has not taken place, Mike, especially as I have urgent matters to attend to elsewhere.' And with that he turned and walked off. This was a favourite trick of his. Avoid making decisions and avoid confrontations at all costs.

When I told Gerry over coffee, he exploded with mirth.

'Jesus Christ, that man is a fuckin' dream. Does he not realise we're mates? What a dickhead!'

And with that, and with an evil glint in both eyes, Gerry

crossed the staff room to corner Davies upon his arrival.

'Now Malcolm, I've been wanting to catch you all day, and I'm hoping you can help me here. One of the boys in my tutor group said something to me this morning about joining the school debating team. Bugger me, I didn't even know we had such a team, but can you point me in the right direction?'

'Mr Redfern runs the school debating team, Gerry. I think you'll find he has a way with words.'

'Mike Redfern!' Gerry exploded again. 'He's got a way with words alright! A way to fuck 'em up and use ten when one would do! Christ, if he ever took part in a debate it would have to go to extra time and penalties just to allow him to finish his first fuckin' sentence! Who the hell'd put Mealy-Mouth Mike in charge of debating? I'd sooner put Ian Paisley in charge of Peace Studies!'

By this time McMullen had attracted the attention of the whole staff room and even Davies realised he was the butt of the joke and, smile weakly as he did, the falsity of the smile was transparent enough for all to enjoy.

'Oh, good one guys, good one, eh? So glad we can all still laugh at ourselves,' he mumbled as he backed out of the room, having completely misplaced both his coffee and his dignity.

'We're not laughing at ourselves,' bellowed Gerry redundantly. 'We're certainly not laughing at ourselves in here.'

Chapter Ten
Derek Humbrell : 2

Vanessa and I are looking forward to the summer break in France. We always take the motor-home. Throughout the term it is locked in the garage, away from the elements and the thieves who would steal it and have it on the roads in Eastern Europe before its absence had been observed. My neighbour lost his that way, and his was a worn out and battered old wreck compared with ours.

I have kept it in immaculate condition, inside and out, and we both adore it. During the last weeks of term we begin running spot-checks on everything and stock up on the essentials we will need for our time in France. Books, games and, especially, painting materials. Many an afternoon we have found a beauty spot, parked, set up the easels and lost ourselves in the joy of our watercolours. Our home is full of our efforts, all dated and labelled as permanent reminders of our travels. In the mornings we might buy a baguette, fruit and some cheese and head off in search of landscape. If only we could spend all of our days in this fashion we would be in permanent bliss, I am sure.

Vanessa speaks fluent French. She loves to chat with the stall-holders in the markets and prides herself on her constantly improving colloquial French. Some years ago she did apply for the position of French teacher at the school. She was not even short-listed as the school does not like to appoint lady teachers, and that odd man Stonehouse was appointed. I am sure he knows his stuff but to hear French spoken in his strangulated Yorkshire tongue is an oddity. Nothing at all like Vanessa's soft and delicate accent with her meticulous attention to both pronunciation and idiom.

Meanwhile, however, there is the end of term to negotiate. The Head's latest bulletin forewarned us of a 'vital' staff meeting at which Malcolm Davies is to introduce the school's new initiative for September. He's calling it the ABC programme, and has announced that there is a three-line whip on staff attendance. I have seen and heard it all before. I shall attend, of course. One does not really have a choice, but I do not expect to be impressed. And as Malcolm Davies is chairing the meeting I do not anticipate understanding much of it. He is such an innocent in some ways: he dresses like a used car salesman and mostly speaks like one, but without the smoothness or conviction that would ever sell a car. He seems to be the Head's lap dog and few of the staff like him.

This is, naturally, the role of middle management – they get it in the neck from both above and below but when I hear McMullen and Redfern slating him in the most vitriolic of terms I almost pity the young man. He has clearly not been prepared to face up to either McMullen's bullishness or the overweight Redfern's sense of his own superiority.

Last term Davies came to watch me teach as part of the school's lesson observation programme. I do wonder what he understands of either Geography or its pedagogy. I attempted to explain to him the nature of self-directed learning, but it was a concept patently unfamiliar to him.

'Thank you for that, Derek, but it wasn't really a lesson was it?'

'I'm sorry Malcolm, how do you mean, not a lesson?'

'Well you weren't actually teaching them, were you, Derek? After your initial instructions they simply got on with their map work didn't they? They just seemed to be copying maps from the text book into their exercise books. Where's the teaching in that, Derek?'

As I expected, he did not have the faintest idea what had been going on. That the boys were not merely copying the maps from the text book but were incorporating into them the information about population, agriculture and exports they had studied in the previous lesson. The man's ignorance of best classroom practice is quite alarming. But I should have been prepared. The week before I had caught Mike Redfern in another of his staff room rants after Malcolm had been to one of his classes.

'When I announced at the start that we would be continuing our study of some of Thomas Hardy's poems from a collection published in 1912, the imbecile interrupted to question whether I had made a faux pas and intended to say 'Hardy's novels' as surely Hardy was a novelist, not a poet. The notion that a creative artist like Hardy might be capable of writing in two genres was beyond his comprehension. Unfazed, I asked the class for a show of hands: 'Who here is of the belief that Mr Davies, who seems unaware of Thomas Hardy's poetry, is strongly placed to assess the efficacy with which we study *At Castle Boterel*?' Naturally not a single hand was raised but I had made my point and moved swiftly on with the lesson. He would not have dared criticise my class after that farrago. And it is my firm belief he understood not a single word of that wonderful poem.'

I really wonder how Davies justifies his salary. Vanessa tells me I should rise above it but she does not have to deal with this man on a daily basis. 'Give it all up, go back to being a postman,' she says, whenever school weighs too heavily on me. 'You know you were happy then.'

And for a long time I was. I had the Oxford degree, the teaching certificate and had covered for maternity leave at one of the local state schools but, contrary to expectation, the woman decided to return to work three days a week at the earliest opportunity and to leave the baby with her mother during those days.

Two days a week were offered to me but I needed more of a salary than that, so took up again with the postal service. This was a job that had supplemented my grant during my undergraduate days. I would pass the time of day with people as I made my round, but beyond that my time and my thoughts were my own. No colleagues giving me grief and no pupils making demands on my time – just me, the mailbag and the morning. These days you see postmen wearing headphones, singing along as they work, but I always preferred the sounds of the street, and I felt alive in the summer, passing from one open window with its snatch of family conversation to the next with a passing radio blast or the smell of a cooking breakfast. I didn't mind the cold days either as I knew I would be home in the warm in time for lunch. But it was a summer day that finished me off – all those babies crying as anxious parents attempted to placate them. I had never really noticed them before, but afterwards it was uncomfortable, and then one day:

'FOR GOD'S SAKE WILL YOU ALL SHUT UP BAWLING FOR JUST ONE MINUTE!'

That was it. Just that one screaming desperate cry from somewhere in the back of a house as I posted a glossy foreign picture postcard. From Florence it was. The Ponte Vecchio. The letterbox was one of those that was installed vertically – I never understood why anyone would do that – and as the sunny card hit the mat I heard her. I dropped my bag and was on the point of hammering on the door when a yappy dog from inside the house broke the temporary silence, soon joined by a child's cries. I picked up the almost empty bag, muttered something nonsensical in the direction of the dog, and with familiar tears made my way to the gate.

Back at head office I found some notepaper and hastily scribbled my resignation. Who needs a job that constantly reminds you of the pai of an empty bedroom?

'Cot death', the coroner had pronounced.

I could have told her that.

Richard was dead in his cot. No warning, no indication and no sense at all. After four years of childless marriage he had arrived. The day Vanessa discovered she was finally pregnant she had cried all morning waiting for my return. When I finally got back for lunch she had put out three table settings. At first I was puzzled, but Vanessa stood patiently smiling and rubbing her belly. No words or explanations! We hugged and cried and forgot about lunch.

Four years and finally…

So when that pious fool Adams starts wittering about God's Will it is as much as I can do to be civil to him. It is easier instead to spend school lunch breaks in the Geography room away from Adams' misguided zeal, McMullen's pigheadedness and Redfern's belligerence.

Some days I consume myself with marking pupils' work, some days I scour maps of France for summer spots, some days I just tidy up the mess left by the morning's classes. Anything not to dwell on Richard's blue eyes, the gurgling noises he would make after a feed and the still empty bedroom.

I believe Vanessa still spends time there when I am at work but I have left it largely unvisited since the painful first anniversary. Better to run from pain. I would rather we had moved home, moved country even. I love France, but no. One time, after a magnificent day's painting overlooking a farm on the outskirts of Carcassonne, I made the suggestion over dinner.

Vanessa's silence told me I had made a mistake, I should have waited, should have let her pain subside. Amidst an aching apology, I told her to tell me when.

Some lunchtimes I do nothing whatsoever. Just sit in the Geography room.

Chapter Eleven
Malcolm Davies : 2

Next week I have to put the ABC programme to the staff.

It doesn't matter how well-prepared I am, I always get nervous before these meetings. I've drafted the powerpoints in detail so it will just be a case of going through them and pointing out the ways the school will benefit but some of the teachers are so sneering and cynical. It always seems like they're just waiting for me to make a mistake or to give them a chance to trip me up.

Time and time again I go through my powerpoints checking everything. Spelling is not my greatest strength and they know it, especially Redfern who seems to think that an MA entitles him to be an expert on everything. I've checked his staff file: his MA dissertation was on some obscure 1960s poet. What is the point of that? How on earth is mankind better off for a few thousand words that nobody will ever read about somebody else whose work nobody ever reads? Being an expert on a minor poet does not give you insights into anything else.

I felt quite confident when he raised his hand at the last meeting and asked if me in which part of the USA I had been brought up. Not sensing the trick I assured him, perhaps too smugly, that I was one hundred per cent English.

'I'm so awfully sorry, Malcolm,' he announced in mock-apologetic tones. 'It's just that you've used the American spelling of 'behaviour', no 'u' before the 'r', and I was curious about your upbringing.'

BLOODY SPELLCHECK!

God, he's a slideball. He knows as well as I do that I am as English as he is. He's had it in for since my first week here: I remember him telling me that most of the kids in the school couldn't spell and that they had no idea about syntax. Being new and keen to make friends I replied something about how knowing how the IRA used it to blow up buildings and people. I tried in vain to pass it off as a joke but he still spent the rest of the week telling everyone about 'Malcolm Davies's famous joke'. He's devious, pretending I knew it was a joke all along. He's so smug and arrogant. He doesn't listen at meetings, he just sits there, alongside his sidekit McMullen, waiting to find fault in others to make himself feel better. At least Derek Humbrell sits there quietly trying to take it all in. McMullen's staff file says he went to Oxford but it's hard to believe. Then again, it was only Geography so I imagine the entry requirements were quite low.

As soon as this term's over I'm out of here. Amsterdam again. They speak good English and the clubs are so much fun. And nobody knows me. You can be a different person every day and I love it. You can wear exactly what you want, wear different clothes and a mask. There is little chance of being recognised. It's not like North Africa, though. They're much more careful in Amsterdam about age, but you can't have everything. At school I wear a smart suit, of course, but in Amsterdam I can get away with wearing nothing at all if I want. A very big part of me wants to present an alternative ABC programme, something like:

A is for Anonymity and Arseholes
B is for Bondage and Buggery
C is for Cross-dressing

and so on.

I can imagine their faces. Even Redfern might be stunned into silence for a while.

And what if I met Simon Gore in an Amsterdam club? Imagine he'd lied about his age to get in and was dancing opposite me in tight rubber trousers and a studded neck collar. I'd have to keep my mask on all night, but oh, what joy!

One has to be careful though. Last year that Portuguese with the tattoos and the piercings stole my Rolex, along with much of my innocence. I had been with men before, but never men like him. All of my previous sexual liaisons had been with men like me and the sex had been predictable and, looking back, rather tame and English. Not so with Carlos. *Carlos the Jackal* as he called himself. The man had no inhibitions and an appetite to match his mighty weapon. Time in bed with him was half sex, half war and I loved every minute. I didn't even begrudge him the Rolex. It was a present from Father and was insured anyway.

I sometimes imagine the expression on Father's face if he'd discovered the truth of how I lost that watch.

Chapter Twelve
Gerry McMullen : 3

Next week is Malcolm Malaprop's stupid ABC meeting.

What the fuck is that gonna do? Teach us all the bleedin' alphabet?

That night, however, is the final rifle club meeting of the year before the summer break and, who knows, I may just decide to take my rifle to school on the way to the club. Just sitting there with the rifle in my lap would keep that dozy sod Davies on his toes. A warning shot over the head for the first malapropism, shoot the fuckin' laser pointer clean out of his hand for the second, and the third? I don't think we'd be needing the third. God knows, I'm sorely tempted.

Let him take note of my ABC:

A is for Accuracy
B is for Bullet
C is for Couldn't miss ya, Davies!

And don't think for a fuckin' second I'd ever be prosecuted. Christ, no, the rest of the staff would swear as one that I'd acted in self-defence and Davies wouldn't have a leg to stand on.

Actually, that could well be my third shot.

Annie hated guns and all of the time we were together I never kept one. If it was a choice of Davies' leg off, or a leg-over for me it would be no fuckin' competition.

But Annie's not here any more and a man must have a release. All that psychobabble about fast cars and guns being dick substitutes, maybe there is something in it after all 'cos let me tell you, I never feel more alive lately than when I've got a rifle in my hands and a target in my sights. Just to feel that tension in the trigger, the pause as I half pull it, knowing I can release or pull it all of the way... In such decisions lies the difference between life and death. The power! I feel like a god with a rifle in my hand. And that moment when you do pull the trigger and you know for sure without looking how good a shot it was. Absolutely no need to check the target. But should you need the evidence, there it is, beyond dispute. Not at all like deciding if it's been a good lesson or not.

Who the fuck decides on the criteria for judging lessons? The Malaprop Man came to assess me earlier in the term and even with sheets of criteria in front of him he sure as hell had no idea what any of it might mean. He wouldn't know a good lesson if it was in bed with him.

He was installed in the lab before me that day, right at the back with his pile of Ofsted junk spread out in front of him as if they were works of holy scripture. Throughout the entire lesson he shuffled them about, making little ticks and comments and frowning like he'd just sat on a fresh turd. Because he was there, the boys were impeccably behaved. Not that they ever dare arse around too much in my fuckin' lesson. One loud 'BEJESUS!' is usually enough to quell any idiocy.

The class went well, and they all got on with an experiment I must have set up countless times before. They cleared up efficiently and got straight down to writing up the experiment and their findings.

At the end The Malaprop Man came over.

'Time for a debriefing, Gerry?'

'Love to Malcolm, but if it's all the same with you I'll keep mine on, bit parky out today eh? Another time, perhaps?'

Malcolm blushed.

'You know what I mean Gerry. Time to go through the attainment levels?'

'Atonement levels?'

Sometimes it confuses the fuck out of him to throw in the first malapropism myself.

'Maybe, Gerry, but let's look at the attainment levels first, shall we?'

'Whatever you want, Malcolm.'

I've a damned good idea what Malcolm wants but, trust me, I'm not the man to give it to him. Not that I'm his type, but you never know.

'Let's start with the warm-up, shall we?'

'Told you it was parky out.'

'Sorry?'

'Cold out today.'

'Yes, indeed, but your lesson-opener. Not much of one at all was there?'

'How do you mean?'

'Well, where was the ten minute task to get the class going, to get them thinking?'

'Like what?'

'Oh, I don't know exactly, Gerry. Some little exercise, say, based on the work from the last lesson.'

'That experiment was building on from last lesson. They knew it was coming and they knew what they had to do. Why go over it all again?'

'Just as a reminder.'

'They're bright lads. I start doing the same stuff I did last lesson and pretty soon they're all gonna be bored stiff and they'd have switched off before they'd even switched on.'

'Just an idea, Gerry, just an idea.'

'Well, a bloody silly one if you ask me.'

'Moving on, I could not help but notice a lack of inclusivity. You didn't talk to all of the boys during the lesson, Gerry.'

'What for? They knew what they were doing. As soon as I start poking my nose into their experiments, they become all self-conscious and anything from me is likely to skew their results.'

What a pillock.

'But some were a bit slower than others to get going, Gerry.'

'Well, surprise surprise! That's the way of the world Malcolm. We all work at different speeds. You put all of the staff in a hundred metre race and you're gonna have winners and losers. Jacko, for instance, not too likely to win any medals, is he?'

'Mr Jackson lost his left leg when he was in the forces, Gerry.'

'Exactly. Even I'd beat him over a hundred metres with a glass of whiskey in each hand and, God knows, I'm not in the best shape of my life.'

'All I'm trying to accurately assess, Gerry, is that all of the pupils have had their needs met.'

'Well why don't you ask them Malcolm?'

'Gerry, if you had read my Introduction to Lesson Observation Programme email last term, you would be fully aware that pupil response to direct staff questioning is unreliable evidence. They are far too easily intimated by someone like me, in a senior position in the school, and they tend to say what they think I want to hear.'

'Do it unanimously.'

Once you start talking to him the malapropisms become difficult to resist.

'How would that work, Gerry?'

'Give 'em all a list of your questions. Ask 'em to write down their answers, but insist they don't write their names on them!'

'Interesting Gerry, quite interesting. But for now we are no nearer establishing if their needs were met today.'

'But what were their needs?'

'I beg your pardon?'

'What were their individual needs and requirements from today's lesson?'

'Well I'd imagine they'd all be quite different. There were about twenty boys in that class, Gerry.'

'Exactly. So in an hour's lesson, when the best part of it is taken up with doing the experiment, say 45 minutes, that leaves me fifteen minutes divided by twenty boys which equals about 45 seconds each to convey to me their individual needs. And let's suppose, against all the odds, that I achieve this task in the limited time available. What might I do with all this information? The lesson's over, they're buggering off to French or History or something else and no-one'll be any better off. Now, in all honesty Malcolm, do you not think I might be better off just teaching them and getting them through the exam?'

'Okay, Gerry, Okay. I'll take this away and give it some thought. I may well put it to the Lesson Observation Committee for their input and feedback. Now what of the way you embedded the school's Equal Opportunities Policy into that lesson?'

'They all had an equal amount of time to do the exact same experiment that was being conducted by the rest of the class, I'd call that equal, wouldn't you Malcolm?'

'But how did your lesson allow for different ethnicities and religious beliefs?'

'Ah, I'm ahead of you there, Malcolm. Maybe you didn't notice from your seat at the back but I made sure that Jacob Fromberg was working with a kosher piece of magnesium.'

Malcolm smiled and tapped his papers with his pen as he closed it.

'You can't fool me, Gerry. You like to pretend to be the staff rebel but when it comes to it, you're fully attentive to different pupils' needs. Well done! And if you could complete a lesson plan pro-forma retrospectively and let have it by the end of the week I think we could be looking at a top grade lesson, don't you?'

What a fucking twat!

Maybe it's as well I'm not allowed to bring my rifle to school.

If Annie was still with me that session with The Man from Malapropland would entertain us all evening.

And if Ian had been here...

Chapter Thirteen
Chris Adams : 3

In coffee break this morning McMullen and Redfern were discussing a visit Redfern had had from a couple of Jehovah's Witnesses.

I don't share their particular views on religion, but it seems Redfern had invited them in with the sole intention of ridiculing their beliefs. He was taking great joy in impressing McMullen with how he had found more holes in their faith than 'in a kilogram of Emmenthal'. McMullen seemed to be taking it all in and was looking up to Redfern with his usual mixture of awe and deference. I am not sure he fully understood all of Redfern's points: I cannot believe he is a man much given to theological debate. This view was confirmed when it was his turn to tell Redfern of his own encounter with the Witnesses.

'In the fuckin' shower I was one Saturday morning when the doorbell goes. I was expecting a parcel so I wrapped a hand towel over the wedding tackle and got downstairs fuckin' sharpish. The look on those buggers' faces when they caught a sight of me in the fuckin' altogether! Couldn't get away fast enough, could they? These days, if I see them coming down the street, I whip off my kit ready for 'em. You should see the look on their faces when they see a real man!'

This is most definitely not an image anyone would wish to contemplate for too long. McMullen is not the fine specimen of manhood he believes himself to be. It would serve him right if he were arrested for indecent exposure.

Not that I personally have any problems with nudity but

as I've told Rachel, there is a time and a place for everything. And it is certainly not to be paraded on one's doorstep for the world to see. I know how some of the boys at school find it very difficult being forced into the communal showers after P.E. lessons.

As a young boy it was something I dreaded. I was a bit of a late developer and every P.E. lesson I feared the looks and laughs of the other boys. I was fourteen before pubic hair started to appear and being slight as well I always felt like a little boy compared with some of the others. It is dreadful to feel self-conscious and the more one feels it, the more, it seems, others seem to notice and mock. It wasn't just me: the fat boys, the spotty boys, the boys whose penises disappeared on winter days. They were all vulnerable and susceptible to the harsh bullying of the fit, the clear-skinned and the well-endowed.

I had thought such bullying would disappear in later life, but it appears that behaviour learned in childhood never leaves. At least, when one considers such men as McMullen and Redfern this seems true. They must have been horrible children.

One member of staff who seems to have had to deal with all sorts of failings is Malcolm Davies. He is not ever one to be exemplified as the typical alpha male but that does not seem to have impeded his appointment to a senior position within the school. He is not a strong physical specimen. At five feet nine he probably weighs no more than ten and a half stones, and he looks as though he has never engaged in any physical sport or exercise in his life. His shoulders are slightly rounded and he finds it difficult to look you in the eye, especially when discussing a sensitive or awkward matter. Quite often he seems unsure of himself. He seems to lack academic and intellectual rigour and one would be a fool not to notice the weak grammar and spelling that typifies so much of his written communication with staff. The spoken word is treated equally badly and his speech is marked by so much incorrect word usage that it can border on incoherence.

In his role as Director of Quality he once came to see me about a complaint he had received from Anthony King's parents over the boy's perceived lack of progress in Biology.

He dropped into my lab at the start of one lunchtime, making out it was a passing visit. It was the first time he had ever been to my room. He has that oleaginous quality that I find so unpleasant. His 'Nice to see you Chris, how are you?' immediately put me on guard along with his comment that he was not on a witch hunt but was simply trying to, 'see things from both sides in the interest of transparency and fairness'.

One does not need a degree in Psychology to see through such a feeble attempt at manipulation of language.

It transpired that he wanted to see my lesson plans and schemes of work. I had no problem producing these as I keep copies both in the lab and at home for easy reference. He then asked if he could look at some of Anthony's work to 'get a flavour of his ability'. This, too, I handed over, knowing that this is not a subject that comes easily to the boy and that his work does tend to be unorganised and lacking in clear logical thought.

After he had been glancing through the pages for a while, I felt the need to offer a gloss.

'As you can see Malcolm, Anthony's work does tend to be rather poorly presented, and he's not at all effective at conveying his ideas.'

'Quite, Chris, quite. I would say this is best described as scatological.'

'Scatological'? The work is flawed but I would never have described it that way.

'I beg your pardon, Malcolm?'

'Scatological, Chris, scatological. As you say, the work here is all over the place. There's no rhyme or reason to the way he's put down these experiment results.'

I was speechless. Should I correct him? Ask him what hge meant? It might seem arrogant and superior to point out the correct meaning to him but on the other hand, how would it reflect on the school if he used this word with Mr and Mrs King? And if they then took the trouble to look it up?

'I'm sorry, Malcolm, but I'm not at all sure that 'scatological' best describes Anthony's work.'

'But of course it does, Chris – it's the very word to describe this mess. Now don't worry, I can see you've done everything most properly here and it is quite obvious to me why Anthony is not making the progress his parents expect. I shall inform them that there really is no logic to his work and that ideas are simply scattered over the page with no attempt at order.'

'I agree Malcolm, and do correct me if I'm wrong, but I am sure 'scatological' means something quite different altogether.'

'How can it? Ideas are scattered illogically. Surely that's the very word for it.'

'I don't think so,' I replied, 'I think you'll find it actually means having an obsession with faecal matter.'

With a smug smile Malcolm reached across to the O.E.D. on my desk and proceeded to prove me wrong. Except, of course, he could not. The dictionary agreed with me. Malcolm spluttered some disbelief and looked suitably embarrassed before asserting that his usage was perhaps an 'archaism' that had fallen out of favour.

In addition to his frail physique and intellect I suspect he is gay and although homosexuality is not an issue on which I have strident views, one wonders about the wisdom of employing a homosexual man in a boys' school. There is no reason, of course, why a gay teacher should be a threat to the boys' welfare in any way, but why put temptation in his path?

There were those staff room rumours about him and Simon Gore but as Gore has now left the school it is impossible to do anything other than dismiss them as the idle and malicious talk of such men as McMullen.

I am no homophobe, but it's not natural is it?

Chapter Fourteen
Mike Redfern : 3

A summons from Malcolm Davies.

What is it about that man that he cannot communicate face to face but has no problems with copious emails?

Dear Mike, If you have a time-window to drop by, we need to discus your policy viz-a-viz coursework submitions. 3.00 today, OK? MD.

Only three errors! Perhaps he is aware that staff are not only noticing his infelicity of expression but that he is very much an object of ridicule. Still, one has to confess a passing admiration for the devious way in which he enquires whether I am free. He knew full well I would be free at 3.00.

At 3.00 prompt I am knocking on Malcolm's closed door. Does he leave it permanently closed to create the impression that he is constantly occupied in major tasks from which he cannot be disturbed? Or is it merely to deter passers-by from dropping in? I know well enough what it is he wishes to 'discus'.

Nathan Spurden in my top GCSE set has failed to hand in his final coursework piece and, in ever so many ways, I cannot wholly blame the boy. Who, of any real intellectual curiosity, could be bothered to stir himself to write 800 words on the nature of the love between those two star-crossed lovers? This is one of the exam board's suggested titles and just about encapsulates the lack of imagination that in their corridors of impotence. What a truly uninspired and uninspiring task!

Nathan is lazy but not devoid of all conceptual thought.

I can wholeheartedly empathise with his reluctance to embark upon such unchallenging drivel. But I am also fully aware that Mrs Spurden – there is no longer a Mr Spurden at home since he set up domestically with a younger man from his office – is a more than protective and pushy mother who has invested all of her time and effort in her only son's academic success since the departure of his no-good, philandering father. Not that I am bothered one iota about the father's absence. These are not my concerns and, as I view it, have no bearing whatsoever upon Nathan's non-submission of coursework.

My primary issue is that the deadline has passed with no sight of a literary view from Nathan, that I have already graded the masterpieces offered up to me by the other boys and I fail to see why Nathan should be allocated extra time when his peers were dutiful enough to meet the deadline. There is every possibility that they may have achieved higher grades with an extra week or two to plan and write, so why should one boy be given an unfair advantage denied them? Were he applying for a position in employment he would have missed the deadline. The same principle applies here. I am confident, however, that Davies does not share my opinion; otherwise, why am I being summoned?

After a perfunctory knock I enter without waiting the full five seconds I know Malcolm allows himself before uttering the command to enter. I count to two and am on the verge of closing the door behind me as he instructs me that my entry is permissible.

I can see this has unsettled him but my timing is such that it is not too obvious an infringement of protocol, and he can say nothing without appearing childishly petty so he lets it pass. But he is rankled and for a moment at least I have distracted him from his pre-prepared opening to what he is surely anticipating to be a difficult meeting. I unsettle him further by taking the initiative and greeting him with an obsequiously polite *Good afternoon, Malcolm* as I take the chair opposite him and smile at him across his ridiculously oversized desk.

Can he seriously believe anyone is remotely intimidated by the size of his desk? Its effect is quite the opposite of the one intended, and I am thinking of penis substitutes when I look at it, exactly as I do whenever I see him drive his BMW into the car park.

'Er, good afternoon, Mike. So… *glad* you were able to drop in at this time.'

'But you knew I was free this afternoon Malcolm. Why else suggest this time?'

'Quite, quite. But all the same, I appreciate we're all busy at this time of year, so many thanks again for dropping in.'

He stood up. He was not quite ready to touch upon the subject of Nathan Spurden's coursework, and I could sense the imminent offer of afternoon tea as a pre-difficult meeting sweetener.

'Please do not trouble yourself with tea on my account, Malcolm. It is not very long since I had one and as soon as we are through here I have an afternoon tea rendezvous in town.'

That's told him. Get on with it, old man.

'As you wish Mike.'

'So shall we get straight down to business, Malcolm?'

Malcolm hates this. All of the middle management courses he has ever attended have taught him to offer a smiling and welcoming face, especially when a difficult agenda lies ahead. He has also been trained to take the lead in one-to-one meetings with underlings, but I too know enough of these facile strategies to be able to pre-empt and dislocate his.

'Busy day, Mike?' he offers.

'Yes, Malcolm, very, and it is not over yet so may we please press on? For what reason am I here?'

'Well, it's a matter of some delicacy, and one where we need to use kid gloves and tread carefully.'

More stalling.

'If we need to tread carefully would not kid slippers be more appropriate?'

Confusion in Mike's head.

'Sorry, Mike? Kid slippers?'

'A private, passing thought, Malcolm. Don't let it concern us now.'

Davies must know that staff mock him behind his back. Lately the pointed comments have been of a more brazen nature and I sense he is more and more frequently feeling publicly undermined.

So I decide to force the issue.

'I imagine you have summoned me here today to discuss Nathan Spurden's non-submission of his *Romeo and Juliet* coursework; am I correct?'

'Oh, come on now Mike, it was not a summons. You're casting me in the role of the courts or the police.'

'Well, if it is not a summons, would you object if I take my leave? As I say I do have to meet someone in town.'

'Well, er, let's call it a summons then, as it's about a call I have fielded from Mrs Spurden regarding Nathan's coursework.'

How on earth does one *field* a telephone call? If only he could speak properly. The Campaign for Clear English would have a full-time job rendering his emails, speeches and notices into something any layperson might understand.

'As far as I am concerned Malcolm, this does not exist.'

'What? You don't believe Mrs Spurden rang me in a state of some concern?'

'Not at all. I firmly believe she may well have contacted you. It is her son's coursework on *Romeo and Juliet* in which I do not believe. In fact, I would go so far as to observe that on the grounds he patently has not done it, so it cannot be said to exist in any material form.'

'You're losing me here, Mike. Let's not get into metapsychics.'

Poor Malcolm. As soon as the malapropisms kick in, he loses the scant credibility to which he may have been clinging. And, to be overly pedantic, why are malapropisms not called 'Dogberryisms'? *Much Ado About Nothing* predates *The Rivals* by some 150 years. As I mentioned to McMullen last week. Another example of some ignorant paddy bog-trotter receiving the acclaim for the inspired idea of an English genius.

'Sorry Malcolm, it was never my intention to lose you.'

'The whole point is that Mrs Spurden is very worried that you have told Nathan that you have given him a mark of zero for his Shakespeare coursework.'

'That I cannot deny.'

'She also tells me that you are not willing to mark Nathan's work, which is why you have given him a mark of zero.'

'Once again, absolutely true Malcolm.'

'But it is your job to mark pupils' work Mike. Mrs Spurden feels it is only Nathan's work that you are now refusing to accept.'

'This, too, is correct, Malcolm.'

'Mike, you must treat all of the boys equally and fairly. Heaven knows, the last thing we want is some sort of scandal about pupil victimisation.'

'Ah, there we do have to differ. This is not a case of victimisation. Throughout the academic year, and, indeed, my whole teaching career, I have treated all pupils with equality, and shown no favour at all.'

'But you won't mark Nathan's essay?'

'Absolutely not. On this point, I insist.'

'I don't wish to come across as heavy-handed here Mike, but refusal to perform designated school duties as specified in your contract might well result in a disciplinary hearing.'

'I am fully versed with the school's disciplinary procedures but I am also fully aware that my treatment of Nathan Spurden is not in contravention of my conditions of service.'

'But refusing to mark a pupil's work...'

'...is not a charge that can be levied at me. I was more than willing to assess his essay on *Romeo and Juliet*. Indeed, I marked all of the other boys' essays on this text. But, and here's the nub of the matter Malcolm. All of the other boys submitted their essays before the appointed deadline. And if the truth be told, I had graded them all within twenty-four hours of the submission date. If master Spurden does not see fit to take heed of my deadline - a deadline which I hasten to point out, has been in the school calendar since September - I fail to see why I should inconvenience myself by accepting it at a date deemed suitable by him.'

'See it as an act of kindness... of charity.'

'Shall I also return the work of the twenty or so boys in the class and afford them this kindness? Several of them, as I noted earlier, may well improve upon their grades with a lengthy extension.'

'Of course not.'

'But if we are to be true to the school's equality policy this would be the logical consequence. Just imagine the outcry when the parents of all the other boys hear that one boy has had privileged treatment. Will they not all be appealing to our sense of fair play and invoking our policy on equality?'

Malcolm sat and toyed with his cufflinks. The ones he always wore. He tried to give the impression of deep thought, but in reality this was panic. He started to drum his tiny fingers on his giant desk and the cufflinks rattled against the wood. Torn between my enjoyment of his suffering and leaving for a non-existent afternoon tea date, I broke the silence.

'Well, if that is all Malcolm, I really must...'

'Extenuating circumstances?' he interrupted. The question was a little too loud and betrayed his obvious desperation.

'Sorry?'

'Extenuating circumstances. Mrs Spurden is a single parent and the father's absence has had quite a detrimoral effect on young Nathan.'

'Oh yes, of course, his father is the man with the late onset of homosexuality. Didn't he set up home with some toy-boy? How the other half love!'

Malcolm's cufflinks were again the object of his fingers' interest. I had temporarily overlooked how Malcolm shied away from any conversation involving such topics. And now he was obliquely playing the absent father card in a misguided effort to exhort me to mark a piece of unsubmitted, and, in all probability, as yet still unwritten, piece of coursework. 'Really Mike, I did think we might discuss this in a professional manner. I see no need for such flippancy. We have a young boy's future in our hands.'

Not the best metaphor perhaps?

I smiled. Malcolm blushed. I enjoyed the moment and my silence said more than any ribald comment might have done.

'Exactly, Malcolm. And *professional* is what I am being here. I set the work, the work is not done, *ergo* no marks. To accept it now would be an unprofessional betrayal of the efforts of all of the other boys. I shall not be grading this work should it now appear.'

'Then I will mark it, Mike.'

Malcolm, mark an English essay? One might equally expect Pol Pot to join The St. John's Ambulance Brigade.

'No, Malcolm. You are not a qualified English teacher and I have to moderate and authenticate all the boys' work. There is, I am afraid, absolutely no way this can be allowed to happen. Should you even attempt to undertake this I shall have no alternative but to seek union involvement.

'And now that my views on this matter are crystal clear, I shall bid you farewell as I hate to be late for afternoon tea. I do love a good muffin, don't you?'

Chapter Fifteen
Derek Humbrell : 3

It is not just the loss of Richard that tears at the very pulse of my heart.

His death created holes everywhere. The bedroom I no longer care to visit; the staff room conversations about children and grandchildren I avoid at all cost; the incessant television advertisements at Christmas, and the empty space in Vanessa which I used to occupy. The reading I have done tells me this is not an unusual reaction but the loss for us both has truly been life-changing. To this day his absence is a continual presence in our lives. Instead we travel across to France and paint its beauty in washed out watercolours. It is not so much art imitating life but art replacing life.

It is as if from the day after the funeral a *Richard Off* switch was flicked that has left us permanently in the dark. Did we blame each other? Superficially, no, but in those dark channels of our psyches who can tell what secret accusations lurk? I am sure I never blamed Vanessa, but I am not one hundred per cent sure and this eats at me. Has this sliver of doubt somehow made itself known to Vanessa? And does she have some unacknowledged desire to lay the blame at my door?

One always looks for scapegoats, so why wouldn't two?

We gave up, we withdrew. To outsiders we coped. The shopping was done and everything packed away in its rightful place; the house was show-house clean. Nothing was untrimmed or unweeded in the garden. We went to social occasions, though these became fewer as the months turned into years. But withdraw from each other we did. Even our painting is not really our painting. It is my painting and it is Vanessa's painting. We may paint the same scene but we do not collaborate.

And of course the sex died, too. It had never been the torrid wild unlikely sex one sees so much on film and television these days, but it was sufficient. We had both been virgins on our wedding day but there had never been the embarrassed fumblings associated with the sexually naive. We never felt the need for exotic and erotic clothing or fantasy role play; we simply took our time and discovered what we both enjoyed. It felt wonderful.

In the early years I felt like some intrepid sixteenth century explorer charting undiscovered country. Our first tentative steps with new positions brought heightened joy and closeness as we shed our inhibitions with our clothes and the darkness. Our mutual discovery of oral sex was a new world, a new universe and a blessing in the months after Richard's birth, but after his death, we simply stopped.

Matters were not at all helped by my relationship with Mary. Mary was, at the time, the school secretary and had had a tragic life herself. She had never married or, indeed, left home. She had left school to attend secretarial college and had, at one point, held a high-flying PA post. When her father had taken almost three years to die from a rare form of cancer, she had resigned her PA position and taken part-time agency work in order to spend more time assisting her mother. Her father's illness and death had inevitably taken its toll on both Mary and her mother, and her mother soon fell into decline so Mary went from caring for one dying parent to caring for the other. During this period she came to work part-time at the school, initially to help out Jean who was close to retirement and looking to train a successor. After Jean's retirement Mary took the post full-time and in the one year she filled this post we became close.

At first our losses brought us together, and we would spend lunch times in mutual lamentation and comfort. After a while we fell into our Monday routine. Vanessa had returned to work by this stage, and on Monday evenings went straight from work to her badminton club, leaving me to sort out my evening meal. It seemed so natural for Mary and I to leave school and take a drink and a meal together at the local *Coach and Horses*, especially with their two-for-one Monday diners' offer.

Mary had spent the weekend alone and I felt as if I had too, so pleasant conversation over dinner helped us both. With hindsight it is a wonder we did not drive each other into even greater troughs of depression, but we did not. We found solace and comfort and a sense that life could still carry on. That was it – dinner and mutual support until the end of the academic year when she had talked herself into emigrating to California after a suggestion from a cousin who had found a good life there, and assured Mary that sunshine and good career prospects awaited her there too.

After she had left, I made the mistake of telling Vanessa about my relationship with Mary. I did so in an attempt to bring us back together, to illustrate to her how low I had been and how talking to Mary had helped and that maybe we should talk together. But Vanessa would not hear my appeal, she would only hear what she took to be my guilt, my need to unburden my conscience of my 'affair' with Mary.

'A secretary! How absolutely obvious!' she accused. 'No doubt you felt powerful and clever and superior and had her over her desk and in the stationery cupboard after hours!'

How does one argue with that? There was no arguing with Vanessa whose mind was set. I was a philanderer, insensitive to her loss, who had not even given her time to mourn for her son before jumping into bed with another woman.

Did she not see my sorrow? Did she not understand that Mary and I used each other as sympathetic ears and that was all? Sex never, absolutely never, entered into my relationship with Mary. In fact, I know for certain that Mary had never slept with a man. She had devoted her life to her parents and she had confessed to me her regret at that. It was neither an invitation to sex, nor an appeal for a quick initiation. Just a sad admission of a fact.

I hope she found love and sex in California as well as the job she was promised.

Months later Vanessa wrote me a letter: I was not to reply or to discuss its contents with her. It was merely her point of view for me to accept. In it she admitted that if I stated that I had not slept with Mary she could accept that. What she could not accept, or forgive, was what she termed my 'emotional betrayal'.

I had thought my life was simple. Vanessa and I had enjoyed a wonderful mutually fulfilling relationship, but after Richard she would not talk to me about this and did not want me talking to anyone else about it either.

How do women work?

And is this why I teach at an all boys' school?

Chapter Sixteen
Gerry McMullen : 4

Ian was such a top bloke. We started here on the same day and even though he was a bit younger than me we hit it off straight away. I saw this lanky bugger in ill-fitting clothes and I guess he must have seen a man of average height, in ill-fitting clothes. Never did bother too much about dress sense either of us and, in my case, not even when I was with Annie. It wasn't her concern either – she saw the man and not the fuckin' clothes. Christ, Malcolm Malaprop can put on a suit, but does it make him smart? Does it, fuck! He looks exactly what he is - a twat in a suit - and it wouldn't matter one fuckin' bit if he put on the royal robes and crown; he'll always be a fucking twat and there's no arguing with that.

But Ian, well he looked like an English teacher at a boys' private school. Always that semi-bohemian look and even when he put on a tie to come to work he still looked as if he had no fuckin' idea how to tie it properly. There was always something of the scruffy sixth form kid about him. He was a joker, too, and I swear he encouraged the boys to behave in more and more outlandish ways, just to be different from what is expected of a boys' private school. He definitely had something of the 'Dead Poets' Society' about him.

Each year the kids would be asked to do a presentation to the rest of their class as part of what he saw as confidence development. He loved it. He told me that when he'd been at school everyone had done something like this but their subjects had been chosen or vetted by Mr Knight, his English teacher. The knock-on of this was that everyone's talk was like an audition for the BBC: The Rise of Cromwell; The Life Cycle of the Whale Shark; Social Conditions in 1900's London; that sort of thing. There had to be an academic basis and the line of thinking was apparently that it would involve plenty of research work in the library whilst stimulating an interest in a new area of study. Did it buggery! Most of the poor kids just stood up and slavishly recited bits of The Encyclopedia Britannica. This ensured that most of the class would be bored stiff throughout the whole exercise. For Ian it was torture and served in no way at all to make the kids more confident speakers; for most of them the effect was the exact opposite: boredom tinged with abject fear!

Ian told me that he hadn't been prepared to go along with that kind of shite; he had told Mr. Knight the title of his talk would be:

The Major Effect of the Luftwaffe's Bombing of Liverpool in The Second World War

Knight had seemingly been impressed with both the serious nature of the subject and the length of Ian's title and, having less able children to deal with, had left Ian to get on with it.

On the day of the talk he had started in the accepted way of all of the other kids in his class, something like:

'Today I shall be talking to you about one of the major effects of the Luftwaffe's bombing of Liverpool during the Second World War, with particular focus on the bombings of Autum 1941 and their long-term effects on the city.'

At this point, apparently, the class was in its normal semi-catatonic state but Knight had sat up and with chin on hands was clearly anticipating a sharply focused and well-researched piece of British history.

Having got Knight's attention Ian then set out to grab all of his classmates' interest.

In a confident treble he started singing a song about how he had no troubles the day before but how today was so different. You know the one.

Everybody listened, rapt. He paused briefly before offering a snatch of another song, this time about some grinning lonely fool parked up on a hill somewhere.

Knight did not respond. Ian assumed he was too shell-shocked but also knew when to stop singing and carry on with his talk as if the singing had never have happened.

'It was late autumn 1941 and Liverpool was the target for one last intensive bombing schedule. The Germans clearly wanted to disable the port and it was inevitable that some bombs would fall on innocent civilians. Mary and James were a local childless newly-wed couple, living in furnished rooms in the Anfield area of the city. Mary clung to James every time she heard the siren and James, ever the protective man, would enfold her in his arms and reassure her in soft but manly tones. Having no air-raid shelter they had no alternative but to pray for the best and hold each other tightly.

James, James… (He did the accent) *I'm scared, what if we get a direct hit? We could be dead by the morning. Oh James, what are we gonna do?*

James held her more tightly and for a while his comforting grip helped. But her fears were so very real and were certainly not to be got rid of with a cuddle all the time the German planes were droning overhead. He began to kiss Mary's neck. James was by nature both a fatalist and a pragmatist who believed that if your number was up, then your number was up. But he was also a very physical man and the proximity to death awoke in him some primal force, maybe the force to continue the family name and line, even at the moment when these parts of his life were most under threat. His kisses on Mary's neck became more passionate and were soon gentle bites. His hands moved from her back and his intentions were obvious to Mary. By this time she too was caught between fear of imminent death and her carnal longings. The mutual longings won the day and on June 18th 1942, when the bombs had ceased falling on their city, Mary and James were no longer fearing for their own lives; they were celebrating the life of the newly-born baby James.'

Mr. Knight coughed prior to finally delivering a comment:

'Notwithstanding the cacophony of your tuneless singing, which I assume was just an unnecessary gimmick, you have simply wasted this great opportunity by regaling us with a sordid account of what I can only assume is some childhood sexual fantasy. What on earth happened to any analysis of the social, historical and cultural effects of the bombing of Liverpool?'

Knight was alone. The rest of the class had been engrossed. The sexual act and music were two things constantly on their minds even if they had never made either themselves. Ian had gripped his audience, but Knight was having none of it. Ian started to sing again, this time Why Don't We Do It In The Road, and this served to tip Mr. Knight totally over the edge.

'That's quite enough!' he bellowed, possibly as a consequence of his own ignorance, as well as his embarrassment at the song. His classroom was not a place for singing and even the songs in Shakespeare's plays were treated as poetry on the page rather than anything that might require a tune.

He was given a mark of zero but it was Knight who had

completely missed the point. Ian had not.

He loved to tell this story - God knows how fuckin' exaggerated it had become by the time I first heard it - and he loved to say how it was at that moment that he had decided to become an English teacher. It was partly the power one might exert over an audience but mostly the sense that there was so much more that could be done to fire up kids' enthusiasm and confidence.

He also knew he could do a better job than Knight. He always used to say that if you had no idea what was happening in kids' lives, you had no way of getting through to them. Knight had patently had no idea about the Beatles' songs and hadn't grasped the notion of using singing to capture audience interest, so alien to his notions of a 'proper' talk.

At school Ian encouraged the boys to find their own subjects to discuss, the things for which they had a passion. As a result, he would say, he had learned more about contemporary culture in the classroom than he had ever learned from television or a broadsheet. His favourite talk ever had been given by a boy called Edi Shaw who, despite his quiet attitude in class and generally self-deprecating demeanour, had announced that his subject would be The Edi Shaw Fan Club.

Amazed and fearing the worst, Ian had sat back to listen to this ordinarily shy boy's talk.

Edi simply stood at the front of the classroom. For over a minute that was all he did - no words, no handouts, no images on the board – nothing. But as the seconds ticked by it became increasingly clear to Ian what Edi was doing: where Ian had used song to gain his peers' attention, Edi was exploiting the power of silence. He knew that Ian and the other boys were expecting a mess-up, and he was giving them the time to let their fears be fulfilled. Once a full 90 seconds of silence and paper-shuffling had passed, the boys by now had sensed that this was not just nervous behaviour: Edi was starting with a mime.

Accordingly, they began to laugh, not viciously but with enjoyment. This spurred Edi on all the more and he twice opened his mouth and looked up as if about to talk, but each time returned to his paper-shuffling.

At the very moment Ian decided he would intervene, Edi began to speak.

With an experienced performer's reading of his audience he had timed his opening perfectly and by this stage his entire audience was desperate to hear whatever he might say. He had them in thrall.

In a flat voice, he began:

'This all started when soon after my birth I was bitten by my neighbour's pet monkey.'

Chaotic and uncontrolled laughter.

His understated and deadpan delivery served only to highlight the comedy.

Edi raised one finger to his lips and silence was magically restored. Ian wished to himself that such a minimal gesture would have such a striking effect on some of his more difficult classes.

'From this point on I was marked out as special. From the moment I was capable of rational thought, I knew I would achieve great things.'

As he watched, Ian pondered the likely reaction of Mr. Knight to this unorthodox presentation. In the playground this would have been met with hoots of derision but in class there were different rules; no-one felt the need to mock. They were being entertained.

'With this in mind,' Edi continued, 'I recently set up The Edi Shaw Fan Club. I did, at first, wish to establish a new religion with myself as a new messiah but I feared being seen as a crank.'

Strangely nobody laughed… or even heckled.

'My first step was to place an advertisement in *The Mail on Sunday* and within a week I had two members. I think the offer of free membership attracted them, though in all honesty, they may have mistaken me for someone else.

On joining, members would receive a signed picture of me, though it wasn't really me but my Uncle Jack who used to be in the army and looked a lot more like a messiah than me. I also sent out the Club manifesto which included my views on such issues as hanging, conscription, immigration and abortion. These are, in that order, for, for, against and against.

Since my one-off advertisement - I can't afford another yet - the membership has blossomed with no further effort from me. I now have over thirty members. Most are from cities up north and in The Midlands and most list their main interests as keeping bull terriers and gay-bashing.'

Here Ian felt he had no choice but to interrupt.

'I'm terribly sorry Edi but you're out of time and I'm going to have to stop you there.'

'Okay sir,' replied Edi. 'In that case it only remains for me to thank you all for listening today.' As he uttered the words Edi bowed to the ground in the style of the great actor-managers. But there was still a flourish to come: as he raised his arms up from his toe-touching position his hands firmly grabbed his loose-fitting school shirt and, in one swift move, whipped it over his head leaving him naked from the waist up to take one final curtain call.

The other boys laughed uproariously and Ian made no attempt whatsoever to wipe the tears of rollicking laughter that were now rolling down his face.

That was the teacher and man that Ian was. Inspiring. He loved to tell stories and they did not all have to be about him. He found joy wherever he could and with his experience of the restrictive Mr. Knight always strong in his memory, he loved it that Edi had felt able to deliver that talk in his class on that day.

Chapter Seventeen
Gerry McMullen : 5

Annie and I were married within three months of meeting each other. Talk about a fuckin' whirlwind romance. Everything about her was perfect. Her looks, her quick-wittedness, the views abouth the world that we shared, and the sex. Believe me, I was no retiring virgin when we met and neither was she. Though we talked of our past loves it was never with any hint of jealousy or with concern that either of us was making unfavourable comparisons. Instead we silently thanked our predecessors for what they had taught us. At least I know I did. But sex alone is never enough to sustain a relationship, as we both had discovered beforehand.

We loved the same music, and just as she introduced me to the Romantic poets so I introduced her to the delights of such great songwriters as John Prine, Tom Waits, Warren Zevon and, would you believe, Bob Dylan? I still find it amazing that she had never really listened to Bob fuckin' Dylan! Oh yeah, she knew the hits like *Blowin' in the Wind*, *Like a Rolling Stone* and *Knockin' on Heaven's Door* but she was genuinely one of the many who believed *All Along the Watchtower* was a Hendrix song.

Until she met me she'd never heard of, never mind actually listened to, *Blood on the Tracks*. What a joy it was to play that to her for the first time. I made it an occasion of religious observance. I disconnected the phone, dimmed the lights, opened a good bottle of wine and pressed play.

Apart from the pouring and drinking of wine, neither of us made a sound. I'd stipulated that short of a house-fire, talking was forbidden. I didn't want her to comment on *Tangled up in Blue* straight after the opening song. I wanted her to experience the album in its entirety and to start discussing track one would have prevented that and would doubtless have eaten into the opening bars of *Simple Twist of Fate*. No, we sat there for the full 51 minutes and 53 seconds from start to end.

She listened, engrossed, taking in every musical and lyrical nuance. I didn't think I'd need to listen in that way having played the album countless times since its release. I thought I'd be watching Annie's reactions, searching for a smile after that wonderful opening to *Idiot Wind* when Dylan sings about his good luck… Or watching her getting to grips with some of the less easily recognisable moments of enunciation that Dylan gives us all of the time.

Some of this I did do, but you just can't help reassessing a piece of work when presenting it to someone else. It's as if you're also hearing it for the first time, while the songs are saying something about your inner self, almost as if it's you singing and playing your own composition. I knew all of the time of course that it was Bob not me but that didn't stop the feeling that in choosing this album for her, in saying *This is the best album ever released*, I was making myself vulnerable. If she didn't like the painful drawn-out syllables of *You're a Big Girl Now* or the heart-breaking tenderness of *If You See Her, Say Hello* where would we be?

Not liking it would not have been enough to drive us apart but it would have stopped us getting any closer.

I had a friend at university, Jack, who, whenever someone visited his flat for the first time, insisted on playing Tom Waits's *Kentucky Avenue* from the *Blue Valentine* album. Just that one track. If you don't know Tom Waits, why not? It's a powerful song from the point of view of one kid to his wheelchair-bound friend in which he tells him of all the things they can get up to when he's cut the braces off his legs. The music rises and rises, the lyrics are filled with all of the naive optimism of childhood pranks but the song never lapses into sentimentality or sugary pity for the crippled kid.

If you don't know Waits's voice, he sings in a deep gravelly tone that on first hearing is not that dissimilar to the voice of Rowlf, the piano-playing dog in *The Muppets*. As soon as he starts singing, some people start laughing; they just don't get it. If this happened in Jack's flat he thought seriously about whether or not he would bother pursuing the relationship. The song was a litmus test of friendship for him. The first time I went to Jack's flat I didn't laugh; I wept unashamedly. And then I went out and bought *Blue Valentine* and three or four other Tom Waits albums.

I didn't want Annie to weep, but I sure as hell did not want her to laugh. As the final note of *Buckets of Rain* faded, Annie looked across at me and raised her forefinger to her lips. She came to me, put her arms around my neck and kissed me before again putting her finger to her lips and leading me to the bedroom. No words passed between us until much later. She too had fallen in love with *Blood on the Tracks* and a new closeness and intimacy had been born. I had had my *Ozymandias* moment. This was hers.

After she left me, I didn't play the album for over a year. The ultimate break-up album was not my soundtrack of choice for our break-up. If I played music at all it was harsh and loud – *Physical Graffiti* and *Exile on Main Street* mostly. Records where the lyrics are secondary to the noise generated by the band. Or, even better, lyrics that are quite unintelligible. Who knows, or cares, what they're singing about on *Exile*?

Even today it's unfathomable to me how we went from sharing the joys of Shelley and Dylan to splitting up altogether. And not long before Ian's death either. I've been over it time and time again, but I never saw the signs, the fault-lines she called them.

Most marriages break up because of infidelity, money problems or arguments over having children. But neither of us was unfaithful, we had plenty of cash and neither of us wanted kids. What was there to go wrong? So many times I asked her if she thought I lacked ambition, but despite her own high-powered job she was not interested in or impressed by career men.

I used to think I was too casual for her – I've never been a collar and tie man, a tailored suit man, a Malcolm Malaprop all-suit and no-brains kind of man. God knows, a shirt can last me years and as for shoes, I wear them until they're no longer on my feet. But again, Annie was never impressed with flash clothes and labels, and outside of work she was a T-shirt and jeans woman who barely bothered with make-up. The blessings of great bone structure.

When she first left I spent hours boring friends and strangers with my pains, interrogating them in the search for likely reasons for my wife's departure. They listened, mostly, out of politeness and with embarrassment but how the hell could they explain to me what I could not begin to understand for myself?

The only thing I knew how to do was to keep on keeping on.

As Dylan might have advised. Fuck me, like Shakespeare

and The Bible, he's got words for every occasion.

I am suddenly struck that the 'fuck me' in the previous sentence is the first time I have used that word for a while now. Just shows you how swear words are just intensifiers, and when you've got something real to say, they're redundant. Fuckin' words!

But she's gone and these days I miss her like hell, but I seal up my loss and my grief by trying desperately not to think or talk about her. The pain aches. There is no cure for the pain, so what alternative do I have?

I considered therapy for a while, but why pay some other fucker to listen to problems when talking to near strangers, like that idiot wife of Chris Adams who offered fuck all help?

Better to have loved and lost and all that.

Yes, my life was richer with her for a while, but that feeling seems a long time ago now.

Chapter Eighteen
Mike Redfern : 4

Quite naturally Malcolm Davies requested my presence in his office again. Whilst he fully understood my desire for equality in treatment of the boys, he also had to consider both sides of the argument.

'No argument Malcolm, my mind is settled, there is nothing about which to argue. What we have here is a *fait accompli*.'

Davies swallowed the bait.

'It is exactly Nathan's fate that I have in mind here, Mike. Without a pass grade in English his career options are going to be rather limited.'

'I would not worry. The BBC will take anyone these days. Lack of proof of linguistic and literary achievement is no great impediment any more to entering their hallowed doors.'

I knew however that it had, to date, prevented Davies's admission to that august institution.

'There is no need for this flippant habit of yours today, Mike and I am sure you know that Mrs Spurden is most concerned, and notwithstanding the school's need to avoid scandal at all costs, we need to do all we can to keep up our success rates. I'm afraid I'm going to have to pull rank here and ensure that this piece is marked.'

'What we have here Malcolm,' I said, using the most tired and bored voice I could muster, 'is an *impasse*.'

One more attempt to confuse him with a French phrase.

'What we have here, Mike, is a new state of affairs. This assignment is going to be marked and form part of Nathan's coursework folder, and there is the end to the matter.'

Davies leaned back in his chair. He was distant across that monstrosity of a desk, but the smug grin was still discernible. He was not playing with his cufflinks or drumming on the desk. His hands were neatly folded together and pointing upwards as if in prayer, perhaps in anticipation of his gay god striking me down even as I sat on my uncomfortable hard-backed chair. The oleaginous toad was genuinely of the belief that mere rank had won the day. I drew breath.

'Forgive me, Malcolm, but did I not inform you on the occasion of our previous meeting that as Head of English and thus the member of staff charged with the moderation and authentication of coursework, that I am not prepared to mark this boy's work at this late stage? Nor, I hasten to remind you, do I permit you, or indeed, any other member of staff at this school to assess Nathan Spurden's work. To do so would be both unacceptable and unprofessional and would necessitate the involvement of the union at both local and national levels.'

Davies did not respond at all in the fashion I had anticipated. He merely remained in his relaxed position, one might almost call it serene, and said nothing for almost ten seconds. When he did speak, it was to offer me tea or coffee.

'Did you not hear me, Malcolm? At this moment we should not be deciding on a choice of beverages! We have a fundamental principle under threat here, and there can be no middle ground. Let me reiterate...'

At that point the telephone interrupted. Malcolm took the call as he always would, even mid-conversation with the person in front of him, sitting in the same room. Such rudeness, but on this occasion it was a lifeline for him, even if, as I suspected, it was Gordon issuing him wih more demands.

'So sorry Mike,' he simpered, upon replacing the receiver, 'but when the Head calls, we all answer.'

Speak for yourself, I thought.

'Now, where were we, Mike?'

'What I was trying to explain,' I resumed, 'is that there is no way that as a pupil at this school Nathan Spurden is going to have that Shakespeare assignment included in his coursework portfolio to be presented to the exam board.'

Davies continued smiling. Had he not comprehended the gravity of the statement? How utterly foolish was this man? I glimpsed at his untouched cufflinks: today they were made of jet but with his initials monogrammed on them in white. His middle name is Andrew, and I silently pondered the pity that the cufflinks were not just that tiny bit larger so as to accommodate his middle initial. Power had clearly gone to his head. He could not want a walk-out by the majority of the staff, so close to the exams. But he was seemingly oblivious to the Damoclean sword ready to plunge itself into his cranium at one command word from me to my colleagues.

'Did you say tea or coffee, Mike?' I had not noticed he had stood up and was rattling around crockery and cutlery on the tray behind his chair.

'Malcolm! Have you not heard a single word I've said! Tea or coffee? I cannot believe you can be so insensitive, so crass, so impervious to my stance and that of the union, which I know will be behind me all of the way. You know I called regional office after our last discussion ended in deadlock.'

'And I too have been busy seeking a resolution. In fact, in light of your continued resistance to helping both the school and Nathan, I have to tell you I have made congeniancy plans, which I am sure will satisfy all parties.'

Congeniancy? Congenital, I would have said.

'And your contingency plan? I cannot imagine any plan that will be acceptable to me in these circumstances.'

'You needn't worry at all, Mike. What I'm going to do is take this whole problem off your hands. After long discussion with Mrs Spurden and the Head we have decided to withdraw Nathan from our exam entry.'

'And that will help the school's success figures? Even without this one piece of coursework there is every possibility of his still achieving a C grade. He is not a stupid boy, just a very indolent one.'

'Let me finish please, Mike.'

Davies sat down again and adopted his serene position. He really seemed to be somehow crediting himself with a victory here.

'Yes, we are withdrawing him from our exam entry. But only for English. Instead he will be entered as a private candidate and we have in place the mechanisms for his coursework to be formally assessed. In fact, the coursework of private or external students is marked by subject specialists appointed by the board. Of course it is going to cost us a little more, but far better this way than all of the bad publicity associated with strikes or lower success rates. He'll still be taking all of his other exams as a school pupil, so I don't suppose anyone will notice much if we include his English grade as a part of our overall figures. And even if we don't, no-one will notice either. Now, how about that coffee? White with three sugars, isn't it?'

I took the proffered coffee and drank it in a state of shock and confusion.

What was I to do?

I had been hoodwinked by Malcolm Davies, or as I would

come to see it, the Malcolm-puppet whose strings had been so cleverly manipulated by Albert.

It was a new feeling and one that left me most discomfited. To have been duped by that fool.

He would suffer later.

Chapter Nineteen
Malcolm Davies : 3

Mike Redfern really does behave in an odd way at times.

Our recent disagreement over Nathan Spurden's coursework must have upset him, especially the way I out-manoovered?... out- manoovaired?... out-foxed him by entering Nathan as an external candidate. I am sure he was not at all happy not getting his own way for once. All of his talk of unions whenever he feels threatened! Didn't hear much about unions after that meeting, and since then he has been very quiet. Hopefully this means he'll be a lot less of a clever dick at my ABC meeting. It will make my job a lot easier not having him throw a spanner in the works every time he feels the world is against him.

I was fine-tuning my ABC presentation today when the phone rang. I answered, fully expecting it to be Gordon with some new orders that he couldnt be bothered to deliver in person, as that would mean leaving his fortress and walking the few yards he'd need to, to see me. But, surprise, surprise, it was Mike Redfern. I was quite taken aback at first as he is one of the few members of staff who normally has no hesitation at all at knocking on my door whenever he feels upset at something.

I had barely picked up the receiver before he was into his stride. Apparently he wanted to talk to me about a book order for next year and get my approval for a number of sets of texts he wished to buy. I hate this part of my job. I don't really have much of a clue about novels and plays and poems but Gordon insists that as part of my brief to maintain academic standards

I keep a close check on the materials used in all classes. How on earth am I supposed to judge one History text book against another or one book on comparative religions against what seems a pretty much identical book? But apparently there had been parental complaints when Ian, the man who had held Redfern's job before him, was teaching some poem by a man called Harrison...

Since then Gordon has demanded some sort of quality control and, like many of the thankless tasks in this school, it's ended up being left to me. It seems the fuss with this Harrison character was over some four-letter word, so I suppose there is a need for close control. I just wish it was someone else, and I initially tried to put Redfern off until later, but he was insistent. (Have I got that right, I wonder? It's not insistant is it? Must look that up later when I check manoover). He wanted to place an order quickly so he could take advantage of some discount sale he had found, and he needed my signature. It seemed a trifle unusual as I know for certain that he has bypassed the system when ordering in the past. I certainly don't recall signing an order for copies of that text with the 'n' word that he was teaching not so long ago.

I suggested he bring along copies of the books he wanted to buy so that we might look at them together but he kept saying there wasn't time for this and as he didn't have copies to hand and how anyway this would be impossible. He then actually brought the 'n' word book into the conversation and assured me how we had reached a sensible compromise on his teaching of that book, and how none of these books used that word even once. Perhaps he was beginning to see how my decisions are for the good of the school and that I am not someone to be so easily trifled with.

I asked him for a quick rundown of the books he wanted.

I had not expected there to be so many, and I was aware of the work I still had to get through with my ABC presentation but he started off with something called *Entertaining Mr Sloane*. This was apparently a family-based drama concerning a brother and sister who both remain single in order to look after their ageing father. Nothing wrong there. His second request was for a book called *Oranges are Not the Only Fruit*, a strange title. One I thought I recognised.

'Oh, I'm not sure abut that, Mike. Isn't that the one about a gang of wild youths who go around beating up old people when they're fired up on drugs and the music of Beethoven played at loud volume?'

I also remembered something about the film of this book and some of the fuss it had caused but was pleased when Mike said I was confusing it with something called *A Clockwork Orange*. A film, he said, which was so shocking that even its director had withdrawn it from public cinema. I was beginning to sense new levels of responsibility and the corporate player in Mike Redfern when he went on to tell me that the plot of the book he wished to buy centred on a religious woman who had adopted a young girl and was bringing her up in the way of the Lord. I felt better. When he also told me that this woman was known for placing Conservative posters in her window at election time, I agreed to the purchase.

I was beginning to feel there was no need to go through all of the titles he had talked about earlier so I asked him to let me have the list so that I might sign it off straight away. He was appreciative of this, but did ask if he might run just one more text by me as he was slightly unsure of its appropriateness. I had so much still to do, but agreed.

'It's essentially the story of a man called Henchard whose troubles centre around the occasion when he sells his wife and daughter and....'

I stopped him there.

'This one does sound a bit of a risk, Mike. Thanks for sharing your concerns with me. I think I am going to say no here. Some of our Asian pupils have got sisters who have been in quite similar situations.'

I held my breath in expectation of all sorts of reasons from Redfern as to why this, maybe above all of the others, had to be purchased. But none came.

'Yes, I see your point of view Malcolm,' he said. 'I'll delete that one from the list right away. How soon did you say I can let you have the order for signing?'

'As soon as you're ready, Mike. Whenever you're passing.'

Almost immediately there was a knock at the door and within a couple of seconds Mike was coming towards me, order form in hand.

'No time like the present,' he beamed.

I was flabbergasted. How had he made it so quickly?

'Here you are Malcolm. Please use my pen,' he announced, pen in one outstretched hand, order still in the other. I signed it.

'But Mike, where were you when we were talking just now?'

Mike pulled his mobile from his jacket pocket.

'Right outside,' he exclaimed.

'But why? Why not just come in and talk to me like this?'

'Oh Malcolm, I appreciate how many important telephone calls you have to field.' He paused. 'And I simply did not wish the petty business of my book order to impinge upon the more pressing duties you have. And I knew that were I to call you on the phone you would have no other distractions. Like a phone call for instance. Thanks again for the signature here. I have left a copy for your records.' And with a swift turn and a cheery wave of his fat hand, he was gone.

I could not quite decipher the title he'd crossed out, but casting my eye over the rest of the list I could see nothing to cause alarm, even if some of the titles were a little odd: *The Wasp Factory*; *The Cement Garden*; *Saved*; *The Well of Loneliness*; *The Romans in Britain*. Surely that last one was more of a History text?

Oh well, I suppose it can always be used as a cross-curricular resource.

Chapter Twenty
Derek Humbrell : 4

All weekend I watched the cricket from Trent Bridge on the television. I tidied the garden a little in between times and went out shopping for food, but otherwise, nothing.

Vanessa went to her sister's on Friday night and did not return until late Sunday so I behaved like a student. I should have marked some homework that I had collected on Friday but why bother? I did it during the morning's classes and glancing up at one stage I glimpsed McMullen outside again. I am not at all sure what he is doing prowling around the school. He is not a man to be trusted.

Last week he and Mike Redfern decided to play a sick practical joke on Phil Stonehouse. Apparently he had set one of his classes the task of composing a piece in French entitled *La Mère Ideale*. Between them Redfern and McMullen wrote some scurrilous filth about a promiscuous housewife who bestows sexual favours on the school friends of her son. On the paper they wrote the name of one of the boys who had been off ill and slipped the rogue essay into the pile Stonehouse had left in his pigeon hole. I am convinced it must have been McMullen's idea and that Redfern wrote the piece. It seems unlikely McMullen would speak much French. Most times his English is fairly limited.

From what I could gather, Stonehouse was in quite a state wondering what to do with the piece. He was pleased with the use of the subjunctive, but shocked that a boy might submit writing of such a sexually explicit nature. At one point he approached Redfern for advice.

'Treat it as a serious approach,' suggested Redfern. 'We are, after all, no longer living in an age when *Lady Chatterley's Lover* is deemed too salacious for one's wife or servant to read. Consider it a work of art and mark it accordingly.'

'And while you're at it, I'd like the number of the mother if you don't mind. I could do with some of that treatment after school myself.'

Unsurprisingly, McMullen felt he had to offer his thoughts.

'But there are real issues here,' Stonehouse replied. 'After all, we do have a duty of care to these boys and some of the descriptions here are very graphic indeed. I'd hate to think of a mother out there behaving in this way with young boys.'

'Get fuckin' real, Stonehouse. If you were gettin' blow-jobs like that after school, you'd not want some interferin' bugger tryin' to protect you. You'd be wantin' more of the same on a regular fuckin' basis!'

'Oh I know it's probably sheer fantasy but what of the mental state of the boy who would, a) hand this in to me and, b) think it was appropriate to write the stuff in the first place? Why, I had to look up some of the terms and I am not even sure about some of what is going on here when I've got it in English!'

And so the baiting of Stonehouse carried on in this vulgar manner for almost a week until the 'joke' had run its course. This level of schoolboy prank leaves me in despair. Surely real men, real gentleman with breeding and class, do not act in this fashion? This sort of teenage behaviour with all of its smuttiness would never have been tolerated in any of the departments Father ran during his career. I appreciate we are talking of a different era here, a generation or so back, but men respected each other's professionalism then and did not feel the need to resort to tomfoolery and sexual fantasies to occupy their working days. Sadly it appears those standards died with the passing of Father and his generation.

Like the loss of Richard, his death is not something I have ever come to terms with fully. I cannot get to grips with the fact that I am a childless orphan.

Father had always been such a healthy man, advocating the values of a strong work ethic and a clean lifestyle. He rose and retired early, took regular exercise and, unusually for those times, did not smoke, and drank only moderately. I don't recall him ever taking a day off work because of illness.

His summer holidays were spent with Mother walking the coastal paths and tow paths of Britain, the country he adored. He maintained he had seen enough of France and abroad during the war and Mother always seemed content to follow in his footsteps, quite literally, along the designated footpaths he so loved. A good map, sound walking boots, a sensible lunch and plenty of water and they would be out all day before taking a light supper and off to bed in preparation for the day ahead.

When retirement beckoned, he already had plans meticulously drawn up for new walking breaks in Scotland and the north of England. So how sick and ironic was it that just three months before his retirement date, when he and Mother were walking the wild but beautiful coastal path near Hartland Point, he suddenly collapsed with what was later diagnosed as the malignant brain tumour that after six months of hospitalisation and futile treatments took him from us?

At first, like everyone else in such awful circumstances, Mother and I clung to every shred of hope we could find in every statement the doctors made. We willed him to recover whilst simultaneously not acknowledging to each other the obvious decline we could see in him at every visit. Hope may well spring eternal in the human heart but hope plays mean tricks on so many of us. And on some of us fate plays a mean card on more than one occasion.

When the hospital could do no more, they moved Father into the local hospice, a place where Mother used to volunteer. This involved reading to those for whom reading, even holding a book, was no longer possible. It was sometimes a case of just listening as dying people tended to find comfort in the presence of a stranger. As soon as the hospital said he was to be moved to the hospice, all pretence of hope disappeared from me and Mother. Even so we never admitted as much to ourselves, and certainly never to each other. My sole consolation by that point was that Father had no real awareness of either where he was or what was happening to him. This belief may have been for my comfort alone. Who knows what little deceptions we practise for our own self-preservation?

The first day at the hospice seemed no different from the last hospital day. A different venue, different medical staff with different faces, but essentially the same situation. Within two weeks, however, he had been moved from the room he shared with three other chaps, and was now in a room on his own. Both Mother and I knew this was preparation for the final moments, but once again neither of us said as much to the other. It was most definitely not a subject we would discuss with Father, choosing instead to comment on his good fortune at landing a private room.

Throughout my life it had always seemed as though Father and I had been close, and that we had spent considerable time together, but the long silences of these visits brought home to me how little we had ever really communicated. Naturally we had talked, there had been words, but about what? Cricket. World Affairs. Politics. But never really about ourselves and each other and so it was in his final days. To break the custom of a lifetime seemed unnatural. And too late. Calm restraint and quiet politeness do not give way to exuberance and an outpouring of bottled up emotion just because someone is dying. It's at these points, in fact, when they remain strictly off limits.

Father's last two days were, and one feels so selfish saying this, the most unbearable. His last moments of consciousness had faded into that sleep that precedes the coma that precedes death itself.

Without the pretence that we were addressing ourselves to a conscious Father, Mother and I were left with only each other for conversation. If I had had little to say to Father in life, I had even less to say to Mother. It was then I realised how I had never really noticed her: she had provided meals, clean clothes, maternal love, even in my adult years, but I now recognised, it had all been a one-way relationship.

She gave me all of those things, and I took them. And apart from the predictably unimaginative presents at Christmas, birthdays and Mothers' Days, what had I given her? Most certainly not any acknowledgement that she was another person, another adult with whom I should have been having an adult relationship. When we knew for certain that Father had finally given up the struggle, I put my arm around her and tried to comfort her but inside I knew I was waiting for the comfort that she, as a mother, should be offering me.

I was grief-stricken and the natural order was for my

Mother to protect me, to tell me that everything would be alright.

Still a child, even at that age? I took control in dealing with all of the officialdom that follows a death, but at night in my parents' house, my Mother's house, I was still waiting for her reassurance, perhaps almost as a thank-you for the efficient way I had sorted out 'the arrangements'.

At the funeral itself I did not cry.

I could not cry.

Back at home with Mother, and later when Vanessa and I were back at our home, I wept uncontrollably.

Chapter Twenty-One
Chris Adams : 4

Not too long after the Anthony King incident the school was subject to two days of 'mock inspection' from some consultancy company that either the Head or Malcolm Davies had arranged. The aim was to sharpen up best practice across the school before the implementation of some new policy for the next academic year. There was much staff disquiet about the likely cost of such a consultancy company, along with the widespread belief that no matter what the cost, the benefits were likely to be minimal.

As always with such matters, there is some misguided fool with his own agenda and a limited imagination that prevents him seeing what anyone else might be trying to achieve. I was resigned. Let it happen and next month there would be another issue to bother and infuriate staff. At times it appears that the school's management is adopting a policy of agitating and upsetting the staff in the belief that creating an air of instability and boat rocking is good for the school.

The consultancy's second and final day was coming to an end when I received a visit to my GCSE class. They are all sound students who work to the best of their abilities, albeit that in several cases these abilities are limited. Being close to the exam I decided to show them a Powerpoint of some exam tips I had picked up at a recent London meeting. These were aimed at teachers so I displayed them and talked through them in an attempt to explain to the boys what the complex terminology and expression might mean for them. I thought the lesson had been useful and the boys all took notes which I hoped would prove beneficial when it came to sitting the paper.

After class, the pseudo-inspector offered me his feedback. He was a younger man who clearly had been caught up in some of the experimental teaching of a previous decade which had since fallen out of favour. He had not enjoyed the class.

'All very teacher-led,' was his first utterance.

My efforts to explain that the points put on the screen had needed a gloss for the pupils' benefit seemed only to annoy and perplex him in equal measure.

'I feel you missed an opportunity there,' he wheedled. 'Far better for kinaesthetic learners to discuss in pairs the exam board's advice in order that they might make meaning for themselves on ways to improve their grades.'

The fool had not appreciated that the very density of the language precluded the boys from otherwise any sense of it all.

'Never under-estimate the potential children have to learn in a constructive way from each other,' was the parroted rejoinder. 'Education is a process of mastering new concepts along the road of the educational journey. They would have worked out for themselves some of the more difficult terms.'

I could not resist.

'Tu crois que c'est possible de comprendre les idées difficiles, même qu'on ne comprend pas les mots utilisés par l'auteur?'

'I beg your pardon?'

'My point exactly,' I beamed. 'Without a clear knowledge and understanding of the lexis used, any comprehension of new ideas and concepts can never be anything more than rudimentary, a series of unlikely guesses at best, and complete non-understanding at worst.'

He was more than a little riled.

'Notwithstanding that,' he continued, 'I do believe you

missed another chance there, the opportunity to introduce technology and I.T. into the classroom. Why did you not suggest to the boys that they use their mobile phones to google any words that were causing them difficulties?'

'Two reasons really. One, it was far quicker to explain, and, two, did you not notice that all of their phones were in a box on my desk? I find that if one does not take them in at the beginning of the lesson, the class is constantly interrupted by incoming calls and naughty boys distracting themselves with games and texts when they think I am not looking.'

That was it. I was a Luddite whose seeming reliance on teacher explanation stood in the way of any possible chance of learning and exam success. What a fool.

He wittered on. A few other 'aspects of the class' that were 'unsatisfactory' and 'in need of improvement' had come to his attention. And that was the last of it, I thought. Another passing 'expert' had been and gone.

Three days later, however, I received the following email from Malcolm Davies which I read with a mixture of anger, annoyance and disbelief.

Dear Chris,

As you received a low grade in the recent mock inspection, you will now be given some support as outlined in the school's teaching policy. This will outline a series of meetings with I in which we shall discus an action plan that will lead to your delivering a more consistantly high level of provision.

Regards,
Malcolm

What was the most appropriate response? To storm into Davies's office and demand a re-assessment by someone who actually understood the teaching of Biology?

To ignore it altogether?

To offer him advice on the standard spelling of 'consistently' and 'discuss? To inform him that the correct grammatical form is 'with me' not 'with I'?

To tell him, as McMullen would doubtlessly have done, to 'fuck off'?

I brooded on it for a couple of days before replying:

Dear Malcolm,

Many thanks for your email.

Of course I always knew that I have been a complete charlatan throughout my teaching career. I am, however, surprised that it has taken the school's management quite so long – ten years in fact - to come to the same self-evident conclusion.

Indeed, so thoroughly has school management been hoodwinked, that I have:

1. *Constantly been given positive feedback.*
2. *Been asked to mentor several new staff.*
3. *On several occasions been asked to run staff training sessions.*
4. *Run a consistently successful Biology department since my appointment.*

But quite naturally, if the school now realises, on the basis of one allegedly weak lesson, that I require support, who am I to disagree?

And, given another ten years' teaching, I hope to attain the school's required standard.

Regards,
Chris

P.S. I fear that the tone of my reply may, by certain folk, be misconstrued as caustic or satirical but please rest assured this was never my intention any more than I imagine it was yours in writing to me.

Once I'd pressed 'Send' I sauntered home with a spring in my step and the knowledge that neither Malcolm nor Rachel would ever grind me down again.

My email barely registered with Malcolm.

At the next meeting he thanked me for it as one might thank a cat for a dead bird before carrying on with his own private and aimless agenda.

Chapter Twenty-Two
Malcolm Davies : 4

I had not long been in from work and my triumphant meeting with Mike Redfern, when Father rang and said that work had brought him into the area and he would be dropping in for a coffee and a bite to eat. Just like that. No request, no 'by your leave', just the expectation that if that was what he wanted, then that would be fine. When I protested that the cupboard was bare, he said it didn't matter: I could take him out for dinner on the fine salary I was earning, thanks to him and his old pals. All of my further comments about workload and preparing for an important meeting cut no ice either, so an hour or so later we were in some local trattoria with a bottle of Barolo and a plate of pasta each.

I don't talk about my family at work. I barely talk about my family to anyone. Yes, Father got me this job and I should be grateful to him for it, but it's not ideal. But if I try to mention this to him, I'm met with total resistance. He is not a man who is accustomed to seeing things from other people's point of view.

As he sat opposite me I noticed his hair was greyer and receding just a little more than it had been at Christmas when we had last seen each other. Otherwise, he might have passed for a much younger man.

He is still in good physical shape, largely I believe, because of the way he throws himself into games of tennis and squash several days of the week. He has never liked to lose and he rarely does, often thrashing much younger opponents. Not that he ever tells them his true age. He's too vain for that.

Sitting opposite him I feel such a slob. When he rang I had ditched my work clothes and wearing a polo shirt, jeans and trainers and could simply not be bothered to change again, but faced with him in that crisp white shirt, striped tie and dark slimline suit I feel like a naughty boy sent to see the Head of House. This may not be Father's intention. I am sure he expected me to still be in my suit, but it is nevertheless a situation he enjoys.

As a child I remember his sense of always being right. If there were many ways of doing something, his was always the right one. Milk or tea in first? The correct way to begin a business letter? What to drink before Christmas lunch? For Christ's sake, even the correct way to peel the potatoes for Christmas lunch one year! These were all matters on which he was expert and everyone else was expected to follow his lead. My poor mother was eventually driven into the ground by his relentless opinions and constant lecturing. Though I miss her dearly, I sometimes feel she wished herself to death just to be free of him.

'No appetite, eh?'

'Sorry?'

'You've not touched a mouthful. Just staring into space you were. Did you actually hear a single word of what I just said?'

'Sorry Father, busy day at work. I did drift there I'm afraid. Terribly sorry again. What were you saying? Sorry.'

'For God's sake Malcolm, sharpen up! You can't take your eye off the ball for a minute these days. I hope you don't behave like that at work. God knows what Gordon must think of you and me if you daydream like that in the staff common room.'

'Sorry, sorry… won't happen again. Sorry, Father.'

'I was speaking about your cousin George. I bumped into Arthur, your mum's little brother, the other day, and he told me George is now engaged to be married. Quite a delightful lass apparently. From up north somewhere, but she did graduate from UCL so that has taken off some of her rough northern edges according to Arthur. Next year sometime, the wedding, followed by honeymooning in St Lucia or Thailand. They've not yet decided.'

'Lucky man. Which was George again? He was the one with the tinted glasses who studied History somewhere in the midlands, wasn't he?'

'Good God, no, that's Keith. George is the younger of Arthur's two lads. Went to Oxford to read Mathematics and now works in insurance or something. Bloody good rugby fly half and pretty handy with a tennis racquet too. Gave me a run for my money a few years' back.'

'Well, congratulations to him. I hope they'll be very happy together.'

'And how about you, Malcolm? Any hint of the sound of wedding bells? And grandchildren? Not that I wish anyone to think I'm that bloody old, but keep the family name alive, eh? It's all down to you, you know. Surely there's some little cutie you've got your eye on?'

What was I supposed to say to that?

This was not the time, not when his head was full of cousin George and his gorgeous young fiancée with the UCL degree. Not the time to break the news that marriage and children were not part of my immediate plans. Not, in fact, of any plans I might ever have. But how would it be, I wondered, if there, right there, over the cold pasta, I were to pour out my longings for Simon Gore, or offer up the details of my time with Carlos the Jackal who, even as we dined, was in all probability wandering around flashing my Rolex at anyone he thought it might impress. Father had not been best pleased at my carelessness with the watch, but he had still made a full claim on the insurance. For a replacement that I never saw.

He leaned across to me and with what would, in almost any situation, have been an unpleasant and leering tone, pressed me on the amount of 'fresh young fanny' that I must have at my disposal what with my good looks, my salary, the BMW… The subtext was that, as his son, an endless supply would be on tap, and it was my duty to sample widely before informing some lucky girl that she had won the big door prize of a life married to me, and the undoubted honour of bearing my children.

Fresh young fanny?

He had actually used those words. And used them in a way that made them sound like this week's best offer at Waitrose. What was it about that phrase that caused me to cringe so much? His use of illiteration? The suggestion that somewhere there existed such a thing as *stale* old fanny? I did not want any fanny at all, not even the fresh kind, and the idea of stale fanny caused me to gag on my puttanesca sauce.

I wished I had ordered the carbonara.

'You're not telling me that you haven't got a string of young fillies just waiting for you to drop round with red roses, a bloody great diamond and the offer of eternal bliss, have you?'

I contemplated the notion of taking red roses to Carlos. Or Simon. Simon would have appreciated them more. Carlos? Well with Carlos I would have probably ended up in A & E in the small hours, having a red rose removed from the orifice of his choice.

'No, Father, there is no lady in mind at present,' I offered meekly. 'Sorry to disappoint.'

This much was the truth. Never lie to your Father had been drummed into me as a child.

'You must still be putting it about a fair bit, though, eh son?'

How to avoid a lie?

'Well, it is really difficult meeting women when you work in an all-male environment all day Father.'

'But the nights, the nights! You're not there all night. Or at weekends.'

'Father, I'm not sure you fully appreciate how very demanding the job is. As I said, I have this big presentation next week, and you would not believe how set in their ways some teachers can be. The mere suggestion of buying a different brand of instant coffee for the staff room is enough to have some of them threatening to walk out. Sometimes it's as much as I can do to stay on top of things.'

Father found this impossible to credit and went off on another lecture about how it was not my duty to consult the buggers, but to tell them instead. It was clear that he saw any kind of negotiation as a sign of weakness. His world view was that one's minions did what one's minions were told to do or else one's minions would pretty soon be unemployed minions. Even for an outsider it would have been easy to see how Father's attitude to the workplace was an outdated one. To have seen that same approach throughout one's childhood was a cause of much bitter sadness.

'Well, don't leave it too bloody late,' he warned. 'Not much point leaving you the family home if you've got no family to put in it. I might be better off selling it now and living the high life around the world on the proceeds in my twilight years.'

'Don't talk like that Father. You've got years of life left in you and you'll need to have somewhere to live. It makes no sense to talk of selling the place.'

At that point the waiter cleared our plates and offered the dessert menu. This was not the same waiter who had taken our order and served us the pasta, but a younger man, almost a boy, in tight black jeans, an equally tight white T-shirt and brown eyes that could leave women tingling.

And me.

I could barely bring myself to look, for fear of betraying the obvious attraction. And though he addressed his questions to Father I sensed that those brown eyes were lingering on me. I muttered something about no pudding for me, Father did the same, and in the particularly curt way he reserved for talking to minions, he ordered the bill.

'Never could stand puds. All that bloody sugar. Especially Italian puds. And I certainly don't want one from that limp-wristed tosser. Did you see him? Strikes me sometimes that half the bloody world's gone gay lately. All these poofs wittering on about 'coming out' and 'gay rights'. Call me old-fashioned but I preferred it when it was illegal. Kept themselves to themselves in those days, not constantly trying to force it down your throat.'

I was used to this sort of tirade from Father but as he proceeded this time I felt myself turning more and more red with embarrassment. His final image hit me with its powerful inappropriateness. I hastily covered for my shame by asking Father to keep his voice down as he was causing embarrassment.

'Embarrassment be buggered!' he exclaimed. 'If these people want to 'come out', so be it. Let's all come out and openly express our views! God knows I've felt embarrassed enough myself at times at some of their public demonstrations of sick affection. On trains, in pubs, anywhere you like. What about offending my sense of what's right and proper!'

Definitely not the time to inform Father of his son's sexual preferences.

I hurriedly rose from my seat, went to the bar and paid the bill by card. I did not want those brown eyes meeting mine again under Father's gaze. (Isn't it odd that if you say that phrase out loud it sounds just like 'Father's gays'? I'm not sure he'd be too keen).

Brown Eyes smiled at me as I paid and as he returned my card his hand lingered while he expressed a desire to see me again, soon.

Next time I would not be bringing Father.

Chapter Twenty-Three
Brown Eyes

I was just finishing off setting the tables when the guy who'd been in the night before with the loud-mouthed older man showed up. I looked up and he seemed to pause with a guilty and embarrassed look. I'd seen that look before in middle class men. Overly religious upbringing, overly dominant parents, overly Puritanical schooling… overly something or other, and never anything good.

He was in an expensive suit, which suggested that he had come straight from work. Something in business. It was just after six and I had not long since opened the door. I had been working on the tables with no real expectation of any of our regular customers for at least half an hour and this man was patently not a regular.

He looked first at me and then at his highly polished shoes. He constantly played with the cufflink on his left sleeve. This trait betrayed any confidence the suit may have suggested. I took the lead and showed him to a table. He didn't seem sure at first. I offered again. I attempted to break the tension by pointing around the restaurant and offering him any place he wanted as we were the only two there.

He selected a corner seat, as far from the door and the window as it was possible to be. I handed him the menu which he studied the front of without opening. Another nervous characteristic. I tried to break the tension with the suggestion of a drink. He muttered something and I awkwardly had to ask him to repeat, before establishing that he would love a glass of prosecco.

He was an attractive guy and I remembered mildly flirting with him the night before, but not in a way that might risk causing offence. This was, after all, my uncle's restaurant and he was allowing me to help out with holiday cover over the spring and summer months before heading off to university.

In the three years since leaving school I had spent time in several casual jobs, returning in March from six months of foreign travel during which time I had grown accustomed to a life of casual sex with a variety of men.

It was so much easier away from this country. Nobody knew me and I could move on the next day if I wished. The anonymity of being so far from home afforded me a freedom I relished. When you come from a large Anglo-Italian family there is constantly somebody close by who knows you or your parents or someone connected with that extended family. If Big Brother was not watching you, the chances were that Big Uncle or Big Cousin probably was. And I did not wish to jeopardise my job as I needed the cash-in-hand I was being paid to supplement the pittance I received for being officially unemployed.

My uncle would not countenance customer complaints about the good-looking young waiter coming on strong to a customer. Of course our Italian blood made it compulsory to flirt outrageously with the female customers but never in any way that might be taken as serious or threatening. Instinctively, it seemed, we all knew when to back off and when to cut out the flirty talk.

We weren't trying to chat up the women, Uncle said, just flattering them so they felt special enough to justify the expenditure on a superior bottle, or even some champagne. And I knew how to put on that little-boy-lost look to make the older women wish to mother me and the younger women to fuck me, even as their husbands and boyfriends were paying the bill in expectation of the carnal delights to follow. So, I had been very careful the night before. My initial excitement at this man's reappearance so soon had told me he did not wish to mother me, but with all of his nervous weakness I was beginning to think that it might not be worth the bother. If he couldn't decide what to drink or where to sit, how weak and indecisive might he be in bed?

I was just going behind the bar to pour the prosecco when I became aware that he had left his seat and followed me. Briefly I feared this might be a nutter intent on attacking me but then looking into his anxious eyes I thought he might be about to have another change of mind about the drink. Or eating altogether, and was simply coming to apologise for wasting my time. Instead he did neither but apologised gushingly for the offensive behaviour of his father the night before.

So, he had not been the 'older man' in that sense, as I had thought yesterday.

It's quite amazing how many of the older gay men feel the need to denounce gays in public, how they have to blurt out these homophobic declarations as if to prove to a suspicious world that they are nothing to do with this under-class of sexual miscreants. Some legacy of a former time perhaps, or some misguided need to maintain a public image. He was beginning to sweat as he mumbled something about feeling the need to apologise to me in person for his father's outrageous comments.

Trite phrases about men of a certain age and his father having drunk most of the bottle of Barolo on top of a couple of large gins beforehand and how he had been equally and embarrassingly just as loud when he'd got on the last train home and other such platitudes, and could he now buy me a drink by way of apology for his father's unacceptable behaviour.

The words poured out of him in such a torrent that it was not easy to take it all in, especially as I was being distracted by a bead of sweat making its way from his hairline and past his left ear before resting temporarily at the side of his chin. He offered the drink for a second time, but with a little less self-assurance than the first time. I replied that drinking at work was frowned upon by my uncle and made some pathetic half-joke concerning how we were both dominated by the alpha males in our families.

He didn't seem to follow my thinking and looked even more crushed, so without fully considering the consequences I blurted out that I should be very happy to accept his offer but after hours. Suddenly his hang-dog face vanished and an impish smile took its place. In no time at all he knew that my shift finished at nine-thirty. He ordered the tagliatelle carbonara and agreed to meet me at nine forty at a wine bar within easy walking distance of the trattoria.

After his pasta and a sizeable and perhaps unnecessary tip, he had left rapidly. We'd not even exchanged names. I began to worry that this might be a mistake.

But outside the bar a bit later on, there he was. He'd changed into a clean dark blue shirt, open at the collar with a new cream jacket that looked as if it never been worn. He extended his hand and said, 'Malcolm' in that way redolent of business meetings and days on the golf course. His hand was soft but his handshake was firm enough. I introduced myself and there followed that awkward moment when we each waited for the other to make the first move into the bar. Simultaneously we both went to speak and this raised the awkwardness level another notch or two. This was not an auspicious start to the evening, so I stepped forward, said, 'After you,' holding open the door.

At the bar I was expecting a repeat of the prosecco moment but to my pleasant surprise he asked if a Shiraz was alright and, bottle and two glasses in hand, we headed off to a table at the rear of the bar.

He poured the wine with the exaggerated swagger of an older man not fully at ease in the presence of someone younger. As we clinked our glasses I was tempted to say 'Bottoms Up' but Malcolm got in first with a simple, 'Well, cheers then,' and we drank to good health. Again he was sweating, not as profusely as earlier, but most certainly sweating even though we were probably in the coolest part of the bar. He apologised once more for his father's loutish behaviour and I made some inane comment about choosing one's friends but not one's family. The evening had not started too promisingly: I did not feel relaxed, but was in a state of complete calm compared with Malcolm.

By the second glass of wine, we had only been there ten minutes or so, he began to loosen up. He had taken off his jacket and the shirt looked box-fresh. Pity about the underarm damp patches that were beginning to appear.

We talked about what I was doing at the restaurant and this led quite naturally to my university plans and my travels. Malcolm seemed interested though I took care to stay silent on my sexploits. I knew he was gay, I just for some reason didn't want him to regard me as promiscuous. I was also wary of sounding arrogant or too worldly in the company of this man who was coming across like a virgin. He then he began telling me of a trip to Amsterdam and I wondered if this was my cue to be more forthcoming, but I held back and we talked of the Van Gogh museum rather than the city's clubs and coffee shops.

He had just ordered a second bottle of Shiraz when I realised it was my turn to seek out his life story. At first he was reluctant to go into detail, saying it was a dull tale of no real consequence, but I pushed him and asked what it was he did in business. Was it banking or some other financial area? He laughed self-deprecatingly as he told me that he was hoping to break into the media when the right post become available at the BBC and sidetracked the conversation into a discussion of the parlous state of so much television output.

He complained about there being so much sports coverage and ranted at length about how football seemed to be on every night of the week. It was beyond him that so many people could spend so much time, effort and money in the pursuit of so little real achievement. It was so tribal and he could not stomach the way in which every game was discussed in such hyperbolic terms. One hundred and ten per cent. Must-win games. Sport always seen in terms of battles. What, he wondered, would happen if a must-win game were lost, as it inevitably was, by one team? Would it be Armageddon? Would civilisation break down and anarchy rule the world?

Of course not! One group of men had lost a game to another group of men. A fucking game, that's all! Malcolm almost shouted as he made his point and then downed what was left in his glass. I like strong opinions but this man seemed on the edge, a little unbalanced. Yes, football commentators and pundits speak in overly dramatic terms, but for a man seeking a career in television he seemed woefully ignorant of the channels' need to sell their shows.

I did not mention that I was a Brentford fan. I could see little point in prolonging this particular strand of conversation, and it seemed prudent to move on. I was also thinking of bed, my own bed, and the previous thoughts of physical intimacy with this wannabe television executive seemed an increasingly unlikely, not to say unattractive proposition.

I moved the conversation on to what I trusted would be safer ground and asked the now calm Malcolm what he did for a living while waiting for the BBC. With an air of mild embarrassment he informed me that he was Director of Quality and the Cultural and Equality Officer at a local school.

'Deputy Head, you mean?'

My attempt to lighten the mood.

Clearly this was not at all the thing to say and he began to sweat and fluster again; he insisted his job title was more than just 'Deputy Head'. He also answered, with an air of superiority, that it was a good local private boys' school where he was currently pushing through a programme to drive the school's impressive academic standards even higher.

I smiled and correctly named the school and asked him if Mad Mullah McMullen the Mick was still teaching Chemistry there. Side-swiped, his arrogance immediately faded. He seemed not to believe that I knew Mr McMullen, and when I told him that I had achieved good grades there despite all the school had done to ensure otherwise, he went very quiet indeed.

I persisted. Was McMullen still abusing the kids, and had

anyone got any closer to proving his IRA links… but Malcolm was fumbling for his jacket and was off.

'I'm terribly sorry,' he rattled, 'but this has been a terrible mistake. Please forgive me for taking up your time and good luck with your career.'

I considered myself fortunate that he had gone from my life more quickly than he had entered it.

The wine was paid for so I took the rest of the bottle home to bed.

Chapter Twenty-Four
Gerry McMullen : 6

When Ian told me of his sickness I thought he was taking the piss. People of his age don't get that ill, they certainly don't die. Especially someone like Ian who had too much of a life force for it ever to be so easily extinguished. Christ, it wasn't even something I recognised – cancer, leukaemia, even AIDS I could have understood. If I'd been told that he'd died in a car crash I could have accepted it: the erratic behaviour of other road users, dodgy brakes, slippery road surfaces; these are all things we live with and over which we have no fuckin' control. Tragic, yes, but also perfectly understandable in the random and careless way they just turn up unannounced in this nonsensical fuckin' world. But this made no sense at all. Ian was fit and young for his age and a bloody top bloke; he was a good teacher, a good mate and a good brother to Annie.

When I first met Annie, she was always telling me tales about their lives as kids growing up together. He was barely two years older than her and living where they did with few other kids around they had naturally spent more time in each other's company than is usual with brother and sister.

The first night I met Annie at the pub when Ian brought her along she told me of the time she had persuaded him to take to the water in their old plastic baby bath that had been neglected in their wasteland of a garden. She had assured him that it would float and that with the aid of an old cricket bat he would be able to row it across their small pond. As the story progressed to the inevitable sinking of the bath, Annie described in glorious detail how Ian went down with the vessel, singing a full-blooded version of the national anthem; neither of them could hold back the laughter and giggles and their giggling prompted even more raucous belly laughter from the other.

This was a tale that had clearly been refined and honed with several tellings over the years but that did not seem to diminish their howls of amusement. I knew the story was being told to entertain me, for the younger sister to say something about her dopey older brother, but their laughter seemed to take on a life of its own, becoming a force field around them and temporarily placing me in the role of the outsider, the witness who could marvel at their childhood moment, but who would never be a full part of that shared experience.

They were trying to bring me into this world of theirs but at the time I didn't see it that way. Soon, however, I overcame my awkwardness and one day when Ian and I were laughing like drains at something that had happened at work I realised that Annie was beginning to share our lives just as I had started to share theirs. They both howled further when describing their mother's reactions to the sinking of the SS Plastic Bathtub and how the poor woman had been unable to stay angry with Ian for very long. This incident was typical of his desire to try new things, especially if it brought joy to others.

On another occasion they told me how soon after he'd passed his driving test he had offered to take their grandmother into town so she could buy a few groceries. On the return journey a bottle of milk had rolled free from its bag in the passenger foot-well and in attempting to pick it up to save granny bending down, Ian had driven into a small wall causing no personal injuries, but inflicting permanent damage on both wall and car. As the story reached its climax they both howled deliriously after they sang out in perfect unison, 'But the milk emerged unscathed!'

There seemed to be endless stories of this kind: stories of Ian's inability to achieve anything of a practical nature; his total confusion when faced with the simplest piece of machinery and, most of all, his love of practical jokes - and anything that highlighted the stupidity of mankind. He was very fond of quoting from Henry Fielding's introduction to *Joseph Andrews,* and this line in particular has stayed with me.

Life everywhere furnishes an accurate observer with the Ridiculous.

If comedy could be found in the human condition, Ian would smell it out. He couldn't stand pretentiousness of any sort, and he could sniff out bullshit at a hundred yards. He positively relished staff notices and took immense delight in drawing everyone's attention both to the idiocies of sentiment and expression they so frequently contained. He was constantly on the lookout for comic ambiguity in the written word.

One time a member of his tutor group, who happened to be the captain of the school hockey team, sought his assistance with the correct spelling of an end of season notice for the sports board. Ian did this, but could not resist rewording the final instruction to team members so that it conveyed his own feelings about Bob Larbey, the Maths teacher who, with Roger Thomas the PE teacher, helped run the team.

Please return all hockey sticks to Mr Thomas and balls to Mr Larbey.

A petty point scored maybe, but I know for a fact that it got an even bigger laugh in the staff room than it did from the boys.

A lot of his spirit was good-natured.

The first time he came to my flat he found a sink full of dirty dishes and a pile of unwashed clothes on the floor. I mumbled some pathetic men's excuse; he simply brushed aside my apology with the simple comment: 'Smells like poteen spirit'.

How can a man with that much devil in him be allowed to die so fuckin' young?

Even with his own cause of death he could not resist the pun. It was an old pun of course, one that had been used insensitively about Asa Hartford, the Scottish footballer, but Ian could not resist commenting on the irony of how a hole in the heart could bring down such a whole-hearted guy.

I didn't even know you could live with a hole in your heart. I certainly find it hard to live with the hole in my heart that Annie left, but there's an all too obvious difference between metaphorical and real holes.

Apparently he had had that hole in his heart since birth.

Like some maniacal terrorist bomb with a very, very long fuse, it was just waiting, just biding its time before a routine check-up highlighted its presence and it was too late to stop the ticking. Funny how people call the heart their ticker. Most people see the ticking as the thing that keeps you going. Very few think of it in terms of a clock running down, or even worse, as a fuse on a bomb growing shorter and shorter.

When Ian's bomb detonated it was not unexpected, since its discovery it had been a case of when, not if. And unlike most sick terrorists' devices this caused only one fatality. The collateral damage was not a limb-strewn street, but what it did to Annie and me. Quite what the extent of her loss was is impossible to say. She was with him when he died. I was not and she told me the inevitable in the short call that I had been waiting for, and which she knew she would have to make. As soon as she said her name there was no need for further words.

At the funeral we barely spoke and, in truth, since Ian's condition was diagnosed we had had less and less to say to each other with each passing day. At the very time I needed her most, she didn't need me. She seemed to resent my presence, my words, my very essence, as if I was to blame in some sort of sick fuck way. As if our love was bound up in some triangle that could not exist without all three of its points.

Fuckin' hell, that last part sounds like some kinky maudlin shite! I wish I'd never said it. There was fuck all kinky about our sex life. It was me and Annie and nothing to do with Ian whatsoever. Christ, even the thought of me in bed with another bloke, even Ian, or Annie in bed with her brother makes me want to fuckin' vomit. There's more to a marriage than sex but I'm buggered if I can give you a list of all the ingredients.

That was it. As a chemical reaction it would be:

Ian gets sick - Annie goes silent – Annie moves out – Ian dies – Gerry lives on, in ignorance and misery.

But you try explaining that to Chris Adams' moronic wife or anyone else and you'll come across as a self-pitying twat wallowing in his own misery.

So these days I don't.

Chapter Twenty-Five
Annie McMullen

Gerry lost it in the end. At first he had been one lively and lovely man, with a great sense of humour and a real zest for life. But the longer he stayed at that school, the smaller became his world and his mind. He shrank. His interests grew fewer, his energies diminished and outside of work his focus was just the gun club and the drink.

Most people drink to escape or to enhance what they are doing, or simply because it makes them feel good. It soon got to the point where Gerry just drank. He didn't get exuberant or reckless or silly, or even violent. He just drank. And the more he drank, the more he lost his identity and became the drink.

When we first met he would love the poetry I read him, the films I suggested watching, the restaurants I took him to. And in turn he switched me on to some of the best music I had ever heard. How on earth had I got through so many years without Tom Waits?

But by the end that joy had gone. Beyond the drink and the guns there was eventually nothing.

When Ian was diagnosed, it crippled me. Everybody says that but there would be days when I could not move beyond getting out of bed, getting to work and coming home again at the end of another uncaring day. And what did I come home to? The shell of a man deadened by the drink and already in mourning for his friend. A man so blinkered by his self-loathing that he never registered the depth of my grief. He knew all those old tales from our younger days and how close Ian and I had been throughout childhood, but once Ian was ill all those things were obliterated from Gerry's mind. We still made love occasionally but with an increasing sense of purposelessness on both our parts.

If he spoke to me at all, it would only be to complain. He was not a man at peace with the world or himself and the subjects of his anger were so small and so sad. They were all about the school. The smug Head, the incompetent deputies, the pre-programmed staff and the disaffected, lazy kids.

One weekend he did not utter a single kind or flattering word on any issue whatsoever and it was then that I knew it was time to quit. I could not watch his suffering whilst I suffered alone in the same house, so I moved out and came to terms with the loss of Ian in my own way. If you know you are receiving no help with a problem you can adjust to the situation. It was the delusion of help that drove me down and far better that I help myself deal with the horror than look to Gerry, a lost and defeated man and no help to me or himself.

It is tough to tell, but I swear he looked better at the funeral than he would have if I had stayed. I know I felt better. I had not only left Gerry, but I had resigned from my job and done voluntary work for a while. After the funeral I headed east and ended up in Sydney.

New world, new country, new life.

Yet at times, I do still miss Gerry. He was not sophisticated by any stretch of the imagination and to look at he could have easily passed for one of the sad homeless who wander the streets or sit on corners, a tin of cheap cider in hand. He had no dress sense, and in fact he owned very few clothes: One to wear and one in the wash, he used to say, but I'm not so sure that before I met him either set ever got to the wash. Why waste money on fuckin' clothes, was his maxim, to which he would add that he had seen so many widows packing up too many bags of late husbands' clothes for charity shops. Doesn't fuckin' add up, he would argue, and I loved him for this simplicity, this lack of vanity.

No, sophistication was never a charge likely to be levelled at Gerry McMullen. And the tragic thing was that most people never saw beneath the belligerent, gruff and, let's say it, scruffy exterior. But, believe me, a vastly different man lived on the inside.

He loved the poetry I read to him and, like all seemingly hard-nosed cynics, a true romantic lurked inside. People used to say to me that it was patently clear what he saw in me, but they were often bemused at what I might have seen in him. But then nobody knows what goes on indoors. The doors we slam, the curtains we draw and the other protective walls we build.

Australian men are a bit like Gerry. Not physically, of course, but in that bullshit macho way they keep it all in.

I have dated a few but it's never gone anywhere.

Both Ian and Gerry, in their own ways, left me and I am not ready to lose another man so soon.

Chapter Twenty-Six
Gerry McMullen : 7

When Annie left I was devastated. I came home one day and every trace of her had gone. Just like that, as if the intervening years had never happened. Her keys were on the side but there was no note. Just a set of keys as if some holiday tenant had left them there.

Before she'd moved in she said it would make sense for us to live together, and though she certainly wasn't skint she did try to point out the financial benefits there were in sharing and stopping having to paying for two places. She even gave me that line about two being able to live as cheaply as one.

'Bollocks!' I remember replying, 'Only if you each eat half as much and share the same bit of bog roll!'

Not that I eat much nowadays. Can't seem to make the fuckin' effort to knock up more than a sandwich or warm up something in the microwave. But, by contrast, we used to eat well together. We both cooked, and it was all good stuff. Some Friday nights it would be a prime piece of steak with ratatouille washed down with a bottle or two of Shiraz. As the first glass hit the spot the worries of the week would wash away and the weekend would stretch ahead just like those 'deserts of vast eternity' Shelley talks about.

When the fuckin' hell did the laughing stop?

Whether alone together or down the pub with Ian and a pile of others, we would howl at the slightest incident or word. Silly card games when half-pissed, telling the same old jokes and, most memorably, the time I came home to a seemingly empty house only for her to leap out of the wardrobe at me.

What the hell possessed her to play a prank like that I'll never know, but I loved that child-like quality. And this is why the bedroom, the house, the whole fuckin' world seems so desolate these days.

These days I feel under constant house arrest.

Yes, she took everything of hers, but her shadow still remains in every room, a persistent reminder that she was once here. And now she's gone. Isn't it enough that she left, without leaving this fuckin' shadow to chase me around the rooms?

I've abandoned the double bed now. You'll find me in the spare room. Waking up for a piss, only to note her absence. No man should have to contend with that. It's like having a twenty-four hour stalker. Even the drink does nothing, the hoped-for oblivion never arrives. Filling the emptiness with a gallon of beer only emphasises that emptiness.

One night recently I woke for a pee in the small hours, and that was it. No sleep, no matter how long I read or listened to the radio. At four thirty I gave in, got up and hoovered the whole house from top to bottom. Fuck knows what the neighbours must have made of that! Mind you, the house needed it. Twice I had to empty the bulging bag. Don't believe that bastard Quentin Crisp when he says the dust gets no thicker after a certain period!

The hoovering worked up my appetite though, and as soon as I'd finished I wolfed down a chicken korma ready meal and over half a bag of oven chips. Some early breakfast! Didn't eat for two days afterwards. I felt like some snake that eats once in a blue moon to keep itself going. Is it any wonder that my shit is a funny colour and a very strange consistency?

Fuck knows how I ended up here. As soon as this term's over I'm goin' on a major detox. And it won't be Malcolm Malaprop's diet of ginger tea and lettuce!

Chapter Twenty-Seven
Mike Redfern : 5

Yesterday I had a free lesson at the same time as Gerry McMullen. This rarely happens, but my class were all on an Art trip to London, so I had the rare luxury of 50 minutes with McMullen in an otherwise empty staff room. With coffee and biscuits on hand we had both intended to catch up on some overdue marking, but opted instead to jaw away the time. It started with a typical McMullen observation about whether or not it was wise for me to be attacking a packet of McVitie's plain chocolate digestives. He is always making comments about my weight, but yesterday, with no audience, he seemed genuinely concerned for my well-being.

'For Christ's sake, Mike, I know I take the piss but seriously now, it can't be fuckin' good for you carrying all that weight around. Think of the fuckin' pressure it's puttin' on your heart for one thing. And when was the last time you took any fuckin' exercise?'

Bit rich that, coming from a man whose sole exercise seems to be loading his gun and lifting pint glasses… But I sensed a different Gerry… a caring Gerry.

'Have you always been a bit on the porky side, Mike? As a kid I mean? Is it the classic fuckin' tale of the other kids takin' the piss 'cos you were a bit chubby and you seeking comfort in even more doughnuts and biscuits?'

McMullen had hit home. With a father who force-fed his family potatoes and sandwiches, and a mother whose sweet tooth I inherited, I was no doubt destined to be overweight. It is reported that these physiological markers are laid down early in life and, coupled with my parents' fat genes, I was doomed.

Sport and physical activity never attracted me much, either. I was usually the kid with the forged note excusing me from games. It wasn't just the physical horrors of wet freezing playing fields. It was the ridicule and the inevitable comments every time I was the last boy to be picked for team games. That pathetic and well-worn scenario. In every class, in every school throughout the country, there must have been a kid like me awaiting this ritualistic degradation. One reads so much about the decline of competitive sports in schools, but for every decent athlete developed there were surely plenty more kids like me for whom the only game worth winning was the one spent convincing the sports teacher that the excuse note was genuine and that the afternoon should be spent in the library instead of the howling wind and rain.

That's probably why I ended up studying and teaching English. All those afternoons engrossed in the world of literature

Early on it was a non-stop diet of Billy Bunter, Jennings and Derbyshire and Just William. By the time I reached my mid-teens it was the classics: Dickens, Lawrence, Hardy and then Orwell, Huxley, Hemingway and Fitzgerald. Dickens and Hardy fed my desire to escape to the past and '1984' and 'Brave New World' got me thinking about the future, though I never got into all that science fiction stuff, Asimov and so on, that so many of my peers raved about.

Most of all I loved Dickens, especially 'Great Expectations'. In particular those early chapters in the book when Pip encounters Magwitch and that truly wonderful Christmas meal with the obsequious Uncle Pumblechook acting just like some of the supercilious morons who had taught me.

And poetry, too. Keats and Tennyson thrilled me with their imagery and I am sure that one year, probably the whole of the lower sixth, I read no poetry except Plath. Not that I understood it all. Some of it passes me by even now but what a way to excite the teenage mind!

Though good as it is for the imagination, the intellect, the development of a wide vocabulary, spending hours engrossed in a book each day does absolutely nothing for one's physique. So, as my reading log thickened, so did my waist. It may even be possible to chart a graph showing the correlation between books read and inches gained.

I told all of this to Gerry whose only comment was, 'Seems to me like both your reading and your eating were ways of makin' yourself feel better about yourself. Pity they're both pretty solitary activities 'cos I bet you went in for a lot of private, secret eating, probably at the same time as you were curled up with a fuckin' book.'

Of course he was right: you don't need to be a genius to see that, but perhaps you need someone else to draw it to your attention. After all, it is never an easy thing to bring into conversation. You can guarantee nobody ever said to Hitchcock, 'So, is it glandular Mr Hitchcock?' But are my reading and eating so very different from Gerry's drinking? They are both just means of temporary escape from the utter unbearableness of much of life? If Gerry was feeling he could be honest and frank with me, then he surely would not baulk at the same line of argument.

'And your drinking, Gerry? How much is that to help you cope with the loss of Ian and Annie?' It was no staffroom secret that Ian's death and Annie's departure had shattered McMullen. To lose a best friend and a wife so close together would unbalance most men.

'Don't go playin' the fuckin' therapist with me, Redfern!' was his initial response but I did not react.

'Gerry, the last thing I am offering is analysis. You brought up the weight issue and you're right to. I'm bringing up your drink issues. What harm can it do to be honest with one another? Male banter is one thing, but why can't we be open for once?'

McMullen visibly mellowed and for an instant he was silent.

'I'm sorry Mike, I know I'm a bit of a gob-shite at times but you're right, of course.

'I drink far too fuckin' much. I've always been a bit of an artist in that area. Started knockin' back the Guinness as soon as I could get served back home, must have been about fifteen or so I suppose, and I've never stopped. And you're right, I have been hittin' the bottle way too fuckin' much for the past few years, and even more so lately.

'And this fuckin' job doesn't help, does it? All that crap with that football I burst, Box-Head and that fuckin' beaker, and, to top it all, that wanker Davies with his constant nosin' into everything we do. What the fuck happened to professional trust? And what gave that wankspanner the right to think he can pass judgement? Christ knows, has anyone ever seen the moronic fuckin' malaprop man teach a single fuckin' lesson?'

For a while we discussed the tragic state of a school that would appoint someone like Davies to a position of seniority, but I sensed the shift down tired old roads, and saw no point in merely complaining about the man. He was in post and no amount of moaning from us was going to change that.

‘So what happened with Annie?’ I had never met the woman.

I expected some gushing account of his ex-partner’s virtues, dressed up in heartbroken mawkishness, but McMullen clearly felt the need to talk in terms that weren’t self-indulgent. He seemed to trust me. For over ten minutes he spoke of Annie’s warmth, her humour, her lust for life and even their compatibility in bed.

He did not go into details and nor would I have wished him to do so but he painted a picture of a vibrant, caring woman with whom he had fallen in love and had been expecting to spend his whole life. All the time he talked I was building up a mental picture of her and in my head she was about five feet eight, slightly overweight, quite plain with a face more full of character than traditional beauty. Gerry was not, after all, going to have been married to a Sandra Bullock lookalike.

‘Bugger me, Mike. I still can’t work it out but she just upped and left at the same time Ian got ill. If she’d only explained her reasons I could have made some sense of it but, no, nothing. Talk about a clean fuckin’ break.’

As the words trailed off, Gerry did something I suspect he had not done in public since Annie had left him. He took out his wallet and fetched from it an old and rather crumpled picture of her. This was one of the most attractive women I had ever seen in the flesh or in a photograph. She actually made Sandra Bullock look plain, and though I know how unwise it is to judge anyone or anything on appearances, especially women, her looks alone, her obvious beauty and character in that half smile, underlined the depth of Gerry’s loss.

Looking across at him, I knew he would never find another

woman to replace her. Certainly not if he kept drinking the way he had been drinking. My eating and his drinking made us two collectively lonely men trapped in dead-end jobs with no hope of ever spending our days with another person. The only females likely to enter our lives now were either fictitional or inflatable.

Time after the honesty to move back to the more mundane.

'Okay Gerry. Well have you ever thought about a different career?'

'Well. Now that you mention it, I've often considered that I might jack this in and keep fucking chickens.'

I smiled. 'And tell me, Mr McMullen, in that sentence, is the word 'fucking' an intensifier or a verb?'

Chapter Twenty-Eight
The ABC Meeting : Beforehand

Malcolm Davies entered the empty school hall and took a while to cast a critical eye over his surroundings. During assemblies one spent all of one's time with at least one eye on the boys to ensure there was no silly behaviour. One never really noticed the room itself.

In the mid-afternoon of a July day in a typically grey English summer the hall looked somehow desolate. Perhaps more suited to what Davies imagined to be a prison out house than an important room in a school. The walls had long ago been painted in a shade that defied colour charts and the fading of time had added nothing to their initial greyness and grimness.

He could imagine this paint seeping into the walls and crumbling off them in dry protest. It was too ashamed to show its face in public, even in such a third rate boys' school as this. In places it was beginning to flake away, and nothing had been done by Charlie Dyer, the caretaker, to mitigate this overall effect of abject misery.

Portraits of the school's two previous headteachers hung on either side of the hall, giving the impression that these two august and outmoded figures were actually staring across at each other. Perhaps they shared some regret at the way in which the school had been allowed to go to rack and ruin since their days when everything had ticked along so well and when standards had been so much higher. The portrait of the school's first head, Arthur Chambers, had been placed on the wall that received most of the sunlight. This had been done in the vain hope that any shafts of golden light might give the effect of a Russian icon and place Chambers in the haloed glow in which some of his contemporaries had viewed him. In post-war Britain when the school had been established, when jobs were rare, he had offered full-time salaries to grateful men whose chances of gainful employment would have been otherwise slim.

Over time, however, years of occasional English sun had faded what had originally been a dark and sombre portrait, and now Chambers appeared less like a proud domineering headmaster and more like some blood-starved vampire figure desperate for new blood. That mere trace of a smile in the portrait now assumed the preternatural leer of a pervert.

As he looked up at the painting Malcolm Davies found himself wishing for the day when all colour and images would be finally bleached out, presenting once again a fresh canvas for a new artist to use for a new portrait. Davies himself, perhaps, in his Armani suit gazing down in perpetuity over succeeding generations of boys and staff. It is most unlikely, however, that he would have thought in terms of 'perpetuity'. He would, however, stipulate - another word he probably wouldn't have thought of himself - that his portrait should be hung away from direct sunlight. Far better to be at the rear of the hall and clearly illuminated with a bright LED uplighter to bring out his noble features. Such positioning would also enable future staff members to gaze upon him from their seats at the front during assemblies and school meetings. The idea pleased Davies greatly and for a while he stood lost in his daydream and forgot anxieties about his ABC presentation to staff.

He briefly turned to face the portrait of George Baxter, the school's second headmaster. He had met Baxter only once, when some time into his retirement. Baxter had returned to the school to present a prize that bore his name, a prize awarded to the boy who had made the greatest contribution to public life and the community over the year. Sadly it had been only awarded on that single occasion.

Baxter had struck Davies as an imposing figure. He had correctly sensed that Baxter would have had little time for him. He could not imagine George as his headmaster. In the brief time he had met him he had been intimidated by Baxter and surmised, again correctly, that Baxter would have seen through his veneer and his Armani suit to the failings and weaknesses in Malcolm's thoughts on a daily basis. Davies still longed for that position at the BBC, but inwardly he thanked both his father and Gordon Albert for providing him with the current income he enjoyed.

He switched on the hall lights. A number of them were not working, adding to the effect of seedy dilapidation. It was too late to call Charlie Dyer to see to them. In any case the chance of the man having the necessary replacement bulbs seemed unlikely. Since the incident with David Gale and the pictures, Malcolm had been convinced that the idle caretaker spent most of his petty cash budget not on the upkeep of the school but on top shelf magazines.

Surely the old fool was approaching retirement? Davies pondered a staff meeting at which someone, probably McMullen, might propose the commissioning of a portrait of Dyer for the hall in commemoration of his many years of service. Malcolm shuddered and for the first time realised that the hall chairs had been set out in serried rows as requested but inexplicably the idiot Dyer had placed them all towards the back of the hall, some distance from where Davies had been planning to set up the screen for his Powerpoint presentation.

Fortunately Davies had arrived early and thus found himself thrust into the role of caretaker charged with chair moving. Davies being Davies, and so very keen for all to run as smoothly as he had envisaged, set about his task with resigned weariness but before long discovered that he was actually enjoying the freedom of manual labour. He had been up most of the night running through his presentation and ways to deal with the objections and difficult questions that he would face from some of the staff, always resistant to dynamic new ideas.

Most of the day had been spent with little focus on his other daily tasks but now the simple act of moving several chairs across an empty floor pleased him, and thoughts of a less demanding job seemed attractive. Most of the school was quiet. Classes of tired boys watched clocks as equally tired teachers droned on.

Surely days spent with inanimate objects would be preferable to dealing with the likes of McMullen and Redfern, Davies thought, as he guiltily kicked into a corner a stray Twix wrapper. Outside a piss yellow sun could just about be made out through the encrusted grime of the hall's upper windows. *Dyer again!* he thought, as he found himself losing the calm induced by his mindless labour. Why did the man infuriate him so much?

It vexed Davies that the caretaker insisted on answering his phone with the loud pronouncement, 'Dyer 'ere!' and on the occasion when he had finally suggested to him that a less informal tone might create a more professional impression with outside callers, the irascible and cantankerous fool had turned on him saying that he had always answered the phone in that manner, and saw no reason at all to change it at this stage of his career. 'And besides,' he had added whilst refusing to move from the sole chair in his boiler room, 'I say it that way 'cos that's how I feel about this job. It's a shit job these days and it's my little joke.'

Irked by thoughts of the lowly caretaker, Davies had failed to see the joke, but decided to keep his lack of understanding to himself for fear of more staff room ridicule. He had once mentioned Dyer's slack telephone manner to his father, but faced with Father's immediate guffaw had decided not to ask him either for an explanation of just what might be so damned funny.

A quick glance at the hall clock and he broke from his thoughts of Dyer and began to set up the laptop and projector.

* * *

Gerry McMullen was in no rush to finish tidying his lab.

The thought of sitting through a meeting chaired by Davies held no real attraction for McMullen. He had had his fill of the Malaprop Man since his elevated appointment in the school and did not think he would be able to make it through the meeting without killing the man.

With this in mind he had left his rifle in his car ready to set off for his gun club meeting but a part of him felt the overwhelming desire to sit in the front row at the presentation with it laid out across his lap like some porch-seated hillbilly keeping a mean lookout. Instead he had opted for making notes on Davies's verbal ineptitude. Perhaps there might be some way he could later use them, and there were sure to be several, against Davies the next time the idiot came to assess one of Gerry's classes.

He decided he would take along a clipboard and a boardmarker and each time Davies uttered some lexical inanity he would note it down with a resounding thump of the pen and beam smugly in order to disconcert him. 'It's too fuckin' easy picking him up on every fuckin' error.' he mused. 'Far better if he has no fuckin' clue what I'm grinning about.'

With the possibility of extracting some amusement from what was otherwise bound to be a dull and pointless meeting, McMullen continued packing away with more than a hint of devilment in his heart.

* * *

Mike Redfern was in a jovial mood. The end of the academic year was approaching. The incident with Nathan Spurden's coursework had been nothing more than a meaningless loss of a skirmish in the ongoing battle with Malcolm Davies. Had Davies won? After all, Mike had stuck to his guns in refusing to mark the wretched boy's essay and had never even set eyes on the piece. It had cost the school hard cash and Redfern had had one fewer piece of work to assess; his only nagging doubt was that the time he had devoted to arguing his case was enough to have marked the bloody essay fifty times over. A pyrrhic victory, perhaps, but he had stuck to his principles. He must use that term in some future discussion with Davies, any of whose victories must surely have been worthy of that qualifier.

Redfern noted with a degree of concern the amount of his time that he seemed to be devoting to ways of confounding Davies; it was bordering on obsession. Similarly, he was a little confused by the way he felt about the wretched Spurden's chances of passing his exam. A pass would improve his success rates, no matter what had been said about the boy being entered as a private candidate because, after all, Redfern had taught the bloody boy for the past two years. And he was very aware how Davies and Albert were constantly on the lookout for weak success rates to put pressure upon undesirable members of staff. But at least the failure would be seen as some sort of vindication for Redfern.

It was a dilemma and the more he dwelt upon it, the angrier Redfern became. Why was he, Mike Redfern MA, reduced to such petty squabbling when, by rights, he should be sitting on a university awarding board making fine distinctions between firsts and upper seconds.

The prospect of Davies' presentation also left him with mixed emotions. The man's track record promised it would be just more specious and half-arsed thinking expressed in something only approximating to English. That it would have little real bearing on the daily realities of teaching in such a school still amused Redfern. Davies' infelicities of expression were always a joy to behold. Redfern preferred to think of Davies as less as a man with a serious mission in education and more as a second rate educational satirist.

Take a huge pinch of salt, imagine you are in a comedy club on open-mic night and see Davies as a struggling stand-up trying to cope with an audience of vicious hecklers and the farrago could be seen in a completely different light. It would actually become first-rate entertainment.

The summer break was imminent and six weeks in Australia lay before Mike when he would drive south from Cairns with several planned stops before spending the final ten days in Sydney. What had prompted him to tour this country which he had never before visited and was somewhere about as far from school as one could travel without actually leaving the planet?

He had researched plenty about Australia and though he was most decidedly not a fan of snakes, spiders and other such unpleasant creatures, he was willing to run the risk. He would be staying in upmarket hotels and surely they would employ menials to rid the rooms of such nasties. With this in mind and his developing 'couldn't-give-a-shit' approach to Davies, Redfern set off for the meeting in a better mood than he might have been expected.

* * *

Don Jones did not like meetings. They were an intrusion into his world which comprised almost entirely of Maths, cycling and country music. But a three-line whip had been issued to all staff, and Jones had been told that this included him. For once he could find no plausible reason to explain his absence. So with a heavy heart and a fully charged and loaded personal stereo, he trudged from the Maths room to the school hall, secure in the knowledge that whilst this would be a waste of everyone's time, he might at least seek comfort in the company of Emmylou Harris and Dolly Parton.

* * *

In the Biology lab Chris Adams had little to tidy away: the boys had sat through a theory lesson with no experiment to conduct, so the lab was free of the detritus of a practical class. He was not at all keen to arrive at Malcolm Davies's meeting too early, but at least it was a reason not to be at home with Rachel.

He was also dreading the summer break, fearing that six weeks together might signal the final collapse of his marriage. With this in mind, he took himself to his prep room where, more in hope than anticipation of a divine response, he offered up some silent prayers. After the amen for an improved personal and professional life, his conscience added an appeal for those whose lives were materially far worse than his. The terminally ill, the world's starving, the homeless and the politically oppressed.

Thoughts of these people's lives had left him feeling both depressed and guilty. He was most assuredly not in the mood for a meeting chaired by Davies at this late stage of the academic year, but attempted to reassure himself that the meeting would be painless and, in all probability, its content would be completely forgotten by September.

* * *

Derek Humbrell was a quiet man with no great desire to change, to rock the boat or to become involved in any of the petty politics of school life. His sole wish was to teach Geography, and it was not that the machinations of school management were low on his agenda but rather that, beyond the teaching of Geography, he simply had no work agenda.

His life had always been like this: he had always kept himself to himself, had always been on the outside of goings on with whatever was deemed the in-crowd. He remembered feeling this way at an Oxford party where others had cavorted wildly to loud music whilst he had sat in an armchair listening to a man singing of how he was 'in with the in-crowd' and how he would 'go where the in-crowd go'.

Humbrell had sat feigning engrossment in the lyrics, firstly to give himself something to do that suggested to others his mind was actively engaged even if his body was not, and, secondly, because the lyrics made absolutely no sense to him. He was not at all sure what the 'in-crowd' was. He knew it did not include him but he was not bothered in the slightest at his exclusion. He was, in fact, rather pleased not to be included. In his eyes, 'crowd' smacked too much of the herd, and a sense of his own superiority, instilled in him since birth, made him feel smugly pleased not to belong to whatever it was the singer and others might belong.

Throughout his life he had always felt this way. Whenever he felt smug about himself he regarded it as perfectly natural that he should look down upon those whose instinct was to seek comfort in group activities. When he was feeling low, however, he could never quite shake off the sense that he was *de trop* in this world. When he felt like this he would wonder how it was that he had had the good fortune to meet and marry Vanessa. From time to time he cursed himself for those months when he had taken pity on Mary, the former school secretary, but he was also angry with Vanessa for having been so suspicious of his motives.

Despite the cooling of their sex life caused by this and the earlier loss of their infant son, Humbrell was constantly grateful and amazed that he had met someone to love and marry. For years he had simply assumed that he would pass his life as a single man.

In his youth, the boys' school and the cricket field had afforded no opportunities to meet girls. Oxford too had been a largely male environment. At least the Oxford inhabited by Humbrell had proved so. Only when he had started to attend Art evening classes did he come into regular contact with women, and it was his wonderful good luck to have met Vanessa there. Had he not, on a complete whim after seeing a placard advertising enrolment at his local technical college, driven in and signed up, he would almost certainly still be a bachelor.

Like all marriages, his had had its rocky moments, but he was grateful to Vanessa for the love life they had once had, and the companionship that they now shared. Whilst she too had been destroyed by the loss of their son, and this was something Derek fully comprehended even if her way of dealing with it had bothered him, she had been a rock at the time of his father's illness and death.

Over time he had come around to accepting the changing nature of their marriage as another inevitable phase of life. Shakespeare's *Seven Ages of Man* speech came to mind. Surely he was not yet at the 'lean and slippered pantaloon with spectacles on nose' stage'? But it occurred to Humbrell that all that remained was the final age of 'mere oblivion' which he had seen all too clearly in his father's final days. He shivered.

Malcolm Davies's meeting did not bother Derek excessively. It was not something to stir his blood one way or the other. He would attend, he would listen, and he would forget it all before arriving home. It was a chore, but like all of the other chores he faced on a daily basis, it was not something about which he could become too aggravated.

Having locked the text books in the cupboard, he closed the door to the Geography room and set off for the meeting. As he made his way down familiar corridors, however, he began to wonder if his life had been imperceptibly losing pace and momentum as that seventh age of man loomed.

There was something not right, perhaps, in spending one's lifetime as a quiet man who passed unnoticed through quiet corridors.

Chapter Twenty-Nine
The ABC Meeting : 'Aspire'

Having cleared the school hall of discarded crisp packets and sweet wrappers, and having arranged the chairs to his satisfaction Malcolm Davies had set up his laptop, projector and screen.

All was now ready, and he stood proudly, if nervously, awaiting the arrival of the teaching staff. Thoughts of Lincoln at Gettysburg and King in Washington fleeted briefly in his mind, but despite his own high aspirations he swiftly banished these as he recollected some tale he'd heard of a chap called Hugh Brice – he thought that was the name – who had taken a public fall after setting out his stall too highly.

It was silly to even think of himself alongside such great orators and he fully realised that a small meeting in a school hall was not in quite the same league as those men's great speeches. But why not aim high? And in his own small way he liked to imagine that the impact of his words might stir his audience to higher things.

But did Dr King have men like McMullen and Redfern in his audience? And if he did, they would have been too far away to make themselves heard, not intimidating presences within a few feet. Davies reminded himself of the public speaking tricks he had been picked up from television documentaries. He would ensure he looked just over their heads and thus avoid direct one-to-one eye contact. This was preferable to imagining Gerry McMullen naked and vulnerable; McMullen was most definitely not the sort of specimen likely to attract longing looks from either women or men. The thought of his scrawny body caused Malcolm to gag slightly. Just as he was holding back the bile, Chris Adams arrived.

Chris Adams: So this is the response to my prayers? How come I am the first here? Now I'll have to be pleasant to him, and he'll expect me to sit in the front row. When I had been hoping to pass unnoticed and even do a little prep for tomorrow. No chance now of that.
Malcolm Davies: Thank God he's the first to arrive – he's dull but at least he's not McMullen or Redfern. This is a good start.

Adams smiled at Davies, said, 'Good afternoon,' in a near whisper, sitting on the end seat of the front row.

'Are you sure it's alright for me to sit here, Malcolm? I mean, if you are reserving these seats for anybody....'

'No, no, you're fine just there. All the better to see the screen I guess.'

'Quite.'

A protracted silence.

'Thanks for coming, Chris. I'm sure you'll find it worthwhile and... exciting.'

'Quite.'

Adams fiddled with his file and the papers he had brought with him; he fiddled beyond the point where the papers could reasonably be said to hold any interest for him.

'Shouldn't be too long a meeting,' Malcolm offered, in overly apologetic tones. He found something fascinating with his laptop to occupy him.

Malcolm Davies: Rest assured this meeting will take exactly as long as I need to impress upon this lot the absolute importance of what I am asking, no, telling, them to do next year.

The two men remained in silence for a couple of long minutes, each totally unable to come up with anything to say to the other. Thankfully Derek Humbrell shuffled in, meticulously avoiding the front row and sitting directly behind Adams: close enough to appear friendly and to talk but actually to set Adams up as some form of human shield between himself and Davies.

Derek Humbrell: So glad I wasn't the first to arrive. Hopefully the front row will fill up and I can sit here without being disturbed.

Other staff began to arrive in numbers. Don Jones took the seat next to Derek Humbrell. Malcolm had looked up at him and uttered another phatic greeting but Emmylou was crying out her heart in the middle of *Boulder to Birmingham* and Don had been putting on some sort of sotto voce harmony and Davies's unexpected words had also passed unheeded.

Phil Stonehouse edged in next to Don Jones and received a smile of recognition in lieu of a verbal welcome. Don had by now moved on to *Before Believing* and was still singing in his head. He loved *Pieces of the Sky*, believing it to be Emmylou Harris's finest work. He had even contemplated choosing eight of its ten songs for his selections in the unlikely event of the BBC inviting him to share his life and music with the nation on *Desert Island Discs*. But which two songs should he omit? Certainly not *Boulder to Birmingham*, nor *For No One* which he loved even more than the original version. He would have to jettison *Coat of Many Colours* for its excessive sentimentality, but which other track?

This issue could well occupy him for the entire meeting without a resolution being any closer. It had occupied too much of his thinking already and frequently his wife would remind him of the futility of time spent on thoughts that would never come to fruition. But what did she know? She tended to leave the room when Don played *Pieces* and he had lost count of the times he had had to eject some awful Cliff Richard disc from the car stereo after she had been shopping. In darker moments he wondered how they had ever found sufficient common ground to marry. She would have been far happier with someone like Cliff and in his heart he lamented the tragedy that he and Emmylou had been born so far apart.

The last to arrive, as Davies might have expected, were Gerry McMullen and Mike Redfern who ignored the couple of spare seats near the back in favour of the two remaining chairs in the very middle of the front row directly opposite and close to where Malcolm had positioned himself.

Malcolm Davies: Why did those two have to sit right there? I suppose I can look over their heads and hopefully ignore them.

McMullen stretched out his legs to the point where they might act as a hurdle to Davies should he wish to walk across the room. He then proceeded to pull from his rucksack a clipboard with a strong metal clip which he began to twang violently with a loud snapping sound until a look from Davies seemed to embarrass him in to stopping. He then took from his pocket a large marker pen and wrote the word 'BULLSHIT' across the top of his paper before underlining it dramatically and adding an exclamation mark with a forceful and loud flourish.

Gerry McMullen: Right boyo, Gerry's here so let's get fuckin' crackin' shall we? The sooner this tosser feels compelled to shut his fuckin' gob, the sooner we can all piss off outa here.

Davies tried to compose himself. The calm that he had suddenly felt when Chris Adams had been the first to come had, inexplicably evaporated just as suddenly. What was it about McMullen and Redfern?

He took a few deep breaths and attempted to compose himself. Pulling himself up to his full height and standing behind the table on which he had placed his laptop, he began.

'Good afternoon colleagues and thank you all for coming along today.'

Someone near the back was heard to mutter, 'You mean we had a choice?' causing a ripple of amused laughter and prompting McMullen to make his first note of the afternoon, which he accompanied with a resonant, 'Ah!'

Davies did not allow himself to be rattled by such levity; he had anticipated such a start.

'I accept that attendance today was mandatory,' - he had checked the word in the OED for this purpose - 'but I do assure you gentleman that this will be a very productive session. One that will help us all over the course of the next year push the achievements of the school up and beyond our already enviable record.'

McMullen made a single-word note 'enviable' which he complemented with a question mark and a emoticon smile. Davies, peering above the front row beyond McMullen, missed the recorded comment. He turned instead to technology and the first Powerpoint of the afternoon which lit up the screen as the letters A, B and C flew one by one into view, each beneath its predecessor so that the gathered staff could read:

A
B
C

with absolute clarity.

Phil Stonehouse declared at volume, 'I can read all those letters perfectly clearly, Malcolm. Does that mean I don't have to go to *Specsavers*?'

More laughter around the room gave Davies no alternative but to wait for it to die down before continuing. He considered momentarily responding with a joke of his own, something along the lines of better glasses might have helped Phil to see the practical joke that had been played upon him earlier in the term by McMullen and Redfern, but decided to keep his approach serious. No point alienating staff so early, and Phil Stonehouse could be quite a touchy character when needled.

After the laughter faded, Davies pressed a button and the letters 'spire' flew into place to complete the word 'Aspire' at the head of his list.

'Right colleagues,' he announced. 'This is the first new key-word of our new ABC policy which will drive up our rates of success from September onwards. Basically what it means...'

'Oh come on, we all know the meaning of the word 'aspire' for God's sake.' Redfern's voice rose from the front row with all of the frustrated anger of a man who has just witnessed the last train home pulling out of the station.

Malcolm Davies: Don't get flustered Malcolm, just put him in his place and show yourself to be the reasonable one here. Show the rest of the staff who is in charge and what a mouthy and arrogant man Redfern is, no matter what his academic pretensions might be.

'Indeed we do, Mike, and thank you for that vote of confidence in us all. Had you allowed me to complete my sentence I was going to say what it means for us all here at school from now on. The Head and I have thought long and hard about this policy, and great care has gone into framing it in a way that is simple, achievable and memorable for us all. By this I mean staff and pupils alike. Of course we know the basic meaning of the word and soon into the next academic year there will be no boy in this school who is unaware of its meaning for him in terms of his time at the school. Let me explain.'

Davies proceeded to talk in great detail about the ways in which boys were going to be encouraged to take a more active role in their learning. He talked of pupil-centred learning and of ownership and of whole days when the timetable would be suspended and each boy would have a twenty minute interface with his tutor to discuss his personal progress plan and set academic targets.

The acronym PPP was soon one which all of the staff felt had been in their vocabulary for years. It appeared that studies in America where high school pupils had had twice-termly discussions with school staff had, in some cases, yielded better exam performance and better in-school behaviour with fewer cases of class disruption.

'I'm not in the slightest bit surprised by those figures, Malcolm,' interrupted Redfern, 'but I would urge you to recall Mark Twain's famous observation and the uses, or perhaps I should say abuses, of statistics.'

The allusion was unfortunately lost on Davies and several of the staff, most of whom found Redfern's tireless allusions to be little more than literary showboating. They had heard too many to be either interested or impressed.

'Oh, for God's sake, that line about lies, damned lies and statistics, of course.' Redfern was already riled and his impatience could not be restrained. 'Of course there are going to be fewer cases of disruption in class if the little darlings are out of class for an extra six days every year. I'd be very wary of trying to emulate our American cousins on the basis of such flimsy and, dare I say, spurious evidence as this. Hardly scientific at all.'

'More to the point,' - Phil Stonehouse this time - 'how are the parents going to react to the prospect of lessons being abandoned for the day? They pay good money for their sons to come here and will probably be wanting a reduction in fees if we're effectively teaching them a week or so less. Notwithstanding the fact that they're going to have to take days off work to look after the ones whose *interfacing* falls on different days. They're not going to be best pleased, at least the parents of the younger boys, at paying extra childcare costs.' Stonehouse was a man whose own childcare costs took up a sizeable chunk of his wife's paltry salary.

A general muttering broke out as staff voiced their opinions on childcare costs and the merits and demerits of closing down the school's timetable for whole days at a time. Whilst many inwardly welcomed the idea and the relief from teaching it might represent, the alternative of setting exam targets with each boy was greeted as nothing more than pointless. Surely all boys should be aiming at the top grade? Why else bother sitting the exam at all?

Most staff were worried about cancelling lessons to tell the students what they already knew and were working towards - it was a completely futile act. Furthermore, such a discussion might well lead to pupil complacency, and the loss of teaching time could only have a detrimental effect on the very chances of those likely top grades becoming a realisation. As for the academically weaker boys who laboured well below the C grade pass mark, why urge them to believe they could aim for a pass that was always going to be well beyond their capabilities?

Instilling such false hope seemed cruel and while every member of staff concurred that pupils should be pushed to the full, silk purses from sows' ears were a proverbial and practical impossibility. Alchemy seemed, someone commented, a more fulfilling pursuit than trying to get David Gale to the point of exam success.

Stonehouse was especially outspoken: 'I'm sorry Malcolm,' his voice rose above the low-level complaints which were threatening to derail the meeting, 'but for some of these boys to pass French at present requires something like a miracle. I would suggest that it's only intensive teaching across the year that gives us any success at all. To take these boys away from an environment in which they are forced to speak and write French and to give them more days when they have no exposure to the language is, frankly, untenable. Far from aspiring to high grades we are condemning them to almost certain failure. It just will not do!'

The general chatter finally subsided and Davies was grateful to Phil for his final interjection; he had never been too assertive in restoring meetings to order and had been worried that having to raise his voice this afternoon might make him look and sound too much like a school teacher.

'Thank you, Phil, for that observation. As you all know, we are very much a listening school and I am grateful to you for your input which I shall certainly factor in to my next meeting with the Head. One immediate thought occurs, however, and it is this. That we stagger the pupil-tutor meetings over a week, say, and that we timetable them into teachers' preparation time. This way, each pupil would only miss about twenty minutes or so of one class in order to meet up with his tutor. The disruption to each pupil's timetable and to the school timetable as a whole would therefore be absolutely minimal.'

'But as you've already said, Malcolm, that free time is our preparation time.' On this occasion it was Redfern, speaking very much as the voice of the union.

'First of all, Mike, I thank you for your contribution. I must, however, take issue with your use of the phrase 'free time'. Might I respectfully remind us all that what we are talking about here is not 'free time' but rather non-teaching time. This does not mean we have this time at liberty. No, this is contracted time and is to be used for the good of the school and its pupils to help them however we can.'

'Of course, of course…' Redfern conceded, 'But 'free' time, 'non-teaching' time, call it what you will, let's not get bogged down in semantics here…'

'Antics? This is not antics Mike, this is a very serious issue we are addressing here. I hope we can keep the discussion at the serious level it deserves.'

'Semantics, Malcolm, the study of different meanings attached to words and symbols.' Everybody turned in the direction of Derek Humbrell's voice, emerging from the back.

Derek Humbrell: Good heavens, Davies is a fool but I cannot bear to see anyone make a fool of himself in this public fashion. And besides, the longer we spend just going round in circles and underlining this man's foolishness, the later I am going to get home and escape this tediousness.

'Malcolm, I believe you must have misheard what Mike said; for a second myself I thought he had said, 'Some antics'.'

'Thank you for that Derek and for clarifying the situation.'

Malcolm Davies: My God, I must be very careful in replying to Redfern. Remember, count to ten, Malcolm, before saying anything unprepared. And I really must be more lenient with Humbrell next time I observe his lesson. After all, they might be learning something as they do all that colouring in.

Davies continued. 'If I might get back on task, I am perfectly open to any suggestions as to how we might implement this policy for the good of all, and with minimal disruption to learning. So, whether or not you agree with the Personal Progress Plan meetings, we are definitely going to trial them for at least two years to see if they have a beneficial effect on pupils' learning and achievement. The only issue for debate here, gentlemen, is how we run the scheme.'

Order had now been restored, and with the unforeseen help from Derek Humbrell, Davies had ridden the first stormy interruption from Redfern. It was time to move on and though he was grateful that McMullen had not yet spoken, the Irishman's silence was disturbing and threatening in its status. And what had he been writing on his pad? Davies pressed on.

'As I said at the start, gentlemen, the first strand of this new policy is the word 'Aspire'.' His red laser pointer traced the word again on the screen. 'We owe it to these boys to instil in them the need to aspire, to believe that success only comes from hard work, digging deep and daring to reach new heights.'

Mike Redfern: How the fuck can they reach new heights while digging deep? Who are these kids? Twizzle? Probably best not pick him up on the mixed metaphor. Everyone else must have noticed it.

'So, from September onwards we are going to build into our lesson plans a clear recognition of methods by which we are going to encourage all boys to aspire to greater exam success in all of their subjects. To this end, all classroom and homework tasks will have built into them some sense of how improvements can be made. Not only this gentlemen,' (Davies was pleased with his choice of the word 'gentlemen': it conveyed exactly the right note of polite superiority he wanted), 'but staff appraisals will also focus, in part, on how each of us is aspiring to greater things in our professional lives.' (Davies was also expressly pleased with this distinction he had drawn between professional and personal lives). 'What I am talking about here gentlemen,' (was he overdoing the word?), 'is the need for continuous professional development – the notion that we should all be improving in all sorts of directions for our own sakes and for the sakes of the young men whose futures are entrusted to us. I am confident we all agree that to aspire to anything less would be a betrayal of that trust.'

A temporary silence.

Then, softly, against this quiet could be heard the gentle sound of a middle-aged man singing the chorus of *Coat of Many Colours*. It was only the eventual realisation, upon opening his eyes, that Don Jones sensed every eye upon him. With no sense of embarrassment whatsoever he kept his left ear leaning on his left hand where it concealed the one earpiece he had been listening to and he simply smiled around the room.

'Not a bad voice for an old feller, eh?' he said, grinning. 'Sorry Malcolm, lost in my own little world there for a minute, hard day and all that, you know. Don't mind me, please carry on.'

Davies had never encountered anyone remotely like Don Jones. The man had no shame. He seemed oblivious to normal codes of daily behaviour. But harmless, if ineffectual. Briefly Davies pondered a later meeting where Jones' professional aspirations would be under discussion. Perhaps this would be a discussion for the Head to have with Jones.

'Does this mean the school will now pay the tuition fees for my MA course?' Phil Stonehouse again.

'I beg your pardon, Phil?'

'My MA. If we are genuinely talking of continuous professional development here, I can think of no better way to improve my subject knowledge than by completion of my master's degree. As I may have mentioned before, Malcolm, I'd be willing to meet the costs of my transport and materials, so it would be wonderful for the school to invest in my development and I'm sure it would be good for the *kudos* of the school to have some staff with higher degrees.'

Having no idea what he meant by *kudos*, Malcolm felt unable to respond. Finally the awkward silence was broken.

'Excuse me, but without wishing to blow one's own trumpet, some of us do already have a higher degree.' That was Redfern.

' 'Some of us'? 'Some of us'? As far as I can see Mike, you're the only one, and well done to you, but I am surely not alone here in wishing to study for a master's degree?'

A cough from Derek Humbrell.

'Oh yes, sorry Derek, but of course yours is not quite the same is it? Don't they just post yours out to you some time after you leave Oxford?'

Humbrell smiled as if to agree and as if to suggest that, yes, an Oxford degree was probably worth more than any master's certificate picked up by the likes of Redfern at some second-rate institution.

Malcolm Davies: Hidden depths that Humbrell. I'm going to have to be more careful with him from now on.

'I'm not in a position to discuss or even authorise external programmes of study,' Malcolm replied to Stonehouse's question, 'but what I can promise you all is an ongoing programme of in-house and online CPD which will benefit us all.'

Mike Redfern: Not another bloody acronym.

'We have,' Davies continued, 'recently acquired a whole range of materials from one of the companies run by one of the school's governors, who assures us of the benefits to his staff and that we too may reap the rewards of this generosity.'

McMullen wrote the words CHEAP SHIT on his paper and grinned.

Stonehouse exploded. 'Most of our governors work in industry! How the hell on earth can materials aimed at insurance clerks, accountants or bloody shop assistants have any relevance or use for us? 'Aspire' you say? Sounds more like 'expire' to me if this is the target we're setting ourselves. Always something for nothing, some bloody nod to improving things but when it comes to the crunch this school suddenly discovers its pockets are empty again. Give me a break, Malcolm. Let's do something properly or let's do nothing at all!'

Exhausted and deflated Phil collapsed back in his chair, a defeated man.

Malcolm Davies: That's one down, I don't think he'll be bothering me again today.

'Thank you, Phil, for what was another thoughtful and valued contribution. I say we wait and see and let's not be too hasty to judge this resource before we've even used it. Always best to keep an open mind to any way of improving both ourselves and the school, eh, gentlemen? And with your permission I'd now like to move on to the next part of our new policy, 'BELIEVE'. '

Chapter Thirty
The ABC Meeting : 'Believe'

'BELIEVE'?

McMullen wrote the word in bold capitals on his paper and, for a second, imagined himself in some Alabama church being addressed by Aretha Franklin's father, or Dr King.

Surely this was not what he had signed up for when entering the teaching profession. 'Believe!' McMullen had always suspected that working at the school required a giant leap of faith but now this faith was being institutionalised. He contemplated a facetious response but decided to bite his tongue. A rowdy response was exactly what Davies would have been expecting and so far his silence did seem to be unnerving him.

The capital *B* on Davies's screen had now been joined by the remaining letters of the word; He was only surprised that the word had not been adorned with angels and cherubim and the flying in of the extra letters had not been accompanied by a few bars of sacred music or Mahalia Jackson.

But then both of these would have been too classy for the Malaprop man; had he selected any music he would have gone for some shite by Queen or some other tired old rock anthem. But no, the word just sat there under 'Aspire', the two words together rendering the capital C hanging underneath like some odd typo. Although Gerry had already worked out his own choices for 'ABC', he now puzzled over what 'C' might represent for Davies.

'Commit' ? 'Control' ? 'Concentrate' ?

Any of these would have been suitably silly and vague

enough to fit in with the fool-of-a-man's misconceived notions of education. For Christ's sake, 'Aspire' and 'Believe' were so woolly you wondered what the poor kids might make of them. In a world that required clarity the last thing they needed was more fuckin' wool.

McMullen's thoughts drifted to sheep. He lost himself in a darkly romantic reverie involving Davies and a particularly ugly sheep; a rain-drenched sheep covered in mud and its own shit. The setting was vivid: a grey day with the rain lashing down and Davies in a pink cagoule struggling desperately to persuade a vehemently reluctant sheep to make the beast with two backs with him.

McMullen's mind was off and running. This was no clichéd scene of comical sheep-shagging with a gurning man in wellies inflicting himself on some dumb animal. No, this sheep was much more clever than Davies and, like some coquettish courtesan, was constantly rebutting all of Davies' gauche advances. In McMullen's narrative Davies had brought flowers and champagne, but the rain and wind had shredded the blooms to buggery and the Bollinger had spilled across the hillside leaving Davies with only his wits to fall back on in his attempt to seduce the coy beast. He had thus resorted to singing to the sheep in some hideous parody of a troubadour wooing a damsel. In McMullen's narrative Davies was making a great effort to imitate the tremulous warble of Charles Aznavour and was crooning in the sheep's left ear, A bastardised version of the old hit which substituted the word 'sheep' for the word 'she'. But all to no obvious avail. The sheep simply tossed her head, defecated once more, and ran off in alarm and disgust at being serenaded by a strange wet homosexual whose lime green wellies clashed with his pink cagoule.

Fortuitously, McMullen's pen dropped to the floor and stirred him from this sick fantasy. What on earth was happening to him? Why should his thoughts be consumed with images of Davies in an unrequited search for love with sheep? Thank god the summer holiday was fast approaching.

'Believe,' Davies announced, and for a brief moment McMullen heard the word 'Bleat'. He tried to think of something else but it was not easy. 'In our pastoral roles we need to be shepherding the boys into a whole new mindset. I'm not saying we need to ram home this strand of our new policy but ewe need to be thinking of ways to change the culture of the school.'

He hadn't said any of that, had he? McMullen wrote on his sheet the words, 'GET A GRIP, GERRY!', shifted his arse and sat more upright, in an attempt to clear his mind. As he did so he caught Davies glancing in his direction and sensing an anxious look, he regained his self-composure.

'It seems to me,' droned Davies, 'that if we are collectively going to ASPIRE.' He pronounced the word in capitals, 'we need to BELIEVE,' (more capitals) 'that we CAN ASPIRE.' (capitals becoming irritatingly tiresome). 'So what I am suggesting, indeed, asking for, is that we adopt a new strategy to reinforce the idea to the boys, and also to ourselves, that we can do better in our aspirations.'

Don Jones who had now switched off Emmylou Harris, nevertheless began singing again. This time it was the chorus of the old Bachelors' version of the Frankie Laine song *I Believe*. His singing was barely audible but to McMullen who was sitting directly in front of him, it was quite clear. Mcmullen considered joining in, but instead merely observed on his notepad: DON JONES, GENIUS.

'In order that every boy in the school takes this idea on board, we are building it into the tutoring programme and the PPP meetings. When we are discussing target grades with the boys we should be aiming high, ASPIRING to the best grades possible. It has been proven that to gain the top grades pupils need to BELIEVE their grades are within their capabilities. It's very much a matter of mind over matter that matters.'

Supressed sniggers were heard around the room at the unintended triplet. Once more Davies had allowed himself to veer ill-advisedly from his rehearsed script and he was all too aware of the clumsiness of his words. Don Jones removed his single earpiece and spoke.

'Now that would make a catchy slogan, Malcolm. The alliteration and repetition make it easy for the boys to remember. Perhaps we should have it displayed on brightly coloured posters in every classroom in the school to drive home the message. Superimpose it upon a background of Rodin's *The Thinker* and even the weaker kids would not miss the message. How about 'The message is very much a matter of mind over matter that matters'? Trips off the tongue a treat that does, Malcolm.'

Malcolm thanked Don and said he would raise the idea with the Head. McMullen amended his previous note so it now read: DON JONES, ABSOLUTE GENIUS.

'Whether we go with Don's idea or not,' continued Malcolm, 'the point is we need to be encouraging positive thinking. It's very much like the role sports psychologists play in getting their clients mentally prepared before a big game or a big race or whatever. The margins in these elite sports are apparently very slim and top athletes are physically all much of a muchness. The one who wins is the one who wants it most;

at least that's what all the evidence and research suggests. I wouldn't claim to be much of a top athlete myself,' he added. Nobody laughed.

'BIT OF A COCK-JOCKEY, THOUGH?' McMullen wrote.

Redfern could contain himself no longer. 'Malcolm, I could spend all day trying to convince myself that a ten second hundred metres is within my grasp but let us please be sensible here. We can both predict with cast iron certainty that such a likelihood is beyond credibility and no amount of saying it could happen increases the possibility of it ever being realised.'

Davies was primed in his response. 'Of course not, Mike, and no-one is expecting to see you picking up gold at the next Olympics. But if you do believe, you may well break twenty seconds for the hundred metres.'

McMullen suddenly erupted. He could sit in silence and swallow Davies's educational bullshit but the notion of his friend Mike ever completing the hundred metres, no matter what his time, was beyond anything anyone could believe. Redfern was very fond of a drink or ten, as his unhealthy girth testified.

'Only if it was all downhill and some fucker rolled him!'

The laughter that Davies had failed to achieve just a few seconds earlier now rang around the room in gales. Redfern, who wore his weight like some obscene badge of honour, stood up, turned to face the assembled staff and took a bow.

'Exactly my point Gerry. It is obvious for all to see that I am, as Howlin' Wolf so eloquently phrased it, built for comfort, not for speed.' More laughter. 'We all have different skills and mine are patently not in the field of sporting pursuits. To tell me otherwise is both false and dangerous and to tell our pupils similar lies, at their impressionable ages, is both reckless and downright irresponsible. Thank you very much but I must sit down again as I do find this uprightness so dreadfully tiring.' With another stage bow he took his seat.

'Gentlemen, gentlemen...' Davies returned to his obsequious self. 'I am not suggesting we tell the boys to believe that absolutely anything is possible but that if one doesn't give oneself the chance to achieve something, one will certainly never do it. All I am asking is that we urge and encourage pupils to entertain different possibilities. It's a case of opening up one's mind to new options.'

'Sounds like some new-wave hippy shit to me,' offered Don Jones. 'And I never did trust the old-wave hippy shit of the sixties. Free your mind, take LSD and you too can be a butterfly. Load of tosh if you ask me.'

'Well, actually Don, and with all due respect, I don't recall asking you, but thank you all the same.'

'Hang on Malcolm,' Phil Stonehouse came out of his shell again. 'Didn't you say earlier that this is a 'listening school'? I think, no, I BELIEVE...' Phil paused, pleased with his usage of the word. '...that Don has every right to express his views. After all, we are not in some totalitarian state here, are we?'

Davies kept silent. 'If only,' he thought. 'If only.' But despite his desire for the school to be some 'totalitarian state' under his supreme control, Malcolm felt great unease at introducing the final part of the ABC trilogy. How was it possible to bring the word 'Challenge' into view immediately after he had put down Don Jones in such a peremptory manner and then failed to respond to Phil Stonehouse's defence of Don?

McMullen could see Malcolm beginning to perspire

just a little more profusely as was usually the case at such meetings, and, like Malcolm's armpits, his sense of well-being was becoming just a little warmer. And just as this glow of self-satisfaction came over McMullen he heard a shuffling just along the row from him and was suddenly aware that Chris Adams was addressing the meeting.

Chris Adams?

Chris Adams never contributed to staff meetings. He was one of those staff who preferred to maintain a stoic silence in the face of whatever management might throw at him. It was generally known that his marriage was not a happy one. He had once tried to confide in McMullen but Gerry had shrugged him off and rushed to tell the rest of the staff of Adams's misery. Nowadays Adams and McMullen barely exchanged greetings and it was obvious to all that these two members of the Science department had little or no time for each other.

'As I see it Malcolm, I fully agree with your plan to make the boys aspire to fulfil their potential. Surely that is a part of the job that is fully understood by us all. If we are not here to bring the best out of the boys, what are we doing here at all? No, aiming high is a fundamental part of what we are doing, or should be doing and I do not feel that an occasional reminder here and there is any bad thing for us or the boys.'

Everyone was quite stunned at Chris's contribution. Most had not grasped the content of what he was saying. They were too struck by the novelty of his speaking at all. But McMullen had taken in every word, and now he had already broken his silence to gain an easy laugh at Redfern's expense he saw an opportunity to attack Adams, albeit under the cover of a debate on school policy. He was, in fact, formulating a response which would afford him the opportunity to attack Adams for his defence of Davies's bullshit and which would also allow him the chance to mock Davies for both his idiotic ideas and the even more idiotic way he had presented them.

But Adams was not finished.

'No, Malcolm, I support to the hilt any initiative that pushes us all to give and achieve of our best.'

Amused smirks were beginning to flash around the room and Davies was now sweating less as a consequence of this endorsement form such an unlikely source. He had not forgotten the 'scatalogical' incident and had since harboured the correct belief that Adams saw himself as superior in so many ways.

'But yet…' Adams continued.

Malcolm's armpits began to leak again, and his throat simultaneously began to dry. How could all that saliva be abruptly diverted from his mouth to his underarms? Why did his body betray him so drastically in times of nervousness and crisis?

Mike Redfern smiled. He knew all too well about Cleopatra's reaction to the Messenger's *But yet* when he came delivering news of Antony's Roman exploits. If only the Malaprop Man were to scream 'I do not like *But yet* and, drawing a knife, follow this up with *Rogue, thou hast lived too long*.' Redfern would attend more staff meetings at the promise of such drama.

Chris Adams continued, still free from the risk of attack.

'Yet I should like to add that my support of your professed intention to push the boys all the way is severely tempered by the preposterous and flawed logic behind your assertions regarding belief. It is no secret that I am a practising Christian and like the followers of any creed, belief is a vital part of the way we lead our lives. It is, indeed, the very bedrock of our lives. But our belief, my belief, is founded not on any ability in ourselves but in the benign goodness of our creator and the belief that a good life on earth will earn us a place in heaven. It is, in many ways, an abstract belief in a divine essence who will grant us eternal life after this vale of tears that we call our mortal existence. It is a belief in a higher being who will offer us redemption and salvation. And whilst I fully appreciate that it is a mystery to non-believers, it is less of a mystery than the gibberish you have been propounding, Malcolm.

'I tend to be a man who keeps himself to himself, and it has to be acknowledged that I do not always see eye to eye with some of my colleagues but I do recognise that we are all trying to do our best for the boys. But to suggest, as you have, that education is a simple case of mind over matter, flies in the face of all educational theory and is, simply expressed, plain ridiculous. And if we suggest to the boys that a simple belief in academic achievement will, without application, dedication and serious study, lead to academic achievement we will be guilty of gross deception at a level that renders it immoral, if not bordering on the criminal.

'I am sorry Malcolm but I can take no more of what Don coarsely but correctly calls 'new-wave hippy shit,' so if you will excuse me, I have better things to do with my time on such a pleasant evening.'

With this Adams calmly left the meeting amidst a hushed silence, and McMullen made one further note: on his notepad THERE'S METHODISM IN HIS MADNESS.

Chapter Thirty-One
The ABC Meeting : 'Challenge'

If Malcolm had been concerned earlier about introducing the third strand of the new policy, he was now beyond worry. From the initial meeting with Gordon Albert he had had doubts over the head's choice of Aspire, Believe and Challenge. He could not voice that it was the abstract nature of these words that bothered him; he simply preferred the simple and more easily understandable sense of his original choices of Arrive, Behave and Complete School, and he knew that these would also have made more sense to the boys.

But the meeting had descended into chaos. The staff were behaving like one of Don Jones' classes or even one of Derek Humbrell's. Laughter and animated conversation were now set out before him, and faced with such a breakdown in order, Davies felt helpless. He could feel the tears beginning to well up at the sense of his own inadequacy. He even began to hear his father's gruff tones from somewhere deep in his being. It was a familiar, mocking voice. All of his life Father's method of encouragement had been based upon ridicule as a means of motivation and, for all of Malcolm's life, this had failed.

A delicate boy with anxieties over his physique, his looks and, especially, his homosexuality, he had never been strong enough to respond as required and Father's macho admonitions had only served to deepen his insecurities. And when Father had not been bullying him, he had been providing for him with the considerable help of his old-boy network. Private school, university, this current job – Father had pressed the flesh, made the phone calls, called in the favours and generally greased the wheels to keep Malcolm at a level that was always just a rung or two beyond him.

Malcolm had hated his schooldays. The miseries of cold food and even colder dormitories had exercised detrimental effects upon his health throughout his time there. He recalled more Wednesday afternoons with Matron than he had ever spent on the rugby field.

Matron had not really wanted him with her. It was enough dealing with the post-match walking wounded without this sad boy with his increasingly feeble excuses for missing games. And yet she had felt pity for 'Drippy' Davies. The name-calling cruelty of some boys was a part of the job she despised and she knew that the rugby teams wanted 'Drippy' on their pitches even less than Malcolm himself wanted to be there. She could not get from her head the notion that Drippy Davies was her own appointed Billy Casper.

For his part, Malcolm had hated and loved Matron in fairly equal measures. Or so it had seemed. But what he had come to realise was that his love for her and the sanctuary she offered was balanced by the self-loathing that arose from his reliance upon her.

In front of him he could see McMullen and Redfern sniggering with laughter, McMullen's face a rictus of contorted hateful hilarity and Redfern's excessive pounds shaking under his shirt. The phrase 'belly laugh' took on a whole new meaning with Redfern. Jones was also out of control as he and Stonehouse exchanged what were obviously mockeries of their Deputy Head. No, their *Director of Quality and Cultural/ Diversity Officer*! The very thought of his full title lifted Malcolm. 'I am Director,' he considered, 'I should direct!'

And so, as he surveyed the pathetic staff of this decidedly

less-than-adequate school for decidedly less-than-adequate boys, he felt the bile rising in him. These teachers were, for the most part, ordinary men towards whom he felt no individual animosity. Of course, Redfern had his master's degree but what had he ever done with it? He was, as were they all, below Malcolm. And didn't all of those clever words and literary references merely hide the man's own inadequacies? The references to obscure poems too - were they actually correct? For all Malcolm or anyone else on the staff knew, Redfern had been making them up for years. McMullen, of course, was a nasty, vicious man, the kind of man who reinforces all English bigotries about thick, violent, hard-drinking paddies, and that was plain for anyone to see. Why, he even kept guns and was a very scary man. Malcolm lived in dread of ever bumping into McMullen outside of school.

But what of the rest? Stonehouse was another empty man with a jumped-up sense of his own importance. Jones was a bumbling fool. Humbrell a sad, ineffective teacher with even less self-esteem than Malcolm himself. And as for Adams, had he not just proved his mental instability to all? Malcolm had never had much time for god-botherers: his own school with its constant Biblical warnings against masturbation and homosexuality had taught him early in life never to trust zealots. They were just one more group out to trouble his life. Just like the types before him today. He knew full well that all the low hum of conversations were about him and Adams. What bothered him was that all of the men in front of him were clearly of the opinion that Adams had just put one over him. That in walking out of his meeting in that way, Adams, the laconic Adams, had made a fool out of him.

The bile in his throat thickened. Davies began to feel

himself choke on his self-loathing. But at least the sweating had stopped, and in its place he felt the unexpected chill of delight. He had never really wanted this post and after Adams's exit he could see no way that he could continue in it with any shred of dignity. The summer break was only six weeks – far too little time for bitter men to forget, or for him to overcome his shame and embarrassment.

The staff chatter showed no sign of abating. Davies moved as if to return to his presentation but instead gave the laptop one almighty shove. As the laptop hit the floor with a resounding crash, silence was restored and staff concern shifted to the broken machine, its shattered screen no longer emitting any light.

Before the silence could again be broken Davies started to speak. At first his voice was barely audible and his audience remained silent, as they strained to catch his words.

'*C*,' began Davies, 'in our new programme is for… well, it doesn't really matter what it stands for because it's very obvious, gentlemen, that you have absolutely no intention of supporting or even considering any new initiative. In this way you are one of the most blinkered and stubborn groups of people that has ever been gathered in one place and it is this resistance to change, to improvement, that makes me feel so sad for you and so sorry for the boys whose futures you hold in your hands.'

No one sniggered at what, at other times, would have been the prompt for smutty innuendo.

'One of the roles of education, in any form, is to open minds, to develop thinking, to explore possibilities. But you men are so stuck in your ways that you cannot even see you are in a rut, never mind get out of it. You also cannot see the rut getting deeper day by day. You prefer to hide behind your own pathetic failings, never seeing beyond the petty to the possibility that something better may be available.'

The staff were stunned but Davies' words had hit home and nobody spoke out.

'Take me as an example.' Davies had lost all fear now. 'Don't you think I know I sometimes get lost for words and get my words muddled? But no, you are all so small-minded and keen to mock that you laugh behind my back. Not one of you has ever bothered to ask why I should have this affliction. Not one of you has ever offered any help or support. The cheap and easy laugh means you don't have to think or do anything. And don't tell me it's just 'banter', that it's harmless, because, believe me, it most certainly is not!

But enough of me; what about you? '*C*' was supposed to stand for Challenge but forget that now. Now it really ought to stand for Cunts, because today you have proved that is exactly what you all are.'

'No one calls me a fuckin' cunt!'

'Oh shut up McMullen and listen for once,' Malcolm retorted before McMullen could really get going, and the force of his reply silenced the Irishman.

'Yes, I only have to look at you all to realise what a complete bunch of cunts you are.'

The use of the *C* word had liberated Malcolm; its brutish Anglo-Saxon tone had sounded good in his mouth and he understood its primal force. It was not a word he recalled having ever used before but he liked it for the way it made him feel. He was on a roll.

'You, for instance,' he pointed at Phil Stonehouse. 'You've no real imagination or talent so you hang around the likes of

Mike Redfern and Gerry McMullen in the hope that one day you will be fully admitted into their little gang. You're a very small fish in a small pond and yet you give yourself airs that are, frankly, laughable.'

Malcolm turned to Derek Humbrell.

'As for you Mr So-Called–Geography-Teacher, I wonder why on earth you ever entered the profession. You never talk to the boys and as far as I can see your classes are just one long colouring festival. Half of the school's stationery budget seems to go on bloody felt pens for your dumbfuck lessons.'

In this deliberate way Davies continued to assassinate the characters of every member of staff in front of him until he got to Mike Redfern.

'Mike Redfern. Ah, Mike Redfern, *MA,* the man who is so principled that he can't make an exception to mark one late piece of coursework for an otherwise excellent pupil. Mike Redfern, MA who can parrot the classics safe in the knowledge that nobody else here knows if he is bullshitting or not. Mike Redfern, *MA,* the man with university lecturer pretensions who is slumming it here with the rest of us. Lot of bloody good that higher degree did you, eh Mike? Or is it your caustic tongue and petty personality that shines through all those failed interviews and enables people to see what a truly shallow, nasty, ego-ridden and bitter man you really are? Mike Redfern, *MA,* who claims to know all of the great writers but who, to my knowledge, has never put pen to paper to produce anything of greater substance than a shopping list. Mind you, when you consider what a fat bastard Mike Redfern, *MA,* truly is, then that must be one long, long shopping list. I wouldn't mind betting that the other half of the school's stationery budget goes on paper for Mike Redfern, *MA,* to make out his grocery lists. Perhaps that is another reason no university will touch him - they are all scared witless he will drop dead with a mid-term heart attack.'

The Director of Quality was beginning to flag but Gerry McMullen had been left for his finale.

'And finally we come to Gerry McMullen, whose middle name must be 'Fuck' as that's the word we most often hear coming from his foul weasel mouth. In Gerry's mouth the word isn't even an obscenity, it's just punctuation.

'Gerry Fuck McMullen – the brave man who smashes beakers on poor boys' heads and punctures boys' footballs. Isn't it a pity we're not all as big and brave as Gerry McMullen? Why, it's even rumoured that his wife couldn't stand his bullying and foul mouth, so she upped and left him.'

'That's e-fuckin'–nough Davies, you ignorant little shit of a bureaucrat,' McMullen sputtered. 'What gives you any fuckin' right to stand there slagging us all off? And you can leave my wife out of this! I never bullied her but I sure as hell am gonna batter the fuck out of you as soon as I catch you on a dark night away from this place – maybe outside one of those fuckin' gay bars you hang around. We all know you're a fuckin' shirtlifter. And don't think we don't all know the reason Simon Gore had to leave the fuckin' school. Too pretty for his own fuckin' good was Simon.'

The sweat was now returning under Davies' shirt, but he was not to be waylaid from his cause.

'Don't be a fool McMullen. The Head and I are on your case, and trust me, you're not likely to be here in September anyway. And you can apologise now for those comments about young Gore – I never touched the boy, and you know it.'

There could be no going back now.

'But yes, I am homosexual, though I fail to see what business that is of yours. We're not living in the Dark Ages now, McMullen. Well, you may be, but most of the country has moved on. It's like I said earlier, most of you can't cope with anything new or different. I am gay, yes, but the chances are I am not the only homosexual member of staff. Boys' schools are renowned for attracting teachers with, shall we say, an extra-curricular interest in their own sex. I was rather railroaded into this job, but all of you actually chose to apply here. So, ask yourselves, which of you has any homosexual tendencies?'

For a moment, silence.

Until…

Until McMullen kicked back his chair, rose to his feet, spat at the floor in front of Malcolm and made his exit muttering something about his gun.

Davies sank back in his chair but comfort came in the unlikely form of Mike Redfern.

'Don't worry, I'll go and calm him down. But you've not heard the last of this, Davies.'

Davies made an attempt to switch off his laptop but it was obviously fit only for the bin since he'd bounced it on the ground before him. With a resigned smile he headed for the rear exit, stopping only to turn to what remained of the staff.

'As for you lot, your jobs are safe for September. After all, where else would this awful school find replacements? This is a bloody awful school, but then you are all bloody awful teachers, and so you belong here. Goodbye, gentlemen.'

The staff were all dazed and confused. In silence they collected their possessions and shuffled from the hall, too shocked for further comment.

In the corridor they passed Gerry McMullen locked in heated argument with Gordon Albert with Mike Redfern standing between them like some boxing referee. Gordon had been on his way to the hall to bask in the glory of his new initiative's reception, when he had encountered the fuming McMullen, heading for his car seat to fetch his gun. Redfern was now playing the peacemaker role and trying to reassure his friend McMullen that he would be better off out of the school, that another job, a better job, was Gerry's for the asking and that following Mike's imminent resignation they may well find themselves better jobs together in a better school. It would also be better for them both if they were off the premises before the police arrived. Gordon had dialled 999 whilst they had been standing there.

That evening at the gun club Gerry McMullen was advised to stop shooting and go for a calming pint or two; Mike Redfern stopped at the nearest pub and took advantage of the 2-for-1 meal offer which he washed down with several beers; Derek Humbrell bought new watercolour supplies and extra felt pens for September.

From his office Malcolm Davies recorded a gushing answerphone message informing his father that he was leaving behind both the school and any pretence that he was straight, and that his father better get used to both bits of news.

As soon as he finished the message he headed out for pollo cacciatore and the most gorgeous brown eyes in town.

Chapter Thirty-Two The ABC Meeting : Afterwards, Charlie Dyer

'What a bleedin' mess they've made of this hall!
'Sod it, this lot can wait until the morning.
'Now, where did I leave them mags?'

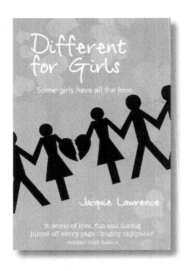

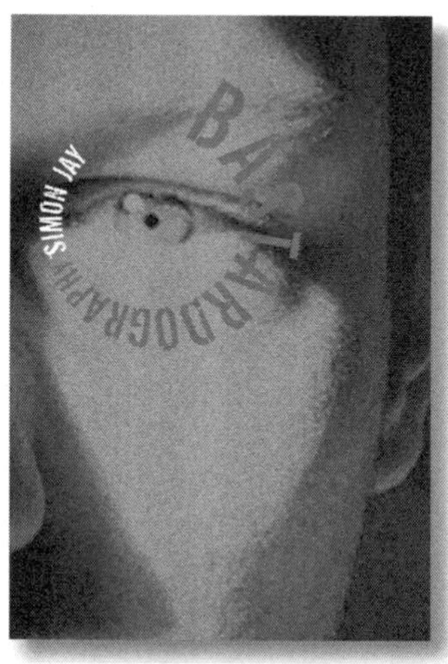
SIMON JAY
BASTARDOGRAPHY

ZITEBOOKS
writing for all time

I THOU
You'd
BIGGER !

A SMALL PERSONS
guide to
FIGHTING BACK

by Kevin O'Hagan

‘I thought you’d be Bigger’

A small person's guide to fighting back'

Kevin 0'Hagan 6th Dan

About the author

Kevin 0'Hagan has spent 30 years studying, training and teaching the Martial Arts. He presently holds the rank of 6th Dan black belt in Ju Jutsu and also holds a black belt in Atemi-Jutsu. Additionally he is a registered self-protection Coach with the British Combat Association.

He has taught people from all walks of life his brand of Combat Ju Jutsu and Self Protection methods, from ex-forces, bodyguards, Security and doormen to ladies, children, the elderly and disabled.

His clubs are based in and around the Bristol area.

Kevin has written many articles for Martial Arts magazines and has appeared on local television and radio, teaching his Art.

Kevin has written four books, this is his first book on the subject.

2nd Edition Oct 2001

Printed by
New Breed Publishing
Po box 2676
Romford
Essex RM7 0WA

Email: jamieokeefe@tiscali.co.uk

Web site: www.newbreedbooks.co.uk

Acknowledgements

Published by

New Breed publishing 1998, 1999, 200, 2001

A CIP catalogue record for this book is available from the British Library

Printed and bound in Great Britain.

ISBN 0 9517567 7 X (10 digit ISBN)
ISBN 9780951756775 (13 digit ISBN)

Please note: The theoretical information and physical techniques outlined in this book are for self-protection and Self defence purposes only. The author and the publishers cannot accept any responsibility for any proceedings or prosecutions brought or instituted against any person or body as a result of the misuse of any theoretical information or physical techniques described in this book or any loss, injury or damage caused thereby.

CONTENTS

YOU'VE HAD IT,
YOU LITTLE
SQUIRT !!
HELP!

thinks size, or lack there off, has any debilitating qualities when it comes to protecting your self and those that you love.

I can tell you categorically that the most ferocious fighters that I have ever worked with have been physically small, like Kevin, but absolute dynamite when the fuse was lit.

I have known Kevin for quite a few years now, not only is he a very personable man he is also a first rate martial artist, one of the few that I really admire and one of even fewer high graded martial artists in Britain that is not afraid to don the white belt and learn off just about anyone that has something of worth to teach.

He is a realist, one of the leaders in the new age of realism, he talks the talk and he walks the walk so I heartily recommend and endorse this text to anyone, of any size or stature, that wants to be better prepared when the metaphoric 'big bad wolf tries to blow your house down.

This is a great book, buy, read it and be bigger for the experience.

Geoff Thompson, Coventry 1998.

Preface

This book has been written for the small person, who feels intimidated and frightened by the larger foe.
Because they lack the inches in height or are outweighed in sheer physical bodyweight, they feel vulnerable and inadequate when having to stand up for themselves or when they have to fight back.

This lack of self belief leads to more harassment and bullying and their lives can become a misery; forever running scared and unable to confront their fears and do something about it.

Now with the help of this book they will learn tactics and techniques that will give them self confidence and 'know how' to stop being victimised or pushed around.

They will also learn how to fight back when required and win!

There are many books on the market covering all topics of Martial Arts and Self Defence but not one properly addresses the problems of the small person at all, although there are many such people out there looking for a tailor made Self Defence system particularly catering for their needs.

Myself being just below average height can identify with the problems, as I have experienced them all from childhood to adulthood.

It was lack of height/physical bodyweight that made me initially at 14 years of age seek out my first Martial Arts class, looking for the magical techniques that would solve my problems!

Some 22 years on I have found my solutions but the journey was a long and perilous one but well worth it.

Am I any taller? Any bigger? Yes physically I have built up my body, but it is mentally where I am the most strongest.

I would like to share my knowledge now with all others out there who want to develop the self-belief to fight back and win. You can do it and the time starts now!

"Some of the Smallest Creatures
on the planet, are the most deadly"

Big guy Vs Small guy
What's the 'Likely' outcome?

Introduction

For countless generations people have believed that in a fight involving a big man and a small man, the bigger would almost certainly win.

We have been brought up with the stereotype fighters in the films and later videos. Men like John Wayne, Clint Eastwood and Arnold Schwarzenegger. All big guys who could handle the troublemakers with ease and pound them into the dust. Everybody secretly wants to be like that, be that big, that strong, that fearless.

With the exception of the late and great Bruce Lee, the celluloid world hasn't done a lot for the small man to show how he would fare against the 'Big Boys'.

One recent example of how people view fighting/fighters was made clear in a film called 'Roadhouse' starring Patrick Swayze. He played the part of a night club 'Cooler' (head bouncer) called Dalton with a legendary reputation for being able to look after himself.

Frequently throughout the film when people met him for the first time they would say, **'funny, I thought you'd be bigger!'**
It became a funny line in the film but it stuck with me, hence this books title.

But it also showed how people in general stereotype fighters to always being big and fearsome and are otherwise sceptical.

In the boxing arena though the smaller fighter has never done well against the larger ones. Even if they were both evenly matched with boxing ability, usually sheer physical strength and bodyweight win in the end.

Let's face it as good as he was, no-one would say give Sugar Ray Leonard even in his fighting prime much hope of beating Mike Tyson in a match up.

So again in the ring, the bigger man rules supreme and people will draw conclusions from this fact also.

But remember these people are fighting to a set of rules.

They know what each other can and cannot use.

This is a world apart from a brutal no holds barred street fight.

In that situation a skilled and knowledgeable little man can turn the tables and win!

When Karate and Judo first came to the Western World, people suddenly realised that these small Japanese Masters could really defend themselves against larger opponents.

After all most of the Westerners were considerably taller and heavier than their oriental counterparts. But this did not deter these little men with tremendous fighting skills and spirit, literally 'chopping' them down to size!

People began to train in these Arts as size didn't matter it was technique. But as these Arts developed, a sporting influence took over. Suddenly there were set rules for sparring, the more lethal equalising techniques the ones that the smaller person needed were excluded for safety reasons.

Weight categories were introduced as in boxing, so people would have a fair fight. Because again it was realised a small man against a bigger one under set rules would not be an even match.

We though are not concerned about fighting under set rules or within the confines of a ring. We are concerned with fighting for Self Protection in the street!

You will not be fighting for trophies, medals or belts; you will be fighting for the supreme prize, your life!

A no holds barred street fight is a different proposition to a fight where a referee is on stand by to see fair play.

No one will step in if you go down to the floor or are being punched senseless!

It will be just you and your adversary, because anything goes in this situation and you can use this play to your advantage.

In this text we will look at the training necessary to survive a street encounter. The techniques shown are pure close quarter combat Ju Jutsu.

No frills, no fancy moves. Just straight forward no nonsense Self Defence.

It's time for the little man to stand tall and fight back!!

Chapter 1

Developing the proper Combat attitude of mind

'It's not the size of the dog in the fight, it's the size of the fight in the dog'!

This above saying can certainly hold true and I have seen it displayed many times not only in the controlled arena of the training halls but also on the streets.

The perception that big goes hand in hand with tough is not always true.

Another favourite quote of the uninitiated is ***'Look at the size of that bloke, I certainly wouldn't want to tangle with him'!***

Now there are big guys out there that are monsters but I also have known big guys who couldn't give your grandmother a decent fight!

You must begin to get rid of the ***'look at the size of him'*** mentality and re-programme your thinking. Sure, still be respectful and wary of a large man but don't be intimidated or feel that he must be superior to you in all departments.

Don't let fear convince you that if you get into conflict with such a person you will not stand a chance. These negative thoughts will always creep into your mind. The more you train physically and mentally to control them the better you will become.

Start thinking small can be dangerous, small can be intimidating, and small can be ferocious when needed.

Think of the animal kingdom, some of the most deadliest creatures in the world are small, spiders, snakes, frogs, insects. Even large predators know when to avoid these creatures and like, because they realise they will have **'bitten off more than they can chew'.**

Look at dogs like a pit bull or Jack Russell. Big dogs give them healthy respect and plenty of distance as they realise their fighting qualities, you can be the same!

Also remember some large people will use their height or body bulk as an intimidating safety net to keep others from them but although the house may look big and strong underneath the foundations are weak and one good wallop could send the lot crumbling to the floor!

So how can you start re-programming your thoughts along these lines?

You must firstly examine yourself and find out what sort of person you are, then you can begin to re-mould yourself.

Basically I have found there to be **<u>3 types of small person</u>**.

One is a person that is quiet and reserved who keep themselves very much to themselves. They lack belief in their abilities because of their size and try to avoid conflict because they feel they are weak and cannot handle it.

The second person because of their lack of physical presence has to make up for it by being loud, cocky and arrogant. They feel this will get them noticed and this is their safety net or mental suit of armour. I am sure you all know somebody like this?

Thirdly the type of person you want to become.
Again quiet and polite, friendly but commands respect when needed. Will know the point where he will not be taken beyond and will communicate it in no uncertain terms!

Will avoid conflict at all costs. But when cornered and has no alternative will be able to flick on that 'killer instinct' switch and become a dangerous and formidable opponent until the threat is removed.

You have to work to master being that type of person, you have to gain that quiet confidence so that if trouble comes your way and there is no avoiding it you will be able to handle it.

This confidence comes through training in proper combat techniques that suit your build and stature. As you progress and learn the feeling of control and confidence, your abilities will develop.

Remember though never be brash, arrogant or big headed and don't under-estimate anyone. Just channel that burning inner feeling of how to cope with a violent and dangerous encounter if it happens.

After self-belief you must learn to build ruthless determination. The next essential ingredient. Once you decide on defending yourself you must go at it a 100%. All thoughts of defeat, injury and pain to your own self must be blotted out and never enter your mind.

If you let these thoughts enter your mind, you will lose the confrontation.

You have to keep on fighting like a savage animal until the attacker is incapable of further action. Don't hold back - see that he is stopped.

The law forbids you to take revenge but it permits you to prevent. Do what you have to do to prevent the assault. Let's face it your attacker is not going to be worried about your welfare. If he is physically bigger and stronger you must not allow him a chance to get into the fight. You may only get one chance so make it count, swarm and overwhelm your opponent.

If you get punched, kicked, grabbed, keep fighting! Don't let the mind give in; as soon as it does you will be beaten. Most fights finish because one of the participants has mentally given up, not necessarily because of their physical injuries.

If after you receive a few blows your mind says 'this hurts, he's going to kill me here', your body will react to and give in. Don't let this happen. Be ruthless and dogged.

Think positive, I will win, I cannot be stopped; I won't be hurt, I will defeat you no matter what!
This sort of determined outlook will give you a distinct psychological edge; it will also give you the advantage to win!

Remember a big guy who chooses to attack you is 100% sure he can beat you. His physique is I'm bigger so I'm better. He sees you as no threat and doesn't believe you can harm him. Blow his stupid and over confident attitude out of the window along with his senses. Turn into that pit bull; blitz him from all angles with blows. Overwhelm him with sheer desire to win and ruthless fury. Make him suddenly think what the hell have I taken on here?

Can you recall a part in the film 'Jurassic Park', when the guy who stole the dinosaur embryos was trying to get away, when he was confronted by what looked like a small playful dinosaur?

Him believing so, didn't treat it with the respect it deserved. Then suddenly it turned into a ferocious, poison spitting, man-eating nightmare!

By the time the guy realised what he was up against it was too late! Get the idea, remember how people might perceive you then prove them wrong.

You see psychologically you have turned the tables. There's nothing worse than when a supremely confident fighter suddenly finds himself on the receiving end of punishment rather than dishing it out! Some don't know how to handle it and won't be able to readjust quickly enough.

So cultivate this mind, set and show no fear, even if your stomach is churning over inside, channel the feeling positively, except them and make them work for you. Wear the mask of a cold and calculating veteran of many such battles. Stare at your opponent with blank, expressionless eyes, like shark's eyes, pull your lips back in a grim determined smile. All these tactics will unnerve your attacker.

Think again how the pit bull will have no hesitation or fear when attacking a larger dog than itself.

That's because it has an inner belief in itself and a will to win, so can you!

Another component to the whole picture is developing a 'killer instinct'. This is the ability basically to finish the fight, to resoundingly defeat your attacker.

You must strive for this, make no mistake your attacker given the chance will finish you, whether it be beat you, stab you or kick you to a pulp!

The days of fair play are gone, the hardened mugger or psycho street fighter will not worry about stooping to the lowest level to beat you.

Unfortunately you may have to stoop even lower to defeat them!

But remember you are doing this for a different motive than them, you are doing it to defend yourself, your family, your loved ones, whatever the case maybe.

You must have no compulsion to going in and ruthlessly finishing the fight, do not let them off 'the hook' you may not get a second chance.

Once they realise you can look after yourself and the essential element of surprise is gone, they will up the stakes and the intensity of their assault, so finish it!

You may say it's not in your nature to be aggressive and that you despise violence. I also hate violence if it can be avoided then fine, but sometimes it comes knocking at your door and you can't hide from it.
Then you have got to summon up courage and defiance and fight back.

Today's society unfortunately is a violent one, robbery, rape, muggings, murder, kidnapping, and terrorism, down to road rage and domestic squabbles. Today's street fighter or thug is different from yesteryear. He may come into the confrontation totally 'crazed' on booze, pills, or drugs.

Nine times out of ten probably armed or 'carrying', he is a biter, a gouger and a stamper, he will not back off when you hit the floor, he will carry on stomping and kicking.

He is a psychopath. You cannot plead to his good or moral side, he hasn't got one, he is an animal, make no mistake.
So when the chips are down and it's you or him who is going to survive, it has to be you, no question!

The killer instinct can be switched on or off at will.

It can lie dormant inside you as you go about your everyday life but when trouble looms you can switch it on instantly. I liken it to having a monster inside you that every now and then you will let off the lease to have the run of the place. But when the job is done it is chained safely back up again. You must never let the monster escape or control you; you must be its master and have control of it at all times. To hope to control another person you must first control yourself!

All these fighting components must come under the heading of 'fighting spirit', or controlled aggression.

Never anger, rage, or out of control. It's not about letting the 'red mist' come over the eyes and 'loosing it'.

In that case you will use precious energy up with no result, you will blindly wade in to deeper troubled water and finally drown!

Look at some of the World Class boxers in their prime like Mike Tyson, Marvin Hagler, Duran, Leonard, Benn.

When their opponent was in trouble, when they sensed victory they were in there and took the opponent out the game but although it was ferocious it was still controlled and when it was done they switched it off.

Former World Middle weight champion Marvin Hagler had a fearsome reputation in the ring and was a terrific finisher but outside the ring was said to be a quietly spoken gentleman.

This is what you must strive for, if these boxers forementioned had hesitated in those crucial times it would have cost them their titles and a fortune of money. If you hesitate it may cost you a higher price, your life!

You can have all the best fighting moves in the world but if you haven't developed the right mental attitude it is like having a handful of bullets but with no gun to fire them!

The techniques are a hollow shell without emotional content.

If you still doubt your ability to develop these attributes then quietly sit down for a moment and visualise your worst nightmare. For instant being held at knife point and being forced to watch your wife being raped or your children beaten.

Visualise now some faceless fiend that you fear pulling up in a car outside. He's huge, aggressive and has a reputation for hurting people. He's now walking up your drive. The doorbell rings and you unexpectedly answer the door and he pushes his way in. Your wife is in the kitchen, your kids asleep upstairs. What are you going to do?

Can you honestly now say you cannot conjure up the necessary mindset needed to survive? Of course you can, you have no choice!

If by even reading these words they have conjured up feelings of fear, repulsion, nausea, panic, then take the opportunity to channel these feelings positively to fight back and win!

Fear is natural, everybody gets it, and it's how you control it that's the key. Under pressure you will get the 'fight or flight' syndrome! The body is preparing and priming itself for confrontation, it is a primitive animal, survival tactic that dates right back to the beginning of time.

Don't be frightened, if you have to fight it will initially powerhouse your body and give you super charged strength and speed but it won't last long until you will get the down side of the adrenaline rush, exhaustion.

Most live confrontations will happen quickly and not last long, so channel the adrenaline into a burst of controlled aggression and take your assailant out.

More about the bodies functioning under stress later.

When you carry the right mental attitude you will surprise the larger assailant and defeat him. But you must have belief in yourself that you can do it. What you lack in physical size make up with the heart of a lion!

A favourite quote of renowned Self Protection expert Geoff Thompson is that you should train to be 20 Stone up in the mind, not in the biceps.

This excellently sums up what this chapter is all about.

If some of you readers have been tempted to skip this chapter in search of the physical techniques then you have made a mistake and missed out on the most essential element of personal protection!

"If you truly believe your
Life is in danger...Strike First!"

Chapter 2

Offensive fighting methods

'Action is faster than reaction'

The techniques described in this chapter are termed offensive, which means you are going to initiate and launch an attack on your opponent before he gets a chance to make a move on you.

Now this particular philosophy may go against the grain with some people, especially practising Martial Artists who are taught only counter-attack moves.

Remember today's enemy is different from yesteryear and most Martial Arts technique is dealing with outdated tactics and techniques.

Today's monster on the street will attack you without any remorse, he will relish beating you senseless. Given the chance he will take you out of a fight before you can draw breath, let alone prepare yourself!

Remember we are dealing with a vicious street thug, not a sparring partner. If you are confronted by a guy 6ft 3ins and 17 stone and you are only 5ft 3ins and 10 stone you better take the offensive and quickly.

If you hesitate and get battered with a big punch or get lifted up and dumped on your head the fight is over, maybe permanently. So if you are sure attack upon yourself is imminent then go offensive and pre-empt his move.

The best time to strike somebody effectively is when they are preparing to strike you!

As I mentioned previously the monster in front of you will be confident, even arrogant about his abilities to flatten you. Use the element of surprise to catch him when his body and mind is not prepared for your onslaught.

When you make your move, go for it, overwhelm him and don't stop for anything until he is down and out and no longer a threat to your well-being. Determination, ruthlessness and killer instinct, the combat mindset, don't weaken.

Tactics

I will now explain a series of tactics you need to employ to make your pre-emptive attack work. Without understanding these tactics your offensive move may never get off the starting blocks. So absorb these ploys fully before venturing onto the physical.

The set up

This is the crucial element for leading up to your attack.

You are going to momentarily mentally disarm your attacker, dropping his psychological guard and prime him for your technique.

In the first moments of confrontation your attacker will verbally abuse or berate you. He may come on fully aggressive snarling threats. All these things are his way of leading up to physically attacking you.

This will be frightening for you and you may wish the ground would open up and swallow you, but you are going to have to override the feelings.

Don't let him trigger your panic button or he will be controlling you and you don't want that. He is looking for you to cower at his immense size, power and aggression, so give him what he wants but be in control.

Now while this is happening keep an arms length of distance between you and your attacker, this will buy you breathing space to launch your attack and also help you see anything he intends to do, don't let him close that space.

There are many verbal ploys but use something along these lines.

Don't worry this is exactly what you want, you have now lured the fly into the spiders web, now it's time to eat him...

Please forgive me if for one moment I digress from the above scenario but I want to give you at this point a short list of the best possible weak points on the human body to inflict damage, even if the guy in front of you is build like a gorilla!

Targets
- A good strong focused blow to the following spots can cause considerable damage.

Knockout points
- Chin/jaw, throat/windpipe, temples, base of skull.

Incapacitating points
- Eyes, nose, eardrums, solar plexus, kidneys, groin, kneecaps, biting techniques.

Attitude adjusters/controllers
- Shin kicking, elbow dislocating, finger wrenching and breaking, soft tissue/pressure point gouging or ripping, biting.

These are the major and minor weak points, study them, memorise them, every human being no matter how big, strong or muscular will be vulnerable in these areas.

Note the knockout points are the ones that can instantly finish a confrontation if struck correctly. The incapacitating areas can stop attacker in his tracks and can be fight stoppers. The last group will give you a distinct advantage and may turn the fight in your favour.

I will expand on how they work as we get back to the techniques.

'Okay we're going now!

Technique 1

Once you have made your verbal ploy make sure you are standing in a small 45% stance. Make sure also that your strongest hand is the one furthest away from your assailant (e.g. if you are right handed, have your left foot forward, or visa versa, if left handed).

Explode forward, bending your knees for balance and smashing an upward punch into assailant's testicles. Use your whole body to punch and torque your hips.
Aim to punch his testicles upwards and give him instant 'mumps' of the neck! If you land this blow right he will pitch forward, presenting his head as your next target.
Quickly grab two handfuls of hair either side of his head and yank the head downwards, at the same time bring one of your knees upward to smack into his face. Keep a tight hold and do this 2 or 3 times.
Then twist his head by the hair to one side so that he drops onto his back on the floor. Then finish if warranted by stomping on his ribs, groin or extremities, like hands or ankles.

If you stomp on the head or neck area it can prove to be fatal, be aware on this but also if the situation calls for it do it. Remember those fearful scenarios we conjured up earlier?

When you have completed your technique, step away from your attacker.
Done properly he will never know what hit him until it's too late! When he regains consciousness England will have won the World cup!!

Pointer - If attacker has short hair or no hair, grab him by the ears or back of the neck.

Face off - Protect your space

Groin Punch

Knee to face

Head/chin twist

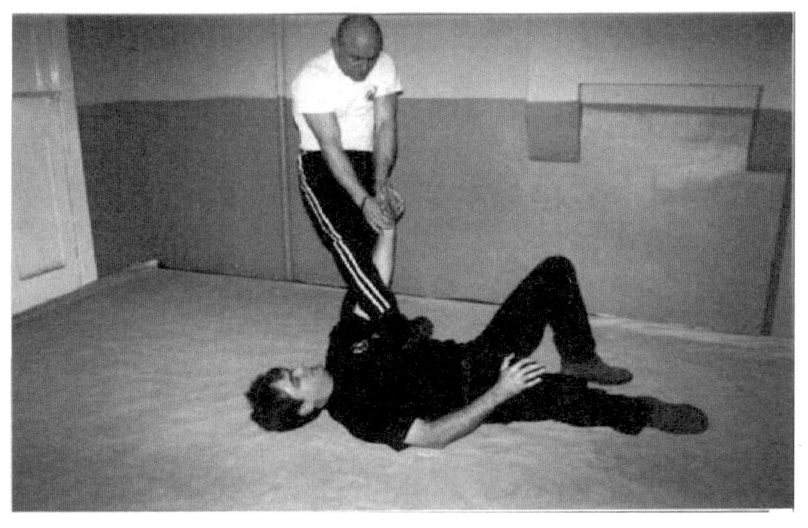

Finishing heel stomp

Technique 2

Begin again with the same rising punch; this is your key strike because it brings your attacker down to your own height, which is of utmost importance.
If you went searching for his head for your opening strike he would see it and counter it before the blow landed.

Once you connect with the groin punch, his head and body will lurch forward. This time grab the hair on the back of his head with your free hand and prepare to use the heel hand strike.

To form the heel hand correctly, you must open the hand wide and spread the fingers. Now flex your wrist and hand backwards so the bottom or heel of your palm, projects forward.

This is the part you will strike with; it is a naturally tough body weapon that needs no prior conditioning or strengthening to be effective.

So from the hold on the hair, retract your groin-striking fist, form it into the heel hand and bring it rising upward to smash hard under your attackers chin.

If formed correctly the heel hand should fit snugly under that vital point! Then quickly retract it and send another this time up under the base of his nose (the philtrum).

If you feel you need another blow, hit him again in one of those vital targets. Remember you have control of his head by the hair so it cannot ride back and lessens the impact of your strike.

If you hit these targets correctly you will cause a 'knockout' to your opponent.

To finish the technique.

From the heel hand, claw your already extended fingers into his eyes and rip downwards. This will cause extreme pain and uncontrollable watering of the eyes plus momentary blindness. Now turn his head with the hair grip and drop him onto his back on the floor. Finish with the stomps previously mentioned.

The palm heel strike is the preferred weapon for striking the bony parts of the head like the jaw/chin. It can hit with fearsome impact and won't damage like the knuckles.

Punching is a required skill that takes a long time to perfect. For instant, 'street' use with minimal training the palm heel is safer, plus regardless of your size it can pack a 'wallop'.

Palm heel to chin

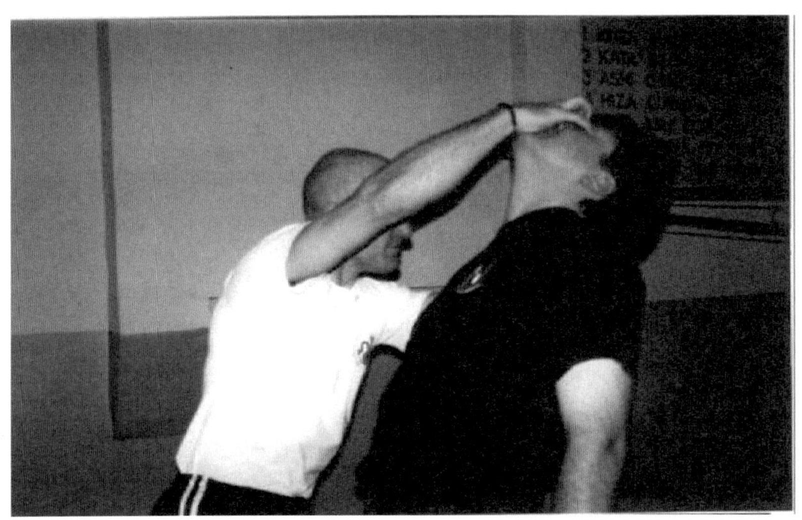

Palm to base of nose with eye claw

Technique 3

Once more execute the groin punch, this time as his head comes forward and down, slap both of your palms over his ears. This causes air to be trapped inside the ear passages and makes a tiny explosion in the eardrums itself. It can cause anything from dizziness and loss of balance to unconsciousness. From the ear strike, grab both of his ears with your hands and lift his head up slightly then execute a head butt onto the bridge of your assailants nose. Make sure you strike with the top of your forehead to prevent injury to yourself and also avoid butting him in the mouth as you might end up with his teeth imbedded in your forehead!

If you are considerably smaller than your attacker then from the ear grab pull his face down onto the crown of your head to execute the butt. Both ways are brutally effective.
To finish still hold onto the ears and bring a rising knee up into his testicles then twist his head by the ears so he falls onto his back on the floor. Again stomp if necessary.

You can also finish with a knee drop, which I favour a lot.

To execute just drop into the attackers body or head with one of your knees, so that your whole body weight is concentrated into the kneecap when it connects. This is an extremely effective finishing technique. Practice must be done with this move so that you don't over balance yourself and fall onto your attacker!

Ear slap

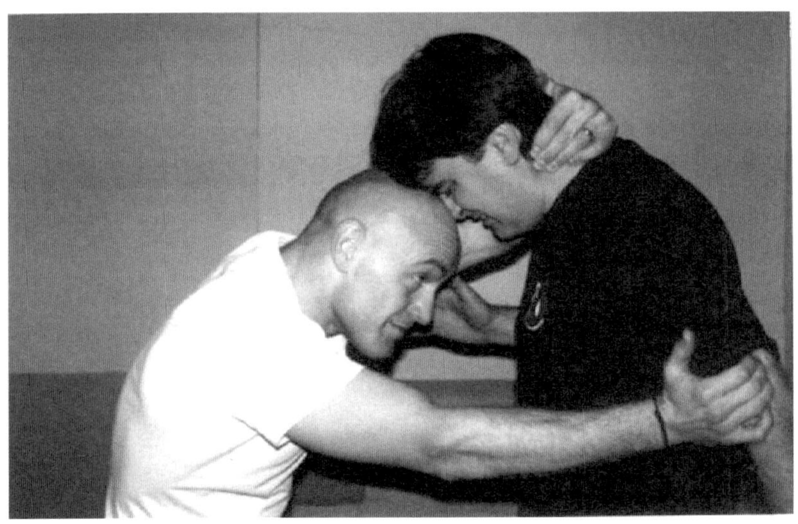

Head butt to nose

Knee to groin

Technique 4

You are still in front facing posture, again execute the groin punch. Move in and with the other hand; grab the back of the hair. Now with the groin punching hand we are going to strike the body with the fist.

Properly executed punches to the body are a must in the persons arsenal they are readily available to you so use them. To develop power and accurate hitting use a punch bag. This will give you the feel of striking into a body and also tell you if you are hitting correctly, so you don't damage your hands.

The rule with punching is hit the bigger and safer targets. Everybody goes hunting for the head in a fight.

The head can be a mobile, hard to hit target, also you can break knuckles, fingers and sprain the wrist against the bony skull or jaw of another person even if you know how to punch correctly (which a lot of people don't).

So my motto is 'hit the body and let the head come to you'. There are many vital organs within the abdominal area. The rib cage shields a lot of them, but good solid punches will fracture the ribs anyway.

If you punch upward under the right side of the ribs when the opponent is facing you, you will hit the large part of the liver a good blow will paralyse the diaphragm for a while and can even stop the breathing.
I have hit a training partner on this spot when sparring and although I pulled the punch at the last minute and didn't use full strength, it dropped him like a stone and he was in some distress with his breathing until I helped revive him.

So I know how powerful this blow can be. Under the left side of the ribs you will probably strike the spleen, another organ, which will have similar effect.

Punch below the belly button and above the groin you will hit the bladder. If the guy who picked on you has been drinking and still has a bladder full of beer a blow there is like bursting a balloon full of water, he will drop in agony.

Remember any well-focused blow around the abdominal area will cause damage. But don't forget to work out on the bag to get the feel of striking. Put your whole body into the blows for maximum effect.

If you haven't worked the bag before wear bag gloves until you hit correctly and then use the bare fists.

If you still doubt the power of body punches study some of Barry Mc Guigan's, the former World Featherweight boxing Champion fights and see his devastating body blows and the effect they had on his opponents, he was only a little man too.

So back to the technique, grab the hair and slam a couple of uppercuts or hooks into the body then as his hand lurches forward. Open the punching hand and spread it wider, palm down. You are now going to strike with the web of your hand between index finger and thumb; this is called an arc hand.

Bring it up the body, just like the heel hand and strike into the windpipe. From there grip the windpipe and squeeze it shut with fingers on one side and thumb on the other. Really dig in so you can work your fingers right around the trachea (windpipe). Now holding the throat and the hair pull the attackers head back and drop a hard butt onto the bridge of his nose.

For lady readers you can substitute the punching for again, palm heeling to the body if you feel you cannot generate enough power with the fist. Remember if the blows don't have the desired effect, drop slightly and punch the testicles again

Body shot

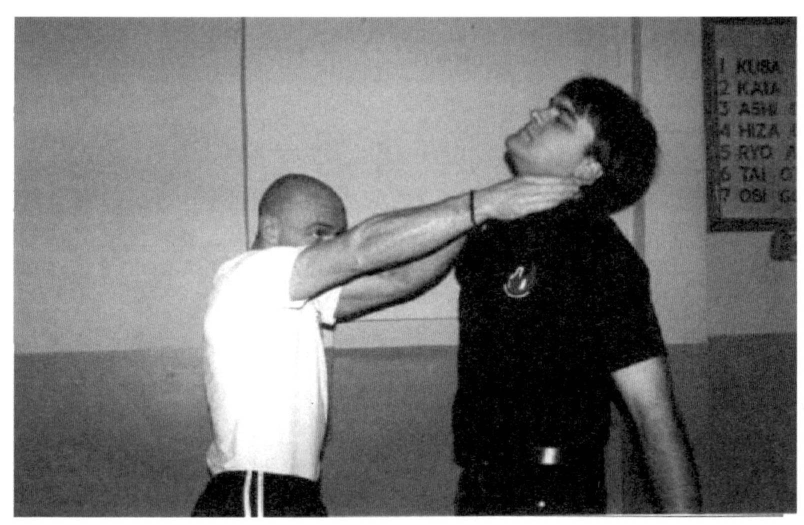

Arc hand to throat

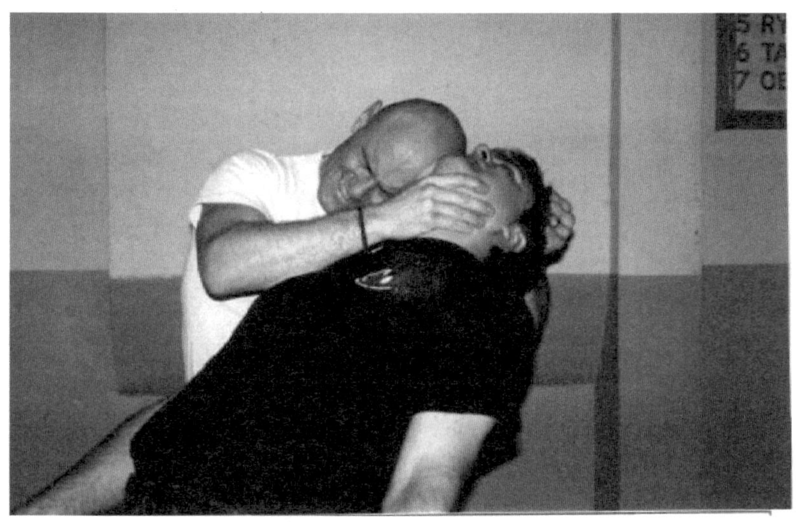

Hair pull back and head butt

Technique 5

This time you are still in the same fighting range but stood side on to your attacker. Again you have made the verbal play and you turn slightly as if to walk off.
From the turn clench the fist of the hand nearest your attacker and swing it downward and into his testicles, connecting with bottom side of the fist, this is termed as a 'hammer blow', as you are striking with the fleshy bottom part of the fist just like the head of a hammer. This blow will bring his head forward and down for your second strike.

From the hammer fist bring the hand up and across your body and slightly beyond your shoulder. Stiffen the fingers with palm facing down and tuck your thumb tightly into the palm.

You are now going to perform a reverse knifehand strike or 'chop'. Bring the hand back towards your attacker cutting the air like a knife and slamming the little finger side of your hand into his throat. The target is the thyroid cartilage, more commonly known as the 'Adam's apple' the protuberance at the front of the throat area.

If struck forcefully this blow can be fatal, as it will crush the windpipe causing suffocation and choking. If struck moderately it interferes drastically with the breathing.

It is one of the most lethal blows in your arsenal of weapons. Remember we are dealing with a serious threatening situation not a quarrel over which football team should have won the league, so the strike is valid.

From that blow, bring the same arm back across your body at chest height, slide in slightly to your assailant and strike with the point of your elbow in a side elbow strike to the solar plexus. The solar plexus is a weak spot located between the sternum (breastbone) and the upper abdominal muscles.

The point of the elbow will seek the target out and if hit correctly will empty the lungs and diaphragm of air.
If your opponent is still attempting to fight grab a handful of his hair and pull his head down into a few rising knee strikes, he should no longer be a threat!

Side guard position

Hammer blow to groin

Knife hand to neck

Elbow to solar plexus

Knee to face

Those are 5 close range offensive techniques that have all been picked especially for the smaller person.

The moves all start with the groin attack to bring the head down for the follow up and finishing blows. The attacks are all aimed at the vital body points.

The next 3 offensive techniques come from a longer distance away, at kicking distance. This means to close the gap on your opponent you must start with a kicking manoeuvre.

We are only concerned in this book with practical combat kicking, not the high, flashy or flying kicks associated with some Martial Arts. We do not kick above the waist for balance and safety's sake.
Also as a well known American close quarter combat instructor says 'the only time you kick somebody in the head is when they're on the floor!'

We are not going to worry too much about proper form and the perfect mechanics of kicking, as you would do in a Martial Arts class. You are just going to learn fast effective kicking with a good pair of shoes or boots on and not the traditional Martial artist's bare feet, as in a training hall.

The three kicks we going to review are the front, round and side kick. They are relatively simply kicks to apply even for a novice.

Remember we will be kicking low so you should be able to maintain a good centre of gravity and posture, this is essential.

Although the high kicks of the Martial Arts are eye catching and dynamic they have no real part in street Self Defence.

When questioned on the subject I always say how well would the high kicker fair on an ice covered pavement after a fall of snow, would he chance a spinning kick or a head height roundhouse kick?

The same could be said of a crammed beer soaked dance floor in a club, a definite dodgy surface for flashy kickers!
Also how would the expert kicker defend himself if he were attacked in a phone box or his car?

A well-trained street fighter will grab a high kick and dump the kicker on the floor. High kicks just aren't worth it in a real life situation, they are far too risky.

This brings us to the point of a small man joining a Martial Arts class and being shown a head height kick as a dynamic Self Defence move.
He pairs up with a taller guy who is having no problems reaching his head with a kick, but when it is the little man's turn he can barely reach chest height, then he is losing balance.

The instructor might say he needs more practice but even then it's not going to be a practical technique for him and he certainly wouldn't rely on it in the street!
He then may get disheartened and leave the club, where if he was shown a simple shin, knee or groin kick he would have got benefit from it.

It must be low, hard and fast kicks in the street, they are hard to see, hard to stop and easy to learn.

Remember also you won't have kicking distance to long as your assailant will be closing down your space, so if you are going to kick make it count!

Now onto the techniques.....

Technique 6

You are stood facing your opponent at kicking distance in a natural stance. You have one foot slightly ahead of the other. Without telegraphing the move, raise your back leg up slightly then lash it out in a front kick as you thrust your hips into the move. Let the toe of your shoe connect with your attacker shin or knee. Both of these targets have no muscle to protect them and are extremely painful.

If any of you have been in a football match and been kicked in the shin or if any of you have walked into a low coffee table and cracked your knee you will know the feeling!

When you have been struck in these areas you automatically reach down and clutch the injured part, it's a natural instinct.

As your attacker does this it will once more bring his head into view, now seize the chance as you move in and slam a rising heel hand strike up under his chin, continue in close, grab his jacket by the lapels or his shoulders and hit him with a couple of rising knees into his groin and then stamp your heel down onto his instep.

Drag him forward onto his knees by the hair and then raise your arm above your head, clench the fist tight and bring the arm downward dropping your body weight, at the same time by bending your knees and strike him at the base of his skull or between his shoulder blades with the point of your elbow in a downward elbow strike, step away, you have finished.

Kick to shin/knee

Palm heel to chin

Knee to groin

Foot stomp to instep

Elbow to base of skull

Technique 7

The next kicking technique we will explore is the sidekick. Again it will be a basic combat kick without any thrills or too much technical excellence.

The way to describe this kick to a novice is to think how you have probably broke a piece of firewood with your foot, when it was leant against a wall, that is the basic workings of the side kick.

The target will be the kneecap, an excellent vital point for this kick. This technique is especially suited for the small man. You can keep at a distance and fire this kick out without going into your opponents punching range.

Also if you take the big guy's legs out he will fall, just like if the foundations of a house are tampered with the rest of the house will fall. Think of the big man's legs, as his foundations plus big men don't like to be off of their feet!

To execute this move stand in a side-facing stance to your attacker. Raise your leading knee slightly as you slide forward and then lean your weight back onto your rear leg which you will bend slightly for balance then thrust your lead leg out and strike into the assailants kneecap.

You must thrust through the leg and not just on it. The kick should send the man onto his back with a badly damaged knee joint.

From there quickly move in and kick or stomp his groin, if it is open, if not stomp onto his ankle joint to totally destroy the legs, then move away.

If the man doesn't fall from the kick then you must carry on with follow up strikes.

From the kick, use your leading hand, whip a reverse knifehand blow into your opponents neck, striking for the windpipe as in a previous technique, or slightly to the side of this area to hit the carotid artery that runs up either side of the windpipe and supplies blood to the brain.

By striking this target you can put the man unconscious because you are drastically slowing down the blood flow to the brain.

From there go to a slight crouch and execute two uppercut/hook punches into body or groin with either hand, using full body twist for maximum power. Then grab your attacker's hair to hold his head still and throw what will look like a short hook punch to the side of his head but infact you will strike the target with your elbow in a circular motion.

This elbow strike is extremely powerful with a full hip twist put into it. Aim anywhere on the head and it will have effect. The elbows are the body's battering rams and they can inflict terrible damage.

After the blow pull the man to the floor by the hair and stomp him if needed.

Side kick to knee joint

Knife hand to neck

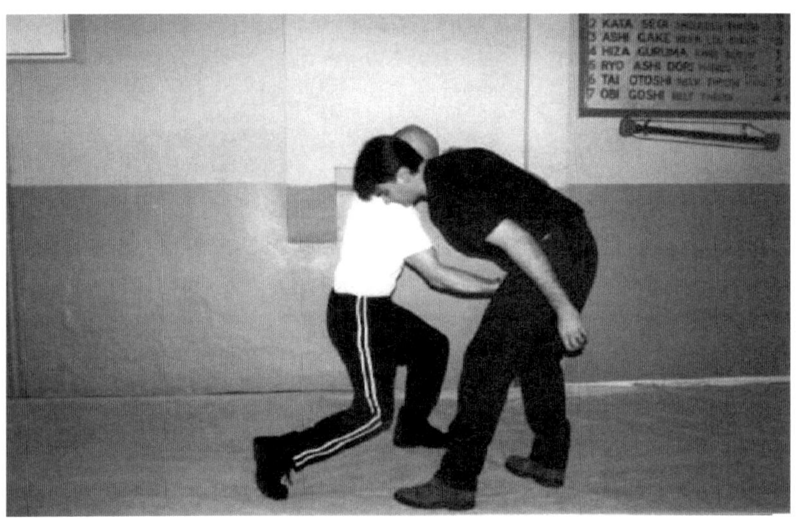

Punch to groin

Elbow strike to temple

Technique 8

The final kick, is the round kick. This requires a little more training to execute than the other two but remember we are not concerned with perfect form, practicality is the main aim.

The round kick will come from the rear leg for power. To execute pivot on the ball of the lead foot, which will turn your body slightly sideways, then bring the rear leg around in a sharp arc, knee slightly bent, at the same time push your hip into the movement for power.

You are contacting with your foot instep or your shinbone. The target being the outer edge of opponent's thigh muscles. Aiming roughly centre between hip and knee. The lateral branch of the femoral nerve is situated here and contact with it causes considerable pain.

The feeling is like the old school 'dead leg' or 'Charlie horse' but much more extreme. You can literally buckle leg and send your assailant crashing to the floor in agony if you get it right. At the very least the sharp pain will give you a chance to follow in with the heel hand or a knee strike.

Thai boxers favour this kick and some of them can generate awesome power into it with dramatic results. If you have access to a hanging bag or kicking shields, time spent practising this kick will be worth it.

You can 'cut' your opponent down to size with this technique regardless how big he may be and have him at your mercy! An essential kick in the small person's arsenal of weapons.

That ends this chapter on offensive striking techniques.

The techniques described were kept simple and straightforward.

They are also as Combat effective as they can come, so that a novice can pick them up and use them with a small amount of training.
There are many more combinations of blows, kicks, etc that can be used, but the ones described are the most instantly effective and combat proven.
Some people may think that they may be overkill moves but in the real world in an actual street confrontation you do not know who or what you may come up against.
An attacker high on drugs or alcohol may not drop from your first blow. There are some born and breed 'hardcases' out there who will keep coming even if you had a good start.
So the philosophy of my Martial Arts system is use continuous flowing strikes until the threat is over.

Also in the heat of the moment you may miss your intended target or glance off it, so you need a follow up to survive!

The traditional Karate outlook of a one-blow finish 9 times out of 10 doesn't hold true in the street.

You must train to keep up relentless pressure and attack to your assailant's weak spots particularly eyes, throat and groin, until you drop him.

That's why you must train on a bag for power and realistic feel and with a partner to pin point accurately the vital points on the body. Because under pressure you are going to have to target in on them like radar and make every blow count.

So practice these moves until they flow naturally and instinctively. Train until they are second nature and you are confident you can use them effectively.

Don't forget the aggressive mental attitude to accompany the moves. Remember you may only get one chance to execute the technique so make it count, if you foul up the big man's going to be twice as mad and suddenly more cautious and definitely more dangerous, so get it right first time, you are fighting to survive!

Shin roundhouse kick

"To demolish a tall building, First
start at the foundations!"

"To chop down a big tree
start at it's base!"

Chapter 3

Combat takedowns

'The bigger they are the harder they fall'!

Throwing techniques are a complete science in un-armed fighting. There is no better sight than a small person tossing a large opponent up in the air and dumping him onto the ground. It's probably every small person's dream to achieve this, but is it a practical reality in a street fight?

First off, you have probably seen demonstrations of Judo on the T.V. etc and watched two skilled Judoka throwing each other about with precision skill, but again you must remember both these Judoka know what each other are doing and they are in no way resisting each other, plus they want to make the demonstration as dynamic and eye catching as possible.

Now in an actual Judo contest you will see a chess match struggle for one man to get the other over in a throw because now they are doing their best to prevent each other from hitting the floor. The reality for a street fight would probably be nearer this way than the demonstration techniques.

There are a vast array of throws, sweeps and takedowns in Judo and my own Art Ju Jutsu but I have long ago discovered even if you are highly skilled in these Martial Arts, some of the throws are impractical and impossible to execute against a strong, large, determined aggressor.

For the unskilled man throwing is virtually impossible to achieve. There are some terrific throws that can be used but you need continuous practice week in week out to get them right and maintain the skill level needed to perform them, especially against a large person.

To repeat myself, training with a partner week after week throwing each other is a totally different world to coming up against a uncooperative and fighting opponent!

Just a point on this subject I have noticed over the years particular with black belts in my travels, that they always stick together to train, even on courses. They usually say it's because they are learning a higher level of technique than the lower grades and also they don't want to hurt a novice with their advanced moves.

Whilst some of this may be true I believe a lot of it has to do with their ego as they don't want a raw inexperienced person messing them up and making them look bad.
When they can't cleanly throw them over! A man who is fearful of being thrown, won't be thrown if he can avoid it!
Anyway back to the point of combat throws for the street. There are a small collection of throws or to put it more accurately takedowns that even a relatively unskilled little guy can use effectively to put his larger aggressor onto their backs.
I will outline these moves in this chapter. Some of them involve going to the floor with your attacker, which isn't always the best policy, especially if he's got a few mates to pitch in and help him. But sometimes this can't be avoided chiefly if the assailant hangs on to you.

My Ju Jutsu system has a lot of ground fighting in it and my students get to feel as competent on the floor as standing when it comes to fighting.
To some of you it may feel alien but as long as you follow the procedures described here you should be fine.
As I mentioned before I have found the big man does not like to be off his feet, remember about the foundations in the previous chapter?
Also don't forget the old saying

'The bigger they are the harder they fall'!

The techniques for throwing will once again be shown in a offensive manner at this stage but later on in the book you will see how they can be used in a counter attack manner also.

Takedown technique 1

You are again stood at close range. Remember a verbal ploy or a simple gesture with your hands, to distract your opponent. Execute the fast punch to the testicles as before.

Now as he bends forward, move right up close. One-hand grabs the hair on the back of his head the other strikes the chin with the rising palm heel. From there keep the hand on his chin and twist his head by rotating the chin around. Keep this move very tight and sharp. Your attacker will have to follow you because if he resists the vertebrae in his neck will snap.

This is a very powerful takedown. Keep rotating head and chin until assailant falls onto his back on the floor.

Keep hold of the head. Make sure you have bent your knees well for good posture and that your face is not too close for him to hit at you.

To finish pin his jaw to the ground with your heel hand and then strike at his exposed temple and ear with your other hand either in a fist or palm heel blow. Step away making sure he is no longer a threat.

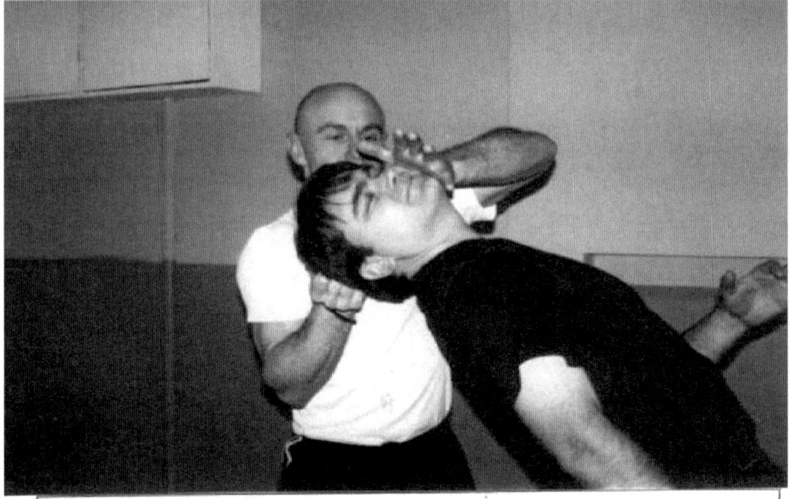

Head & chin twist

Takedown technique 2

This time your opening blow is going to be a stinging finger claw to your opponent's eyes. To do this effectively, make the gesture of running your fingers through your hair. Then suddenly in a loose, snappy fashion fire the claw hand out. If you connect with the eyes it will cause profuse watering and temporary blindness. If not it will still cause the distraction that you need to execute the throw. (I.e. throwing key, coins, a newspaper etc can have the same effect).

Move into your attacker and put one of your legs between his.

Press your nearest hand onto one of his thighs and reach down and grab the back of his ankle on the same leg with your other hand. At this moment drive your shoulder into his body and as this breaks his balance lift up viciously on his ankle and push his thigh. This is a single lea takedown and the assailant will be thrown heavily onto his back, maybe even cracking the back of his skull on the floor. From this position with him on the floor, you holding his leg, immediately toe kick, then stomp his testicles to make sure he isn't going to get up again! Then swing his leg across his body and step out and away.

Single leg takedown

Takedown technique 3

Use the same claw hand distraction technique as before.
Move in to the aggressor. Kneel down on your right knee right up close to his legs. Hook your right arm behind his right ankle and then roll your body into his straightened kneecap.
As you have anchored his foot he will not be able to keep his balance and he will be thrown onto his back to avoid damaging his knee.
You will drop with him and pivot your body circularly so you turn into him and hit him squarely in the groin with a back elbow.
Now quickly regain your feet as you continue a barrage of blows to his body, so at no time can he attempt to grab at you, if he still has any fight left in him!
Just aim the blows to solar plexus, windpipe, nose and eyes as you regain your footing, you can even knee drop his groin as you are getting up from between his legs!

Reclining leg throw

Takedown technique 4

This time you are stood at kicking range. From a relaxed posture explode forward with a sidekick into your targets lead knee. Make sure that if for instance your attacker is stood in right stance, you kick him with your right foot or visa versa.
The reason being you want to end up on the outside of him so you can move behind him for the takedown.
Assuming your attacker has not fallen from the kick but has lost his balance or his leg has buckled. Move from your kick instantly behind him. From there grab a handful of his hair or the collar of his jacket/shirt (if wearing one) and again sidekick the hock of his knee (the back fold of the knee).
As you forcefully kick, yank back hard on the hair/coat etc and you will send him crashing to the floor with a sharp and abrupt takedown.
As he hits the floor you will be in a perfect position to knee drop his face/or neck, to finish the move.

Rear Knee kick

Takedown technique 5

Start the takedown with the same kick to the knee, then move right behind your attacker. When behind reach up and grab his hair with both of your hands.

Try and take the hair from the front hairline on the forehead.

Now yank his head backward, if you take the hair as explained above, you will have locked his neck backwards, destroying his balance completely. Now from this position bring your knee up in a hard strike to the tailbone of his spine (coccyx) just above the crease of his buttocks. This will not only cause extreme pain it will arch his body and pull it further back.

Now place the sole of your foot against the hock of his knee and fold his leg as you yank back hard on the head. Again he will crash to the floor. If he falls completely on his back finish with the kneedrop or stomp. If he falls to a sitting position, stand behind him, clamp his nose and mouth with the palm of your hand and strike with a downward elbow with your free hand to the top of his skull. That ends the move!

Knee to spine, head pull back

Takedown technique 6

Once more move behind your opponent after the kick and strike him in the kidneys with an uppercut punch or a straight thrusting palm heel. The kidneys are situated just on the belt level.

This blow will arch his back and bring his body backwards now reach over and get your fingers into his eyes with both your hands. Now press in and pull opponent viciously backwards, the pressure to the eyes combined with the pull will take him down hard onto his backside. Now release eyes, pull back his head and drop the downward elbow between his eyes to finish. Instead of eyes, you can also hook the nostrils and rip back as you takedown opponent, if desired.

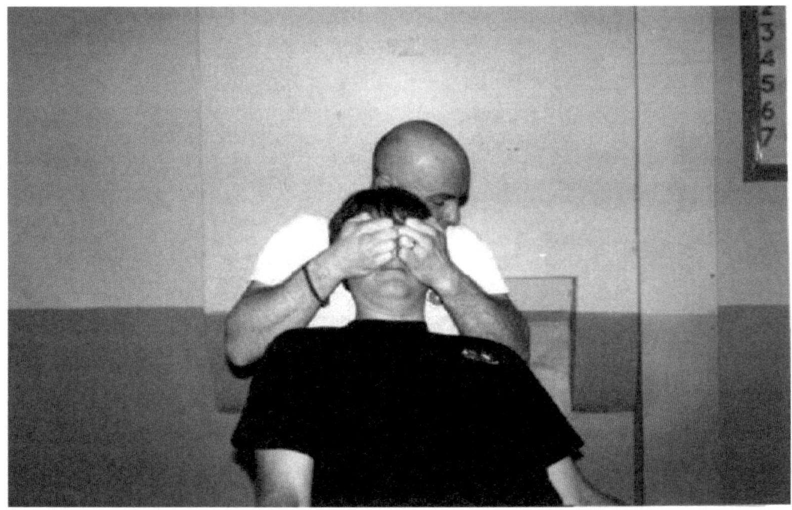

Eye grab takedown

Takedown technique 7

Once more from behind drop to one knee and bring your stiffened forearm up between his legs to strike testicles. As he falls forward grab the front of his ankles with both your hands and drive your shoulder into his upper thighs and buttocks this will send him crashing to the floor.

Immediately regain your feet and stamp down onto his spine with the heel of your boot to finish him.

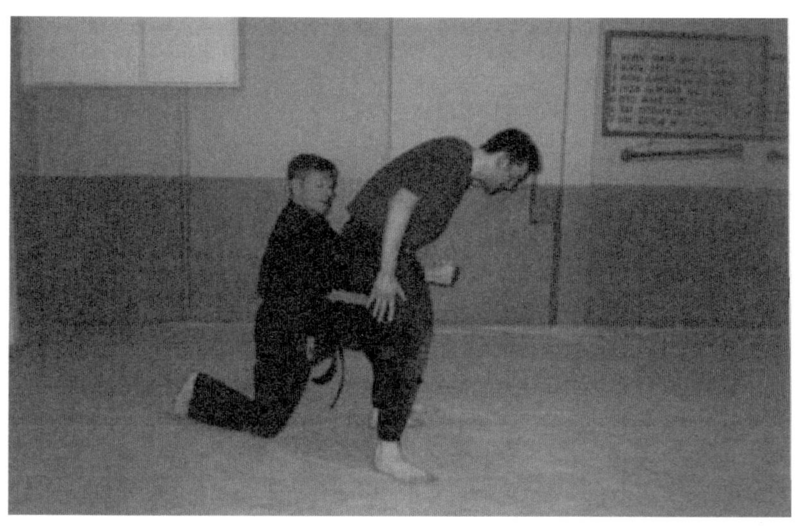

Takedown technique 8

From the opening strike, or kick move behind quickly.

Grab hold of your assailants, coat collar or hair with one hand then reach between his legs with the other and grab hold of his testicles. Squeeze and twist them as you jam your head into the lower vertebrae of his spine. Now lift and pull back on his testicles as you push down on his head/collar. This action plus the agony of the testicles grab will tilt the man forward to crash onto his belly in a face down position.

To finish stomp down hard with your heel between his shoulder blades attacking the thoracic vertebrae, then step back towards his feet and stomp down again squarely in the middle of the back of his thigh, attacking the sciatic nerve/artery. Both blows will insure you that the attacker will not get up for a second shot.

Rear groin takedown

Takedown technique 9

This takedown is called a double leg takedown. From front facing stance, shoot out a hard front kick to opponent's shin/knee area. Then rapidly close in. Drop down on your lead knee, roughly between his feet. Now grab the back of his knees and drive your shoulder into his thighs with your whole body weight exploding forward. This will topple him onto the ground. Immediately follow up with 3 or 4 punches to the testicles and regain your feet and make your escape.

This is a popular takedown in Ju Jutsu and wrestling and with practice you can certainly take the biggest of opponents down with it, when you use that moment of unexpected explosive energy into their legs. Work on it and you can cause a mighty fall for your assailant. If the back of his head hits the pavement as he falls the fight will instantly be over!

Bear in mind being taken off your feet and crashing to the floor is physiologically as damaging as physically, it really does shake you up. The big man is going to be stunned more so because he just isn't used to being on the floor, and as I said before, they don't like it, especially if a small man puts him there.

Double leg takedown

I can remember my first experience of being taken to the floor in my Martial Arts training and it was a big shock to the system! I was training in the Korean Karate style of Taekwondo and I sparred with a guy who was also taking some Judo training at the time, although I didn't know this until later.
As I moved in on him to throw a punch he swept my lead leg perfectly. I went about 3 foot up in the air before crashing onto the wooden floor, luckily physically I was alright but it mentally shook me up and I learnt a very important lesson in how valuable throws and takedowns can be.
Later as I began to train in the grappling Arts I realised just how good it was to execute the throwing methods as well!

Those are 9 practical takedown methods that have been picked solely for the small man. Each of them can be learnt and executed with minimum training even by a complete novice to be effective in combat use.
Note that the takedown either takes the foundations of the attacker away by attacking the legs or either by twisting the head or grabbing the groin. At no time are you involved in heavy body-to-body contact as in some throwing methods.
Because in these types of throws there is always a chance the attackers superior body weight or strength may counter you!

Other throws will be discussed in later chapters from a defensive viewpoint.
For now though these are the throws to learn, they are quick and sharp in their application and can be used offensively or defensively.

Work at the takedowns and you will find just how effective they can be to cut the big man down to size and bring him down to earth with a bump!

Chapter 4

'The sleeper hold' - 'Let sleeping dogs lie'!

Even a novice I expect has heard the term **'sleeper hold'** mentioned sometime or the other in the television 'wrestling bouts'; unfortunately they don't portray the reality of the hold.
This chapter will explain in detail the workings of the hold along with the important anatomy of the neck and throat area to understand exactly what you are doing.
The hold is a prime weapon for the small man to have in his arsenal because you can restrain a big opponent quite easily with no strength involved.

The sleeper hold has been used by the American Police forces for many years and they have found just how effective it is in a real life situation. They found it was a great 'equaliser' for the small officer or lady officer to control a large aggressive attacker. Officers have even reported in cases against drug-crazed assailants where body functions were immune to standard strikes and locks were successfully restrained with the 'sleeper' hold.

So let's first take a close look at the anatomy of the neck and how the vital arteries, veins etc. work.

Firstly the neck is the most 'vital point' on the body for attacking in serious combat. Any attack to the throat or neck will have a profound and immediate effect on your opponent.

The main area of concern for us in this chapter is the major arteries of the neck. The aorta is the bodies main and largest artery rising from the heart. It starts the network of arteries for supplying blood all over the body.
As the aorta rises it gives off important branches to the neck, the most important are the common carotid arteries, these run up either side of the neck close to the windpipe.

THE MAIN STRUCTURES OF THE NECK

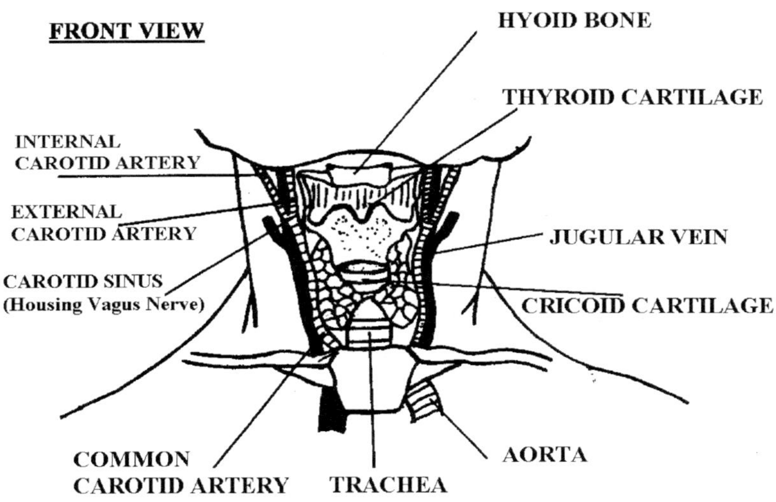

NOTE THE CAROTID SINUS AND ITS LOCATION

THIS IS THE POINT WHERE YOU PRESS TO APPLY THE "SLEEPER HOLD"

If you put your fingers close to the windpipe you should feel the pumping of the carotid pulse. Have a go now and learn how to immediately locate it.

THE MAIN STRUCTURES OF THE NECK

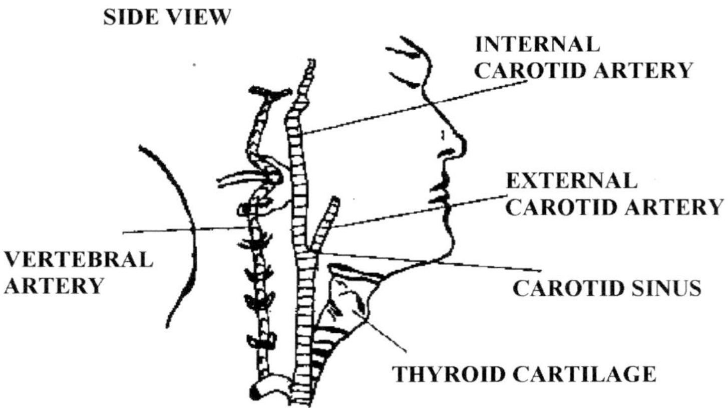

NOTE THE LOCATION OF THE VERTEBRAL ARTERIES THESE CONTINUE THE BLOOD FLOW TO THE BRAIN EVEN WHEN CAROTID SINUS IS CLOSED OFF

As the carotid artery rises to the level of the Adam's apple (thyroid cartilage) it divides into the external and internal carotid arteries. The inner artery supplies blood to the brain and eyes, the outer to the face and scalp.

The point where these arteries originate from the common carotid is called the 'carotid sinus', this is a sheath which houses the important 'vagus nerve centre'.

The vagus nerve has a direct link to the heart and plays an important part in it's functioning.

The carotid sinus is the point where we shall apply the sleeper.

It is incorrectly thought in a lot of Martial Arts circles that by squeezing the carotid sinus in the sleeper choke that it stops the flow of blood to the brain. Even if you could stop the flow completely, running a little way from the carotid arteries are the vertebral arteries, these enter the brain through the base of the skull and continue the blood flow to the head.

To correctly apply the 'sleeper' we are going to stimulate the vagus nerve in the carotid sinus to perform a very clever manoeuvre. We are going to disrupt the normal bodily functions of the blood flow.

By squeezing on the vagus nerve it will send a message to the brain telling it blood pressure is getting dangerously high. So the brain sends a message via the vagus nerve to the heart telling it to slow the blood flow and reduce the pressure. Seeing this really is an incorrect function to take because of our disruption, when the heart slows the blood flow, the brain gets deprived of blood rich in oxygen so the person blacks out due to oxygen starvation.

You can now see why this is such a clever hold because you are feeling the body mechanisms. Regardless of your opponent's size or bulk he cannot fight a natural bodily response, this is why the hold is so vital for the small man.

Check the diagram on the next page and study it so you fully understand where the vital arteries are located in relation to other major parts of the neck and throat.

Now how do we actually get the hold on and apply it correctly?

Move behind your assailant. If you can't get to his neck with your arm, then try these following moves.

Reach and grab a handful of hair and yank his head back and down, or stomp with the sole of your foot into the back of his knee, to fold it and bring him down to your height. You can also drive that uppercut we have been using into one of his kidneys; this move will weaken him and arch his body backwards.
Now encircle his neck with your complete arm. Make sure the bicep is on one side of the neck and the thumb side (radius bone) of the forearm is against the other. The fold of your elbow should be in front of the aggressor's windpipe but not crushing it or interfering with his breathing.

Now with your free hand grasp your strangling arms wrist in a tight grip and begin a scissors action with the forearm and bicep, so that you are squeezing the carotid arteries on either side of the neck.
As you do this turn your body away from your attacker, so that your hip pushes into his lower back, now step away so he is hanging by his neck in your grip. This move totally reinforces the sleeper and stops him using any counter attacks. Also turn your face away incase his flailing hands might poke at your eyes.

You now have the 'sleeper' on and it won't take long to take effect. Wait to the struggling ceases then take the attacker to the floor, the technique is completed.
This move can also be applied from the side and front of opponent but there is always a chance of being countered before you can effectively get the hold on.
Stick to the rear method and at anytime you find yourself behind the attacker you can move in for the 'sleeper'.

A word of warning: when you practice this move, you must do it carefully and sensibly. Don't rush or jerk any movements and avoid pressing on the windpipe as you can easily rupture the cricoid or thyroid cartilage, which can be fatal.

If you have to apply this hold in the street then keep it on no longer than necessary. If you keep the hold on for 3 minutes or more the subject may die or have severe brain damage.
Remember if he 'blacks out' without prolonging the hold he should regain consciousness normally later. But if you are under a violent street attack then your priority is saving your skin, so just keep the hold on until he is physically subdued.

Once mastered you can effect this hold from 5 to 15 seconds, that is a very quick effective technique!
I have used this hold in training 1000's of times and 9 times out of 10 it has worked almost instantly. I have also been on the receiving end of the 'sleeper' and can testify for its effectiveness!

Please read and study this chapter carefully you have at your hands information on one of the best combat moves ever invented!

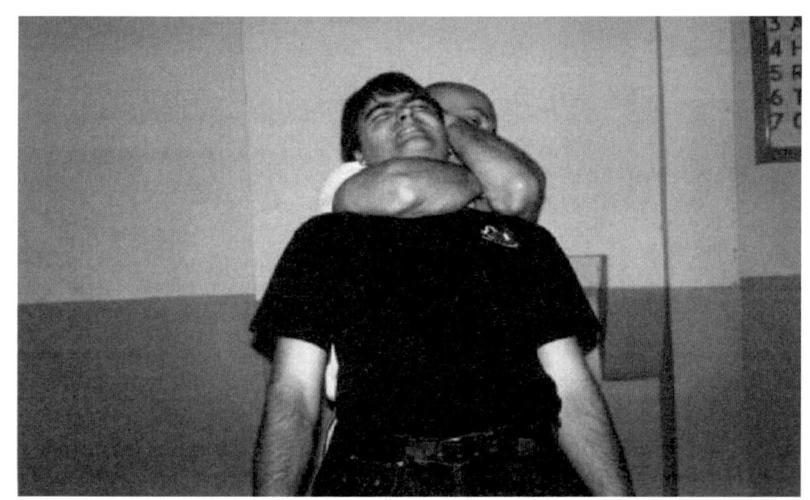

Sleeper hold 1

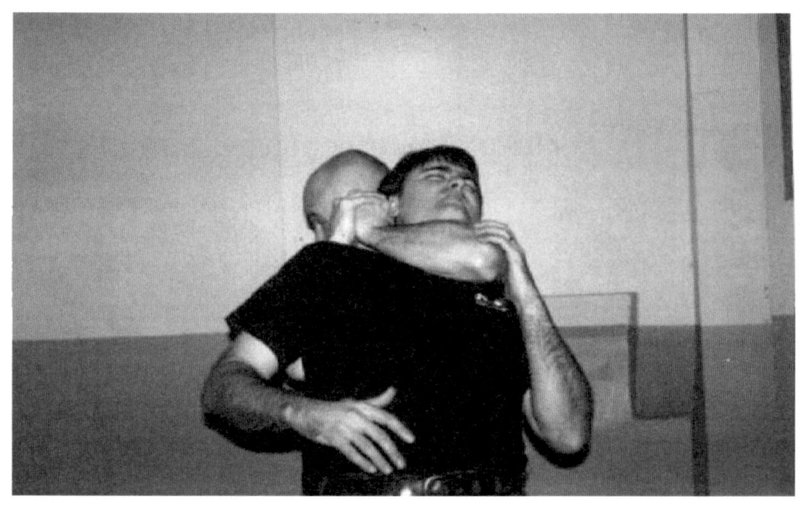

Sleeper hold 2

**“Don’t fight strength with strength
use cunning instead!”**

Chapter 5

Counter's to holds & grabs

'Grappling with reality'

We are now going to look at some counters to holds and grabs. We are especially going to deal with holds that the big man likes to apply on his smaller target. They are what can be termed as 'strength holds'. This means they are basically unskilled moves but by using sheer physical strength and body weight the large man can make them very effective.

Obviously the best defence is not to let yourself be grabbed at all. In which case you would use the offensive techniques discussed earlier at the mere threat of an attack.
This isn't always possible if it's a surprise attack by your assailant. So now you are going to have to learn defensive tactics and counter attacks.
Again we are going to deal with quick, sharp and decisive counters. There will be no fancy locks, throws etc.
Remember what a less than serious training partner will submit to is not always what a street hardened thug will give in to!
The moves are designed to put the bigger adversary away quickly without getting involved in grappling and wrestling where his superior strength and body weight will win.

Some of you will think the techniques are brutal and savage, but remember you are fighting for your life.
It is surprising what a determined attacker can take in the way of punishment. When you are being choked or having the air squeezed out of your lungs in a rib crushing body hold you have got to make sure the techniques you use will get an instant response from your assailant, otherwise it could prove a costly mistake on your part.

Now to begin the techniques

The first hold we will deal with is the big man's favourite. A hold where he can show off his superior strength and not feel that he can be threatened or hurt in anyway. We are about to prove him wrong!

Defence against a front bear hug (your arms are free in this instance)

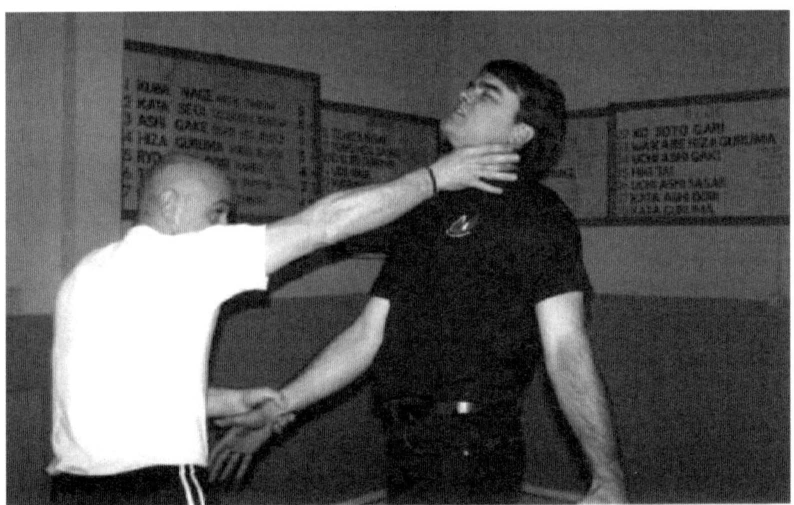

If you can, counter-strike before you are grabbed

1. The assailant has encircled your waist from the front in a crushing bear hug. Your arms have not been pinned, but you have been lifted off the floor. You can see his face in front of you, it is in easy reach.
Immediately slap your cupped hands over his ears and then drive your thumbs into his eyes, in a double attack. Push his head backward with the thumb gouge, until he let's go and you drop to the floor. As you land, still with thumbs in his eyes, drive 2 or 3 rising knee strikes into his testicles. Finish the move by now twisting his head with the chin/head twist throw described in chapter 3.
Once on the floor you can stomp or knee drop assailant if necessary.

Breaking frontal body hold – arms free

Second response to same attack as No.1

2. Clench both fists and slightly extend your middle knuckles to protrude from the others. Now simultaneously smash them into your attacker's temples in a sandwiching attack. This should make him release the grip and drop, if not then go for the follow up. Insert your thumbs in either side of your attacker's mouth, making sure they are not near his teeth and then rip outwards to tear the corners of the mouth out. This is bound to now get the release. Immediately follow up with the groin attack with your knee and the head/chin twist throw. Finish with stomp if needed.

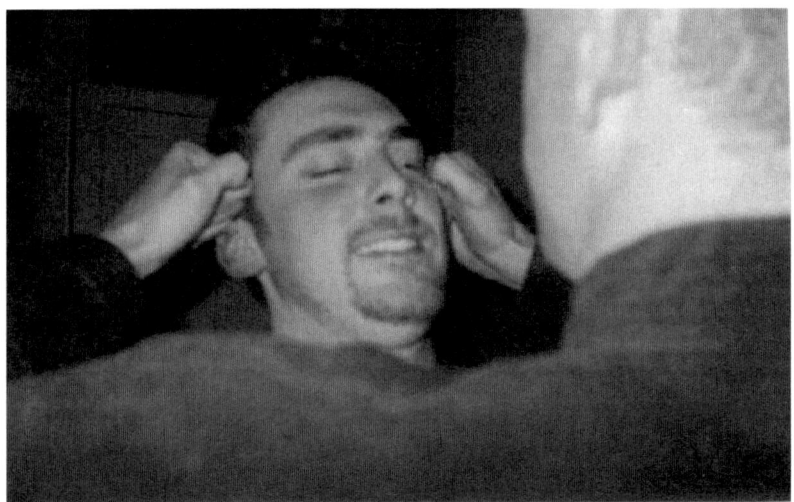

Temple Gouge

3. On this occasion your assailant has grabbed you in the same manner as the previous techniques but his face is not easily reached. It is beyond one of your shoulders. All you have a view of is the top and side of his head.

Begin your defence by grabbing his hair and yanking it back from the front hairline. Do this with the hand furthest away from his face, you can gain more leverage this way.

From there bring your other hand upwards and claw into his eyes to push his face back further and to temporarily blind him.

Now take the eye clawing hand away and then return it either with, depending on the amount of room between you and your attacker, a downward hammerfist, forearm or elbow to the bridge of the nose (septal cartilage) and continue hammering there for the release.

Once you have been dropped down or let go of, follow in with the knee shots to the groin and the head chin twist.

1. You are in the position as for technique No.3 Again grab for the hair and yank back, then bite into the ear, neck, trapezium muscle (muscle which runs from the neck to the shoulder joints) or the nose. Clamp the teeth on the target and **shake your head just like a dog with a bone.**
Physically this technique is brutally painful and psychologically it will put the fear of God into the attacker.

Obviously people have reservations about biting. One noticeably because of the HIV infection involved around open cuts, blood, saliva etc. The other because they believe civilised people don't do these things!

Well so-called civilised people shouldn't brutally beat, mug, torture, rape or kill other human beings but they do! Some people like nothing better but to prey on another person.

So if it's the only option to save yourself, then **bite and do it hard** like a wild animal, totally devastate your attacker.

While you are biting you can bring a hand up and grip the assailant's windpipe, fingers one side, thumb the other.

Now squeeze the windpipe together if needed. If the big guy hasn't let you go after biting him he will now. Soon as he does, slam a knee or punch into his groin and step away.

Defence against a front hear hug (arms pinned) You now have been attacked with the frontal bear hug and the use of your arms have been taken away, as they have been encircled in your attacker's grip. Once again he has lifted you, in a show of strength.

Technique 1

Immediately butt at his face if accessible, aim for the nose, at the same time kick at his shin's with your feet and slide your hand down to grab, squeeze and twist his testicles! If he is wearing tight trousers this may not always be possible. You can try also to pinch a small portion of flesh high up on the inside of either of the attacker's thigh's, this is surprisingly painful. Keep up this barrage until he has released, then follow up as before. Also don't forget to bite!

Breaking front body hold (arms pinned) with a butt

And a bite

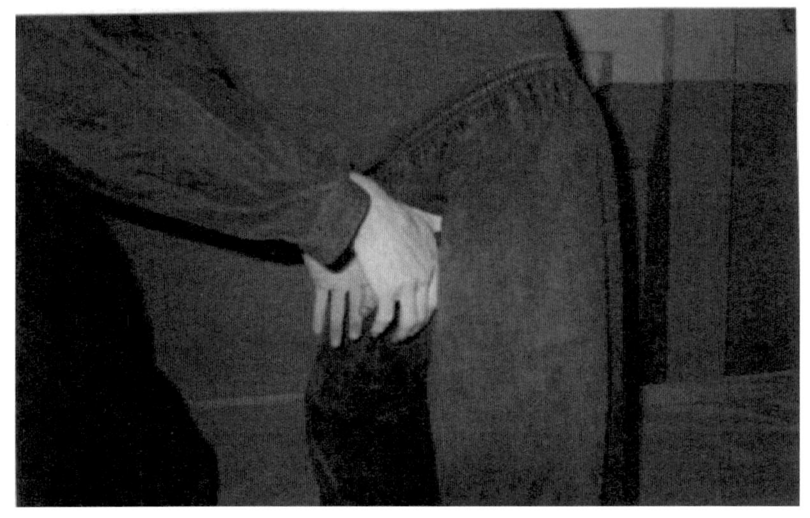

Thumbs to bladder

Technique 2

If he hasn't lifted you off the floor you can stomp down heavily onto his insteps and use your head once more to butt. If his face is hidden then use the bite to his ear, neck, etc.

Make a gap between his body and yours to execute your next move. Clench both fists and hold them vertically, then extend your thumbs out and support them on the top of your fists.

You can then jab them into the bladder region for a painful blow and to widening the body gap between you more, then use the knee attack or punch to the testicles to finish.

These bear hug attacks can also be performed from behind you.

They are a little more difficult to get out of but you must remember, if your attacker's hands are around your waist they cannot do anything else to you.

So try and relax a little, take a deep breath then make your counterattack.

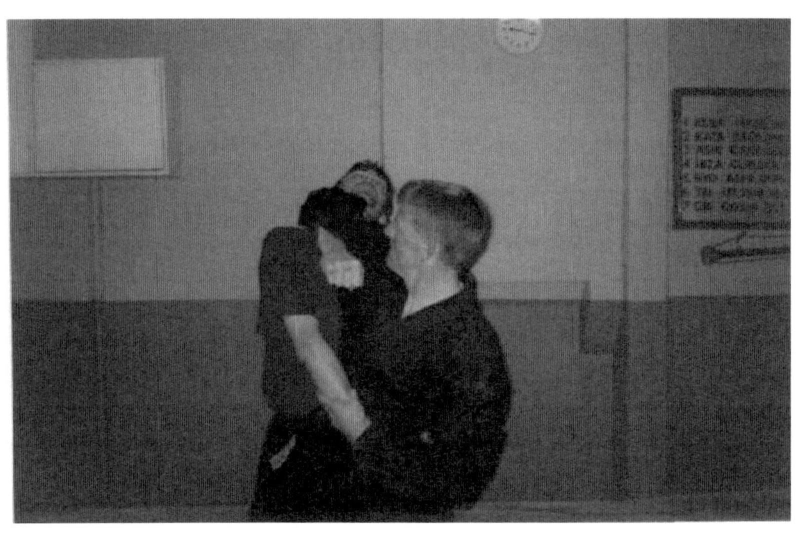

Back Hooking Elbow

Rear bear hug (your arms are free)

Technique 1

The attacker has not yet lifted you up, so immediately stomp hard onto his insteps, this not only creates extreme pain but will also bring your attacker's head down and forward.

Now pivot from the waist and execute a back hooking elbow into the side of his head and immediately pivot the other way and smash an identical elbow strike with your other arm into the other side of his head.

If you have connected with these blows you will have a release. If not then thrust your buttocks back forcefully into the assailant's groin area and then back heel kick his knee or shin.

The back kick is performed simply by rising one leg slightly bending the knee then thrust the leg back connecting with your heel into his knee, to finish the move.

Technique 2

This time you have been lifted off the floor. In this instant snap your head back in a rear butt to the face as many times as needed, also kick backwards with your heels into his knees or shins. Then reach down and prise attacker's little finger away from his grip with both your hands and bend it up and outward in a fast snapping motion to break it. Keep hold of the damaged joint as you pivot out of the hold and around to face your assailant. Raise him up onto his toes by putting upward pressure on the damaged finger joint, to intensify the pain.
Now while his mind is trying to cope with the agony of the finger hold, kick him full in the testicles with a front snap kick to finish the move!

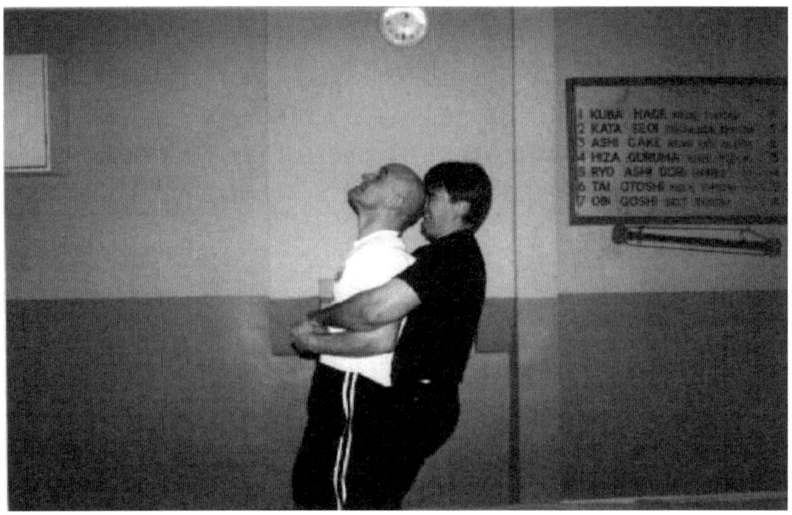

Rear body hold escape – back head butt

Rear bear hug (arms pinned)

The techniques against this form of attack is similar to the hug with arms free. In this case use the foot stomps and rear head butts, along with pinching, squeezing or twisting the testicles or flesh on inner thigh. You will find your hands are in easy reach of the groin when the arms are over grabbed.

Grab testicles

You can also use the finger break technique as well. Also the back kick and back elbow can be used after attacker's grip has loosened.

Remember you must keep up a vicious barrage of fast, brutal techniques against these grabs to gain that release before you get your ribs crushed or get smashed into a wall.

There are lots of other fancy moves against the bear hug involving throws, trips, leg pick-ups and armlocks. But for a novice and for practicality against a powerful person moves shown will work and gain you the release.

Remember also once the grip is broke; keep following up until the attacker is no longer a threat.

Finger Break

Defence against a running body tackle

This is another favourite move of the big guy. The technique is most likely used by a large man who plays contact sports like rugby or American football, which involves taking opponent to the floor with the body tackle.

Your strategy is not to get caught with the move. You have to use your assailant's forward momentum to your advantage. It is obvious you as the smaller or lighter person cannot hope to root yourself to the spot and also absorb your attacker's forward rush, that would be suicide!

You must stand your ground until the last possible moment to make your attacker believe he has you then you can move your body off the line of attack and counter attack.

Technique 1

As your attacker rushes in head down, arms extended to tackle you around the waist, you hold your ground, and then at the last possible moment move your body out of the way. As you do this grab your assailant's hair with one hand and hook his arm up with your other hand, from here flip him over by pushing down on his head and up on his arm. This move combined with his forward momentum will throw him heavily onto his back.

You can control the throw to project the aggressor a distance away or make him land at your feet. This can be done by controlling the circular motion of the throw. If you make a large circle, the attacker will be thrown away from you, if the circle is tight he will land at your feet for a follow up stomp, knee drop etc.

This throw perfectly describes the Martial Arts principle of using your opponent's force against him. The result the harder he attacks the heavier he will fall.

Tackle defence – head & arm flip

Technique 2

You can also use the force principle in this fashion.
As he attempts the tackle again side step and guide the back of his neck and head into a solid object, like a wall, car door, bar-front, tables and chairs etc. This again describes the attacker going to his own down fall for stupidly rushing you while your back is against one of these objects. If you perform the move right the assailant will crack his own skull open and put himself unconscious by his self-inflicted move.

Always be ready to follow up with a few well-placed kicks if he still has any signs of fight about him.
Also if you get the timing right as the assailant passes you after your body shift you can bring your elbow down onto the base of the skull or upper vertebrae between the shoulder blades. Of course you can follow up the move with kicks and stomps as he hits the floor.
The next 2 moves are executed if you have no room to manoeuvre to the sides of your assailant. In this case the only option is backward.

Technique 1

As he charges, step back slightly and encircle his head in a front headlock and quickly slide your body back and spread it out as you go to the floor on your belly. This will drop the attacker down onto his belly very quickly otherwise his neck will snap. Once you both hit the floor, lie your upper body onto his head, pinning it to the floor and make sure the headlock is tight with your forearm against attacker's windpipe to effect a choke. Spread your legs under for good balance so you can't be rolled off to one side. Hold on with everything you have got!
This way you can control a big man properly and subdue him with the headlock/choke. If you can't effect a choke, then get on top of opponent and smash elbow strikes down onto his head/neck until he is subdued!

Technique 2

This technique is identical to the above up until the point of the headlock. Now instead of going to your belly, sit back and go to the floor on your back. Because of the neck lock and both yours and your attacker's momentum he will be flipped over onto his back.

From there you will be laying roughly head to head in opposite directions and you will still have the headlock, strangle on. Keep it on and squeeze the neck tight to effect the strangle to subdue them. Hold tightly and don't allow attacker to manoeuvre out of the hold.

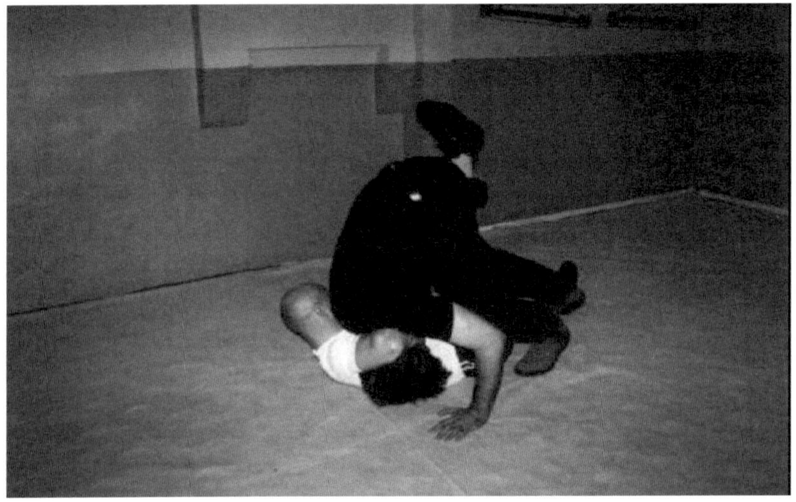

Tackle defence throw

Remember the 2 above techniques are to be used only if you can't move to the side. Going to the floor is not the best option but sometimes it could be the only one!

In ending the tackle defences. If you do get caught unawares and slammed to the floor you must try and control your head so it doesn't smash into the floor.

This is easier said than done because being hit by a tackle will shake you up and knock the air out of you. But if you control the head you will still have enough awareness left to fight back.

You can do this by immediately grabbing the attackers hair and jabbing a thumb into his eye and twisting his head to one side to get him off you and onto his back.

When you have achieved this remove the thumb from the aggressor's eye and strike with a heel hand up under his philtrum a few times to subdue him.

Floor – Fighting

Defence against the side headlock

The side headlock is executed by the attacker clamping your head under his armpit and joining his hands together to lock your head into position, then use his superior strength to squeeze your head or neck.

Fortunately most people don't know how to apply a proper side headlock by squeezing the temples or the carotid arteries, so you have a little more time to counter.

Biting to release

Defence 1

The attacker has a side headlock on you and is squeezing your head, which is clamped, against his chest. This is a high side headlock, which hasn't bent you over as yet, so try and counter immediately.

Bring your hand up and over your assailant's nearest shoulder from the rear and claw into his eyes, ripping back. This will loosen the hold; now turn your head into his chest and bite deeply into the side of the pectoral muscle (obviously if the attacker is wearing a heavy jacket the bite won't work, so stick to the eye claw).

The bite will immediately give a release because of the agonising pain it causes. Soon as your head is free, slam a couple of uppercut punches into the groin as you still claw at the eyes.

Escaping a side headlock

Defence 2

You are now in the side headlock but your head is further down, about level with your attacker's waist. From this position you are in danger of being hit freely in the face by the aggressor.

With that point in mind immediately bring your rear arm upwards to smash a rising forearm blow into the assailant's testicles.

From there retract the hand and bring it up and over his near shoulder and push the edge of your hand or thumb up under the base of his nose. Push back hard to arch his body and release the hold on you. From this position bring your free hand up the front of his body and slam 2 or 3 arc hand strikes into his windpipe.

If he is still standing after that which is doubtful, bring your striking hand back down his body and punch or grab his testicles.

A variation on the base of the nose punch is to hook your index and middle fingers up his nostrils and rip up and back.
Alternatively you can grab and yank back on the hair or rake back the eyes. All these moves work effectively.

Also if you are using one of the above mentioned moves and with the free hand you reach between his legs and pinch and hold the flesh on the upper thigh nearest you or grab the testicles, this will make him lift his leg.
That combined with the other hand manoeuvring his head back, you should be able to topple him back onto the floor and follow down with a few knee drops etc.

These again are the most simplest and effective techniques to use against the side headlock.

Surprise groin strike

Defence against a frontal grab or strangle

If the big man lunges forward and grabs for a handful of your shirt or jacket, instantly react with a punch or knee to the testicles. Follow up with the heel hand to jaw/arc hand to windpipe or eye claw. Don't get involved grappling or attempting joint-locks. These require great skill, if you haven't got the experience don't attempt them.

Fast, instant strikes to vital points will get you free and away. If he pulls you in real close or up off your feet with a double lapel type grab, then you can react with the following techniques.

Palm slapping ear, thumb gouging eyes, head butting his face, biting his nose, ears, and neck. When he releases knee or punch testicles and stomp his foot insteps.

The assailant may lunge in for a strangle against your neck instead. Normally this is a type of furious, angry, reaction.

Be ready - if you have room and are 'switched on' kick his groin or kneecaps then close in with knee strikes or elbows as described earlier. If he gets a good strangle on, then take a large step back to regain your balance and at the same time 'bowl' your arm in a big circle over his arms, you will break his grip and momentarily have his wrists caught in your armpit.

From there drive back a series of vicious back elbows into face, then follow up as you see fit.
Try not to panic when hands are at your throat, think rationally and strike back effectively.

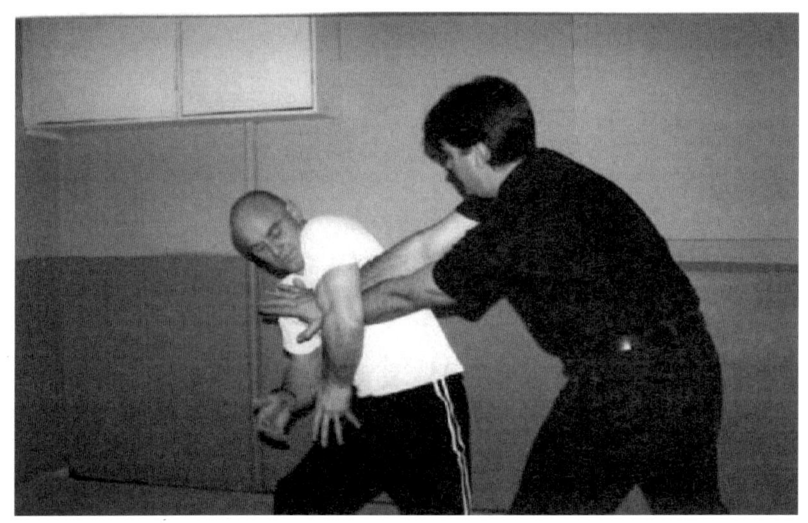

Front strangle counter

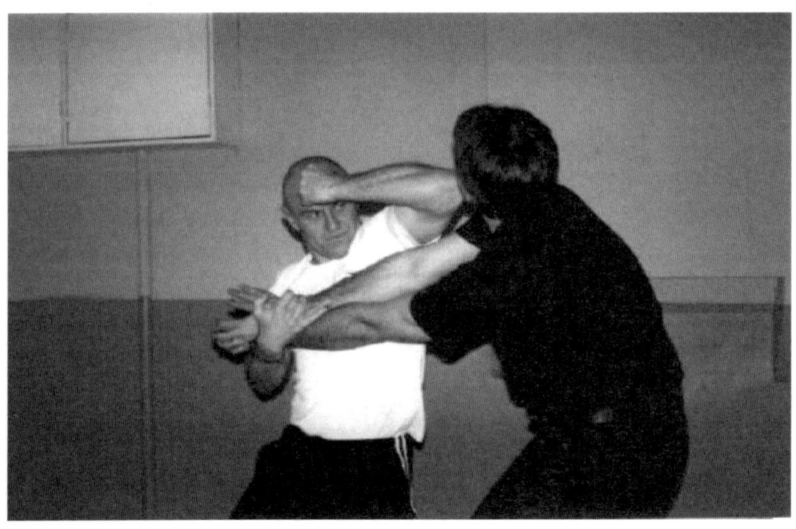

Break grip & strike back with elbow

Defence against a rear chokehold

This is a defence against a crudely applied rear choke very similar to the 'sleeper' we discussed earlier on.

If the guy isn't an expert then the 'sleeper' will not be applied. But having said that he can easily rupture the windpipe with rough choking methods!

Technique 1

Attacker has just snaked an arm around your neck.

Immediately grab his forearm and bend your knees to sink your weight, which will aid better balance. Shoot a back elbow with one of your arms into attacker's solar plexus.
Bite down and into his arm or if that has heavy clothing protection, bite into the muscle between thumb and index finger. From there reach up and wrench down and out on his little finger joint. Keep hold on it; pivot out of choke and around to face your assailant and front kick him in the testicles.

Break grip and strike back with elbow

Technique 2

Attacker has a firmer grip on you.

Here is a beautiful throwing method for the small man, which works a treat! The technique is a shoulder throw, which works perfectly against this form of attack.

Grab the choking arm and pull it down slightly to aid your breathing and at the same time shoot a couple of back elbows into attackers solar plexus. This will lurch his body forward, now grab his arm with both your hands, back up close to him, bend your knees slightly and then bow your upper body forward from the waist.

If you have timed it right the attacker will go crashing over your head and down onto the pavement with a terrific force, he will not trouble you no more obviously. A follow up knee-drop or stomp will give you extra insurance. This is one of the classic Ju Jutsu/Judo throws that can be used effectively in the street from this particular hold.

Biting and finger break to release choke

Technique 3

Choked and being pulled back off balance.

Again this is the worst possible position to be in and a very difficult one to counter. You must straight away drop your weight and balance low, take a large step back and get your leg anchored firmly behind your attackers. Bend your knees deeply to get below his centre of balance, now reach down grab the back's of both of his knee's and throw your body weight back so you both crash to the floor. (If you can't grab the legs, then let both hands grab the testicles and lift up then throw back still holding the groin). If you fall on him all well and good, if not then immediately shoot your elbows to assailants groin, body, throat and face for release, also prise at the little finger joint and bite his forearm if he hasn't released.

The fall though is a heavy backdrop and if the attacker isn't suspecting it he will probably damage the back of his skull or spine on impact with the ground. Again this throw involves using the principle of his own bodyweight against him, you don't use any lifting strength.

Double leg drop against a chokehold

Defence against a full nelson

This is another big guy's strength hold, applied from the rear. This move was made popular from the T.V. wrestling. Unfortunately most people apply it like the T.V. wrestlers, so you have a chance of countering the nelson.
A properly applied full nelson can snap the neck quite easily before you have a chance to react.
The full nelson is applied by the man approaching you from behind and slipping his hands under your armpit and interlocking them behind your neck. From here he can put downward pressure against the cervical vertebrae at the top of the spinal column.

Defence 1

The attacker has put the hold on but has yet to force your head forward. Immediately stomp his instep and step your foot back behind his legs and perform the backdrop throw I showed for the third defence against the rear choke.

It works equally well from here and is just as devastating.
Remember the stomp first to loosen the hold and give you a chance to reach for his legs.

Defence 2

This time the attacker has forced your head forward and down. Do not fight against the pressure but instead drop to your knees and roll your body forward. If the attacker is holding on tight he will roll over your back and land underneath you. Immediately back elbow groin and solar plexus and keep striking until you can get to your feet.

Again this throw demonstrates the principle of using your opponent's force against him. This move will work a treat and if you land on top of the assailant your body should wind him sufficiently for a release.

Defending against a full nelson

Those conclude then the most common grappling holds that a big man will use. We could of course go on with the variables indefinitely but if you apply these principles to any front or rear hold you will get a release.

In closing don't forget to react instantly before he can really use his strength to the utmost. Always remember he doesn't expect you to counter, so when you do, do it rapidly and viciously to put him out of the fight. Don't mess up, you only get one chance.

Countering holds aren't as hard as they first might seem at least you know where the attackers hands are.

Also most of the holds the untrained big guys use, are pure strength moves and not too scientific. They will leave you some sort of opening simply because they believe you cannot match their pure brute strength!

Once you use the counters shown in this chapter it will be too late for the big man to readjust, you will have used the 'good old' element of surprise and you will have taken the advantage, keep it and finish the assailant off for attacking in such a manner.

Now practice these moves diligently and safely until they are second nature.

"Learn to fight from the ground
but don't go to the ground to fight!"

A word on ground fighting...

At present in the martial Arts ground fighting is a popular subject. People are beginning to realise the benefit of the many chokes, locks and submissions involved in floor grappling.

For you as a self-defence student, looking for instant response and straightforward technique in the shortest time possible, we will just literally touch on the rudiments of what to do if you hit the floor.

If you go down and your attacker is standing, curl into a protective ball, pulling the limbs in tight to protect the head and body.
Now shoot out your feet kicking at assailant's shins and knees to prevent him kicking at you or stepping over your legs to straddle your body. Kick until he backs off or is momentarily hurt then get back to your feet quickly.

Avoid at all costs going to your back on the floor with a large assailant on top of you; this could be your worst nightmare. If it happens immediately start striking by thumb gouging his eyes, spearing his throat with your fingers, slapping the eardrums, palm heeling the chin or head butting if up close and biting anywhere available.

Hair grabbing, gouging or ripping the face or testicles is also a must to escape.
Try to prevent the larger man using his superior body weight.

Fight fast and fight viciously and you will survive. For greater knowledge and to expand your ground fighting knowledge, seek out any of the many books videos available on the subject at present.

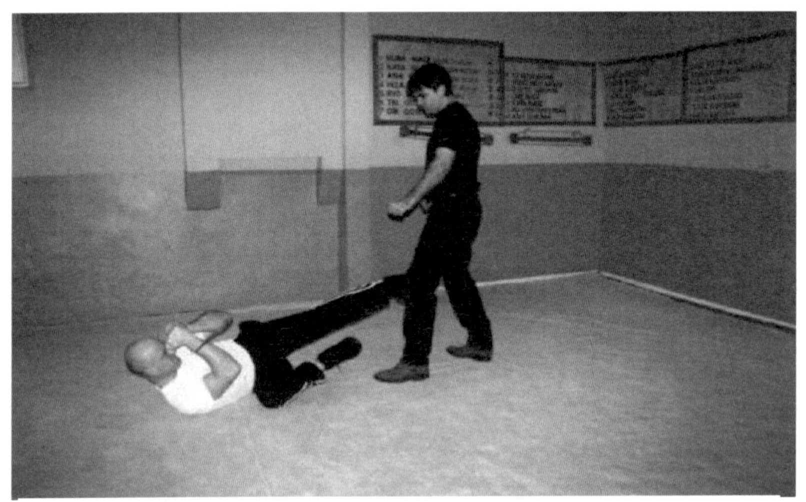

Kicking to legs if you are on the ground

Get it over with quick

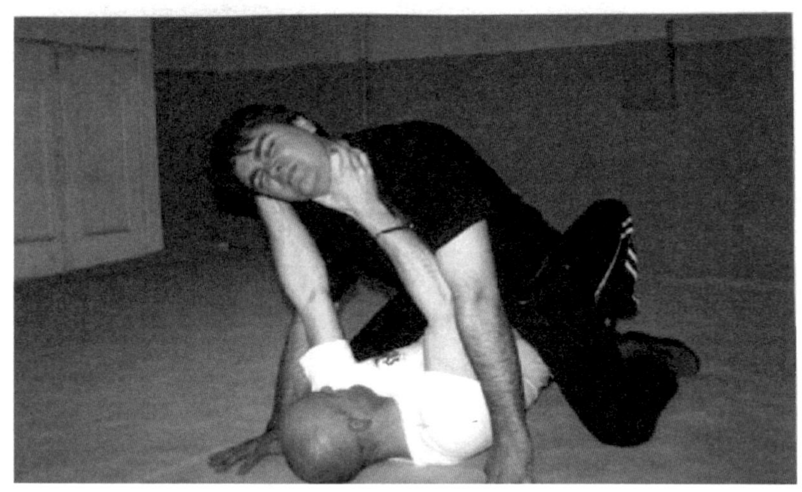

Ground-fighting

I DIDN'T SEE THAT COMING!
PROTECT YOURSELF AT ALL TIMES

Bang! K.O.!

Chapter 6

Handling the sucker punch!

'It's important to keep your head in a fight....literally!

We looked in detail in the offensive technique chapter about taking the fight to your assailant when he confronts you with violence, and there is no other option.

But what happens if you hesitate or are too slow? What if he is a wily street veteran that knows the game and tries to get the drop on you?
We have to address this problem and do something about it.
Firstly as mentioned before keep an arms length distance between you at all times. Do not get any closer to assailant or let him any closer to you. This will give you a chance if he decides to take a swing.

The average street fighter will probably throw a big right hook/swing or a large over hand punch, any closer he will use the head butt, these are his main artillery. If he knocks you to the floor he will follow up with brutal kicks and stomps to your head and body.

So protect that space at all times and look for the signs of the would be attacker preparing to hit you. How can you do this? Study the following cues and clues; they will help you understand the rituals of the sucker puncher.

Face of aggression – see the signs?

Verbal cues

Offensive and insulting language
Loud screaming and shouting
Threats
Disjointed and unintelligible speech
Abnormal stuttering
Rapid Speech
High pitched voice
Single syllable answers to questions

Non verbal cues

Red face from blood surge
Increased breathing
Vein protruding from face/neck
Clenched fists
Extreme body tension
Hunching of shoulders
Wide eyed stare
Finger pointing
Finger prodding
Hand concealment
Shift of body
Chest puffed out
Hands/arms splayed
Neck/head pecking

Seems a lot of things to look for, doesn't it?

But remember it won't be them all at the same time.

Any of the listed things can alert you though to an on coming sucker punch.

Now if you are faced by a big, dangerous assailant, you as a small person will not be trying to block his on coming limb strength to strength or you will lose. Most of the Martial Arts blocks don't work at the best of times, so if you have little or no training do not attempt them at all.

The first defence we are going to explore is the 'Bob'.

I am reluctant to use the word duck because it conjures up pictures of somebody throwing themselves to the floor as another person is throwing some sort of projectile at them. The 'Bob' if you like is a sophisticated method of 'ducking', this is how it works. As say, the big guy winds up a right hand punch. You bring your hands/arms up to guard each side of your head, like a boxer. Then bend the knees lightly and lean your upper body forward, leading with your right shoulder. If you have timed this right the attacker's swing will skim harmlessly over your head and you will be in a perfect position for a counter attack.
Don't bend too low with the Bob, otherwise you may risk a knee in the face and also you will not be able to see opponent clearly enough to counter attack.

Now if the large assailant puts all his might into the swing and missed, his own momentum may well send him crashing, off balance into some obstruction. If this happens all well and good. If not then from your crouched position fire a punch up into his testicles to help him on his way. Or move to the rear and execute the groin takedown or any of the other rear takedowns previously described depending on the situation.
Once you have avoided the punch whether you fight back or make a clean getaway is up to you, whatever you do, do it right away, don't hesitate, the advantage is with you!
This move of the 'Bob' will also work against a straight type of punch. Cover the same and move in or outside of the punch, crouching down.

Then explode the groin punch and follow up with the rising palm heel to chin, an eye gouge, throat attack or knees to face. Don't forget also the frontal takedowns previously described.

If all else fails and you don't get to execute the 'Bob' then you will have to cover up, by bringing your hands up to either side of your head, pull your elbows in and move inside the punches. Don't stand off, or the big man will launch you into orbit! Move it so you don't meet his force or attempt to block limb to limb. Let the sting of his punches be dissipated behind your head. Then react as viciously and quickly as possible.
Go again for the groin shot with fist or knee, as his head comes down, slap his eardrums, thumb gouge his eyes, butt his nose or grab his head and bite his face, whatever it takes, the head/chin twist will work well from here. If you hesitate it will end up in grappling and you will probably find yourself back in one of the holds in previous chapters or worse on the floor!

Bear in mind, having to defend a punch is a last option, being pre-emptive and being first is crucial against a large assailant, you do not want to have to contend his strength or feel the weight of his punches. You will not last long if you do.

In closing if you get caught with a glancing blow and you have been dazed, grab hold of your attacker. Clinch around his waist and hang in there, attempting to move behind him away from anymore punishment. To help you, bite in and clamp your teeth onto any part of his body and reach down and squeeze the testicles.
All these moves will help you buy time to clear your head.

Never ever back off when struck otherwise he will be all over you. If you are serious about handling and defending punches some basic boxing sparring would be beneficial, as it will give you a feel of realism. Remember at all times under pressure try and keep your head!

Weaving under a swing & countering

Blocking the hook punch

Cover up from punches

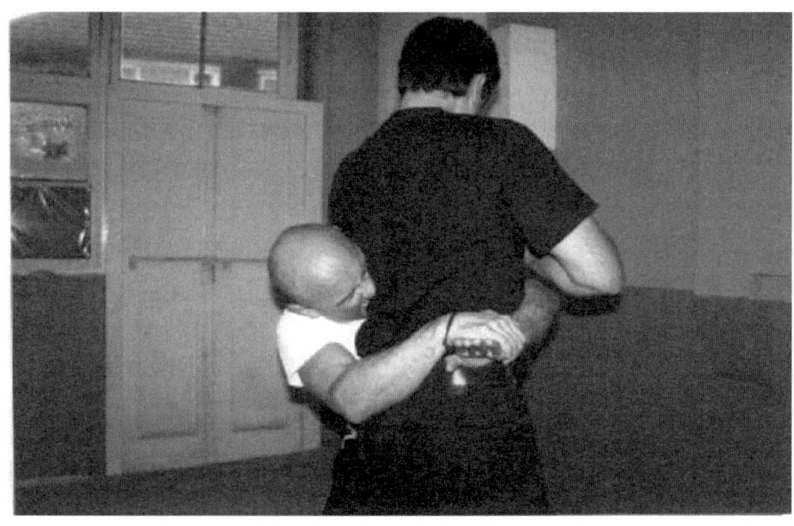

Body clinch & bite

Could these items help save your life?

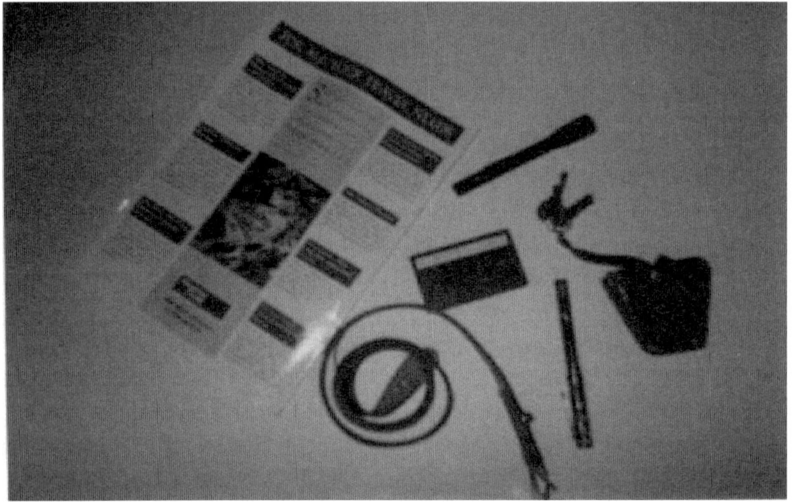

Read on................

Chapter 7

Equalisers

'A weapon in the hand is better than....none!

In an emergency you may have to use anything at hand as a weapon to defend yourself. If the attacker is big, aggressive and overwhelming you and you can reach an object like a table lamp, kitchen knife, heavy ashtray, whatever then use it, your life may be on the line so you will have no choice. Also if the situation warrants it you may brandish an object immediately to equalise the odds against the 'big guy' i.e. umbrella, pool cue, pool ball, crook lock etc etc. There are many equalisers; with a little training and imagination anything can be turned into a weapon.

In feudal times in Japan, farmers and peasants were not allowed to have or carry any weapons. Only the warrior class, the mighty Samurai could have swords, knives, etc. With this ruling the lower classes decided to construct their own weaponry from everyday farming tools and practise in secrecy to develop and hone their skills.

Weapons that are now practised by today's Martial Artists are actually classed by law as weapons, like the Nunchaku, Tonfa and Sai were no more than farming implements that were used as makeshift or expedient weapons when needed, really the same as tools today like a hammer, chisel or screwdriver could be used.

It's important to understand that although the Kobojutsu weapons of Okinawa and Japan are now thought of as deadly martial art weapons that were not their original intentions, they were born out of the necessity to defend life and limb in the violent wartime era of Ancient Japan.

Today in Britain, we are not allowed to carry weapons by law. Even as violence increases across the country at an alarming rate, if you are caught with any sort of weapon whether it be a knife, baton, or firearm you will be in big trouble.

Indeed, if you carried for instance a pair of nail scissors in your coat pocket with the intention of using them to stab a 'would be' mugger you could still be prosecuted by law for carrying a particular implement with sole purpose of using it as a weapon!
Unless you have a good and valid reason for carrying a weapon or a 'fashioned' one you again will be in big trouble with the police.

Some people realise this but fear of actual mugging, rape and assault will have them weigh up the odds, still carrying a weapon, depending on the circumstances they are in.
This chapter is not written to discuss the moral issue of you the individual, nor am I suggesting or advising either way what to do, I'm just bringing your attention to what the 'law of the land' states! So if you can't carry weapons you can do what those farmers did centuries ago and in times of danger use makeshift weapons!
Personal items that you may carry on you in everyday life can in an emergency with a little training be turned into an improvised weapon for defence. With training and imagination any personal or 'house hold' item can be turned into makeshift weapons.
Firstly these items can be totally legal by law and cannot be constructed as weapons, if they have a normal everyday function and you have a reason for carrying them, i.e. belt, credit card, pen, magazine, etc.
Secondly, if you develop skills in their use as a self defence tool you can draw tremendous confidence and comfort from knowing you are not empty handed, this is particularly true of ladies, the elderly or disabled. (I have been able to show these people many useful and effective techniques).

Now there are some drawbacks, which we must consider with makeshift weapons. One is that they were never designed to be weapons so they may well, after a couple of impact strikes, break, buckle, bend or fold, so be aware of this.

Make your first strike count, in case this happens, also don't rely 100% on the 'weapon' if you have the ability to back it up with 'unarmed' skills then do so. Sometimes as a weapon gets broken or you drop it, the confidence goes with it, be aware of this too!
Finally the weapon is only good if it can be brought into play quickly. On some Ladies Self Defence courses I have taken, ladies said they would spray hairspray in the attackers eyes to foil them. That works great but it's no good having the can at the bottom of your handbag, buried cap on.... They are not the ideal makeshift implement as in recorded cases, for example people under the panic of pressure in an attack situation sprayed it in their own faces by aiming wrongly!
If you have a chance as in the case of 'impending violence' or you sense or evaluate danger then you will have a chance to have that weapon at hand and be ready to use it.
In cases of surprise attack when you have dropped your awareness you may not be able to use or get a makeshift weapon.
Remember if you get one good shot it could be enough.

Now let's examine a few items and their uses. The list can be exhaustive from throwing the contents of your coffee mug into attackers face, then smashing the bottom down onto the bridge of the nose, or cracking a walking stick across the shins of an assailant then thrusting the end into the solar plexus, if you are in your own house try fashioning a 'blackjack' from wrapping a bar of soap in a tea towel, tying it in a knot then you will be ready to administer a mighty blow with this.
One item you may have on your person and use regularly is a credit card or cash till card. Most 'hole in the wall' cash tills can be a haven for muggers and you would do well to keep aware whilst with drawing your money.
If grabbed and spun around whilst using the card, turn and whip it across the face in a slicing motion. The thin and the surprisingly sharp edge can cut into the skin to foil the attack, then follow up with a knee to the groin to make your escape.

Also the card's edge can be rammed up into the philtrum (base of the nose) this is a good and highly painful method of breaking a front hold. Also slicing it across the same area will do the trick. The corner edge of the card can be thrusted in the eye or throat or in the mastoid behind the ear in a close quarter grapple. Even if the card snaps you will still be left with a jagged and uneven piece, which can rip flesh with ease.
Definitely a flexible friend!

A rolled up newspaper or magazine is an excellent expedient weapon. You can carry this in your hand without raising any suspicions and instantly bring it into play.

Rolled tightly the ends are as strong as a baton particularly on big glossy mags, or travel brochures. Jabbed or thrusted into the eyes, throat/neck, solar plexus or groin can have an instant effect on your attacker. Circular strikes to floating ribs/kidneys or temples can also incapacitate easily. If grabbed from the rear thrusting back into the groin or jabbing over your shoulder in a backhand fashion in the eyes will get you a release.
At high skill levels with a sturdy magazine you can choke, strangle and lock also. This is a very versatile weapon.
Your ballpoint pen can also be used as a 'Yawara Stick' to jab and thrust into the bodies soft points up at close range, so can a sharp pencil which can puncture and then be broken off to leave in the attacker, if you are in a life threatening situation. Finally a belt is a good equaliser especially against a knife assault. Wear a belt, which will slide easily through the trouser belt loops for quick excess.
If you cracked the belt in the fashion you used to do with your school tie (yes you did) it can be highly distracting and stingingly painful against the eyes. This will buy you time to kick the knee joints and gain control. Also wielding the belt in figure 8 circles and simultaneously kicking the legs can keep a knife attacker at bay.

Heavy belt buckles can be awesome weapons.

It's been known for certain individuals to file the edges down to make them razor sharp flailing instruments, very effective against a knife hand or wrist.
At close quarters the belt can be used to choke and strangle with great effect. From the front one such move is to encircle neck and choke, follow up with a head butt to the nose and knee to the groin.
Think about things you may have on your person in your everyday working life or things at hand where ever you may be.
If sat in a restaurant/cafe and you are under threat, think about unscrewing salt or pepper pots and flinging the contents in attackers face to buy yourself some time, if he is still dangerous drive your fork into his leg or hand and make a get away possibly up turning the table in assailants tracks.

Hot tea or coffee thrown to the face is also a sound tactic.
In a pub throwing the contents of your glass in the face is a good opening move, (what a waste), spirits particularly sting the eyes and impair the vision. Contents of ashtrays or ice buckets will also buy you valuable time and space.

A brief case or shopping bag can be a great shield against knife attacks, as can dustbin lids or chairs or stools. A good heavy-duty 4-cell torch is an excellent expedient weapon to carry in the car. The list goes on and on....

So if a time comes when you have to improvise under pressure **use an 'equaliser'!**

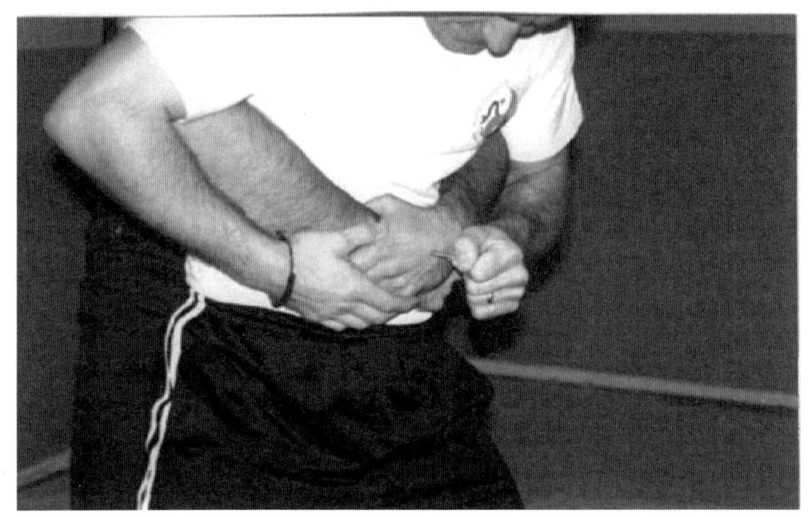

Car keys to nerve point

Rolled up magazine to groin

Credit card pushed under nose

Pen jabbed into eye

"Should I stay or should I go?"

Decision is in the balance

Chapter 8

Law and Self-Defence
'Better be judged by 9 then carried by 6'!

In learning Martial Arts of any type you are basically learning how to defend yourself. This is really the bottom line of training no matter what other qualities you get from your style.

But in a self-defence situation do you know by law how far you can go in defending yourself or others dear to you?

It is a very complex subject and at times a little confusing, but every Martial Artist must know and understand the law and self-defence.

The law states in the **criminal law Act of 1967** that you may use

"a reasonable amount of force in defence of your life, of others and of your property".

The important word here is 'reasonable'. Who can exactly say what is reasonable, who can decide this?

The police or a judge if it comes to it must decide and whether they make the right decision or not is one of today's sad facts concerning criminal law.

So how do you stay in the guidelines of the law?
For example if a barman knew that the lad drinking at the bar was under age and shouldn't be in the pub, went over to him and shot him because he was breaking the law. He would have a hard job convincing anyone that he was acting reasonably.
Sure the youth was committing the offence of drinking under age, but the barman's reactions were totally out of hand for the crime the lad was committing.

On the other hand if the barman was confronted with a youth armed with a knife demanding money from the till and in opening the till drew out a gun and shot him. No one could say he was not acting reasonably. Nobody wants to be threatened at knifepoint and robbed.
Even if when the police arrived and they found the youth was a prankster and the knife was plastic, the barman would still be able to claim reasonable self-defence, because in the moment of fear he wasn't to know the knife was plastic and he was sure his life and lively-hood was in danger, so he acted to save himself.
So it shows how complex the subject is and how difficult it can be to determine 'the reasonable amount of force'.

A guide would really be to say 'let the punishment fit the crime'. For instance, if a drunk came up to you in a pub and grabbed your wrist and you decided instantly to gouge his eyes and rip his throat out, taking his life along the way, you would have a hard job convincing anyone you acted reasonably within the law.
Look at the scene again, a man drunk and probably not capable of any effective danger grabbed your wrist and you killed him for it. Not a very nice situation to be in.

Where as on the other hand a guy at the bar smashes a bottle and comes screaming at you ready to jam the broken end in your face. In defending yourself you took his life, the law looking at the situation would probably take your plea of self-defence.

Because if the bottle had connected with you, you surely would have been maimed or killed and you acted reasonably under terrifying and extreme conditions.

The law doesn't expect you to stand and get beaten up because you were frightened of the consequences of fighting back, nor does it expect you to wipe someone away for bumping in to you on the street!

If possible in a situation where there is a chance to run away or to avoid trouble then you are expected to do so.

But if you can't then obviously you must defend yourself, no one would say otherwise.

But if you blocked an attackers punch and struck him back, knocking him to the floor and all the fight out of him, there is no reason to go and stomp on his throat, a dozen times!

You could see the danger was over and he wasn't capable of fighting anymore so there was no need for that final move. You have then crossed the thin line between attacker and defender. You have now become the attacker and the law will prosecute you.

You have got to know when to stop and different police will take different views. Someone I know was prosecuted for punching an attacker twice after he had blocked his initial strike. So it shows different views of 'reasonable force'.
There is a saying though which goes like this I'd rather be judged by 9 people than carried by 6!!

What about in defence of your property? Everybody has the right to defend what is theirs.
If an intruder breaks into your house in the middle of night and you are awoken by him moving about. Then you have the right to find the burglar and defend your property. You may have your wife and children sleeping upstairs so you also wish no harm to them. You don't know whey they've broken in it may be a simple burglar or there may be other more sinister and terrifying motives. So you must act how you feel.

In this type of situation awakened from your sleep and someone in your house, the police will understand the need for maybe in some cases extreme actions.

In defence of somebody breaking into your car to steal the radio. You again can defend your property but this time you will probably be required to shout 'stop thief', or something like.
Creeping up behind the burglar and strangling him will not give you a plea of reasonable self-defence.
If after you call stop thief and he turns to attack you. The defence law that we mentioned earlier on comes into play.
From your point of view being a 'little person' if you are confronted by a 6ft 4ins 18 stone monster with the intent of ripping you limb from limb and you defended yourself with an 'equaliser' or some of the more vicious hand to hand technique in this text, you will probably get more leeway than say somebody your attackers size.
If you truly believed your life was in grave danger then whatever you had to do, could be viewed as reasonable.
It is essential to know where you stand with the law, but you must not let it cloud your judgement when you are defending against a violent assault.
You must act first and save yourself, then weight up the consequences later. In this day and age you must look after yourself the best way you can.
There unfortunately won't be many good Samaritans coming to your aid!
Some of the techniques described in this text may seem extreme. But remember we are dealing with life threatening encounters mugging, rape, battery, GBH, murder, not fighting over whose round it is next! When you are in one of these encounters you will have to do what you see fit for survival.
If you hesitate it could cost you your life!
The techniques I outline in this book give you every opportunity to survive. If your first blow does the job and your assailant is finished, then great, job done. If not then you will have to have all the back up techniques at your disposal to survive!
The law and self defence is a 'grey area' but when it comes down to the moment of truth and you have to defend yourself, there will be no judge, jury or police, just you and your large, angry, aggressive assailant, you will have to make the choice?

Chapter 9

'True Encounters'

'Big surprises come in small packages'!

Throughout my Martial Arts career I have come across some great exponents of their particular fighting systems that are small in stature but truly big in mind and fighting spirit.
These people have made up for their lack of height or muscular body weight with pure fighting skills, honed and perfected through years of training. This has given them a special presence that they carry with them, an air of quiet confidence and tremendous fighting heart. Their lack of size in the end does not present a problem; they do not even consider it when they go into action.
One of my first instructors was an Aikido Sensei (teacher) named John Bennett. I was then a young man around 16/17 years of age. Full of myself, looking to be the next Bruce Lee! (Now there's an example of what a small man can achieve!)

John Bennett was a small red haired man around 5ft 5ins and maybe at the time no more than 10 stone. Basically he didn't on first glance look much. But boy can appearances be deceiving?

In the next 6 or 7 years I trained with him, I found him to have incredible mat presence for one so small.

He commanded respect. When he barked out instructions he as like an angry Jack Russell! It made you sit up and take notice.

He was strict on discipline and no-one skived on his training mat! I witnessed him on many occasions have training partners twice his size screaming in pain and helplessness, being held in an extremely painful joint lock or being flipped over onto their backs with a devastating throw.

The Japanese use a shout in their Martial Arts training called Ka-ai, which translated means 'spirit shout'. It is a method of expelling air from the stomach, into the lungs and out through the mouth in a roar! It is not just a shout from the vocal cords but a complete emptying of the lungs of air.
Japanese warriors have said to have frozen their opponents in battle with Ka-ai and then dispatched them.
The Ka-ai not only channels adrenaline in the right direction to be used as a shout to increase explosive body power but also as an unnerving psychological weapon to frighten your attacker.

John had a powerful and impressive Ka-ai. I have seen him not only freeze a training partner but the whole class as he released an unexpected Ka-ai! People could not believe that this small man could release such explosive aggression.
He explained to me that Ka-ai should be like a lion's roar and when heard, it would strike immediate fear into your opponent's body. I have always remembered this I have used it to great effect many times myself.

John Bennett is a prime example of a person conquering a weakness and finding other avenues to develop strengths.
John still teaches and although somewhat older is still a formidable character!
One of the greatest warriors I have ever had the fortune of learning off of was again from the Art of Aikido. This Japanese Master is a living legend and anyone who is anyone within the Aikido world will have heard of his name and had a tremor of fear in their bellies, his name Kazuo Chiba.
A man of small stature who seemed to grow and grow as he demonstrated his very powerful, abrupt and dynamic Aikido.

At the time I trained under this great man, I was just a relative novice. I watched in disbelief as this small Japanese would hurl the biggest of opponents through the air with ease or have them on their knees screaming for submission in one of his many holds and locks.

He was like a small tornado when he was in motion, awesome to see. The biggest and "most brave" in the Aikido world would far from relish being on the end of his technique.

Sometimes the mere mention of his name was enough to drain the blood from their faces! Chiba Sensei was a Samurai thrown into the modern world; he still lived and trained like one. For a small man he had incredible presence.

Even before he entered the training hall the hairs on the back of your neck would stand up in anticipation of this true warrior.

He again is an example of what can be achieved at the highest levels. His reputation for effective technique on and off the mat was without question. He could fill a room with an aura and strength although he couldn't have been any more than 5ft 6ins in height! But to everybody who met or trained under him he was big, very big!!

These Martial Artists and others have given me huge influence in my training over the years.

Most of my training I have faced people bigger than myself (I am 5ft 7ins) and at first I felt intimidated but gradually as my skills, strength and confidence grew I didn't worry about my size.

I developed a very aggressive fighting spirit, where in the end, people were intimidated by me! Looking back in some aspects I may have been too hard, but I was developing and enjoying my new confidence.

You see right back to school days where I can say I was never really a victim of relentless bullying, I did have an inner fear of being confronted by 'bigger lads' and I did feel inferior.

I hated the feelings and decided at 14 years of age I was going to change this and then started my Martial Arts journey after reading a magazine on the legendary Bruce Lee, a man who stood around 5ft 6ins and weighed no more than 9 stone, yet he was awesome, and I wanted to be like him.

Needless to say I am still trying to reach his incredible standards some 22 years later!

Going back to my school days, I can remember a classic incident of a David verses Goliath confrontation. I will not use the names of the people involved, as that would not be right. So I will call them David and Goliath!
Goliath was a big lad for 14 years of age; he was also a troublemaker and a bully of the worst kind. He intimidated kids smaller than himself extracting dinner money, sweets, etc from them with menace. If he couldn't get them that way, then he would do it with his fists. Everybody tried to stay clear of him if they could.
David was just an ordinary lad, good for a laugh and a bit of fun, but not a troublemaker or a fighter. Although some of us had heard when pushed he had a fiery Irish temper.
He wasn't big in any form, just your average kid.
For reasons I can't re-call he had in some way offended or upset Goliath. He was on the warpath, the word had gone around that Goliath was after David to give him a good hiding when the time was right!

One rainy dinner time some of us boys including David were in the 'new block' of classrooms away from the main school just larking around, as you do, when suddenly the door of the class room we were in burst open. Framed in the door, foaming at the mouth like a raging bull was Goliath. We all froze, we knew what was on the cards, so did David, there was no escape!

'You', bellowed Goliath, pointing at David, ***'I'm going to 'ave you'!*** As he said this he moved menacingly towards him. Confidence shining in his eyes, as he homed in on his prey, ready for the kill. We all waited for the inevitable out come.

Suddenly David moved into action, he picked up a wooden classroom chair and as Goliath closed in, David swung it powerfully and it whacked into the bullies' head. He howled in pain and disbelief as he cowered back trying to protect himself. Another blow rained down on his head and he sank to his knees.

All his confidence and arrogance drained away, replaced by fear. ***'Stop, stop'*** he pleaded, ***'I'm sorry David I didn't mean it, leave me alone'***, he wailed. David stopped. Breathing hard he shouted, ***'Go on get out and don't you come near me again'.***
Goliath got up and staggered out, fear still in his eyes.
When he was gone we all cheered and clapped an unbelievable show of courage from the 'small guy'. Needless to say 'Goliath' never bothered him again!

Some years later when I had left school I decided to take up weight training and went to a local well-known gym. Here I was yet again to witness a giant slaying act. At this gym was a rest area with tables and chairs and a T.V. on the wall. Also a bar that served fruit juices, energy drinks, that sort of thing.
A lot of the guys would hang around here after their 'workouts'.
The guy employed to work behind the bar could be described as looking like a bit of a 'wally' although. I was to find out that he wasn't!

He was small, slight, glasses with a 'teddy boy' hairstyle. He was always the butt of some joke or 'piss take'.

One-night two big body builders were sat at one of the tables and had been taking the 'mick' out of this little guy for some while. Again they were confident in the knowledge that he was no threat and that they felt superior because of their muscular stature.

Well I suppose it got too much for 'wally' as one of the body builders made a 'crack' and turned to his mate. 'Wally' suddenly let out a ear-splitting roar and vaulted the counter.
He launched himself into the big guy like a wild cat and began pounding him. The body builder was so shocked he didn't know what had hit him! He fell from the chair he was sitting on and hit the floor with 'wally' clinging to him like a leech. 'Wally' continued the beating until two other big guys pulled him off the battered body builder.

Everyone else stood silent in shock. Then 'wally' still breathing hard from his exertions said ***'Well, he just pissed me off'***!
As illustrated here, sometimes the false confidence of thinking your size is enough to handle situations can be sorely proved wrong. The little guy certainly proved it wrong, so never judge a book by its cover!
Through personal experience I have found when a 'new comer' comes to train at one of my classes and he's a 'big lad', he will eye me with scepticism, thinking how can this bloke be any good, I'm much bigger than him, he doesn't look much!
I have seen this look a thousand times, and I smile inwardly. That arrogant self-confidence that will soon be shattered!
I had two such 'lads' recently come along with this disrespectful attitude, so normally I get them to hold the focus pads or polystyrene block that we use in developing striking power.

Now I have been fortunate to train with two prolific punchers, Mr.Geoff Thompson and Mr. Peter Consterdine, of the British Combat Association and I have learnt much about the art of striking. I can hit hard with my full body weight behind a blow and although I am around 12 stone, it probably feels like 15.5 stone hitting you!
When these 'disbeliever's' go staggering back with a look of sheer pain and surprise on their faces, I know they now see me in a different light and if their arrogance had been in a 'street' situation I would have knocked them clean out and they suddenly realised this.
I hate having to prove the point, but most of my life in or out of the training hall I've had to on occasion do it because situations would have escalated.
I remember another time when a tough Karate man and a bit of a handy street fighter came to train at my Dojo. He was sceptical about joint locks saying that I wouldn't be able to put one on him and that he was too strong. I took the challenge up and we faced off, he came in with a thunderous straight reverse punch towards my head and if I had been caught with it I would have been launched to the moon!

As it was I slipped it, grabbed his wrist and cranked on a vertical wristlock (sankyo).
The guy first went up onto his tiptoes screaming in pain and then found himself face down on the mat in more agony and he tapped out a submission signal on the mat like a drum beat!
He got up a converted man, I was glad to say and we became good friends.
Sometimes you have to back up your claims even if you don't want to, but I must confess it is a satisfying feeling when you do!
These are just a couple of many such incidents that I have experienced.
In closing this chapter 1 would just like to give a mention to two other practising Martial Artists instructors who I greatly admire them.

They both come from my hometown of Bristol their names **Neil Bartlett of Ju Jutsu** and **Martyn Hurd of Muay Thai**, both true 'little warriors', keep up the good work lads!

These stories just show that with the right belief and confidence, being small doesn't have to be a problem.
A lot of the time we have been programmed and conditioned by society to believe that it does!

It takes time to re-programme your outlook but do it now, once this book is finished decide as from then you will step out and be confident, remember big is in the mind!!
You can look at many great sportsmen for instance that if they had listened to certain people would not have achieved what they have done because of their size, and others from all walks of life.
Be positive you will definitely be able to handle defending yourself with the knowledge you have been given.

Knowledge is Power!

Chapter 10

'Final tips & tactics'

'Knowledge is power'

In this final chapter we will just review and suggest major points and tactics in your personal Self Protection plan.

1. Remember, belief that you can perform the technique is important

2. Remember the eyes, throat, groin, kneecaps have no muscular protection no matter how big your opponent may be.

3. Cultivate a hard mental attitude and an undying fighting spirit, without them the techniques are hollow.

4. Work on your distraction/set up talk and tactics. Practice in front of the mirror to see if you are convincing and give nothing away in your face or body language.

5. A certain level of fitness will make the techniques work better and stop you from getting fatigued under pressure. Adrenaline can tire you badly. Whatever exercise you do make it in relation to what you want to achieve. Remember having the fitness to run a marathon will not necessarily help you in an 'all out' combat encounter.

6. Develop Ka-ai or spirit shout. This is a powerful weapon that can momentarily freeze your attacker and make him believe he has taken on a 'crazy person'. It may be just the mental edge you are looking for

7. Don't ever feel intimidated or inadequate because of your stature, remember have the heart of a lion and it's bite!

8. Always bring your assailant down to your height never reach up or stretch to get at him.

9. In our set ups we worked on the defensive plea, of pretending we were not a threat before we attacked. On the other side of the coin you can be ultra aggressive, if it's in your nature psyche your larger adversary out, this way, but be prepared to back it up physically if he takes your challenge! You could say something like,

'C'mon then, I ain't frightened of you, let's see what you've got?'
or
'Let's go then, your all mouth, c'mon, I'm here let's do it, now'!
or
'Right, I've had it, I ain't scared of your size, pity your brain ain't as big as the rest of you, let's go'!

Anything along those lines, make up your own, but when you say it, be positive, snarling and vicious, leave your opponent with no doubt in his mind if he tackles you he will come off second best!

10. Always maintain a 45-degree angle stance from your assailant, even when talking.

11. Always fight back with 100% commitment and strike through body targets, remember it's not necessarily how hard you hit, it's where you hit!

12. Always if possible strike first, strike fast and strike with authority.

13. Always remember your mind is your greatest weapon!

14. Learn to use ' makeshift weapons'.

15. Learn to 'tap' your killer instinct.

16. Avoid wrestling with a bigger assailant.

17. Don't get into potentially dangerous situations through foolish arguing.

18. Don't ever give up, keep the will to win.

19. Don't start fighting, unless it's the last resort, then finish it. Do everything in your power to avoid trouble initially.

20. Avoid trouble at all costs. Be aware and switched on when you are out and about and you can cut down the chances of being a victim of violence by 70%. This is true, think about it.

21. Remember no one on this planet has the right to offer you violence.

22. Self-defence begins with Self-esteem!

23. Learn to command a presence, regardless of your size!

24. Battles are won by offence not defence, aggressive attack wins.

25. Understand the difference between fiery aggression and icy aggression. The first is just blind anger, it can work against you, you are not thinking rationally. The second aggression is calculating and thought through, the better option to win!

26. Do not fight a larger aggressor on an equal footing. You will not get a second chance to win a fight.

27. Attack is your best method of defence. If you confront a lion or almost any wild animal, their response to danger is attack, their defence is attack, let it be yours to!

28. Remember keep an arms length distance between you and your aggressor, do not allow him to get too close to you.

29. If an aggressor comes towards you and their hand(s) are hidden, deduce that they are probably carrying a weapon.

30. Lastly but not least, remember the old saying 'size isn't everything'!

Conclusion

'A parting shot'

This book on it's own will not guarantee your safety in today's violent society. Once read and then put onto the bookshelf, it will not give you some invisible force field of protection against all that is 'evil'. You will have to practise the techniques over and over again and deeply study the mental aspects of combat, also, until they are ingrained in the subconscious.

If you don't make this effort, then the book will be wasted. It is like having a shelf full of the World's best cookery books showing you the secrets and delights of food, but only at the end of the day all you can practically do is boil an egg. Don't just be a reader or a thinker, be a doer. Whatever you want out of life you have to work for and put in some effort, it's no different with self protection/Martial Arts.

A quick read and a few hours training won't help you stand your ground against a violent assault, robbery, rape etc, etc.
So set sometime aside to learn, the information there is, it cost me a lot more than the asking price of this book to find it, so that I can share what others are looking for, to confront their fears, doubts, vulnerabilities and fight back.

Remember though the techniques are last resort moves, if you can't walk away or talk your way out of a dangerous situation then you use them, with no reserve. If you hesitate you will lose the fight, maybe lose your life!
Fighting is not the exciting and glamorous filled action that the films might lead us to believe. Real fighting is fast, brutal and bloody. The pain is not just physical, it is also psychological. The former scars heal well before the later.

There is nothing 'macho' about fighting at the 'drop of a hat' over foolish trivial matter; you can end up doing hard time or in a hospital bed.
You only fight when you have to and then when you do move into fighting mode, do it fast, hard and effectively.

Remember as stated before no body has the right to offer you violence. When they do, put up your barriers, your mental chalk line, where your opponent should not cross, if he does, take him off the planet and go home safe.

Remember the size of the assailant infront of you will not matter as much as your desire to win at all costs and not quit even when hurt. Use the techniques described to suit you personally, not all maybe for you but take what you need. In a street fight technique, guts and heart have more to do with winning than a 52-inch chest and 20 inch bicep!

To go over an earlier point most street fights start and finish with a big looping right hand punch or it ends up on the floor. This should alert you to the fact that the first person who gets the telling 'shot' in will win. Let that be you, the last thing you want is to be rolling around with a large, powerful opponent on the floor, 9 times out of 10 you will lose.

I am far from an expert on street fighting and I don't know all the answers, but I have seen a bit and done a bit, maybe more than some of those other 'so called' instructors around, I can only tell you how I see it, it is up to you to experiment and find your own personal way. I hope this book goes some way to help all of you 'little people' out there?

Good luck!

Kevin 0'Hagan   1996

Bag work – Essential strike training

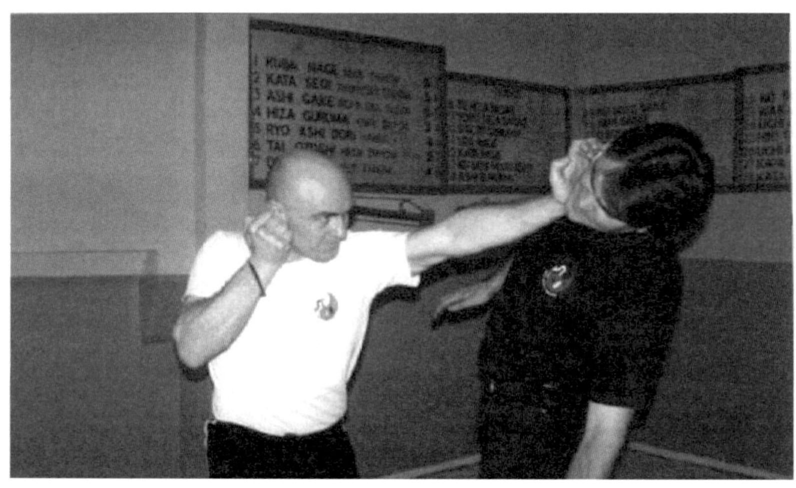

For knockout power

Don't let your attacker get to close

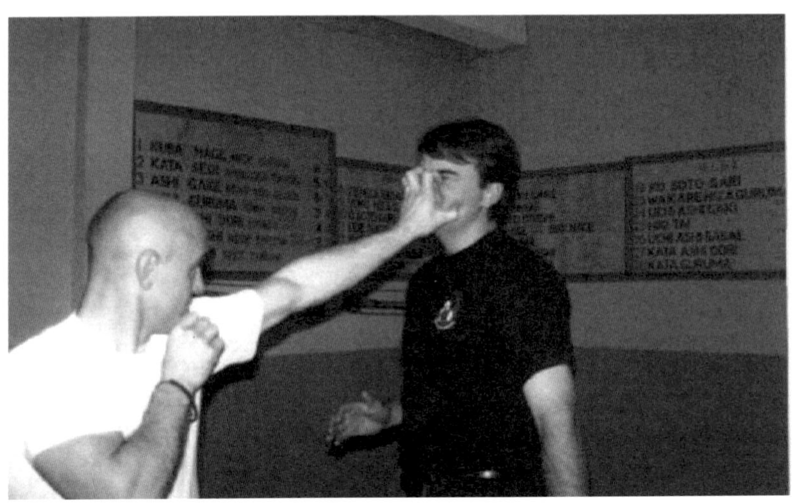

Always – if possible – strike first

Bring assailant down to your height by Whatever means

The End

Adverts

Will the reader please note that the following advertising section of the book is included to let you know of other Self Protection related merchandise.

You the reader, have not been charged for the printing or paper used in this section. The cost for this has been absorbed by New Breed Publishing.

The price that you have paid for this publication is for the knowledge, information and advice given by Kevin O'Hagan throughout the rest of this book.

Thank you

Jamie O'Keefe

Email

Jamieokeefe@tiscali.co.uk

Web Site

www.newbreedbooks.co.uk

Please check our online shop with secure credit card ordering.

'Down & out'

Grappling and groundwork is the 'in thing'
Within Martial arts at present.

If you want to expand your knowledge within this area, this video is for you.

It's loaded with basic and advanced throws and takedowns, with a Multitude of ground submissions and finishes.

"DOWN AND OUT"
STANDING TO FLOOR JU-JUTSU TECHNIQUES

Featuring Kevin O'Hagan 6th Dan

"50" Throws and takedowns with a multitude of finishing holds and submissions!! Hard to find information and techniques on just one tape (60 mins)

Excellent value at **£14.00**

(*Please add **£1.00** for postage and packing*)

Please make cheques payable to "**Kevin O'Hagan**" and post to

23 Chester Road, St.George, Bristol BS5 7AX
Genuine 60 minutes of action guaranteed

"DOWN AND OUT" Vol 2

More dynamic Strikes, throws and submission techniques.

Learn advanced combinations, joint locks, leg locks, chokes, strangles, and much more. This tape is loaded with first class technique.

Modern Combat Jujitsu at it's best

Price £15 inclusive of Post and Packing
Contact Kevin O'Hagan for more details.

"If I wanted to learn something new – this is the video that I would choose. In fact, Kevin O' Hagans videos are the most used tapes in my own personal collection. I have not released any videos of my own because I do not feel I could improve on Kevins instructional tapes!"

Jamie O'Keefe 7th Dan
'Hall of Fame Awardee 1999' & 2001
'Founder Fellow of the Society of Martial Arts'.
'Self Protection instructor for Seni 2000, 2001 Birmingham Expo'

In the Face of Violence

'Understanding and combating the human predator'

by

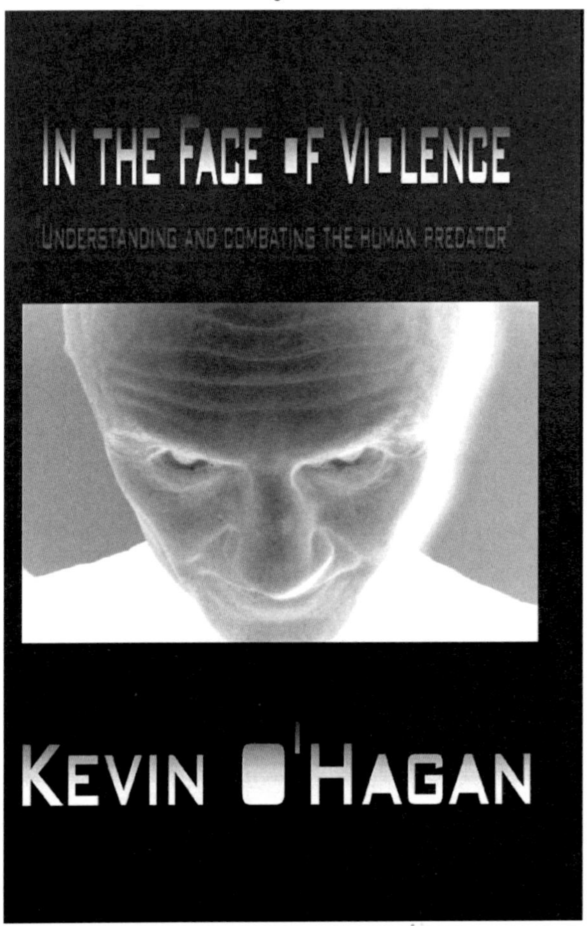

Kevin O'Hagan

£14

<u>Buy it direct from Kevin O'Hagan</u>

And ask him to autograph it!

PREVENT YOURSELF FROM BECOMING A VICTIM
'Dogs don't know Kung Fu'
A guide to Female Self Protection
By Jamie O'Keefe **£14** including post & packing

Never before has Female Self Protection used this innovative approach to pose questions like. Why do Rapist's Rape? Why are Women abused? Why do Stalkers Stalk? This book takes a look at all Simple, Serious, and Life threatening aspects of Self Protection that concern us daily, along with **PREVENTION** of Child abuse and Child Abduction, Emotional cruelty, Telephone abuse, Road rage, Muggers, Date rape, Weapon attacks, Female abduction, Sexual Assault & Rape, Self defence law, and what it will allow us to do to protect ourselves, plus much more. With over 46,500 words, 77 pictures and 200 printed pages 'Dog's Don't Know Kung fu' is a no nonsense approach to women's self defence. It covers many realistic scenarios involving Children's abduction as well as typical attacks on women. Besides quoting actual events, the book explains how to avoid trouble and how you should react if you get into a situation.

This book is a 'must read' for all women and parents.

It is also important for teenage women, but, due to some of its graphic depiction's of certain incidences, parents should read it first and decide if it's suitable for their child.

Foreword

Dogs don't know kung fu

I'm not usually known for writing forewords to books on self protection, and not because I'm afraid of competition, on the contrary, the more people offering good advice in the fight for better protection be better:- rather its because most of what I read on the subject is crap.
I would never be happy putting my name to something that does not represent my own views, and that's putting it mildly. Not only are the proffered 'self defence' techniques in these manuals unlikely, they are also, very often, dangerous and opinionated.
I have written some 20 books to date on self protection and related subjects so you'd think that there would be very little left for me to learn. I rarely if ever find a manuscript that inspires me or even one that offers something new, a fresh perspective, an innovative approach.
Jamie's book did all the latter. He offered inspiration and sensible (and in retrospect, obvious) solutions to the many enigmatic 'grey areas' that had long perplexed me, a so called expert.
Questions that I have been pondering upon for years were answered at the first reading of this text. So I not only commend Mr O'Keefe on writing probably the best self protection book for women on the market but I also thank him for filling in the gaps in what is, at best, a very intangible subject.
What makes this book even more unique is that Jamie is a veteran instructor with thousands of hours of women's self protection under his belt, he is also an empiricist in that he has put his training to work in real life situations. Now while this may not say a lot to the lay man/woman, to those in the know, it speaks volumes.
Most of the instructors out there teaching self protection have never been in a real situation and so garnish unreal scenarios with un-workable, hypothetical technique.
You will get no such balderdash from this cutting edge instructor. What is offered on the menu in this text will prepare you, of that I have no doubt.
Self protection in the very violent 20th century must now, out of necessity be viewed as an environmental seat belt, it can no longer be down graded as a recreational pastime that comes third down the list of priorities after basket weaving, people are being attacked and killed, every day of the week, in un-provoked, un-solicited and bloody attacks.
My advice to you the reader is to take on board what Jamie has to offer as preventive measures and make them part of your life. Being aware will help you to avoid the majority of attack scenarios, for those that fall outside the periphery of avoidance, the simple, yet effective physical techniques on offer in this book will, if employed with conviction, help to neutralise even the most ardent of attackers.
This is a great book that makes great sense.
The best of its kind.
Geoff Thompson. Coventry 1996

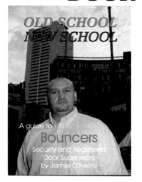

Foreword

Old School – New School

Whether you want to call them Bouncers, Doormen or Door Supervisors, they are still the people with the most thankless job I know.

Constantly under pressure from their own employers, local authorities, the police and especially the general public, it is no wonder that on occasions their self control is taxed to its ultimate. At times, even the best can lose that fine sense of perspective that allows them, night after night to take the constant barrage of banal and often alcohol influenced verbals whilst still keeping the smile in place.

I'd like to think that even going back some 23 years when I first started working on the doors that I subscribed to the "**new school**" approach so creativity described in Jamie's latest book. At that time I weighed eleven and a half stone at six foot one and despite having been on the Gt. Britain and England Karate Teams for some years I knew my traditional marital arts had limited value in the very particular conditions one finds in a night-club.

My weapons were politeness, humour, intellect and large doses of patience and, at times, even larger doses of pre-emptive strikes when occasion demanded. I'm the first to admit, however, that the conditions which applied in the seventies are different to today.

I saw the change begin in the eighties when, as a club owner, it was apparent that the nature of violence, the carrying of weapons, even handguns and the influence of drugs, was going to exact a heavy toll and so it has.

Twenty years ago when someone threatened to come back and shoot me, I slept easy knowing that the next day he wouldn't even remember where he had been the night before - now you'd be reaching for the ballistic vest.

Gang warfare, drugs, control of doors, protection rackets are all now part of the club scene and in the middle is today's doormen. Some are corrupt, some are vicious, some are plain thick, but the majority are honest, well intentioned and keen to do a good job in the face at mounting pressure from many quarters and increased violence and all this with "officialdom" now peering over their shoulder.

Often lied to by the police as to their correct rights of self defence under the law. This book should re-educate people about not only the law, but the many other complex issues.

Expected to be amateur psychologists and perfect man managers versed in a whole range of conflict resolution skills, doormen are still on the 'front line', both male and female.

Door licensing schemes are supposedly the answer to the problems inherent in the profession, but they only go part way to solving many of the issues which still give cause for concern.

Old School, New School clearly defines the gulf between the two approaches as to how the work should be carried out and it should be obligatory reading not only for all door people, but also the police and anyone who has an interest in the leisure industry. By doing so they will get a very clear and honest idea about the difficulties of this work.

Old School, New School isn't just a book about doorwork. It is an effective manual on modern methods of conflict resolution. Over the past few years there has been a substantial rise in the number of companies specialising in delivering courses on conflict resolution in the workplace.
If you read this book you will have all the answers to the management of conflict and aggression.
Doormen have been doing this for years, the only difference being the fact that they have developed their skills from intuition and experience of interpersonal skills in often very violent and

aggressive environments.
Now we know that this is a science just as any other form of social interaction and '**Old School, New School**' sets out to educate on the complexities of what is required.
The book recognises, however, that learning these very specialised skills will still not be any guarantee that you can create a person who can be capable of operating in this increasingly dangerous environment. The job is harder now than it ever was and don't let anyone tell you otherwise. Doing this job puts you under a microscope and an official one at that. `Big Brother' most certainly watches over your shoulder and, many would submit, quite rightly so.

I know many doormen who should have no part to play in the industry and many people to whom the recent changes will be hard to adjust to. What I know for a certainty is that the inherent dangers of the work increase every year.
For those doormen and the people who control them to resist the pressure from others to become another drugs distribution outlet takes courage and confidence from everyone in the organisation. Many crumble and give in to the pressure and violence, but equally many don't and I hope that **Old School, New School** will give people not involved in this work, a clear insight for once, the dangers and complexity of the work. For those people who are in the thick of it, I believe that this book is a "blueprint" for the future.

Peter Consterdine
7th Dan Chief Instructor – British Combat Association

Author of :
The Modern Bodyguard
Fit to Fight
Streetwise

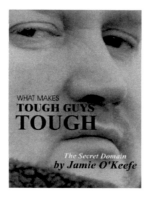

FOREWORD

DAVID TURTON 8th DAN GOSHINKWAI COMBAT SENIOR INSTRUCTOR.. BRITISH COMBAT ASSOCIATION

When I was asked by Jamie to write a foreword to this, his latest book, I was both pleased & honoured, and a little intimidated by the prospect.

The first seemingly obvious thing I did, was to read it..

Sounds obvious, but I mean **REALLY** read. On doing so, I found myself being drawn quite deeply into Jamie's thoughts and ideals.

Jamie tends to venture into fields that few, if any, other authors have entered. In doing so, he lays open many often-unanswered questions. He makes those of you-who have asked themselves these soul searching questions, feel that they are not alone.

Having known Jamie for more years than both of us care to remember, I have the advantage of being able to 'hear' his voice, whilst reading his words. I can hear the inflections that show his passion in his beliefs, and the sheer sense of honesty of his words.

Read this book with no other distractions, and give it the respect of doing so with your full attention. Only then the effort will be rewarded with the insight you will get.

I first met Jamie 0'Keefe around twenty years ago. I was a Guest Instructor on an All-Styles self-defence course, and Jamie was a participant on the course, a very noticeable one at that.

I thought here was a talented Karate-Ka, a bit brash, but Oh, so very eager to learn. He was mainly into what we thought of as 'Free-style' Karate back then, but searching for something more. His thirst for learning was nearly insatiable. His Black Belt status was of no real consequence to him. He simply wanted to get stuck in and learn.

He's still doing just that. ... **THE SAME ENTHUSIASM IS PARAMOUNT IN HIS WRITINGS.**

I have looked for a way to go past the usual platitudes, and try to give; what I feel is an honest appraisal of what I feel Jamie is

trying to give.... Then it registered ... That's the word ... **HONEST**.. That's the man and his writings.
Jamie always 'tells it like it is'. No holds barred, and no respecter of the many fragile Egos so prevalent in the Martial Arts these days. In this, he ranks along my two other favourite HONEST Combat Authors ... Geoff Thompson and Peter Consterdine.
Don't read this book for 'ways to do it', Don't read this book and be offended by his honesty. Read it, because NOT to read it, will leave a massive hole in your understandings of the World of Man & Violence.
Make it part of your collection, but keep going back to it to read it again and again.

I RECOMMEND THIS BOOK,
I DON'T RECOMMEND MANY... '**READ IT**'

DAVID TURTON 8th DAN GOSHINKWAI COMBAT.

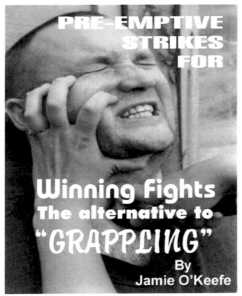

Foreword
Pre-Emptive Strikes

On first meeting Jamie O'Keefe, I was struck by his warmth and humour. I was then struck by his fists, head, & knees... Having been on the receiving end (though thankfully only in training) I can attest to the extreme effectiveness of the techniques he teaches. However, as I got to know him better, I was even more impressed by his integrity, honesty and commitment to teaching. Like many of the finest instructors and toughest fighters, Jamie is a gentleman.

These days I consider Jamie a good friend, but that's not why I agreed to write this forward. I believe he writes some of the best material available on modern self-protection, material, which can be, quite literally, life-saving.

I am proud to be able to associate my name with such valuable work

So what is the value in devoting a whole book to the pre-emptive strike?

Be in no doubt that this is one of the most important concepts for personal protection you will ever learn. Over the years I have read about, trained with and worked the door with many individuals who have vast experience of real violence. Every single one of them *without exception* recommends and uses the pre-emptive strike as the prime tactic for self-protection when a physical assault seems inevitable.

This book thoroughly dissects the theory, training and practical application of the pre-emptive strategy. From legal and moral ramifications to pre-attack indicators, from action triggers to Jamie's unique 'Strike Storage & Retrieval System', this book is the most exhaustive, insightful and thought-provoking treatise on the subject I have yet seen.

The lessons contained within these pages were learned the hard way, with spilt, blood & broken bones - this book was written so you don't have to take that route.

Read, absorb, and live by Jamie's advice. You'll be stronger and safer for it.

When talk fails and escape is impossible or impractical, the pre-emptive strike is your best option. I'll let Jamie tell you why.

Simon James
Instructor, Close Quarter Combat Systems

Thugs
Mugs
&
Violence
Jamie O'Keefe

Thugs, mugs and violence
The story so far

In this true account of his journey, Jamie O'Keefe unveils the reality of living in the East End of London. From childhood to adult this compelling, harrowing and often highly amusing story tells of his encounters with street fighting, crime, drugs, violence and the martial arts. It goes through the trials and tribulations of boyhood right through to his days of working on the door in the heart of London's nightlife. Read how each of his confrontations and experiences have played a major part in making him the well respected authority in the fighting arts that he is today.

This book is sure to intrigue and fascinate you so much it will be hard to put it down..

The names and places have been changed in order to protect the guilty

The late Reg Kray telephoned me from prison, after having just undergone eye surgery to talk through the foreword for the re-print of this book. Due to time restraints and the restrictions that he is bound by, I asked him if he could sum up his thoughts, on this book in a lone paragraph, rather than a lengthy foreword. Although Reg has given me his consent to quote him in length on all the good things that he has said about this book. I have decided to just go with the lone paragraph which was written by Reg himself. *'Thugs mugs and violence'* now has a permanent place within the cell of Reg Kray and is also read by the other inmates.

Thank you Reg for you phone-calls, sometimes three a day, to share your thoughts, ideas, opinions and philosophies with me.

Your friend
Jamie

"Jamie's book 'Thugs, Mugs and Violence' is an insight into the violent times of today and should be read" **Reg Kray – Kray Twins**

Photograph kindly supplied to me for inclusion by Reg Kray

REG KRAY – 32 YEARS SERVED 1968 – 2000 HM Prison.

Foreword

When I was asked by Kevin to write the foreword to this, Kevin's third book, I was both honoured and surprised. Honoured, because it is a great privilege to write for such an esteemed leader in the field of self-protection. Surprised because, although I have trained and practised various styles for many years, the last four with the Bristol Goshin Jutsu Combat Academy, I am, by no means, an authority on self-protection or the martial arts. I was simply a student of Kevin's who happened also to be criminal defence lawyer. What then could I, a humble lawyer, possibly have to contribute to a book on self-protection by this renowned exponent of the art?

A clue was found in the foreword to Kevin's first book, I Thought you'd be Bigger, which along with his second book, In Your Face, holds pride of place on my bookshelf. In that book, Geoff Thompson, describing Kevin as a 'first rate martial artist' stated that Kevin was one of the few highly graded martial artists who is not afraid to learn from just about anyone that has something of worth to share. This insight into Kevin's personality is precisely what makes him a truly inspirable instructor and self-protection expert. Unlike many mainstream styles whose techniques would be more at home in 17th century Japan, Kevin looks to the streets and people of today's inner cities for inspiration for his own unique and brutally effective style.

Samurai swords do not feature greatly on the streets - bottles, knives and heavy boots do - and Kevin knows it! And unlike many other styles, Kevin doesn't teach techniques as individual acts, but rather he advocates a manner of self-protection that is both fluid and responsive to the environment.

Kevin refers to the techniques of his style as parts of a jigsaw puzzle, each piece (technique) part of a larger whole. If the attacker doesn't respond to one technique, then you move into another.

In this way, each of us was taught to respond to what was physically happening, not to hope that the attacker did this or that and execute the technique regardless. Again, this is the real world - no formal rituals, no time to think. Every technique that Kevin teaches is designed to deal with a real life, in your face, situation.

And with each technique that I learnt and practised, I could see, in my opponent, the faces of the defendants that I saw in court each day (no offence to any of my opponents intended!). And that's how I came to be asked to write this foreword.

You see, as a criminal defence, lawyer, I spent years in police stations, prisons and courts representing the very kind of people that Kevin's style is designed to defend against - real-life murderers, muggers, rapists and robbers. In the evenings, I would attend Kevin's classes and I would delight in telling him, just after he had demonstrated an attack and how to deal with it, 'Yeah, that's the kind of attack that my client used the other night on some poor bastard in the city centre'. I would delight in it because I knew that it meant that what we were doing was real. This wasn't 17th century Japan stuff. This was real-world, real-time self-protection. I'd be thinking that this is what could have happened to me last night if I'd been in the same place, at the same time, as the particular victim that my client had chosen. Kevin was an enthusiastic listener and was always very interested to know the details. Each day that I sat in court, I would hear tales of violence and intimidation perpetrated by thugs and muggers and every time I would hear the details of what they did, I could see in my mind how Kevin's style and training, had it been known to the victim, would have enabled him or her to turn that threat around and put the attacker on the back foot, (or indeed, as with most of Kevin's techniques, on the ground in pain!).

As a lawyer, I had the unique opportunity, unavailable to most students of self-protection, of spending hours talking with my clients, probing them on what they did, and how they chose their victim. And what I learnt from these people is what I can contribute to this book.

I can tell you, without hesitation, that there is not one technique that Kevin teaches that is unrealistic nor one attack that he drills each student, or reader of this book, to protect him or herself against, that has not been used in real life somewhere on the streets of Britain last night or that will not be tried again tomorrow by some thug. What you will read and learn in the following pages, happens. People are knocked to the ground. People are kicked senseless on the streets.
I have seen so many victims in court, who, if only they knew how to effectively protect themselves and to grapple once on the ground, could have saved themselves a beating. If you end up on the ground on the street it is a whole lot different to a competition arena. You will need to know tactics and techniques within this text to save yourself a trip to hospital or worse!

Read this book. What you will learn from it is 'reality' of the streets and how to survive.

Matthew Adkins, Solicitor, 1999

NO
ONE
FEARS
when
ANGRY

Rare!! book by Alan Charlton

Awareness Fears And Consequences

An insight to understanding what you can do to stay safe.
You may have only one chance and only one choice

By Alan Charlton

Forward
By
Darrin Richardson B.Sc. CMS

I have known Alan Charlton for many years, I have trained with him taught and been taught by him. He is undoubtedly one of the jewels in the art of self-protection in the United Kingdom. In well over 28 years I have seen many instructors, not all can live up to their reputation. Alan however is one. He has trained with some very notable instructors learning his art and developing his own approach to the subject matter. He like many of his kind did not wake up one day an expert instructor, practitioner and author, His skills have developed over many years, and some two years ago he decided to write down many of the lessons he has learnt.

In today's society we live with the fact that we may at anytime be exposed to some sort of violence. This is not just a statement to scare you it is an every day occurrence; all you need to do is open your local paper or watch your local news. It's out there for all to see, just staring you right in the face.

Awareness, fears and Consequences are your Highway Code. We all read the Highway Code before we take our driving tests; we don't remember it all (well I don't) but we do remember the basics. It is those basics that help us drive round in relative safety.

It's the same with Self-protection; Alan Charlton has waded through all the unnecessary ideas and skills that have become the myth of the martial arts and self-defence. We the reader can quickly learn many valuable lessons from this book, without the pain of having first hand experience. This book is crammed full of information and humour and is a must for the library of those who take the subject seriously.

Darrin Richardson 4th Dan

Want to write a book?

Want to have a book on sale via Amazon?

Want to have your work, ideas, story put in print?

New Breed Publishing are the largest U.K. specialist of Self Protection books.

Five or our authors have appeared on prime time TV shows and two have achieved major publishing deals after releasing books with New Breed.

We do not hold anyone back or make you sign any contracts. Your book remains yours and we insist you keep full copyright and 100% of any money you earn from selling your books.

We have spent 10 years building our reputation and getting it right!
Then email jamieokeefe@tiscali.co.uk
For further details.

www.newbreedbooks.co.uk

Some other New Breed titles to look out for

ISBN	Title	Author
09517567 10	Dogs don't know kung fu –	J.O'Keefe
09517567 29	What makes tough guys tough –	J.O'Keefe
09517567 37	Pre-emptive strikes for winning fights –	J.O'Keefe
09517567 45	In your face –	K.O'Hagan
09517567 53	Grappling with reality –	K.O'Hagan
09517567 61	Old School New School –	J.O'Keefe
09517567 7x	I thought you'd be bigger –	K.O'Hagan
09517567 88	Thugs Mugs and Violence –	J.O'Keefe
09517567 96	No One Fears when Angry –	J.O'Keefe
09538555 2x	Kicking it –	P.Francia
09538555 38	Awareness Fears and Consequences –	A. Charlton
09538555 46	Bad to the Bone –	K.O'Hagan
09538555 70	Bullied to Black Belt –	Simon Morrell
09538555 89	Trust Me I'm a doorman –	Kev Fisher
09538555 97	On the Chin –	Richy Horsley
1-904432 05-0	Relentless –	K.O'Hagan
1-904432 00-x	The Pugilist Quest -	D'Lambert Mensah
1-904432 02-6	A foot in the door –	Tony Simpson
1 904432 06-9	In the face of violence –	K.O'Hagan
1 904432 01-8	Martial arts, muscles & mayhem -	D. Turton

The above titles are available from www.amazon.co.uk or direct from New Breed Publishing. Signed copies are also available direct from each of the individual authors.

Coming soon in 2006

09538555 11 The Glory Boys – J.O'Keefe (not yet in print)

1 904432-03-4 Survive and Stay Alive (how to develop your own personal self protection system) – J.O'Keefe (not yet in print)

1 904432-07-7 'Stabbed (an in-depth look at the experiences, dangers and damage of edged weapons) (not yet in print)

DVD – Silence the violence – J.O'Keefe (not yet available)

www.newbreedbooks.co.uk

Please check our online shop with secure credit card ordering.

BRISTOL GOSHIN JUTSU COMBAT ACADEMY

Training in:

- Mixed martial Arts & limited rules fighting
- Combat Jujutsu (16 years +)
- Street Self-protection
- Conflict management
- Combat Grappling
- Children's Jujutsu 6-14 years

Sunday 10.30 – 12.00a.m.	Impact gym (lifestyles fitness studio) Clouds hill Rd, St. George (MMA training)
1.0 - 2.30a.m.	Impact gym (lifestyles fitness studio) Clouds hill Rd, St. George (Combat Jujutsu/Street Self-defense)
Monday 7.15 – 8.45 p.m.	Kingsdown Sportcentre, Portland Rd, Kingsdown (Combat Jujutsu)
Tuesday 7.30 – 9.00 p.m.	Impact gym (lifestyles fitness studio) Clouds hill Rd, St. George (MMA Training – open mat training)
Wednesday 6.30 – 8.15 p.m.	Horfield Sportcentre, Dorian Rd, Horfield (Combat Jujutsu)
Thursday 7.30 – 9.00p.m.	Impact gym (lifestyles fitness studio) Clouds hill Rd, St. George (Open mat/Private lessons)
5.00 – 6.15 p.m.	Horfield Sportcentre, Dorian Rd, Horfield (Childrens Jujutsu 6-14 years old)

In Your Face
'CLOSE QUARTER FIGHTING'
by
Kevin O'Hagan

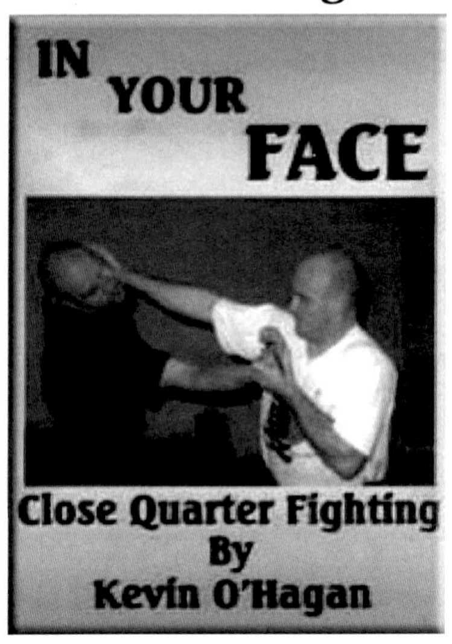

£14

from

NEW BREED

Or even better

Buy it direct from Kevin O'Hagan

And ask him to autograph it!

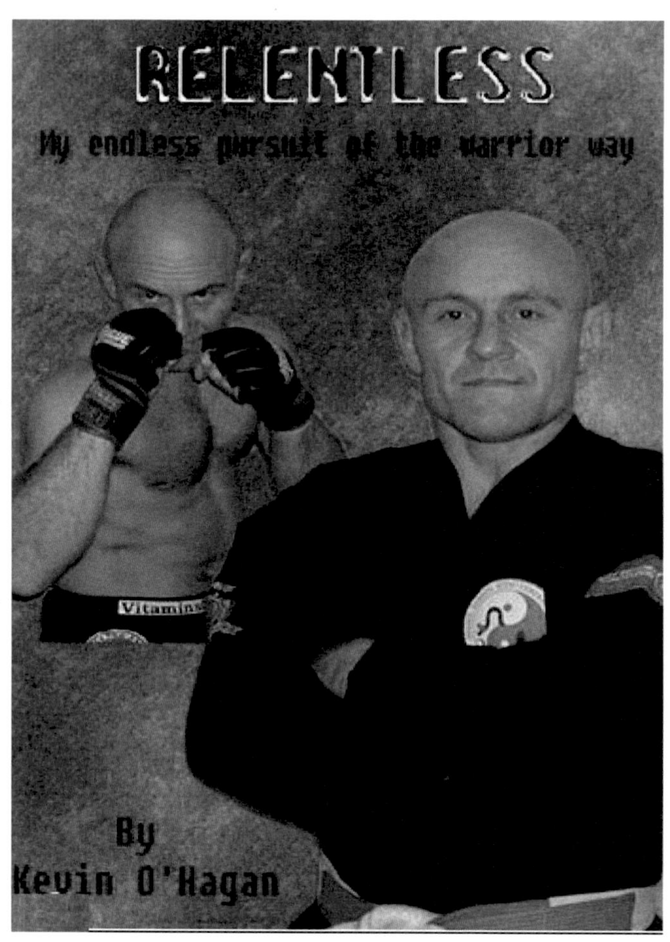

plus in our other books

£14

from

NEW BREED

Or even better

<u>Buy it direct from Kevin O'Hagan</u>

And ask him to autograph it!

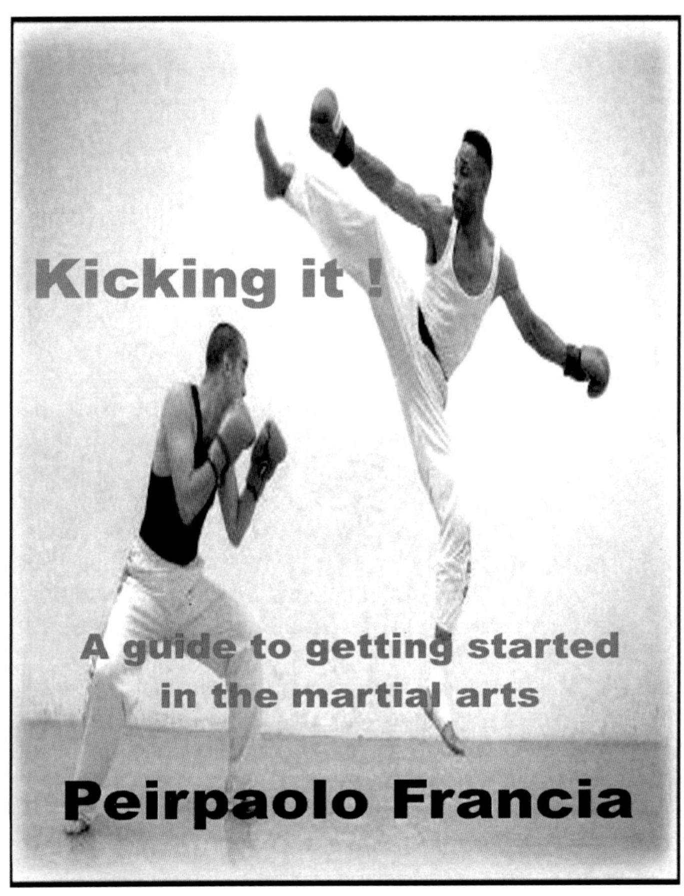

£14

from

NEW BREED

Or even better

Buy it direct from Peirpaolo Francia

www.pierpaolofrancia.com

And ask him to autograph it!

Kicking It!
A Guide to getting started in the Martial Arts
By Pierpaolo Francia
New Breed Publishing

Excerpt

Where to start

As I said in the introduction, I have heard and spoken to very many people wanting to start practising a Martial Art, visiting different clubs and getting hold of the wide range of literature available on the subject. More often than not this turns out to be a daunting task given the vast amount of information available – books, videos, magazines, the Internet etc. – and the beginners may find themselves more doubtful and confused than before their search even began. Which Martial Art to choose? I hear you cry. Which one is the most effective? Which one is more suitable for me? These are all plausible questions when you think that most arts seem to profess to be the be-all and end-all system. Since, as you would expect, the field of Martial Arts as well as the issues, arguments and opinions surrounding them is incredibly vast, I think it is important that you sit down and carefully do some constructive thinking as to what you want to get out of the art you might choose. I say this because no Martial Art possesses all the answers in terms of the acquisition of all-round fighting skills – i.e. those that are punching and kicking orientated will more often than not lack grappling skills and vice versa. Nor are they likely to address all the aspects needed for what concerns self-defence. In this regard, I believe it is worth making a few useful distinctions.

Martial Arts, Self-Defence or Self-Protection?

It would appear, as I mentioned earlier, that the most common reason why people want to start a Martial Art is to learn how to defend themselves, along perhaps with the other benefits that come with them. This is an area ridden with a great deal of confusion and misunderstanding as to what constitutes a Martial Art, a Self-Defence System or a Self-Protection System; thus, before we go any further, it is essential that we contextualise these differences.

The term Martial Art is generally associated with fighting skills that originated many centuries ago (the genesis and development of which are still open to much debate and controversy today (1)) and were practically tested and proven both in the battlefield as well as in the entertainment arena. The Greek Pankration, the Roman Gladiators, The Chinese Kung Fu, The Japanese Karate and Judo, the Korean Tae Kwon Do. . . the list is endless. For very many reasons (which I will skim over as they are beyond the purpose of this book), most European Arts disappeared over the years, whereas the Oriental Arts have survived and remained quite popular to the present day (2). Most of these arts you are likely to come across in your search. Some have various styles and different facets, some have evolved and modernised, some have blended with other forms and systems, some are very similar to one another, a great deal of them have remained very traditional.
Although I acknowledge that this may be a bit of a generalisation, I think it is fair to say that most Oriental Arts have remained very traditional in their approach. It would appear that they have somehow stopped evolving and got trapped in a state of stagnation, particularly when teaching self-defence techniques. You will have to expect that all instructors claim that their art is street-effective and combat-orientated. They will all emphasise the fact that most of the techniques they teach are practical and effective for real street-encounters. The reality is somewhat different. In fact, most traditional techniques have become pretty much redundant in today's world and have very little application against the modern attacker in our streets (3).

This is not to say that they should be discarded. For example, to learn the mechanical operations and the workings of a Ford Escort will not give you a full understanding of a Triumph Herald; but will ensure that your basic general knowledge would aid you in finding a fault or solving a problem if you broke down in a Triumph Herald, even if you haven't been in one before.
Most arts, in fact, offer an invaluable array of benefits, of which I will go into further detail later on in the book (this being the purpose of the book in the first place!).

This is only to clarify that if you are looking to learn effective and practical skills to defend yourself against the modern attacker, you will have to look for a modern response, which most of the traditional arts (unless subject to re-adaptation) will not be able to provide – just as the more modern and technically advanced medical operations could not be dealt with by the knowledge, skills and resources available a century ago, let alone many centuries ago!

The next essential differentiation to make is that which regards Self-Defence systems and Self-Protection systems. Generally speaking, the term Self-Defence refers to an attack that has already occurred and needs to be dealt with. Unfortunately, once you have been attacked (especially if by someone who knows what they are doing) it will most probably be too late to react effectively, leaving very little you can do to defend yourself.
Self-Protection, on the other hand, attempts to emphasise the importance of avoiding an attack to happen in the first place. It focuses on awareness, evaluation and avoidance of threats and how the understanding of such parameters will enable you to avoid dangerous situations and potential attacks altogether.

The theoretical knowledge is of paramount importance, far more important than the physical skills, particularly in relation to the law and what you are allowed to do in order to protect yourself (4).

Martial Arts in print – Book review
COMBAT June 2001

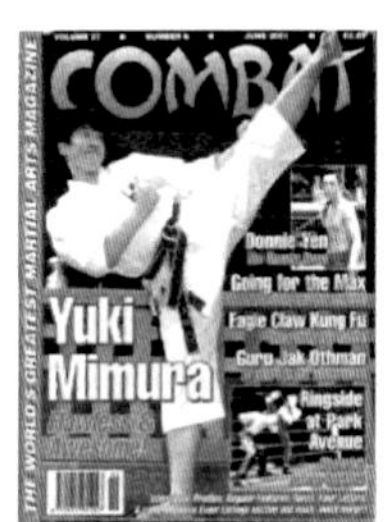

"'Kicking it!"
A guide to getting started in the Martial Arts
New Breed Publishing – London 2001
By Pierpaolo Francia

With the sheer volume of martial arts books now widely available, the majority of them 'how to' manuals, authors need an edge to get noticed, a marketing ploy that will distinguish his/her effort from the ever increasing crowd.

With Kicking it! Mr Francia has found his angle, namely the potentially confusing range of arts available to the fresh-faced new student.
In the good old days there was karate, karate, judo or karate to choose from, but in the 21st century the list is as long as your arm. So with this in mind, Pierpaolo has written his lively reference guide, and a good job he's made of it too!
The strength of Kicking It! is the book's simplicity of structure and presentation, as an average beginner does not want to be bogged down with detail overload when trying to decide what art to take-up. Francia sensibly keeps the constructive information at sound byte level, clearly and concisely introducing the various points for consideration in straightforward layman's terms. The structure takes the form of problem solving, in terms of answering pertinent questions, the most relevant being why do I want to start the martial arts? Here Francia differentiates between fitness and philosophy, sport and spirituality, tradition and evolution, self defence and self protection whilst finding a nice balance between the levels of information needed by a beginner.
The writing style is conversational, an approach I've always liked, as it allows a sense of the author's character to come through, and Francia's enthusiasm is translated to the text. Once the reasons for wanting to start are established he then introduces the arts themselves. Recognising the impossibility of categorising the myriad sub-divisions, Francia wisely confines himself to the most popular and well known general headings, known to even the

most (martially) ignorant of the populace. Each art is given between 2-3 pages of text, brevity once again being the key.

There is a useful list section, detailing important contact numbers for the various arts, as well as sections on equipment and weapons, but to me the most intriguing and beneficial part of the book was the question and answer section with various professional instructors, designed to give the beginner a better insight into what they may wish to learn as they reflect on the answers given. This section takes up a hefty chunk of the 160 odd pages but is well worth it as the piece defines and discusses most elements of the martial arts through the eyes of such luminaries as Geoff Thompson, Jamie O' Keefe, Dave Turton, Dave Briggs, and Kevin O'Hagan. Francia wisely includes the female perspective in his Q and A with Lizzie Clark and many potential buyers might be attracted by these candid mini-interviews.

Pierpaolo Francia has obviously enjoyed writing this book and if you are one of those flummoxed by the avenues open to you, then I can wholeheartedly recommend Kicking it! to you. Similarly, if you have already chosen your first art and are feeling unfulfilled (for whatever reason), this book will open your eyes to a world of informed choice and it is in this respect that the interviews are so important, as they really do give food for thought. Why, the man even manages to give "Combat" a plug. What more can I say?

COMBAT Martial Arts Magazine
June 2001

For Credit card orders please buy you books via

www.newbreedbooks.co.uk

To order by Cheque or Postal order

Please order direct from the relevant author or from

New Breed Publishing
Po box 2676
Romford
Essex RM7 0WA

If you order direct from author you can also get them to include a personalised message and sign the book!

OTHER NEW BREED BOOKS

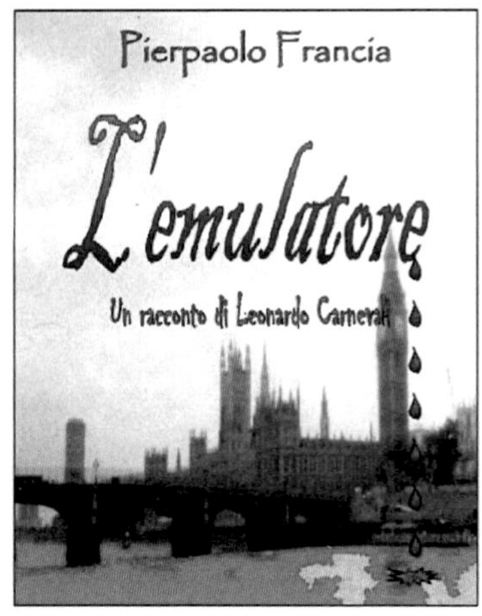